SILVER DOLLAR DUKE

SILVER DOLLAR

DUKE

HEARTS OF ARIZONA BOOK 1

SALLY BRITTON

Published by Pink Citrus Books
Edited by Jenny Proctor of Midnight Owl Editors
Sensitivity Edits by Salt & Sage Books
Cover design by Blue Water Books

This book is a work of fiction. Names, characters, places, and incidents are either products of the author's imagination or are used fictitiously. Any resemblance to actual persons living or dead, events, or locales is entirely coincidental.

Sally Britton
www.authorsallybritton.com

First Printing: February 2021

For Herbert and Douglas,
My Favorite Cowboys.

And for Sally's Sweet Romance Fans:
Thank you for believing in me.

CHAPTER ONE

January 1895
Bristol, England

One never expected to find the son of a marquess at a pub of questionable reputation, which explained the exact reason Evan A. Rounsevell occupied a stool at the Llandoger Trow. Evan had no wish to *be* found.

Especially with his knowledge that the marquess—his *father* — had arrived in London with the express purpose of forcing Evan to take up family responsibilities.

Without raising his eyes from the amber liquid in his glass, Evan put more coins on the slick and greasy counter to pay for his drink.

A shine of one particular silver coin caught his eye. Evan snatched the coin up again, his heart thudding against his chest, just before the barkeep scooped the rest of the money into his apron pocket.

With a single careless action, he'd almost parted with his most prized possession. He clutched the coin tightly in his palm, feeling its edge press into his skin. Slowly, he opened his hand

and studied the glimmering silver. The head of Lady Liberty faced upward, the year 1879 stamped below her.

What a remarkable year that had been.

Although he hadn't been as tall then as he was at present, Evan had the same features in place. Angular chin, sharp nose, dark hair, and copper-green eyes. He'd been a strapping youth, well-practiced in every art an English nobleman's son ought to master. Which was why he had pleaded to go to the performance the Americans had put on for Her Majesty, Queen Victoria, the moment he'd heard of it. Evan could shoot as well as any Englishman—but he'd heard the Americans did it better.

Evan turned the coin over to the side bearing the eagle, its wings widespread, talons clutching arrows and olive branches alike. Americans made strong, bold statements with everything, even their coinage. He smiled to himself as he remembered the day he had received the coin, eight years previous, from a man wearing more leather than one found at a tanner's booth.

The man who had wrestled Indians, fought in a war, rode wild horses, and could shoot a gun and throw hatchets with equal skill. A man who challenged everything Evan knew about the world simply by existing.

A hand landed upon Evan's shoulder, startling him into clutching the coin tightly lest he drop it. He looked up, ready to give a set-down to whoever dared disturb him, when he met the shrewd eyes of his elder brother.

William D. Rounsevell, heir to their father's title as Marquess of Whittenbury, smirked down at him before perching on the stool beside Evan. "Thought I'd find you here. You always have preferred the more interesting pubs." His eyes lingered on the dusty glasses on the shelves, his nose wrinkled with distaste.

"Perhaps." Evan hastily tucked away the coin, having no wish to give his brother reason to mock him. The family thought Evan's interest in the American West no more than a sign of eccentricity, and a shameful one, at that.

Of course the marquess would send William after him.

William was the least annoying member of the family, which consisted of his father, an uncle and aunt, his brother, and a handful of first cousins.

Although William was not a bad sort, he tended to share their father's views on Evan's behavior. So it was no surprise that he immediately took up their father's cause. "You need to come home, Evan. Father has a particular interest in speaking with you about your responsibility for the Shropshire estate. You know he wishes you to show some interest in family matters, but if you continue to neglect it—"

"I know." Evan rubbed at his forehead before taking hold of the drink in front of him. "But I have no wish to settle on that land and look after sheep until the end of my days."

"Father thinks if you marry you will settle." William folded his arms, eyeing the barkeep suspiciously when the man came forward to offer William a drink. "Have you a brandy worth more than a few pennies?" he asked loftily.

The barkeep bowed and went in search of a bottle and glass.

Evan encircled his glass in his hands but did no more than stare into it. If only one could divine the future in the bottom of a cup.

"I have no intention of marrying. What is the point to a union for me? Even if I tend to the Shropshire estate, it goes to your heirs, not mine. Why spend my life toiling on another man's property like a blasted tenant farmer?" He snorted into his cup before taking one last sip of the drink. He much preferred a strong cup of tea but trying to get that sort of drink at a pub as rough around the edges as the one in which they sat would only get him laughed out of the building.

William accepted a glass of his own and turned a bored sort of smile onto Evan. "It is the way things are. If you marry well, your wife's funds will see to any children you may have. It is not as though I will turn them out into the cold the moment you die."

"But if you go first, your son might." Evan tapped his fingers on the smooth wood, worn down from years of patrons sitting in his exact spot. "Or if I irritate you. Or if I die, what will happen to a widow and children too young to have chosen their paths? The situation is intolerable, William."

"Second sons have braved such circumstances for centuries." William eyed his drink dubiously before taking a small sip. He winced and put it back onto the counter, pushing it away from himself with enough force to make the liquid slosh over the brim.

"Not in America," Evan muttered, his eyes on the swirls in the woodgrain.

A deep laugh made him jump in his seat, his gaze coming up to see his brother's head thrown back as he roared. Others in the pub turned to look, some appearing annoyed that the quiet, smoky atmosphere had been disturbed.

Finally, with a last guffaw, William reached out to clap Evan on the arm. "Your sense of humor does you credit, Evan. America." William snorted and picked up his glass, but he must have remembered he held the liquid inside in contempt, for he lowered it again. "Land of the self-made man. More like land of illiterate, unwashed, uncultured upstarts."

Saying nothing was safer than arguing. And less likely to get him laughed at again.

"Come home. Father wishes to speak to you." William scattered coins upon the bar without regard to denomination, then stood. "It is time to accept your responsibilities, little brother, and to stop living in a fantasy of cowboys and outlaws. You are a man of ancient and noble blood. Our family line comes first." Then he saluted with two fingers and strode leisurely out of the pub.

Blood always came first. The family honor held more value for the marquess than the wealth of his estates combined.

Lord Whittenbury, their father, would not rest until Evan came to him, bowing and scraping, accepting his meager inheritance and responsibility for one of the family's lesser estates. Evan's only hope to escape managing his father's Shropshire estate was to take up the practice of law, which he had no interest in, or marry an heiress, which he desired to do even less.

The silver dollar in his pocket reminded him of yet another option. The so-called fantasy his brother mocked. The American West, where fortunes were won or lost in a night, where a man could work to accomplish what he wished, and where expectations and futures were self-made.

Without familial support, he couldn't afford a ticket to cross the Atlantic. Everything he had belonged to his father. Everything—no. Not everything.

Evan pulled out his gold pocket-watch and examined it. Worth a small fortune. A gift from an uncle. The stickpin in his cravat, his cuff-links, all real jewels. All his to do with as he pleased.

The idea that had been no more than the seed of a dream his whole life sprouted and grew like climbing vines upon his mind.

A slow smile stretched across Evan's face as he took out the silver dollar, a gift to him from none other than Buffalo Bill himself.

An electric thrill ran up his spine, and a slow grin spread across his face.

Despite the faint light in the pub, Lady Liberty seemed to wink at him.

It wouldn't be forever. But it would be *something* that was his and his alone. Not his father's, not a responsibility, but a dream the likes of which few could ever attain. An escape from his title, his duty to his family, and the chance for a real adventure.

He left the pub, his pulse thrumming with the cadence of a galloping horse, and he didn't look back.

CHAPTER TWO

May 1, 1895
Tombstone, Arizona

Raising dust with her boots to search out her little brothers was not how Daniella Bolton wanted to spend her time in Tombstone. The city crowds unnerved her, though during daylight hours everything about the town was perfectly safe and respectable. Tombstone was nothing like Boston, but the hundreds of people shuffling down the boarded walks still reminded her entirely too much of that hated period in her life.

She'd needed to come. Tombstone, as the county seat, was a place of business. With her father still recovering from an illness, it fell to Dannie to send telegrams on his behalf to their buyers in California. Running a cattle ranch meant doing a lot more than riding herd. It meant doing a lot more math and cozying up to strangers than she liked.

She headed down Safford street, peering through each window until she spotted her brother, Travis, leaning in the barber's doorway. The seventeen-year-old boy didn't even notice her, his attention completely arrested by something inside the shop.

Dannie adjusted her straw hat, hating the round-brimmed, brown-ribboned thing when she could have on a sensible working hat. Her blue calico dress had enough dust on its skirts to appear nearly the same shade as the ribbon. Dressing up to come to town always irritated her. She liked to look as nice as the next woman, but it just wasn't practical when the roads were a dusty mess.

"Travis Lincoln Bolton," she snapped when she was still several steps away. The boy jerked upright and nearly fell out of the doorway in his haste to respond.

"Dannie." He cast a glance into the shop, then gave her a grin which suggested he hadn't any idea how long she'd been searching for him. Or how much she wanted to drag him away by the ear. "You need to come hear Mr. Rounsevell."

As she'd never heard of, nor seen hide of, any Mr. Rounsevell, she didn't care a lick about whatever the man was saying. "Where's Clark?" Their fifteen-year-old brother usually stayed glued to Travis's side.

Travis pointed inside the barbershop. Dannie narrowed her eyes at him and went to the doorway. Walking into a barbershop wasn't nearly as scandalous as walking into a saloon, but it was rare a woman needed a barber's services. She peered inside the shadowy interior, her eyes adjusting from the brightness of the afternoon sun.

A crowd of men stood along the walls, everyone's attention riveted to a man sitting in one of the barber chairs having his hair trimmed.

He was tall. She could tell by the way his boots stuck out from under the barber's tarp. He had dark brown hair and a strong jawline. But what struck her immediately was the sound of his voice. Cultured. Deep. *Foreign*. His had to be a British accent, given its nearness to the New England tongue she was all too familiar with. He was holding court like a king, surrounded by drovers and stock boys.

"Yes, it's true that Her Majesty is a woman of diminutive stature, but she has a presence about her that fills the room with her prestige. She is an empress, a woman of fiery spirit and a brave heart. She has survived assassins and mothered all the crown heads of Europe."

Dannie snorted. Loud enough in the awed silence following the stranger's pronouncement that everyone turned to where she stood framed by the doorway. Including the British man. The boy at his feet turned, too.

"Clark." Dannie narrowed her eyes at him but tried to keep her tone even. "We need to get on the road if we're going to be home in time for evening chores." She wasn't about to take him to task in front of so many of his peers, but he'd get an earful as soon as they were in private.

The man in the chair raised one dark eyebrow at her as he stood, sweeping off the white cloth from his shoulders as he did. He wore a full suit and vest, white shirt and dark blue tie. His boots were well shined, his face clean-shaven. Everyone followed his movement, then realized the Englishman had turned his attention away from them. A few cowboys frowned, likely irritated she had disturbed their entertainment.

The Englishman bowed. As though they were in a drawing room and an old cowhand hadn't just spat his tobacco into an urn on the floor. She wrinkled her nose at the stranger.

The people of Tombstone might be used to people coming and going, and this man's accent and charm might make him particularly interesting to the average citizen, but she didn't trust him even an inch-worth.

Travis came forward and bumped shoulders with her. "Dannie, this is Mr. Rounsevell. He's from England." He grinned at her, then nodded to the man still standing in the middle of the room. "He's looking for work. Think we could take him back with us?"

After sparing a glance to the man who dressed like he was

going to Sunday church rather than looking for a job, she leveled a hard glare at her brother.

"Travis, get Clark and meet me at the wagon." She cast the tall stranger one last look, then spun on her heel and left, her boots hammering the wood in a staccato rhythm.

Mr. Rounsevell was as out-of-place in Tombstone as a peacock in a chicken run.

It didn't take long for her to hear the quick clomp of her brothers' feet behind her. But a harder step came after theirs. Dannie stopped and turned around, hands on her hips. Travis. Clark. Mr. Rounsevell, now wearing a felt hat nicer than anything her father owned. All three came to a stop under her glare. Then Rounsevell moved between the boys, and another step put him directly in front of her.

"Miss Bolton. I hope you will forgive my forward behavior, especially given our lack of proper introduction, but your brothers have encouraged me to speak with you regarding employment on your ranch." His vowels rolled like gentle spring hills, not with the stretched-out drawl she'd come to expect from the local cowboys and merchants, or the twang which characterized her father's words of wisdom.

She gripped her purse strings tighter, her stiff-clothed gloves creaking. "You may have noticed, sir, that my brothers are boys." She glared at Travis. "A might young for talking business." And lacking her experience with charming men who said one thing and did another.

Travis squared his shoulders. "I'm learning, Dannie, and Dad said we could use some extra hands."

So he had. But there was a reason they were short on help. All their hands had taken part in the spring cattle drive, taking the animals all the way down to Benson for the best prices, where they had collected their pay; most hadn't come back. She didn't blame them. After the drought of '91 and the second in '93, ranchers were desperate for cash. They all lived with tightened belts and long-faces.

Mr. Rounsevell stood still as a soldier, shoulders back, expression calm, gripping the brim of his hat in his hands. He had an air of sophistication she had only seen in a handful of other men, all of them the sons and husbands of socialites back East. It wouldn't surprise her at all to learn he came from a wealthy British family.

The man had to be as green as they came.

"What are your qualifications for ranch work, Mr. Rounsevell?" She kept her gaze on his eyes, watching for falsehoods or weakness. "We can't be nursemaids to every Brit who wants to play cowboy." She barely kept the accusation out of her voice. Her way of life was no game.

To his credit, he didn't bristle up like a polecat, but offered her a friendly smile. "Miss Bolton, I'm an adept horseman. I grew up in the saddle. I'm an excellent marksman, too, should the need arise. I'm also a dedicated scholar."

Dannie did not groan aloud, though she wanted to. "So you know nothing about cattle. Have you ever mucked a stable? Roped a steer? Branded a heifer? And have you ever shot at a cougar looking to make a meal out of your herd? Those are the kinds of skills I need, Mr. Rounsevell. Not looking pretty on your horse and shining your six shooter." She turned her glare to Travis. "You still want to offer him a job?"

Travis stuck his chin out. "Why don't we let Dad decide?" The boy had a tender heart, but this was the first time he'd wanted to exercise it on behalf of a full-grown man. Travis was as like to adopt an orphaned skunk as he was a hound dog.

Rounsevell, for his part, still appeared confident. When Dannie cocked her eyebrows at him, he nodded to her. "I would not mind speaking to your father."

He wouldn't, would he? Dannie sniffed and turned on her heel. "Let's get a move on. Evening chores wait for no man, even if he's English."

She led the way to their wagon, which the boys had loaded with the supplies before disappearing. Tombstone was a three-hour wagon ride from home. There were a few small trading posts, and Fort Huachuca, between King Bolton Ranch and Tombstone, but some things they could only find in the large city. It was a day trip, which meant limiting the trip to every month or two, but the boys always came along hoping to see a bit of fun.

Dannie had once been as eager as they to get off ranch land. These days, though, she hated to step foot off her father's property. There was too much work to be done and not enough people to do it.

Abram Steele waited for them, already seated on the buckboard wagon, whittling at a chunk of mesquite. The wood wasn't easy to use in most respects, but Abram swore up and down it was a dream for woodworking. Of course, Dannie figured he was partial because his peg-leg was made from the stuff.

"Dannie," he said when he saw her, a bright wide smile appearing upon his dark face. Abram had been a Buffalo Soldier, a member of an all-black cavalry regiment decades past. It was hard to picture him as a soldier, given his gentle ways. His eyes flicked to the boys walking behind her, and the Englishman must've caused Abram's sudden frown. "Have we got company?"

"Abram." Dannie stopped on the boardwalk, irritated she had to take further time to explain the situation. "This is Mr. Rounsevell. He needs a job, so he's coming with us to speak to Daddy. Mr. Rounsevell, this is Mr. Steele. He owns a fifth share in the ranch."

The old soldier tipped his hat. "Good afternoon, sir. They warn you it's a long ways to the spread?"

Mr. Rounsevell tipped his hat back to Abram, which was a sight more than a lot of men did when greeting the older man, no matter how he was introduced. "I understand it will be near sundown when we arrive. I am certain my horse and I will be fine."

"Better get that horse then, Mr. Rounsevell. We're on our way out by the western road, Charleston. You can meet us going that way. We won't get too far ahead." Abram gave a look to the boys. "You two best saddle up."

Dannie climbed into the wagon next to her dad's oldest friend. She'd rather have ridden like her brothers, but it was easier to wear a dress and look the part of a lady when she went to the bank in Tombstone. She was accorded far more respect than if she came in denim, and only a fool would ride side-saddle through the Sonoran Desert. She opened her purse and found Abram's bag of lemon drops, purchased at his request. He took them with a nod of thanks before tucking them in his jacket pocket. He'd dressed better than usual, too. They both had to look decent if they wanted to be treated with respect.

The boys untethered their horses from the rail in front of the general store. Then they mounted up and led the way down the street, the wagon following. Traffic was light in the middle of the week. Most of the townsfolk were at work until supper time.

After a few minutes of quiet, Abram leaned closer to Dannie. "How'd we pick up a stray Englishman?"

"Travis," she muttered quietly, keeping her hands folded tightly in her lap.

"Ah. That boy would nurse a rattler back to health if he found one with a bent tail."

Dannie's lips twitched. "Let's hope he never finds one, then." She took in a deep breath but was rewarded by the urge to sneeze. "All this dust. The time between the winter thaw out and summer rains—"

"Most call it spring, Dannie." Abram chuckled, and she glowered at him. He knew what she meant. Everyone in Arizona territory went near crazy in May and June, the driest part of the year. Hottest, sometimes, too. Then the rains would come, simultaneously stirring up dust and muddying up roads. But the rain broke the tension and soothed the citizens of Arizona, whether they were ranchers, farmers, or grocers.

"Spring. Honestly, I think we only had about a week of spring last year." She shuddered. There hadn't been much of a spring for several years. The whole territory and all the plants and animals in it were still recovering from two droughts too close together. Many ranchers had pulled up stakes the year before, rather than hope their luck would change.

Not Dannie's father. He'd buried her Mama on King Bolton land and would never leave her behind.

With no wish to dwell on the past and its uncomfortable history, Dannie changed the subject to the price of sugar and whether or not Abram's wife, Ruthie, might make them a cake come Sunday.

She did her best to put the English stranger out of her thoughts, though she fully intended to have a word with her daddy regarding Travis's behavior. The boy needed to understand that fully grown Englishmen had to look after themselves, and their ranch wasn't so far gone as to need the help of a greenhorn.

GIVEN HIS PLACE IN ENGLISH SOCIETY, EVAN HADN'T EVER BEEN turned down with such vehemence as Miss Bolton expressed when she tried to send him on his way. Americans snapped out their orders like angry dogs, lacking the cold superiority of the English nobility who used to tell him what to do.

Reflecting on this as he hurried to the stable yard, Evan questioned his sanity. While working alongside actual cowboys had been a dream of his since childhood, the reality of the situation had thus far proved unpleasant. He'd spent most of his funds traveling from one side of North America to the dusty, arid Arizona territory in search of the landscape he'd only known through books and photographs. He'd been determined to find a way to join up with a cattle outfit, as they were called in his books, and take part in a real cattle drive.

But no one in Tombstone wasted time telling him the spring drives were over. There'd be no more cattle moving across the desert plains until autumn.

At least that meant more time to work on a ranch—a positive that may very well outweigh the negative of arriving too late in the year.

Evan retrieved his horse, paying a few of his last remaining coins to the liveryman for the trouble of stabling the large bay beast. He'd bought the fine bit of horseflesh in Texas, then paid to have the gelding brought along on the train to Benson. From Benson, he'd ridden to Tombstone to see the infamous O.K. Corral for himself.

It wasn't much to see, to be honest. Though the entire town of Tombstone was interesting, laid out and managed differently than any town he'd ever seen in Britain. Even the mining was nothing like the operations he'd toured in Wales.

His sense of adventure, which had deflated after a few days walking through town, returned full force when he mounted his horse and went looking for Charleston Road.

Luck and tenacity had brought him that far; it would see him through this latest turn in the road.

It didn't take long to catch up to the Bolton wagon. The two boys were on horses ahead, out of the way of the dust churned up by the wheels. Still, it didn't seem polite to bypass Miss Bolton and Mr. Steele, so Evan came up alongside them.

Miss Bolton sat as though her spine had frozen in place, which was quite a feat considering the bumps in the road. He knew ladies who had graced his late mother's parlor without posture that perfect.

She barely looked at him from the corner of her eye.

Mr. Steele spoke around her, leaning forward a few inches in his seat. "What'd you say your name was?" he asked.

"Evan Rounsevell." Evan lifted his hat just off his head as he had seen cowboys doing all day long. Introductions required a full lift, a simple acknowledgement was a tip of the hat, and a brief touch was reserved for close acquaintances and friends. At least, he thought he had that right. It seemed Americans had an entire language with hats alone, whereas in England one kept his hat on outside and removed it in, and that was usually that.

"That's a mouthful. Folks around here usually have just the one name, and if it's too long then we call 'em by something easier on our jaws." The old man chuckled and nodded to the woman at his side, who steadfastly ignored them both. "Take our fine lady here. Full name's Daniella Abigail Bolton. Too fancy. Doesn't suit her excepting on Sundays. So we call her Dannie."

"I think Miss Bolton will do for now," the young woman said, shooting Evan another glare as though he'd been the one to suggest using the over-familiar name.

"For now." The old man chuckled and jabbed his thumb against his vest. "Abram Steele's my name. Most call me Abram. Simple. Biblical. My wife is Mary Ruth but call her anything other than Ruthie and she won't hear a word you say."

"So people just prefer a more easily spoken name?" Evan asked.

"If you're lucky," Miss Bolton said, almost too quietly for him to hear.

Abram chuckled. "Sometimes, a fellow gets saddled with something else. I can't tell you how many Slims, Sidewinders, Reds, Cookies, Lizards, Whiskers, or Kids I've known in my time." Abram adjusted his grip on the reins and nodded to the boys ahead. "Those two haven't grown into any names other than their own. Usually takes something special, or foolish, for a cowboy to get christened."

How intriguing. Of course, he'd heard of Wild Bill, Calamity Jane, and had met Buffalo Bill himself, but they had only had adjectives tacked on to names already their own. "It sounds like an interesting cultural phenomenon. I have read several books in which outlaws are given strange names, but I was not aware the system also applied to those on the correct side of the law."

The woman crossed her arms and turned to face him. "You've read books about outlaws? Let me guess. Cheap novels published to sensationalize the wild and unruly west? What do they call those on your side of the ocean?"

Evan's ears burned. "Penny dreadfuls might be what you are alluding to, Miss Bolton." And he had read his fair share of those books. But he'd also read American newspapers and searched out more reliable accounts of what the west was really like. He'd even exchanged letters with Wyatt Earp once. Not that he needed to advertise his obsession with all things American West.

She waved a dismissive hand. "Some of those books aren't even written by people who've ever left the comfort of their parlors, Mr. Rounsevell."

"Understandable, Miss Bolton. They are, after all, fiction." He was ready to join the boys ahead, as they seemed as eager to hear about England as he was to learn about their ranch, but they circled their horses and came back to ride alongside him before he thought of a polite reason to excuse himself from beneath Miss Bolton's icy glare.

The road wasn't exactly wide, but that didn't prohibit the boys from riding near him. Sage brush here and there dotted the stretch of land and hills before them. He saw a line of scraggly trees ahead, too.

"Mr. Rounsevell," the older boy, Travis, said with some excitement. "Tell Dannie about the Queen of England. Have you really met her?"

"Of course. My father is one of her advisors in matters of agriculture," he answered easily enough. The boys both appeared impressed, but their sister snorted. When he turned to take in her expression, her pert nose wrinkled, and her eyebrows drew together. "It is true, Miss Bolton. My family has been intimately acquainted with the Crown for generations. One of my aunts even served as a lady-in-waiting for the queen for several years, before she was excused to see to family matters."

"Right. And the First Lady asked my opinion on her cutlery," the woman muttered.

Abram chuckled and tugged the brim of his hat further down

on his forehead. "Best you and the young'uns move on up the road, Mr. Rounsevell. I don't think Dannie cottons to your stories."

"I don't." She looked past Evan to her brothers. "You two mind yourselves and don't believe everything coming out of a stranger's mouth just because it sounds good."

There was something in her eye, for all her sternness, that he caught sight of for a moment. A hint of something he hadn't seen evidence of in the lady before—vulnerability. Perhaps she had a reason, something deeper than he could guess at which had nothing at all to do with him, for her distrust.

Had she been a man, Evan likely would have called her out for implying he spoke falsely. Lady or not, he could not let her accusations stand; he threw his shoulders back before speaking as sternly as ever his father had spoken to him.

"Miss Bolton, I assure you I am a man of honesty and integrity. That you would doubt me speaks less to your desire to exercise caution and more to a prejudice of which I cannot understand. Perhaps with time, you will understand I am a man of my word."

The expression on her face, including the way her skin paled beneath her freckles, told him well enough that she understood the dressing-down. He looked to Travis and Clark. "Gentlemen? Shall we move forward?"

The boys exchanged startled looks before putting their heels to their horses, moving ahead by several yards. Evan followed, not deigning to look back at Miss Bolton again.

If the woman insisted on treating him with distrust, he had no reason to attempt further conversation with her. Her opinion did not matter so much as her father's, and if Mr. Bolton had more in common with his friendly and open sons, Evan's place on the ranch was as good as secured.

CHAPTER THREE

Swallowing back her pride hadn't ever been easy for Dannie. She didn't lower her head until the Englishman had ridden upfront with her brothers. But when they were far enough ahead that the dust they kicked up didn't drift into her and Abram's faces, she tucked her chin. She knew what was coming.

"Dannie, you can't keep doing that to yourself, nor t'others." Abram flicked the reins, no more than a reminder to the mules that they were expected to keep up the pace. "Not every fine-looking fellow is going to treat you like Robertson. Not every fancy-talker is going to be like they were in Boston, either."

She shivered, despite the warmth of the desert sun. Her hat didn't shade much more than her eyes this late in the day, and they faced near full-on west most of the way home.

Abram knew she didn't talk about David Robertson or Boston. Both of those subjects were off the table, indefinitely. For him to bring them up meant she had misbehaved in a big way. There were few people in the world she took correction from. Her dad, Abram, and Ruthie, and their housekeeper were just about it. Maybe the reverend, so long as he wasn't going on about women wearing trousers.

"It helps to be cautious," she said after the silence hung between them too long. "He's a stranger. And you can tell as plain as I can that he hasn't worked a day in his life. He's claiming to know the Queen of England. The man's stretching the blanket too much with that one. He's probably some kind of actor or silver-tongued thief."

When her father's oldest friend raised his eyebrows at that, she huffed and crossed her arms tightly across her chest. Abram didn't approve of her picking up the slang that the hired hands batted around like kittens with a cricket.

"The Good Lord said 'judge not,' Miss Bolton. Pretty sure that directive applies even in this particular situation." Though he spoke in his usual steady way, the words stung Dannie as much as a harder rebuke.

Before she could think of an argument against his statement, Abram started whistling one of his favorite old songs. Most of them were mournful-sounding, learned from his mother while they were slaves in Georgia. The whistling was a sure sign he had dropped the subject and had no intention of taking it back up with her.

The sun sank lower, and with her brothers ahead and Abram no longer in the mood to chat, Dannie opened up her purse and fished out the slim volume of poetry she'd bought at the bookshop in Tombstone. The front cover only said *Poems*, by someone named Emily Dickinson. It was the fact that the poems had been written by a woman that had drawn her attention to the battered little book.

She loved words. Not that she'd ever consider herself a poet. Quite the opposite. But beautiful words drew her in, and when they described what she felt in her heart but couldn't speak, she loved them all the more. Of course, her problems with David had started out with his pretty words. *The rat.*

But no harm could come from poetry written by another woman. She opened the book without regard to the page and read the first poem her eyes landed upon. Before long, she was engrossed in the imagery of everyday things.

When Abram finally tired of whistling, he told her to read a few poems aloud. She read a few to him, including one that sounded mournful to her.

His mind had always been sharp, and he turned a poem or two on its head. "Don't think she meant it to be read that way. Try again, like you're saying it with a laugh." He had a gift for perspective, and when she read that particular poem again, she saw the fun where she'd seen a frown before.

The boys stayed ahead, as sure of the way as anyone who lived on King Bolton property. When the sky started turning gray behind and purple ahead, they reached the turnoff with the arch over the lane. KB swung from the vine in stylized iron letters, with a three-pointed crown above the initials of their father's brand.

From the archway, it was another mile to the homestead, curving around the first of the rolling hills covered in long spring grasses, all brown and waiting for the monsoons before they turned green again. The elevation of the ranch was too high for cactuses to grow, and it was easily ten degrees cooler at the ranch than in Tombstone, thanks to the mountains peeking up on three sides of their land.

Travis looped his horse back to come alongside them. "Want me to take Mr. Rounsevell in to talk to Dad?"

Dannie's suspicions immediately rose. "Why you?"

Travis's chin jutted out. "I'm the one that invited him to try for a job."

Though she was ready to say she'd rather be the one to make introductions for the stranger, Abram cleared his throat. Her cheeks warmed all over again when she thought of her harsh criticism from before.

She nodded tightly. "All right. Y'all go warn them we're coming, but make sure you wash up before stepping foot in Ruthie's kitchen."

Travis sat up straighter and grinned. "Sure thing, Dannie." He nudged his horse to get her moving, but barely slowed again long enough to tell Clark and the stranger to come ahead with him. She saw the Englishman look back over his shoulder at her, but he followed Travis down the trail to the house.

It took another ten minutes for the mules to get them all the way to the old adobe building. It had been the first permanent structure on ranch land, built by her father, Abram, and a few Mexicans who knew the art of making adobe brick. Her father loved talking about those first years living in the house, sleeping on the roof in the summer.

They rode through the zaguán, the long airy corridor leading them into the stone corral. Despite over twenty years passing since the adobe house was first built, it was still one of the cleverest things Dannie had ever seen. No one could steal a horse or mule without passing by the main house, the partner's house where Abram and Ruthie lived, or through the adobe house that now served as storage and bunk rooms.

She climbed down from the wagon as soon as it stopped, and Abram followed suit a bit slower. He'd been wounded as a young man, when he was still a soldier, and his bones ached more every year. Or so he said.

Ruthie came out of the main house, wiping her hands on her apron before settling them on her hips.

"Abram Steele, you bringing home more mouths for me to feed?" Anyone who didn't know Ruthie might think she was complaining. Dannie heard the delight in the accusation.

"Yes, ma'am. And more food to cook." Abram swept off his hat as he approached his wife, then looped his arm around her shoulder. She was much smaller than he was. Dannie had passed Ruthie in height when she was only thirteen years old. Diminutive or not, Ruthie was still a force to be reckoned with when she had a mind to be.

A ten-year-old boy swept out the door and came to the wagon, eagerly scooping up crates of supplies. "Did you get my candy, Dannie?" Lee darted a look at his grandfather. "You didn't let her forget?"

Abram snorted. "You reminded us about a dozen times yesterday. Couldn't forget if we'd wanted to." He kissed Ruthie on the forehead. "Send those other boys out to unload. I'll go clean up before supper."

"I have a bath ready for you, Dannie." Ruthie came to inspect the wagon full of goods. "And Lee can empty the crates into the pantry if he expects to get the candy you brung him."

Lee grinned without apology and hurried inside, calling for Travis and Clark to help now that the wagon had arrived. Dannie shook her skirt, though it was unlikely it would dislodge much of the dust she'd collected on the road. She scooped up a small carton of baking powder and a bag of cornmeal before going in through the kitchen. She put both items on the table before going through to the front of the house.

She passed the open doorway to the parlor, then stopped in her tracks when she heard her father's deep baritone.

"You don't say. Met old Buffalo Bill, did you? I always wanted to catch one of his exhibitions."

Her temper flared. Had Mr. Rounsevell laid claim to another famous acquaintance? She turned around to the mirrored hat-tree near the front door and took in her reflection quickly. Her cheeks were pink from riding toward the sun for the last hour, and her hair showed signs of the wind that had come up just before they reached home. Nothing about her looked intimidating at the moment.

The Englishman's low, cultured voice reached down the hall to her. "It was a grand sight to see, Mr. Bolton. The display of expertise in marksmanship and horsemanship would have been enough to thrill the Royal Court, but Mr. Cody has a flair for showmanship. I dare say his charm won over as many hearts as Annie Oakley's ability with a rifle."

That did it. Dannie pulled her hat pin out and hung her straw-brimmed hat on a hook, then smoothed back her dark curls as best she could. Her father had a love for folk heroes, which was why she and her brothers bore the names they did, and Rounsevell must've figured that out quickly enough to exploit it.

She swept into the parlor, ready to do battle.

Her father sat in his favorite armchair, a luxury shipped from Austin ten years before. The Englishman was on the sofa across the rug, and the instant the man saw Dannie, he stood. Her father stood, too, and immediately opened his arms to her. His lungs still pained him enough that he minimized his movement whenever possible.

"Dannie, welcome home."

"Dad." She stepped in to his warm embrace and received his whiskery kiss. Her father's beard had been as black as her hair when she was a child, but it was a sight more gray now.

"Everything go well in town?" He stepped back, and his smile gentled.

"Yes, Dad." She turned to face their guest, who still stood, his head now bare. Why'd the man have to be so tall? Taller than her father. With those green-brown eyes and walnut hair, he looked far too respectable. No wonder her brothers had been taken in.

"Mr. Rounsevell and I were just getting acquainted. Did you know his father's a marquess? I'm not even sure I know what that is."

Dannie narrowed her eyes at the Englishman, but she kept her tone flat when she spoke. "A marquess is below a duke but above an earl." Just a marquess? Why not a duke? Or the crown prince, come to think of it.

The Englishman didn't so much as shift his weight or bat an eye. "Lord Whittenbury, yes. But that's of no consequence here, is it? I'm a second son, so come to think of it, it's not of much consequence in England, either." His smile wasn't so much self-deprecating as it was irked.

"Around here, a man's known by his deeds rather than his birth. We can't take the time to check pedigrees when we need hands." Her dad's voice, coupled with his slow Texan accent, had always soothed her in the past. But not in that moment.

"Dad." She turned so fast her skirts flared around her ankles. "The boys don't really understand the ranch the way you and I do. I'm concerned Mr. Rounsevell has been misled. Not purposefully, of course. But we aren't exactly in a position to bring on more help right now." She didn't add what she hoped her father already knew. *Especially help that doesn't know the first thing about ranching.*

Her father wasn't one to pat her on the head and send her along like a good little girl. In fact, he'd taken to discussing all the ranch's business with her at the end of each day. So when she spoke, he listened, his eyes upon her face.

She knew they had enough for another year, maybe two, before they'd need to sell out. The boys didn't know they'd come down that far in the world. Their father denied the possibility to them with every chance he got. But even he would give in if it meant the difference between poverty and a good future for his children.

"I know you're worried, Dannie. Remember, we've been through tight spots before." He released a deep sigh that seemed to come straight from his bones. Then he looked up at Rounsevell.

"You've been out in the dust for a few hours, Rounsevell. Why don't you clean up and join us for supper? Ruthie's made some stew and cornbread as good as anything you've ever tasted. We can talk over the situation after everyone's fed."

Good. Maybe they could feed the man, put him up a night in the bunkhouse, and then send him on his way.

Heartened by her father's level head, Dannie shot a triumphant glance at Rounsevell. "That sounds like a fine idea. If you'll excuse me, gentlemen." With the decisions postponed until she could take part in them, Dannie had things to do. Removing the dust was at the top of her list, and she had a bath waiting for her.

CHAPTER FOUR

Whatever Evan had done to upset Miss Bolton, he needed to undo it. He'd never had a woman take such an instant dislike to him before. Though he was a second son, he usually merited at least polite behavior. Feigned interest, even.

He glowered at the basin of water he'd been directed to wash in, using the towel to dry his hands and pat at his neck. The grit from the road had somehow gone beneath his collar, and he missed his valet for perhaps the dozenth time since leaving England.

But he'd made it. He was on a genuine ranch, in the middle of Arizona territory. It was a place so wild the nation had yet to claim it as a state. The people talked differently, reminiscent of the Americans he had met in the eastern states, but the way Mr. Bolton drew out his words fascinated Evan. He'd seen cattle as they rode in, some with the longhorns the Texans had been so proud of when he went through that state. He'd caught a glimpse of antelope, too.

The sunset had appeared like a painting, with colors he couldn't recall seeing anywhere else before, and it had been with reluctance that he had entered the house before seeing the entire sky darken and fill with stars. Perhaps after his chat with Mr. Bolton, he could go out and see for himself how big the sky was. The Texans had claimed their stars were somehow superior to everyone else's, but there was something about the dry air of Arizona that made Evan think he might have a clearer view in the desert.

Evan stepped out of the bedroom which likely belonged to one of the Bolton sons and back into the kitchen. He hadn't been made aware of a dining room. Perhaps Mrs. Steele—Ruthie, he corrected himself—could point him in the right direction.

When he entered the kitchen, he saw the full-length table that had been empty when he arrived covered with pots and pans of food. There was a tablecloth, too, over the boards. There were eight plates at the table, eight cups, and he briefly wondered if there was more family he had yet to meet.

Ruthie set another platter on the table, and it bore squares of a thick, yellow cake-like substance. He saw beans in another bowl, stew in a pot, potatoes, and a pie, though he couldn't tell what kind. He'd never eaten any of the dishes spread before him. They were simplistic. The type of fare an English farmer might enjoy, or that a poor inn would serve.

Travis and Clark came from outside with the brown-skinned boy Evan hadn't heard named. They grinned at Evan and stood behind three of the chairs. Even the youngest boy. Abram appeared, too, and came around to the side where Evan stood, still trying to understand the etiquette involved in a meal like this.

"Normally, Ruthie, Lee, and me, we eat at our house." Abram pointed out the door, as though that would help Evan orient himself. "But not on supply night, and not with Loretta gone."

"Loretta?" Evan asked, still confused.

"Loretta Perkins. She's our cook and housekeeper," Clark said. "She's gone to visit her sister."

That meant Ruthie wasn't a servant in the household. Evan thanked whatever angels were watching over him that he had found out before making a fool of himself. "Who else lives on the ranch?"

Miss Bolton walked in at that moment and went to one end of the table, her father close behind her. He took the other end.

"I apologize for keeping y'all waiting." Mr. Bolton pulled out his chair, and everyone moved to do the same.

Evan hesitated. He had wound up standing on Miss Bolton's left. Should he get her chair for her?

She seated herself before he decided, then he realized everyone was seated and staring at him. After swallowing the awkward desire to clear his throat, he pulled out his chair and then took a seat. "Pardon me. I am not accustomed to taking dinner this way."

He heard Miss Bolton mutter just under her breath. "I bet not."

Perhaps it was his upbringing she objected to.

Mr. Bolton bowed his head. "Travis. Please say grace."

The whole family bowed their heads, and Evan had to stare. Prayers at meals were unusual in the larger houses, though he'd been in a few wherein the head of the family made a point of giving a minor speech on one subject or another. Sometimes a vicar would give a sermon or a prayer.

But Travis's words were humble, his words direct.

"Lord, we thank Thee for our safe return from town. We thank Thee for this food, and for Ruthie who prepared it for us. We thank Thee for our blessings. Please help us to be good servants unto Thee, that we can be tools in Thy hands. And please help Mr. Rounsevell to find what he's searching for in our territory. Amen." A chorus of amens followed the young man's, and it took Evan another moment to speak his own.

No one reacted as though the words the boy uttered had been extraordinary. They seemed to accept the simple supplication as a normal part of their routine. Yet something had shifted in Evan. A weight pressed upon his heart.

He'd never been prayed for, not within his hearing. Surely, his mother had prayed over him. Perhaps a nanny when he was young. The sensation of hearing his name in an address to God was something he couldn't immediately define.

"Would you pass the potatoes, Mr. Rounsevell?" Abram asked.

Evan started and found the dish, serving it to his left.

"Aren't you having any?" the old man asked, raising his eyebrows. "Here we pass clockwise. You take what's in front of you, then pass to your left."

Wordlessly, Evan served himself a boiled potato and passed the dish. Then he turned to see Miss Bolton holding the steaming platter of yellow cakes. But they couldn't be cakes. Surely even Americans didn't serve cake with their evening meal.

"Cornbread?" she asked, ready to serve him a slice.

It was a type of bread? "Yes. Thank you." Might as well give everything at least a taste. It would be impolite to turn down anything offered to him by a hostess in England, and it was logical that rule had to apply here.

Before long, his plate was full; there was even stew upon it. Thick stew that looked like gravy. The boys across from him mostly used their spoons to eat the stuff, but he did see them get the last of it up by swiping a forkful of cornbread through it.

There was only one fork, one spoon, and one knife. No dishes were taken away as they were emptied, and no new ones brought out.

Everyone at the table talked at once to one another. The boy, Lee, was asking Travis and Clark questions about Tombstone. Abram spoke to Mr. Bolton as though they were equals and friends. Ruthie listened to their conversation but only spoke when she needed to correct the boys' manners. Apparently, elbows were not permitted on the table and one should chew with his mouth closed, but she seemed little concerned about anything else.

On the ship that carried Evan across the ocean, he'd had dining companions. The same every night. And they'd eaten according to the etiquette he'd been raised with. In the towns he passed through on his way west, he ate in hotels with fine tablecloths and waitresses in black dresses and starched aprons. In the dining car of the train, he'd been treated to plainer fare than usual, but there was still an elegance to the service.

But at this table, for the first time in his life, he noticed a complete lack of ceremony in every aspect of the meal. Sitting at table was something of an art form, or so he had thought. Here, there were different principles at play.

DANNIE ADJOURNED WITH HER FATHER AND THE ENGLISHMAN BACK to the parlor after the meal, throughout which the Englishman had remained a quiet observer. Likely he thought they ate like animals, given what she knew of proper table etiquette. It didn't matter that they were polite, or that they tidied up after themselves. Simple eating was somehow equated to uncivilized eating by the elite of the world.

Her father did not retake his seat, though he did gesture for Dannie and Mr. Rounsevell to be seated. She chose a chair at the corner of the rug, far from anywhere the man might sit.

"Mr. Rounsevell, I always say starting business by breaking bread with a man is a wise move. It allows us to size each other up and enter into negotiations on friendly terms and full stomachs."

Before the Englishman could respond, Dannie spoke. "Dad, these aren't negotiations. I realize Mr. Rounsevell has been introduced to us as a guest, but the man is looking for a position of employment. We ought to start this conversation as you would with any prospective drover."

SALLY BRITTON

Mr. Rounsevell sent a surprised glance her way, and it took Dannie a moment to realize she'd sounded a tad too citified when she spoke. Business did that to her. She might have grown up with a Southern drawl, but the eastern finishing school in Boston had tainted her accent in certain matters.

She wrinkled her nose at the Englishman and was ready to accuse him of staring when her father released a deep sigh.

"Dannie's right. As much as I might enjoy a conversation with you, young man, you have come to us with the purpose of obtaining gainful employment. We'd best satisfy things on that end." Her father lowered himself into his favorite chair, elbows on the arms of it, and leaned forward. "Where should we start?"

For the first time, Mr. Rounsevell appeared uncomfortable. He shifted upon the sofa cushion like a boy about to confess a wrongdoing. "I had rather not speak of my family—"

"No one asked you to," Dannie said, crossing her arms over her chest. If he was about to exercise false modesty to throw around important-sounding English names or more claims to royal connections, she'd not hear a word of it.

The man's puzzled expression returned. "Is that not part of this interview process? Family connections?"

Her father answered that one. "Not in the west." He stroked his graying mustache downward, his eyes flicking from Rounsevell to Dannie. "Out here, from the beginning of an acquaintance, you trust more to how a man behaves at present than whatever his past has been. I've known men who were thieves in the east, but I trust them with my life and valuables out here. You worry less about where a man comes from than you do where he's going, and what he plans to do to get there."

That was true enough, in most cases. Dannie smirked at the Englishman, certain they'd ruined his scheme to rattle off a list of important contacts.

If anything, the man appeared relieved. "I understand the sentiment. One wishes to be judged based upon his own merit, not dubious rumors or pedigree."

32

Her hackles raised at that word. Pedigree. As if people were racehorses.

"Are you an experienced horseman?" her father asked, his eyes sharp. Dannie relaxed. She needed to trust her father. Despite his recent illness, he was still a shrewd businessman. He wouldn't do anything that would harm the family.

"I have ridden since childhood." Mr. Rounsevell spoke with confidence. "I am a fine horseman. I have won cups in a few shows, and I can hold my own on any beast."

"He came in on a thoroughbred," Dannie added, darting a look at her father to see what he made of that news. "A horse fit to go to church on Sunday and little else."

Rounsevell cast her another confused look. The fellow needed to stop doing that, or she'd have to think him less than intelligent. When her father nodded for her to go on, she wanted to retract her statement. Why did she have to spell it out for the greenhorn?

"Your horse looks nice, but he's probably never cut through a herd in his life. He's pretty, might make a good carriage horse or calvary horse, but he's not meant for work. You need to ride animals made for this life. Rangy horses. Small. Quick. The kind that can go a day in the desert without water if need be. And you need more than one."

He blinked at her. "More than one? But I thought a man needed a single good, dependable horse?"

"We take care of our animals," Dannie's father said, his tone amused. "But that's something those books of yours likely got wrong. A good drover rides several horses, and they have different purposes. You don't use the same animal to ride herd as you do to cut an animal out. Most cowboys have three, sometimes up to five animals they can use for various purposes. Sometimes a mule, too, if the creature's well trained."

"Oh." Rounsevell's shoulders fell. "Then horses aren't considered companions, of a sort?"

The man sounded so let down by the idea, Dannie almost felt

sorry for him. "There are probably a few people out there with special relationships to their mounts. And we all have to have a certain amount of trust in our horses." She smiled a touch. "But they're working animals. They have jobs to do. They aren't pets."

"Have you ever had experience riding herd?" When her father asked that question, Mr. Rounsevell slowly shook his head. Her father sighed. "Do you know what that means?"

"It means to ride alongside the cattle and keep an eye on them." Rounsevell shifted as though he sat on buckboard instead of their comfortable furniture. "I have not done that before."

"Have you ever attended a branding?" her father asked.

"No."

"Roped a bull?"

"I've had practice. On sheep."

The cattleman paused a moment, but continued his line of questioning.

"Mucked a stable?"

"No."

Her father bit the insides of his cheek and narrowed his eyes. "Are you a decent shot with a weapon?"

The Englishman perked up. "I am. I've won several competitions, in fact, and I do well during hunting season."

Dannie dropped her face in her hands. She almost felt sorry for him. "Hunting season? Do you mean when Englishmen get all dressed up in red coats and go tearing through a stand of trees after a helpless little fox? With about a hundred dogs in front of you?"

Silence was her only answer. The man was even less qualified than she expected. "Dad. You can't hire him." She directed her frown at her father. "We've got three cowboys. We can make do on that until the fall cattle drive."

Ranches didn't have to have a full stock of cowboys to run, most of the year. And when it came time to drive the horses to the train depot, the ranchers worked together. They'd have enough men when the time came. She hoped.

"Frosty's leg is still on the mend," her father reminded her. "And Buck's a hothead as likely as not to get a job with another outfit if he thinks the food is better. That leaves Ed. You telling me you think Ed can handle things on his own?"

"You've got me," Dannie countered, avoiding answering his question. "And Travis and Clark."

"They're just boys," her father said, fist thumping on the arm of the chair. "And they're both studying so they can go to college. You know that. I will educate my children, Daniella, and they'll ride roughshod over every mean-spirited cattle baron in this territory once they are."

Dannie shrank back into her chair. Her father's views on education were as stubborn as he was. No amount of kicking up a fuss had kept her home when he decided she needed a more delicate touch. Her mother had died when she was young, and a housekeeper from Tennessee couldn't teach Dannie French. Though why she'd ever need to know that language, Dannie couldn't say.

"As for you, young lady, you and Ed by yourselves can't handle all the work."

"A greenhorn isn't going to be much help. Roping *sheep*, Dad?" It was mutinous to keep digging in on her position, but she'd not give up. Even if the stranger was watching the father-daughter argument with wide eyes and an uncomfortable tilt to his head.

"Leastwise he's not likely to have bad habits." Her father looked the Englishman over again. "You sickly?"

The man fumbled for his answer, surprised at being addressed abruptly. "No, not ever."

"You get along with others or you prone to fights?" Her father puffed out his chest.

"I prefer not to engage in fisticuffs." Rounsevell attempted a smile. Dannie glowered at him. Did he not know how to fight? And—*fisticuffs?* What kind of a man couldn't throw a punch when necessary? It seemed his height and broad shoulders were a product of breeding rather than exercise. Shame.

"Do you drink?" Her father raised both of his hands, palm-up. "I don't mean to say you can't ever, but we run a dry outfit when we're working. You drink only when you don't have work the next day and I'll not care how you spend your free time."

The response to that was a quick nod. "Of course. I would never do anything to impair my judgement while in your employment."

Nothing about the Englishman sitting in her house made a lick of sense to Dannie. He dressed well, sounded dandified, and had never done a day's work in his life. What was he doing on a ranch in the middle of nowhere looking for a job? Maybe he'd made eyes at the wrong lady back in England and was on the run. That was as likely as anything else.

But being saddled with a greenhorn all summer didn't sit well with her. They needed someone who already knew what he was doing. How was she going to get her father to see reason?

Guilt gnawed at her, even though this man's arrival wasn't her fault. Even though he didn't look like David Robertson, and didn't talk like her former fiancé, he had a natural charm so similar that Dannie couldn't help the comparison.

Robertson had hurt her, and through her had hurt her father. Couldn't her dad see that this Englishman would prove to be the same? A sharp dresser, smooth-talker, and ready to leave them in a pit if he didn't out right push them in.

There had to be a way to keep her family safe.

"You ought to let the men vote," Dannie said as quick as the idea came to her. "If he's inexperienced, it's the others who will have to train him up. They should get some say in it."

"You make a fine point," her father agreed. He stood with a groan, and Dannie winced. Her father was a man large in stature and life, but a recent spring bout with pneumonia had weakened him. He wasn't as filled out as he'd been before the illness, and there were more wrinkles around his eyes and along his fore-head. "Mr. Rounsevell, might as well take you on out to the bunkhouse."

Knowing Frosty, Buck, and Ed, they'd resent an uppity Englishman in their midst as much as she would.

CHAPTER FIVE

The bunkhouse was part of the adobe structure Evan had ridden through to get into the stable yard. They walked into the open corridor. Mr. Bolton rapped on a door on the same side as the animal pen. There was a window facing into the corridor, but only a little light flickered through the curtains covering it.

The door swung open almost immediately, revealing the outline of a tall man with suspenders hanging from his waist-band. The man saw Dannie, who had insisted on coming out with Mr. Bolton and Evan, and he hastily pulled on the bracers over his shoulders.

"King," the man said, dipping his head. "Can we help you, sir?" He spoke with a drawl that stretched a lot longer than Mr. Bolton's proud Texan accent. Evan was not at all an expert on American dialects, but he immediately wondered where the man had come from.

"We've come on a matter of business, Buck. Everyone inside decent?"

"I think so." Buck took a step back and opened the door wider, looking over his shoulder. "Frosty, Ed, we've got company."

Evan had to duck to enter the doorway, as did Mr. Bolton, but his daughter came in without trouble. It took a moment for his eyes to adjust to the dim light. There was a lantern on a table, where a man sat in a chair with his right leg stretched over a stool. He didn't appear much older than Evan, and another glance at Buck showed that man to be a bit younger. A third cowboy was standing from a cot, book in hand. He was shorter, with high cheekbones, bronzed skin, and black hair.

The room wasn't exceptionally large. There was a bunk bed against the wall on the right, a cot to the left, windows facing the corral, and an iron stove between them. Miss Bolton stepped over to stand in front of the bunks, her hands tucked behind her back and her expression closed.

"Mr. Rounsevell, this here is Frosty. He's been with me the longest. Best drover in the territory, and my foreman these last five years." Mr. Bolton gestured to the man still sitting, and the cowboy nodded deeply but said nothing. "He was near-trampled not too long ago, but he's just about healed up."

Mr. Bolton gestured to the man holding the book. "This is Ed, whose full name takes about a day and a half to say." That cowboy chuckled, tipping his head in acknowledgement. "He's a good hand. He can cut out heifers the way most of us carve butter."

"I'll accept that compliment. Thank you, King." Though the man appeared to be of Spanish descent, he spoke English as well as any American Evan had heard so far. Well enough to make sense to an Englishman.

"And this here is Buck. There isn't a horse this side of the Mississippi he can't ride, or so he says." King sounded like he was amused by the statement rather than a firm believer in Buck's boast. "He's proved a good hand, though he's been with us only since October last."

Buck puffed out his chest and slid his thumbs beneath his suspenders. "I'll keep proving my worth, sir."

"I have no doubt of that, Buck." Mr. Bolton gestured to Evan. "Gentlemen, this is Mr. Rounsevell. He's come about a position.

Mr. Rounsevell, why don't you tell these fine fellows your qualifications."

"Pardon?" Evan looked from Mr. Bolton to his daughter, who smirked, then back to the three men with their eyes glued on him. "Oh." He cleared his throat. "I am from England, where I have had years of experience in riding, and shooting, and hunting. I do not yet have the experience of a drover, but I am a quick study. I will learn all I can and take orders without complaint." His father always seemed to think that the best sign of a hard worker. Perhaps such a trait would translate the same way to Americans.

Buck snorted. "So he's a greenhorn."

"That's what I said," Miss Bolton agreed, her countenance as stern as before.

Evan's dreams had led him to that moment. If he wanted to work a real Western ranch, learn from cowboys, participate in a real cattle drive, he had to get these men to accept him. He was out of money, and he wasn't about to send a letter home and admit his hopes had proven foolish.

He squared his shoulders, then relaxed his hands to hang down by his side. Confidence had gotten him out of trouble before. "It is true that I know nothing of the work you do. But I am willing to work and learn as I go. If you gentlemen will grant me a trial basis, you will see well enough that I mean what I say. If, when the trial is over, you feel I have not done adequately, I will go on my way without pay. But if I prove myself adequate, I will ask that you allow me to stay."

Ed crossed his arms and raised his black eyebrows. "It's brave of you to suggest such a thing."

"Sounds about as useless as a one-legged grasshopper." Buck watched Miss Bolton as he spoke, almost as though he hoped for her approval. She did not even acknowledge him.

The man seated at the table started to stand, pushing himself up with a wince. At his full height, he was nearly a match for Mr. Bolton. He came forward, somewhat stiffly, until he stood no more than a foot away from Evan. He looked Evan directly in the eye.

Perhaps this cowboy's name had come from his hard gaze. Frosty had eyes as cold and blue as a winter morning.

When he spoke, his words were matter-of-fact. "Every man oughta get a chance to prove he's worth his salt." He didn't so much as blink when he swung his stare from Evan to Mr. Bolton. "I reckon we give him two weeks." The finality with which Frosty spoke, and the way both Boltons reacted to his words, meant his was the deciding vote. Mr. Bolton nodded once, and Miss Bolton's shoulders dropped in defeat.

Two weeks to prove himself a capable cowboy. More had been accomplished in less time, Evan knew. He started to grin.

"Ain't calling him by his name," Buck muttered. "More of a mouthful than Ed's."

Evan perked up at that. Perhaps he'd receive what Abram had called a christening sooner rather than later if his surname proved too troublesome. A real cowboy name. The prospect perhaps carried more significance to him than it should.

Ed tucked his book onto his cot. "Let's get you a bed, greenhorn."

Evan immediately wilted. Surely that would not be it.

Miss Bolton frowned, then walked out the door. Her father watched her go before holding his hand out to Evan. "Welcome to the KB Ranch, Mr. Rounsevell. I hope this proves a good bargain for both of us. Now, I'll leave you to Frosty and the bunkhouse. Goodnight, men."

"Goodnight, King," Ed and Buck said together.

"Goodnight, Mr. Bolton," Evan responded with a nod.

Frosty said nothing but stayed where he was, staring at Evan. Only after Mr. Bolton's steps had receded, the echo of his boots on the hard-packed dirt no longer heard in the adobe corridor, did the foreman speak. "Go with Ed. Get your gear."

Ed went to the door, bringing a second lantern with him.

"There's a spare cot and bedding in the room over one. We'll bring it into the bunkhouse. What else have you got?"

"A spare set of clothes." Evan shrugged. "My horse tack." What else did a man need in the west? "I've got a pistol, too. Brand new Colt." He'd left it in the saddlebag, not certain he wanted to be seen carrying a weapon in Tombstone.

The tall man clicked his tongue on the roof of his mouth. "That so? You'll want to carry it on the trail for vermin, snakes, coyotes. I find a rifle a sight more useful against the bigger predators. A weapon should never be out of your reach, of course."

"Of course." They entered the room on the same side of the corridor as the bunk room. He held the lantern high. "See what you can find to haul back to the room."

Evan saw stacks of equipment on shelves against the wall, ropes hanging from hooks in the ceiling, and other tools he didn't know the use of given the darkness. But he did find a wooden bedframe against the wall. A straw tick was folded over the top of it. With a bit of shuffling through the room, he had a few blankets stacked on the bed, too. He hauled it out behind Ed.

"Might I ask what your full name is, sir?" Evan asked. "I am somewhat curious after what Mr. Bolton said."

Ed stopped in the corridor, not opening the bunk door right away. Instead, he held his lantern higher, illuminating the sharp planes of his cheekbones. "I will tell you my name because you are new, and I do not mind. But it is dangerous, Englishman, to ask for such personal details out in the West. Some people are likely to get the wrong idea about you. I keep my name to myself in a lot of places, too." His white teeth flashed in the lantern light. "Eduardo Blackfox Ramirez Byrd."

Evan, arms full of his new bedding, immediately voiced his first thought. "That name tells a story. Might I hear it?"

The other man chuckled, the sound somehow ominous in the shadows of the corridor. "Not tonight. Around here, you earn stories after hard work." He pushed open the door and ducked through the low doorway. Evan ducked his head and followed.

Despite the weight in his arms, and the uncertainty of his future, he felt the blood in his veins quicken.

All his life he had waited for an adventure to find him. Imagined riding through the deserts and mountains of the west. Finally, he had done it. He was in the wild deserts of Arizona.

Not everyone lived their dreams. Evan intended to give himself over to the experience in full. It would end soon enough, after the cattle drive in the autumn, and he intended to enjoy every moment of it.

CHAPTER SIX

Evan woke to the strong smells of coffee and something burning. He pushed the blanket off his face and sat up, rubbing at his eyes. Buck had snorted and grunted in his sleep all the night long. The other two men seemed to sleep through the noise without trouble, but Evan couldn't be sure he had ever fallen fully unconscious.

"C'mon, Duke." A kick to his cot made him look up to see Frosty standing next to the low bed, a tin mug in hand. "Drink up."

His stomach twisted. *Duke?* He did not protest the title out loud but accepted the cup. The coffee smelled bitter, but the cup was warm, and Evan was not about to show even a hint of dislike. He would push himself through every difficult moment up to the autumn cattle drive with a smile.

The coffee didn't burn his tongue, but it was difficult to get it down without cringing. Had they mixed dirt into the pot to make it grittier? He finished the cup, then went to pull on his boots.

Ed stopped him, shoving a metal plate into Evan's hands. There were beans, biscuits, and a pile of yellow eggs beneath it all. That answered his question about breakfast. Apparently, the hands did not eat with the family. It was a shame, given how filling Ruthie's dinner had been the night before.

Buck was gone already. Ed sat with a plate at the small table, scooping food into his mouth at a speed that would have horrified Evan's mother. Frosty sat on the stool he'd propped his leg on the night before, pouring another cup of coffee for himself.

Ed started talking between bites, and it took Evan a moment to realize Ed's words were directed toward him. "You'll be with me today. We're going to show you the way things work around the homestead. You'll do the chores I give you, and if you do them right we can get you on a horse by the end of the week. But you're the new hand. And we're gonna treat you like you're the new hand. *Comprendes*?"

"I wouldn't want special treatment." Evan had to choke out the words. The bottoms of the biscuits had been what he'd smelled burning. Had they cooked them on top of the little stove? The pan of eggs came from there. However breakfast had been constructed, it hadn't been with a deft hand.

"Good." Ed scooped up the last of his beans. "We've got a bet going as to how long you're going to last." He shoved the beans into his mouth.

Frosty took the opportunity to speak at last. "Shake your boots out before you put them on, Duke." Then he stood, grimacing when he put weight on his leg.

"Shake out my boots?" Evan looked to Ed when Frosty didn't say another word.

"It's not mating season for the tarantulas, but scorpions are almost a year-round trouble." Ed shrugged, as though the repulsive creatures he mentioned were of no concern. "It's a good habit for the territory. Up here at the ranch, it stays cooler than in Tucson or Tombstone, so we don't get as many of the crawling types. But it's still a desert. Your boots look like home to a lot of critters."

Evan eyed the boot he had nearly pulled on with sudden uneasiness. "Do they?" He put his plate down, his food hardly touched, and lifted his boot to look inside before shaking it out. Nothing came out of either boot, but he wasn't exactly easy about it until the boots were on and nothing had attacked him from the inside.

Frosty didn't say another word as he left the room, but Ed waited patiently until Evan had on his hat and his only other shirt, a navy blue he hoped wouldn't ruin easily.

"You'll want a coat to start the day." Ed had already pulled on his own thick coat with a wool collar. "It starts out about fifty-five degrees in the mornings. We'll hit eighty-five by the afternoon. It's a big swing, but you'll get used to it."

Picking up his coat, Evan followed Ed out of the bunk room and to the outhouse outside of the adobe building. Ed sauntered toward the stables, appearing impressively relaxed for someone with such speed. The long building was also made of adobe brick, at least halfway up, and it had metal sheeting on top for the roof.

The ranch house was made of wood, with normal shingles for a roof, but Evan had noted a lot of adobe structures since coming out to the territory. He hadn't seen many trees, which likely explained the choice of building materials.

There were stalls along one side of the structure, horses in each of them, including Evan's gelding. They stuck their heads out and perked up their ears when the men came through.

Ed started talking, his words coming rapidly one after another. "You're going to muck out stables today. Every third day, in fact. Shouldn't take you long. Turn the horses out to pasture, clean up, bring them back in at night when you've got the fresh straw down." He outlined where all the tools were for that necessary bit of work, and the hay in the loft above. "The horses spend most of their time out to pasture this time of year, until the monsoons start. So it doesn't get too bad in here just yet. You got lucky there."

"This is not the first time I have heard mention of monsoons. I was not aware they were a problem in America."

"I can't think it's something many advertise. Didn't know about it myself until I came here from Oklahoma territory." Ed tipped his hat back and folded his arms. "But they're a thing of beauty. Rain every day, like clockwork, for a month or even two if we're in a good year. We've had more than our share of dry spells lately. Even the atheists have been praying for rain." Though he said it with a smile, some jauntiness had gone from his tone.

"But that's worry for another time. For now, you'd best get to work on the stalls. I'll be over in the blacksmith shed." He'd shown Evan that small structure before entering the barn. "If you finish before I do, come find me there." He clapped Evan on the shoulder. "Good luck, Duke."

Evan winced again. "Duke?"

"Yep. Frosty worked it out for us."

Given that Evan had hardly heard Frosty say more than a few sentences, he didn't think the foreman was qualified to *name* him.

"Might I inquire how he did such a thing?"

Adjusting his hat, Ed shrugged. "The accent did it. We've got ourselves a King already, and Miss Bolton would throw a right fit if we called you any kind of prince. So Duke it is. Better than the name Buck had in mind." His grin stretched wider across his face. "It ain't so bad, Duke." He slapped Evan on the shoulder again, then went on his way.

Looking from his retreating form to the row of horses staring at him, Evan sighed deeply. Then wrinkled his nose. Mucking stables. It made sense. At his father's country seat, Evan had seen more than one new groom broken in by tending to the least enjoyable chores.

He found a rope lead where Ed had said they would be. First, he had to get all the horses out of the way. Then he could clean up their mess.

THE EARLY MORNING WEATHER AGREED WITH DANNIE. SHE KEPT her window open a crack most nights just so she could wake to the scent of cold, clean mountain air. She breathed deeply, then opened the window all the way and started her day.

Dressed in her favorite divided skirt—the dark brown nearly the same color as her father's leather chaps—her boots, and a flannel shirt over her long-sleeved blouse. She wouldn't set the fashionable world on its ear anytime soon, but the clothing was serviceable and comfortable. Nothing else mattered on the ranch.

Dannie came down the stairs at a fast clip, already taking in the smell of warm biscuits and bacon. She entered the kitchen to see Ruthie laying everything out on the table.

"You're up early," Dannie said brightly. "Mrs. Perkins never has the table set before six."

"That's because your poor Mrs. Perkins has about a dozen chores to see to beforehand." Ruthie filled a mug with coffee, then put it down in Dannie's spot. "Eat up. Those brothers of yours will be down any minute and they'll not wait for you to fill your plate before they fill their stomachs."

Dannie laughed but didn't hesitate to do as she was told. A ranch ran on its stomach, like most of the world. With a full day ahead, she needed a solid start to her morning. "Can I get some sandwiches to take with me today? Frosty wants me to see the fence line near Middle Canyon. Rustler season will be here soon, and we want to be ready for it."

"These are desperate times for desperate men." Ruthie shook her head and lowered herself into the chair nearest Dannie. "And after the droughts, there are more than a few such folk out there."

"Regardless, they can't have the cattle we've managed to hold on to." Dannie's smile didn't last long. Cattle rustling was a serious offense anywhere in the country, but with most ranchers in the territory living hand to mouth after the drought, everyone viewed rustlers as worse than snakes.

As long as Dannie could remember, cattle thieves on both sides of the border regularly stole mavericks from each other, rushing across the invisible national line to strengthen their claims to the herds. People got hurt sometimes, and worse. But with her father's poor health and their lack of manpower, anything they lost that year was unlikely to be regained.

"We'll have to keep men out with the herd as much as possible." Dannie buttered a biscuit and then sighed. "I just don't know how."

Ruthie narrowed her eyes and leaned forward. "You certainly won't be out there with them, Dannie. Don't think Loretta and I will let you. No matter what your pa says." Invoking the name of their disapproving housekeeper made Dannie wince. Loretta Perkins had regularly bemoaned Dannie's lack of appropriate female company.

That hadn't stopped her from leaving to visit her sister over a month before, and she still hadn't sent word as to when—or whether—she would return.

The argument over watching the herd would keep until it was time to worry over such things, so Dannie stayed silent and enjoyed her breakfast instead.

Travis and Clark appeared, dressed except for their hats and boots, bleary-eyed as though they hadn't slept the same eight hours Dannie had enjoyed. The days were getting longer and harder, and so was their work to keep the ranch alive.

"What are you two boys up to today?" Ruthie asked, affection in her voice. She'd been part of the family since before Dannie's birth, and she had a tender spot in her heart for both of the boys she'd watched grow.

"Studying," Travis muttered. "After chores."

"We're supposed to be working on calculus." Clark snorted. "When does a rancher ever need calculus? Dannie, you don't know calculus, do you?"

She narrowed her eyes at her youngest brother. "A ladies' finishing school doesn't worry about mathematics beyond keeping household accounts. But you can bet if I would've learned calculus that I'd be using it." She looked down at her plate, mostly empty. "It would prove a sight more useful than the French lessons I took."

Ruthie stood and gave Dannie's shoulder a pat. "Don't you go belly-aching about that school. You loved what you learned there. As I recall, your only real complaint was that it was too far from home."

Dannie wasn't about to argue that with Ruthie, either. Of course it had been something of an adventure to go to the eastern states and learn things like languages and dances, singing, and all the subtleties in the art of conversation. But it had all proved useless when the drought came, and her fiancé had up and left her, and her father had fallen ill. Absolutely useless.

"I'd rather not apply for Baylor next spring. But with Dad's health—" Travis glared at his coffee before adding several spoonfuls of sugar to it. He'd started insisting on drinking it the year before, though he obviously didn't like the bitter drink much. He wound up putting more sugar and cream in his cup than coffee.

"I'll be joining you the next year," Clark put in. "What's going to happen to the ranch while we're gone? That's what I want to know."

Dannie bristled. She'd take care of things, like she always had, but her brothers kept ignoring her contributions to the family. If they didn't wise up to all the work she did soon—

A heavy footfall had all three Bolton children turning to the door. Their father came in, wearing everything but his hat, which he held in one hand.

"Do I hear the ungrateful grumblings of my posterity?" he asked, eyebrows lowered with mock severity. "You'd think I was sending you boys to prison, the way you talk."

Dannie had heard this lecture enough times. She knocked back the rest of her coffee and jumped up from the table just as her father settled into his seat. She hurried to his side to place a kiss on his cheek. "I'm going with Frosty to check the fences near the canyon. I'll be back around noon."

Her father nodded his understanding. "Take your rifle and extra water."

"Yes, Dad." Dannie turned to the door, and Ruthie intercepted her with a wax-cloth folded up.

"Sandwiches for you and Frosty. Grab a couple of apples from the barrel, too."

In minutes, Dannie was out the front door with a packet of food, canteen, and a rifle slung over her shoulder. "You'd think I was going on a safari," she muttered to herself, smiling anyway.

Frosty waited outside the corral, two horses saddled up and ready for their ride. His eyes were on the large barn where they kept the best horses, hay, and most of the tack. There was a hay barn, too, and a blacksmith shed, and other outbuildings. Most were deserted at present. A fact which made her shudder if she stopped to think about it.

Gone were the days of the military forts offering protection. Fort Buchanan had been empty when her father arrived, and Fort Crittenden had been abandoned the same year her father put down roots in the territory. Fort Huachuca was the closest thing they had to military protection. It wasn't as far away as Tombstone, but it wasn't near enough to make the soldiers inside of any practical use.

"Frosty." Dannie approached, following his stare. "Something wrong with the barn?"

"New hand." Frosty never said much if he could help it. He was close to thirty years old, which was older for a cowboy without his own spread. Droving was a young man's game, her father often said. Dannie had never quite learned enough about Frosty's background to know why the life of a cowboy held appeal.

"You worried about him?" Dannie asked, sliding her rifle into its sheath and tucking her food and water into saddlebags.

"Nope." Frosty put a foot in one stirrup and mounted. "You?"

Dannie looked into the shadows of the barn where she saw the outline of a man with a shovel. She grinned to herself. "Nope."

She'd mucked the stalls out hundreds of times. While not the most pleasant chore, it was essential, and even a child was capable of getting the job done. But something that small might be enough to scare off someone of softer breeding.

She mounted up and followed Frosty out through the zaguán. The morning promised clear skies and a good ride. And most of the day free of the handsome Englishman.

CHAPTER SEVEN

May 9, 1895

Hunched over an account book in her father's study, Dannie studied the numbers before her with blurry vision. The flickering oil lamp was all the company she had, its steady flame doing little to comfort or warm her. She pushed her fingers into her hair, not caring about the strands she inadvertently pulled from her braid.

No one else would be up for hours, but Dannie hadn't been able to sleep. On their ride the week previous, she and Frosty found evidence of fences cut near the canyon. As she suspected, someone had been picking off their cattle and leading them out through the narrow stone passage. The canyon went northward, leading eventually to open hills and flat desert, all the way to Tucson. But there were any number of mountains, foothills, and gullies where someone could hide along the way.

Rubbing at her eyes, Dannie turned another page in her father's ledger. Everything had been written in either her father's firm hand or Abram's looping letters. Every sack of flour, calf sold, and bag of sweets noted.

They needed to cut costs, at least until the next cattle drive in the fall. If only there was a way to get more money for their animals. But with the drought, fattening up the cattle enough that they retained their size even after driving them to market proved difficult. Impossible, almost.

Dannie closed the book and leaned back in her chair, folding her arms over her checkered-green shirt. She looked out the window into the darkness. She knew the view well enough to picture it without the sunlight to help.

Twenty feet from the study window, her mother's tree grew, with branches stretching out to shade the flowerbed beneath it. Mother had carried that tree with her from Texas, and the Spanish oak had flourished despite the Arizona heat and dry air. Beyond the tree, long native grasses were trying to return. It hurt Dannie's heart to see how many dry patches there were still. In the distance, mountains hemmed it all in, creating a sense of safety Dannie had never questioned as a child.

Things were different now. The mountains hadn't kept them safe from her father's illness, drought, rustlers, or her mother's death ten years before. The grasses weren't coming back quick enough, or in enough abundance. The only steady thing outside that window was her mother's tree.

Dannie rose from the chair and re-shelved her father's account book. She extinguished the lantern. The entry hall to the front door was quiet, the only sound an old long-case clock ticking away the time. Dannie opened the front door, knowing it wouldn't even squeak despite its lack of regular use, because Mrs. Perkins oiled every hinge in the house with diligence.

The housekeeper had been gone for over a month, and Dannie missed her steadying presence. Surrounded by men as Dannie was, Ruthie and Mrs. Perkins were the only people who seemed to understand Dannie. And both of them were old. Mrs.

Perkins was old enough to be her mother, and Ruthie old enough to be her grandmother.

As soothing as it would be to stand beneath her mother's tree, Dannie remained on the porch. She leaned against the rail and closed her eyes, listening to the leaves flutter in a barely felt breeze.

She wasn't wearing boots, so there'd be no stepping off the safety of the wooden planks.

Even near the house, she knew better. Snakes, spiders, scorpions, and other creatures roamed freely through the desert night. But the porch was fairly safe, and all she needed was the sound of the tree to ease the familiar ache in her heart.

"I miss you, Mama." Dannie wrapped her arms around herself as the chill of night crept through her clothing and made her shudder.

She went back inside when she could no longer ignore the cold. Dawn was perhaps an hour away; there was no use trying to sleep. She went to the kitchen and made coffee, working in the dark until she stoked the fire to boil water. Once she'd warmed herself with the drink, she found her coat and boots.

She didn't need to wait for the sun to start work. The barn had plenty for a restless woman to tend to, if Dannie had a wish to stay busy.

With a lantern in hand, Dannie went out the back door and to the largest of the outbuildings.

She was halfway across the expanse from corral to barn when she glimpsed flickering yellow light coming through an open door. Someone was already in the barn. Dannie briefly debated turning back. There was no telling which hand would wake that early for work.

Buck had started to make her uncomfortable of late, because of his pointed attempts to please her with his opinions and his compliments. Not that she thought he'd do anything dishonorable, but she had no wish to give him a set down if he pushed his interest further.

"I'm not about to let anyone keep me out of my own barn," she whispered, then rolled her shoulders back and went forward with as much confidence as ever. Sometimes, a woman's bravado was all she had to get through uncomfortable experiences.

Dannie walked in, holding her lantern high, her eyes searching out the other human occupant of the barn. Their milk cow lifted her sleepy head to the light, but she looked away again. Lee was the one who milked her every day and night, so the cow wasn't about to get her hopes up for Dannie's attention.

The light came from a lantern hanging above one of their wagons. Dannie walked closer, still not seeing anyone inside.

If one of the men had left a lantern unattended in the barn, her dad and Frosty both would skin the perpetrator with their tongue-lashing.

A man grunted. Then she saw him stand.

It was the Englishman. His back was to her, all his concentration on something in his hands. The lamplight cast an orange glow over everything, but she could still see the angry red sunburn on the back of his neck. She winced in sympathy. It wasn't uncommon for even experienced drovers to get burnt once in a while, but most knew how to keep their skin covered well enough to avoid doing more than browning.

Startling people in the Territory was frowned upon. People had been shot for it. So Dannie reluctantly cleared her throat, and the man stilled before turning around. His hair was sticking up at odd angles; a smear of dark black grease under his chin made her narrow her eyes until she saw it on his hands, too. He held a wrench and a rag, and dark half-circles shaded the skin beneath his eyes.

Those eyes widened upon seeing her. "Miss Bolton." His lips quirked upward only briefly with his greeting. "I see I am not the only one eager to start my day." The quip sounded more tired than amused, but the effort at humor gave her leave to relax.

Dannie dropped her free hand to her waist. "What are you doing in here, up before the roosters?"

"I have a list of things to attend to." He shrugged and lowered his gaze to his hands. "As you are likely aware, there are many things to accomplish on a working ranch. Your men are determined I learn and fulfill as many chores as possible."

Mr. Rounsevell really was a gentleman. He was saying, with all politeness, that the cowboys were sticking him with every unfavorable job they could think of in order to avoid it themselves. Though she had hoped the Englishman would prove too soft for ranching, seeing his bedraggled state made her feel the weight of her selfishness.

It wasn't his fault he was born on the other side of the world with a silver spoon in his mouth.

"Time never hangs heavy on our hands out here." Dannie smiled when he raised his eyebrows at her, and she shrugged. "If we did half the stuff that needs to be done, we could work from dawn to dusk and still never finish. I'm afraid waking up early won't mean you check everything off the list. Most likely, they'll just give you even more to do."

His shoulders sagged, and he looked at the wagon. "Nevertheless." He lowered himself back to the ground, and she heard metal scrape metal as he worked upon the axle. "It would be better to be given more than to not accomplish the tasks I've already been set."

With a sigh, Dannie turned and went back the way she had come. It wouldn't take more than a minute, and while she told herself she ought to let well enough alone and let the Englishman run himself into the ground, she couldn't ignore his efforts. She'd made it a point to ignore Mr. Rounsevell, and whatever work the cowboys gave him, but there was enough evidence of hard work that she had to do something to reward his efforts. If only to ease her guilty conscience.

It took her a few minutes to fill a mug with the coffee she'd brewed before, and she gathered some of Ruthie's biscuits in a napkin along with a thick slice of cured ham. She wrapped the whole of that together to carry both the mug and food in one hand. Then she trekked back to the barn, entering as Mr. Rounsevell stood, wiping his hands on the rag.

Dannie hung up her lantern, then approached with the mug of coffee outstretched. "Here. If you're going to be up early, you should fortify yourself with more than a stiff breeze."

He stared at the mug, his lips parting as though he wished to say something. Then his green eyes darted up to hers. "Thank you, Miss Bolton. That is kind of you."

She lowered her gaze to the cup as his hand took it, shame squeezing at her heart again. She hadn't been kind to him. She'd meant to be the opposite from the first moment she'd laid eyes on him. When his hand took the mug, he was careful to accept it from the bottom, his fingers not touching hers at all. She could see the red-rawness of his skin and the black grease and dirt in the creases of his knuckles.

The man had likely never worked with his hands a day in his life before coming to the ranch.

When she looked up, he drank the coffee, wincing as he did. Dannie's grip tightened on the napkin full of food. "Is something wrong with the coffee?" She might not be as good a cook as Ruthie, but she knew how to make a fortifying cup of coffee.

He lowered the cup from his lips, and she caught the slightest of smiles from behind the rim. "Only that it isn't tea, Miss Bolton."

Her jaw fell open. "You can't be serious."

The chuckle that escaped him made her relax. "Tea is a drink for English parlors, Miss Bolton. I am well aware how far I am from one of those." Though his expression relaxed, she sensed no chagrin or even self-pitying in his words. "Thank you. This is much better than what Frosty serves us in the morning."

Dannie leaned her shoulder against the wagon. "Frosty's coffee isn't known to taste grand, but it gets his cowboys moving." Her gaze fell to where his hand gripped the mug, wrapping nearly all the way around it. His size ought to have intimidated her, but he held himself with something she mentally labeled as grace. There was confidence there, certainly, but not the swaggering kind she was used to seeing in men of the West.

"What brought you out to the barn before dawn, Miss Bolton?"

The question brought her gaze back to his eyes, and Dannie shrugged one shoulder. "I couldn't sleep. And there's always something to do in a barn."

"True enough." With a moment of stiff hesitation, he eyed how she leaned against the wagon and then did the same, mirroring her stance. "What chore are you after? Perhaps it is on my list." His green eyes twinkled at her through the semi-darkness.

"I hadn't made up my mind yet." She tipped her chin up, pretending to glare at him. "You wouldn't take credit for my work, would you?"

"I wouldn't dream of it." The smile that had teased at his lips appeared fully, and she noticed for the first time how white and even his teeth were. It was a pleasant smile, without guile or teasing behind it. Charming, in fact.

Dannie pushed herself upright. She wasn't about to be charmed by anyone, not ever again, least of all an Englishman intruding where he wasn't wanted. Dannie thrust out the tied napkin.

"I brought you some breakfast. Try to return the cloth without grease on it." He stared at her, likely puzzled by her abrupt change in demeanor, but accepted her offering.

"Thank you, Miss Bolton."

With a tight nod, she turned on the heel of her boot and retrieved her lantern. He could work in the barn all he wanted. She'd go find something to do in the house. Because she wasn't about to make anything easier on him by doing a chore Frosty, Buck, or Ed had assigned to him. Let them run him ragged. She wouldn't—didn't—care.

The Englishman didn't belong in Arizona Territory, and he certainly didn't belong on her ranch.

Dannie had better things to do than coddle a greenhorn. Especially when that particular greenhorn had a smile far too easy on her eyes, and an accent she refused to admit she enjoyed hearing.

EVAN WATCHED THE CATTLEMAN'S DAUGHTER RETREAT, AS surprised by her abrupt departure as he'd been by her kindness. He put his coffee mug on the wagon bench and carefully opened up the napkin, finding biscuits and ham inside. As thoughtful as the gesture was, making sense of her actions proved impossible.

Still, spurning the food would mark him as a fool. The biscuits, cold as they were, tasted better than anything he'd eaten with the other ranch hands. The salty taste of ham made him nearly groan aloud with gratitude. Evan might not know how to cook for himself, but it seemed like the cowboys didn't generally know how to prepare more than beans and eggs without burning things.

After he'd finished every crumb of food, Evan folded up the napkin and tucked it into a pocket of his denim trousers. Then he finished off the coffee, even though what was left was ice cold. He went to the back porch of the house and left the mug with the napkin tucked inside. Someone would find it and take it in.

Then he turned to the east, realizing he'd left the barn without his lantern, and he hadn't even noticed it. The sky had gone from gray to yellow while he'd spoken with Miss Bolton.

A strange woman. Not because of her split-skirts and crooked smile. Those he had seen elsewhere in the wide world. Nor was it because of her apparent ease working on her father's spread. He knew several women back in England at home on a horse enough to attempt jumps while riding side-saddle. He wasn't about to doubt any of her abilities when it came to ranching.

Still, the way she had reacted to him, from the moment they met, didn't sit well in his mind. He had been nothing other than respectful to her, and that morning he had seen hints of kindness in her actions and her words. But she had taken a rather determined stance against him.

Evan needed to find out why. If he did everything Frosty asked of him, put up with Buck's smirks and Ed's amused instruction, they might let him stay after the required fortnight of hard labor. But Daniella Bolton's opinion held more weight than anyone else's in the eyes of her father. The way the men spoke of her showed their respect for the rancher's daughter, too.

If he could get on her unpleasant side before she even knew him, perhaps Evan had a chance of changing her opinion by showing her he was worth the effort of her approval.

He had one week left to prove himself so he could stay through to the autumn cattle drive.

A soft whine from behind Evan brought his attention around to the barn again. Sitting in the doorway, head tilted to one side, sat the cattle dog he'd seen following the other hands around. What had Ed called her?

She stood and approached him, walked a loop around him out of reach, then went back to the barn door and sat. Evan followed, and when he neared, she stood again and went into the barn, where she looked rather pointedly at his lantern and whined.

Evan looked from the dog to the lantern, then picked up the oil lamp and put it out. The dog's mouth popped open, her tongue lolled out, and she looked at him with what could only be a grin.

"You cannot be clever enough to tell me to put out my light." Evan crouched down and held his hand out to her. "No dog is that smart."

Travis's young voice answered him. "Fable might be."

Evan looked up at the same moment the dog tucked her head beneath his hand for a pat. "Fable?"

"That's her name. She's the mama to most of the cattle dogs out here. The man we got her from in Benson said they raised her for sheep, but she never seemed to mind bossing cows instead." Travis hefted a saddle from its place in a row along the wall and approached a stall. "She works hard unless she's got a litter on the way. Dad says this will be her last, though. He doesn't want to wear her out."

"She has pups on the way?" Evan scratched behind the dog's floppy black ears.

Travis started work on a horse, preparing it for a ride. "Yep. She sticks closer to the house, sleeps on the front porch when she's gettin' to the end of it."

"I thought I saw her out with Frosty and your sister yesterday."

"Nah, you saw Gus. They're a bred pair. Gus has brown patches above his eyes—looks like he's frowning at you with 'em. Fable here, she's a friendly girl, only black and white." Travis came to the stable door and rested his elbows on it. "What're your plans for today, Duke?"

Evan stood and stretched, his muscles sore and reluctant to move. "Repairs around the stable and barn. Inventory in the blacksmith shed. I think Buck wanted me to sharpen a few tools." A scythe, knives, and strangely shaped bits of farrier equipment, from what Evan could tell.

Travis wrinkled his nose, his boyish disgust written all over his face. "None of that sounds pressing. You should come with Frosty and me instead. We need someone to drive the wagon."

Before Evan could ask for more details, Frosty came into the stable, followed by another dog. Evan saw the difference in the two animals. The one following Frosty not only had eyebrow-like patches above his eyes, like Travis had described, but he was larger bodied than the agile female dog near Evan's feet.

"You ready, Travis?" Frosty asked, barely glancing at Evan.

"Sure. Maybe Duke can drive the wagon for us, though. He ought to learn his way around the ranch."

Frosty paused and looked from Evan back to the boy. "You're

just tryin' to get out of driving the wagon yourself, aren't you?" The man's tone didn't indicate whether he disapproved.

If Evan could get off the homestead for even a short time, he wanted to take the chance. "I'm happy to assist you both however I can."

Frosty went after his saddle. "Get the mule hitched to the wagon then, Duke. Travis, get the doctorin' bag."

"Yes, sir." Travis left the stall, going to another shelf along the back wall of the barn.

"Doctoring bag?" Evan repeated, hurrying to the wall full of bridles and harnesses. "Is someone sick?"

"A cow. Ed and I glimpsed one of our beasts limping and bellowing yesterday. I reckon it's a bad hoof." Frosty pushed his hat up on his forehead. "I suppose this will be good for you. We need to see how you handle the beasts up close."

"As you say, Frosty." Evan started to turn away, but Frosty's next words stopped him mid-step.

"Bring a rifle from the bunkhouse."

Evan turned around. "A rifle?"

Frosty shrugged. "Or your revolver, if that's more to your liking. But you never know when you'll need a weapon out here. Rabid coyotes, skunks, or bears who feel a might too friendly. And those are just the four-legged troubles you might meet. This here is still a territory, Duke. There's trouble in every ditch and gully."

With another nod, Evan went back to the bunkhouse. He strapped on his gun belt, checked his revolver, then fastened it in with the hammer loop before tying the leather leg ties around his thigh to keep it in place. Then he took up a box of ammunition, too.

Evan had the mule team and wagon ready to go in short order. Though he had never driven mules before, it wasn't all that different from a team of horses. Except the mules weren't as spirited as Evan's thoroughbreds at home. And the wagon's wood-plank bench was not nearly as comfortable as his father's well-sprung carriages.

They traveled over the terrain, too. There were no paths or roads. As the house and outbuildings grew smaller, the surrounding mountains loomed taller. Antelope sprang through the long dry grasses in the distance.

Travis rode alongside Evan, pointing out landmarks and the way the mountains dipped in certain spots. "There's a spring up there. The water's colder than frost. It runs down the other side of the mountain until it joins up with smaller creeks, then goes down into the gorge. That-a-way"—the boy pointed southeast—"are the Mustang Mountains. Up north about a half hour's ride is the old mine that Abram and Dad tried to prove for a while, but nothing much came of it. Dad still talks about getting a geologist here to look into the area again. But since the price of silver fell so much, it might not be worth it in the long run."

Frosty had ridden up ahead to find the cow he'd noticed the day before with Ed. While Evan didn't think it likely they would find one cow in the wide expanse of land, Frosty had possessed no doubts. Given Travis's easy conversation, he wasn't concerned about it, either.

The male dog, Gus, had followed them out and eventually jumped into the back of the wagon.

"When did your father and Mr. Steele start ranching?" Evan held the reins loosely in his gloved hands, wary of giving himself more blisters. The mules were well behaved enough that they didn't need more than light direction, for which he was grateful.

"Eighteen-seventy-seven." Travis grinned proudly. "Dad married my mama and used her money to get the ranch started. She stayed in Texas with Dannie, since there wasn't a house, and Dannie was only two. Dad didn't send for them for a while because the Apache were still restless. When Mama finally came out with Dannie, she lived in the adobe house where you bunk. I was born there, too. First one born on the land." The boy's chest puffed up and he threw back his shoulders. "Dad says it's fitting, since I'll be the one to take over someday."

Miss Bolton's determination to work her family's land made Evan wonder how she felt about giving way to her younger brother. Americans weren't as strict about inheritance as the English peerage, he'd thought. Though it wasn't any of his business, his curiosity got the better of Evan. "What about your sister? Does she inherit anything?"

"Sure." Travis shrugged. "Abram owns a fifth of the ranch, and he's leaving his piece to Lee. Dad's shares will come to us. I'll get two of them, as controlling shares, and Clark and Dannie will each get one. Then they can stay and work it or sell out."

"Would either of them do that, do you think?" Evan couldn't imagine anyone trading away their birthright, especially if it was land. There was no free land in England anymore. Every snatch and patch of grass was owned by someone, and likely had been in a family for generations. Land didn't exchange hands often enough for a man like him to even hope to establish a living. The cost was too dear.

Travis skirted a thorn-covered bush with his horse, then came up close to the wagon again. "Clark might. He talks about trying his luck in the Northwest or going all the way to California. But I don't know about Dannie. I guess it depends if she ever meets another fella."

Evan turned his head at that, unable to cover his surprise. "She had a beau?"

The woman was pricklier than a hedgehog. Perhaps as prickly as the cactus plants he had seen outside of Tombstone.

He hid his grin. He was starting to *think* the way Miss Bolton *talked*.

"She doesn't like us to mention him." The boy appeared sheepish for a moment, but then a smile snuck through the contrite expression. "I guess you oughta know, though, so you know the truth if you hear talk about it. She got engaged. They were only days away from their wedding when Mr. Robertson hitched his wagon to some other girl he'd met out in Oklahoma territory. Turns out he was as crooked as a snake in a cactus patch, and he'd only been after Dannie's share in the ranch." Travis stared ahead of them, quiet for a long moment. "After the second drought hit, I guess he figured the ranch wasn't worth much anymore. Didn't matter that my sister's worth all the land in the territory. I don't think Dannie's really been the same since."

"A lady would take something like that hard." Evan hadn't ever devoted much time to finding a wife. He'd left no one behind, in terms of a sweetheart, when he fled his father's demands for his try at a cowboy's life.

Travis cocked an eyebrow up at Evan. "She didn't just take it hard. She changed. It's like she put on a—a suit of armor." He frowned. "Do they still have those in England?"

Evan had to chuckle at that, then spoke in as high-and-mighty a tone as ever his father had used. "Why, of course. In every respectable castle. Whether they know who wore them or not."

The boy didn't even crack a smile. "You won't tell Dannie I told you about Robertson, will you?" Travis asked, a touch of worry to his tone.

"Of course not, sir. I am a gentleman."

"Dannie said we should be calling you Lord Evan," Travis countered. "So that makes you a lord, not a gentleman. Right?"

Evan blinked. "A technicality." He hadn't expected anyone in the west to understand the proper forms and address for British nobility.

Frosty appeared on a rise ahead of them, riding his horse at an easy lope in their direction. When he was near enough to talk, Frosty leaned over the pommel of his saddle. "Found her. She's near to calving, so if we can fix up her hoof and get her back with the main herd quick-like, she'll be safer."

It was one of the longer sentences Evan had heard from the foreman. "Is she far from here?"

"About half a mile that way." He jerked his thumb over his shoulder. "It'll be work to keep her still long enough to help her.

Range cattle are already a little wild, but you get a cow as uncomfortable as she is, and things get trickier. Gus will help, though."

The dog in the wagon barked when he heard his name, then jumped up on the bench next to Evan. The dog only had a stub where a tail should've been, but his entire rear shook back and forth to make up for the excitement a tail would've shown. Then the dog bounded down from the wagon to the ground, showing no sign of trouble with the height.

Frosty chuckled and spoke with genuine fondness. "Never seen a hand as eager to work as Gus."

"I don't think you've ever liked anybody as much as you like Gus," Travis put in, a broad grin stretching across his young face.

Frosty's good humor immediately disappeared. "Like I said. Cowboys don't work like this dog does." He whistled. "To me, Gus." Then he turned his horse around and went in the direction of the wounded cow.

Travis pulled his bandana up over his mouth and nose to protect himself from the dirt before following at a slower pace.

The mules and Evan brought up the rear of their party, his eyes sweeping the vista before him with appreciation.

The mostly brown land didn't have much in common with England. Dry, arid vastness made it the opposite of his homeland in every way. Yet something about the mountains in the distance and the expanse of clear blue sky above made Evan breathe more deeply than he ever had before.

The continual weight of his responsibilities, of his father's expectations, had lifted for the first time in his life.

CHAPTER EIGHT

Dannie stepped out onto the porch at sundown, her eyes on the purples of the sky. She wrapped an arm loosely about a porch column, leaning against it. When she'd gone to Boston for school, Dannie spent hours learning about art and watercolors—a skill with little use for her way of life. But she'd practiced dutifully. And she'd tried, many times, to capture her memories of the sunset over the desert mountains. Vibrant purples and oranges, yellows and blues, had never looked right on canvas or paper.

And her art instructor, with a thick European accent and permanent scowl, had refused to believe a sky could ever look the way she described it. Not in the American wilderness she so loved.

Why had no one captured the landscape as it deserved?

She smiled somewhat wistfully, tipping her forehead to rest it against the chipped paint of the post.

Her father's voice rumbled from below her as he climbed the porch steps. "When you smile that way, you remind me of your mother, Dannie-girl."

Dannie's eyebrows arched upward. "She always said I was the spitting image of your sister."

"There may be a touch of my family here and there, but your smile is all your mama's." He turned toward the western sky and leaned heavily against the rail. "Never seen a sight so beautiful in all my born days as your mama. Even a night like this can't compare to her. The velvet of the sky reminds me of her hair, the stars are her eyes, and the bright colors are like the music of her laugh, thrilling me to my very core."

Dannie's heart ached. Her father wasn't a poet, and though he enjoyed reading, he had never been a man all that creative with his own words. To hear him speak as tenderly as he did about her mother made her wistful. Partly on his behalf. They lost her mother too soon. But it also pained her to know how she had once thought herself close to having that same deep love in her own life.

Breathing in deeply of the mountain air cleared her head, thankfully. Dwelling on the past would get her nowhere.

"How are you feeling, Dad?" she asked, lowering her gaze to the dirt and scraggly grass of their yard.

"Oh, about like a dog got hold of me and dragged me through the dirt." He turned and came the rest of the way up the porch. "Speaking of dogs—where's Fable? I figured she'd be trailing you around."

"She's too close to her time. She's been on the porch." Dannie tilted her head in the direction of the dog's chosen den, tucked beneath a bench along the wall. The dog had peeked out at the sound of her name but didn't move any further.

"Ain't it something?" Her dad lowered himself to the bench and reached beneath it, scratching the shepherd dog's ears. "Even after all the trouble with the droughts, there's still much to look forward to. Our whole way of life is hard work, from sun up to sun down, and still there's new life coming along every day."

Something about her father's tone didn't sit right. Dannie turned fully around to face him, her back against the column. "It sounds like you mean more than just pups and calves. Is something on your mind, Dad?"

He gave Fable one last pat on the head before he swept off his broad-brimmed hat, dropping it to the bench beside him. "We need to talk about something—something the boys are yet too young to understand or worry over. But you've been helping me with our accounts and paperwork long enough that you won't be shocked by what I'm going to say."

Dannie's spine stiffened, and her fingertips went cold. They had danced around the topic enough that she knew exactly what he meant to tell her. An irrational, childish part of her wanted to cover her ears and refuse to hear him out. Instead, she pushed away her fear, took in a steadying breath and nodded. "Yes, sir. I'm listening."

"You've always been a brave girl. You'd look a bear in the eye without so much as flinching." His smile was fond, but his eyes were troubled. "Dannie, I don't know that we can make it much longer. Not unless we change something about our outfit, and darned if I know what that would be." He rubbed the back of his neck with one hand, lowering his gaze to the dust on the ground. "If it'd only been the one drought, we'd be back on our feet. But the second coming so soon after the first, and everyone else pulling up stakes like it was a race to get out of here..." His words trailed away into a sorrowful sigh. "The railroad changed things, but our cattle are still too thin when we get them to market. We're barely making enough to keep going, and there's no profit coming in, and nothing to put aside in case of more lean times."

Her throat closed up, so her words sounded near strangled when they came out. "We aren't selling, are we?"

"I don't know."

The admission sent her heart plunging. "Daddy. You said you'd never sell. Not with Mama buried on the ranch." Her words came out pleading, though she'd meant them to sound firm.

He stood and came to her, his hands going to her shoulders. His tone was gentle, though his words hurt like a hailstorm. "If your mama was alive, do you think she'd want you to live in poverty and dust? There are men out in California who've been after my land for years. I have half a dozen letters in my desk this very minute, all from interested buyers. Maybe we could just sell a few shares, take on another partner."

Everything in her rebelled at the idea of letting a stranger have a say in how they ran the ranch. Especially someone without a lick of experience, someone who'd want to tell them what they could and couldn't do with the invested funds.

She kept her gaze on her father, her eyes burning with unshed tears. "What other options do we have?"

He considered her closely, the fading light reflected in his eyes. "Bank loans, maybe. I don't know what bank would be willing to bail us out of this trouble. Not without a hefty interest rate. But either of those options are no good to us if things don't change or improve." He released her and went to the porch rail, crossing his arms over his chest. "The world is changing. When I came out here, it was common practice to drive our cattle to market. Sometimes, all the way to Texas or California for the right price. That's folly, now."

She knew the truth of that. Ranges were closing up, and cattle weighed half as much at the end of a drive. Not to mention how many they lost along the way, and the danger of river crossings and rustlers. No one drove cattle farther than the nearest train station.

Hauling cattle by train wasn't cheap, either.

They needed fatter cattle to sell, to make back their money that way. But the beasts that bore the range and travel best were thin breeds. Their own mixed breed were mostly Mexican, and the Long-Horned breed favored in Texas.

"I don't know what the answer is. Maybe, with a little time, we could figure something out." Dannie put a hand on her father's elbow, the cotton of his shirt well-worn and soft. She'd patched the elbows in that shirt herself, the previous summer. "I've seen the books. We've got some time."

His shoulders drooped, a sight that made tears prickle at her eyes. Her dad was a proud man, and to see him lose faith along with that pride would hurt too much for her to even think about.

"Daddy? Isn't there some time?" She didn't call him that often anymore. But she needed him to be the hero of her childhood, making everything right again.

He didn't meet her eye as he spoke. "After the fall cattle drive, we must start making decisions. And we might not like our options."

Dannie leaned her head against her father's shoulder. "I'll do some talking with people. Get some ideas together. We'll figure it out. We always have in the past."

"Just remember, Dannie. As much as we love this place, as dear as it is to us, our family is what matters most."

Family. People she had thought of as family had left them high and dry over the years. "Dad?" Dannie peered up at him. "That last letter Mrs. Perkins sent. Are you sure she didn't say when she was coming back?"

Her father's frame stiffened momentarily, then he relaxed again, his arm going around her shoulder. "Nope. She said she was enjoying her time with her sister and her family. We gotta let Loretta have her space."

The housekeeper had left as soon as her father was on the mend from his illness, looking worn out and sad. Dannie'd thought, with the rest of the family, that Mrs. Perkins needed a little time off. She'd visited her son plenty in the past several years, but she always came back with more spring in her step.

Dannie wanted to ask if her father thought Mrs. Perkins would ever come back, but something about the way he'd said her name, and fixed his eyes on some point in the distance, made Dannie keep her lips closed over the question.

Dad kissed her forehead. His words came out lighter when he spoke. "I'm going inside to read some of that Doyle fellow's book. He's an Englishman, you know. Like our friend the duke."

Her nose wrinkled. "I have nothing against people being English, Dad."

"Then what do you have against him? The man's trying to make a living."

"No. He's trying to have an adventure. Something to brag about later, maybe, the way he boasts about knowing the Queen and Buffalo Bill." She snorted.

Her father stepped away, fixing her with his most disapproving frown. "You don't have any evidence he's twisting truths into lies."

She ducked her head. "What would a man with his background be doing out in Arizona territory? On our ranch? It doesn't make any sense. I won't call him a liar because you're right. There's no evidence that way, either. But we've seen his kind before, Dad." She gritted her teeth together, hating that she alluded to David. She'd been reminded of him far too often of late.

"I brought you up to be a good judge of character," her father reminded her. "But based on a person's words and merits, their actions. Give Duke a chance to prove himself. Maybe he's gotten in a scrape and being here will be of some help. Maybe he is a liar, or a cheat, or a side-winding snake. Then again, he could be a soul in search of some peace, a man needing to work with two hands and a full heart."

Her father's words warred with her natural prejudices. She didn't want Evan to be anything other than what she'd decided.

But her mother would have wanted her to be kind. And her father was asking her to give Evan a chance to prove himself.

When Dannie had been in Boston, at that fancy school with more heiresses and snobs than fleas on a coyote, they hadn't wanted her there. They'd said she didn't belong in their cultured city, didn't belong with their kind. Dannie had worked for four years to prove them wrong. She'd done well enough that David Robertson had followed her home after the drought of '91. Not that she'd been enough to keep him. Not long. He'd abandoned her two years later, during the drought of '93.

Some hurts went too deep to forget.

"I'll give him a chance," Dannie said at last, the words weighing her down like a promise.

Not that it would matter. He would still leave. Just like she had left Boston when her family needed her home. Just like David had left when he realized there wasn't as much money in their way of living as he'd hoped. Maybe Mrs. Perkins had left, too.

"That's my Dannie-girl." Her dad went to the door. "Now, I'm off to solve a mystery with Mr. Holmes."

She waved him inside. "Enjoy your book, Dad. I think I'm going to take a walk around the homestead. I'll say goodnight before I turn in."

Night had fallen fully after their talk, and the moon had risen in the east, given the silver-white dancing between the shadows of her mother's tree.

Dannie stepped off the porch and walked south along the outside of the adobe building that had once been her family's home. She could almost remember when they came, her mother and Dannie, before the main house was finished. They had lived in one of the adobe-brick bedrooms, which had since become her father's study.

Not long after Travis came into the world, the family was in the main house, the hands in the other half of the adobe structure.

The housing structure had grown with the business and with their family.

She came to the zaguán's entrance. The large sliding doors were open enough for people to come and go, but if a horse or cow got out of the corral, they wouldn't be able to slip through. She kept going along the fence of the paddock, her boots barely making a sound against the packed earth.

When she neared the corner of the fence, she saw a figure leaning against the post, head tipped back. She hesitated.

Turning back would be easier than having another confrontational conversation with Mr. Rounsevell. Duke. Whatever people called him.

A furry head appeared, and Gus yipped a welcome at her.

No use pretending she didn't see the Englishman now.

GUS HAD FOLLOWED EVAN MOST OF THE DAY AFTER THEY HAD returned from tending to the limping cow. The poor creature had lodged a rock deep within the cleft of her hooves, causing a wound to appear where the stone rubbed at her. Frosty had removed the stone, shaved a portion of the hoof, and dumped iodine over the whole thing.

When the dog followed Evan outside after the evening meal, he had wondered if Gus thought him in need of a protector or a keeper. Obviously, the dog didn't think Evan capable of managing himself.

He looked up when Gus yipped, the sound friendly rather than threatening, and he saw Miss Bolton in the moonlight coming toward him.

Her head was uncovered, and a long braid hung over one shoulder. She wore one of her long split-skirts, a plaid shirt little different from what the men wore, but with a waistcoat atop it that cinched in just enough at her waist to show her feminine figure.

The woman had a way of walking that Evan couldn't help but admire as she approached. There was confidence in her step, and a sway that no Englishwoman would ever attempt, though it seemed natural as breathing to Miss Bolton. Perhaps it was due to her riding or growing up surrounded by the swagger of cowboys.

"Good evening, Duke." She used his nickname as casually as the ranch hands, drawing out the single syllable with a smile in her voice, and for the first time, he didn't hate it.

He swept off his hat and bowed, his gesture a mix between Western politeness and English civility. "Miss Bolton. What brings you out here this evening?"

"Just wandering." She stopped a few feet shy of him and bent to scratch Gus behind the ears. The lucky dog's lack of tail didn't stop him from wriggling in pleasure. She laughed when the large herding dog dropped to the ground and rolled over. "I see you've made a friend."

Evan smiled and went back to leaning against the post. "I feel more like I have a new keeper. Gus doesn't seem to trust me out of his sight."

"If he didn't trust you, he'd keep an eye on you. He wouldn't lay down at your feet when he's got a bunch of animals to look after in the barn." She gave the dog a final pat, then stood and brushed her hands along the sides of her skirt. "Travis told me about your work yesterday. He said you were mighty helpful keeping that cow still."

"They don't seem in a great hurry to move when you have hold of one leg. Or when they're a day or two away from calving." He shrugged and suddenly wished he had done something more impressive with his time away from the house. He'd practiced roping animals in England until his father had forbidden the activity, accusing Evan of making himself an object of ridicule.

At least he'd been allowed to shoot. He'd spent hours practicing, going so far as to try the mirror trick he'd seen Annie Oakley perform—well, he'd only tried that one once. He shot much better looking directly at the target rather than its reflection.

Why couldn't he prove himself capable of the things most valued in the wild west?

Not that he'd seen anything particularly wild yet.

Miss Bolton came a step closer and leaned against the fence next to him. She directed her gaze upward to the sky. "It's amazing to see the stars like this, isn't it?"

He looked upward, staring at the river of light above them

with a contented smile. "The Milky Way is incredible. I have only seen it clearer once before, when I was permitted the honor of looking through the Leviathan telescope in Parsonstown."

She didn't even bother hiding her skepticism. "You don't say."

"But I do, Miss Bolton." He released a sigh. "I do not understand why you doubt my word."

"Force of habit." She sounded more amused than repentant. "I know it's not fair, and I'm sorry for that. But even if everything you've said is true, I still don't understand your need to brag about it."

"Brag?" Evan turned to her, startled. The moonlight showed her expression, the lift of her eyebrows, the curve of her smile. "I have been called a great many things in my life, Miss Bolton, but a braggart has never been one of them. Where I am from, discussing such things as who you have met, things you have experienced, is considered a social nicety. We call it *making conversation.*"

"We call it throwing too much dust."

He had to chuckle at that. "Descriptive language, Miss Bolton. I assume throwing too much dust is a bad thing."

"It conceals a person's true intent. Their direction. Think about it." Her tone changed from amused to something more casual, almost accepting. "If you're following behind someone, and they're kicking up dust, they're obscuring themselves. Making it hard to follow them. Hard to see where they're heading."

"The language of the west is oddly poetic." Evan folded his arms over his chest and looked away from her. "But I take your point. A person intent on talking of things that are grand and glorious is hardly living in the moment and attempting to be judged not for who they are, but who they know."

Her tone was dry, but not necessarily unfriendly. "An astute observation, as your Sherlock Holmes would say."

"You've read Doyle's work?" Evan didn't hide his surprise. His father mocked the popularity of the fictional detective, but Evan had devoured the mysteries almost as faithfully as he had the tales of cowboys and bandits.

She laughed, a low sound that made something inside his chest twist. "Are you shocked that I can read, or that I've read something written by an Englishman?"

"Neither. I am delighted. I have enjoyed Doyle's work for some time." Then he bent toward her and lowered his voice. "You seem to be under the impression I doubt your intelligence, Miss Bolton. I am not certain how that came about. It isn't at all true."

The dim lighting hid the nuances of her expression, but her widening eyes were easy enough to make out.

He kept talking before she could splutter another of her quick-witted explanations or excuses. "If we are discussing observations, I have another to make. I believe you are holding me accountable for another man's misdeeds. Perhaps you knew another gentleman of a similar privileged background. Perhaps he boasted too often of things he had seen or done." It wasn't quite fair to use Travis's revelation against her. But Evan needed her approval, not her prejudice.

He leaned closer still, bending enough to bring their eyes level, their noses inches apart. "Miss Bolton, whoever he was, I am not he."

She swallowed and tilted her chin up. "You might be cut from the same cloth."

"Doubtful." He stepped back, and when she took in a quick breath, he realized his lungs had grown tight.

She turned away, looking back the direction she had come from. "Duke. Why are you here, really? Are you running from something? Or just trying to amuse yourself at our expense?"

He remained silent until she looked at him again, her eyebrows drawn tightly together and the smile gone from her face. "I am here because I have always dreamed of seeing the American West, of experiencing life the way you live it. My funds ran low, and when I met your brothers, I thought there would be no better way to replenish them than by doing what I have dreamed of since boyhood—working as a drover. A cowboy, wearing denim and a bandana, a wide-brimmed hat, with a six-shooter on my hip. I used to lay awake at night and imagine going on a real cattle drive. This is a dream come true for me, whether you believe it or not."

The silence hung between them for several long moments until her gaze dropped from his. "It was my dad's dream, too. Now it's our life and livelihood. If you can remember that your dream is our living and dying, maybe the two of us can get along after all."

"I would like that." Evan relaxed for the first time in her presence, and his hope rose. "I have nothing but the highest respect for your way of life, Miss Bolton."

Quiet stretched between them, with no sound but the whistling and creaking of insects in the night. Finally, she spoke, sounding hesitant. "What happens after you've satisfied your curiosity, Duke? If you go on that cattle drive in the fall?"

Evan looked down at her, the moonlight revealing a steady stare directed at him. "I suppose I go back to England, Miss Bolton. Perhaps after seeing the Pacific Coast. But eventually, I will return to my family."

She nodded once, as though she had expected his answer, then stepped away. "I had better turn in. Morning comes early."

The phrase made him chuckle. "I suppose it does. Good night then, Miss Bolton."

"Dannie is fine." She spoke hastily, as though on impulse alone. "It's what everyone else calls me."

Evan grinned and bowed. "Good night, Dannie." He had gained more ground than he thought possible with one simple conversation.

"Good night, Duke." She turned on her heel and strode away, taking long steps, the wide legs of her split skirt fluttering.

Gus whined at Evan's feet. He looked down to see the dog staring after her, then the animal looked up at Evan and huffed.

"I know. I could've enjoyed her company longer, too." Evan scratched the dog behind its floppy ears, then leaned back against the fence again, staring up at the river of stars and the islands of constellations while a measure of tranquility entered his heart.

CHAPTER NINE

Although Evan didn't see much of Dannie the following week, when she passed within sight of him, she had smiled and nodded. Since he was usually in the midst of some menial chore, all he could do was nod back.

The fortnight had passed during the week, with Evan anxiously waiting a formal review of his work. Instead, the fourteenth evening he'd been with the cowboys, Frosty had found Evan doing chores. "Bolton says you stay if I like your work. I said you'd do." Then he'd walked away. The complete lack of ceremony hadn't squashed Evan's joy, though.

He'd wondered if his starlit conversation with Dannie had played a part in securing his employment.

When Evan woke that Sunday morning, his third since his arrival, he immediately remembered what that particular day meant on the ranch. King Bolton decreed only the most necessary chores ought to be performed on Sundays, calling for a day of rest for his family and all his employees. The family's farm animals would need tending, which Clark and Travis saw to, and the horses would spend the day in the corral.

Evan sat up and saw Frosty already awake, sipping at a cup of coffee and reading a book. Buck was snoring in his cot, and Ed put a hat upon his head near the door.

"See to the stock, Duke," Frosty said from where he sat, not even looking up from his book. "Then the day is yours."

Evan barely restrained a groan. Every muscle in his body felt ready to snap. "Yes, sir." He slid out of bed and went through the mechanics of getting dressed. He splashed water on his face from the basin near the door, grateful it was cold and clean. The cracked mirror hanging over the porcelain bowl showed his thickening beard, and he winced. His father hadn't ever allowed his sons full facial hair, claiming it made them appear uncouth.

Evan turned his head to the side, looking over the whiskers. It wasn't *much* of a beard yet. It merely looked as though he hadn't shaved in a fortnight—which he hadn't.

He'd make time today.

Once he had his hat on his head, Evan went out to let the horses roam and pitched them fresh hay. He saw to the water trough, then a few other minor chores, and was about ready to turn back to the bunkhouse when he saw Dannie come out the back door from the house.

Evan paused, waiting for her notice. Her gaze directed at the bunkhouse took her steps the same direction, but then her head turned, and she caught sight of him. To his relief, her stern expression altered, changing to a smile. Her path changed, too, as she aimed directly to him.

"Good morning, Duke. They stick you with the Sunday chores?"

"For the third time, Miss—Dannie."

Her hazel eyes sparkled with mirth as she came within arm's length of him. She stopped there, and he realized she wore a dress, and high-heeled button-up shoes instead of her practical brown boots.

"I'm afraid that's your luck until Frosty decides otherwise, but given your hard work, I doubt you'll have all the grunt work to yourself for much longer." She held up a straw hat, the same one she had worn that day in Tombstone the first time he saw her. "I'm on my way to visit some neighbors. Travis and Clark are coming, and they'll stay out longer than I want to, so Dad says I need to find someone else to come with me."

Before Evan could offer his services, Buck's voice came from inside the zaguán. "I'd be happy to accompany you, Dannie."

Evan didn't imagine the slight downward shift of her brow or the change of her smile. It appeared more forced as she looked over her shoulder to the corridor of the adobe building. "That's nice of you to offer, Buck." She slanted a quick glance at Evan. "But the Duke here has already agreed to come, and I think that would be best. The neighbors ought to meet him."

His lips twitched, but her eyes pled him to go along with her. "I'm relieved you thought of me, Miss Bolton." He folded his arms and met Buck's gaze across the dirt yard. "This is one greenhorn task I'm happy to perform."

Buck frowned, then shrugged and turned on the heel of his boot to disappear back into the bunk room.

"That was impolite," Evan muttered, narrowing his eyes at where the cowboy had disappeared. "In England, a gentleman would take his leave of a lady before disappearing. Disappointed or not."

"Believe it or not, it's impolite here, too." Dannie's drawl drew his attention back to her. "We do have manners from time to time, Duke."

"I believe it." He gestured to his shirt. "Mind if I put on a clean shirt?"

"Do you have one?" she asked, her head tilted to the side. "I've only seen you wear the two."

She paid enough attention to him to know how many shirts he owned?

"Maybe I could borrow one from Frosty."

Her gaze swept across his chest. "You're a might broader than him, I think. Let me see if Daddy has a shirt you could borrow."

Evan's jaw fell open at the same moment she seemed to

realize what her words implied—that she had given enough attention to his physical appearance to size him up for a shirt. Red flared up in her cheeks, but she raised her chin higher.

"You come to the kitchen; I'll find what you need. I can't have you meeting my friends looking like you just mucked out the stables."

"That's one chore I didn't do today," he corrected with a chuckle.

She sniffed and whirled around, leading the way into the house. She walked fast enough that he had to stretch his legs to keep up with her. He caught the door as she opened it, but she kept moving.

Evan stepped into the kitchen and saw Ruthie and Lee sitting at the table, a book between them and a plate of scones in front of them.

Ruthie's eyes followed Dannie out of the kitchen, then came back to rest on Evan. "What's got that girl riled up?"

He shrugged. "I could not say for certain, madam."

The older woman's warm smile appeared. She pushed the plate of scones toward him. "Have a biscuit."

"Biscuit? It isn't a scone?"

"Nah, isn't that fancy. Just a flour biscuit." She nodded to her grandson. "Lee here likes them with honey."

The boy picked up a small jar Evan hadn't noticed, a spoon already inside of it. He held it out. "Split it in half, drizzle a little of this inside, and it's heaven, Mr. Duke."

Evan went to the sink first, running the pump to wash his hands. "That sounds like a wonderful breakfast."

"There's coffee on the stove, too, if you want some." Ruthie sounded nothing but welcoming, her mellow tone of voice soothing. "How did you get lucky enough to be invited into the kitchen this morning?"

Evan dried his hands on a towel hanging from a hook above the sink, then went for the coffee. "I agreed to escort the Boltons to visit neighbors. Is that a regular Sunday occurrence?" If it was, he would be certain to volunteer again. Especially if it meant better coffee and food than he received in the bunkhouse.

Never mind that he had a sudden interest in keeping Dannie Bolton company.

"I'd say it's common enough since we lost the preacher." Ruthie glanced at her grandson. "We haven't had anyone permanent at the church in Sonoita since last June. The preacher up and left at the start of monsoon season. We get a circuit Methodist preacher every fourth Sunday. So, people worship as they can at home, and if they hanker for a get-together they make it happen themselves."

"Is the community very religious?" Evan asked as he sat in front of the plate of biscuits. He picked one up and split it down the middle.

"Yep," Lee answered, and Evan realized it was a Bible open between the two of them. "Grandpa says you have to be when you live out here."

Ruthie nodded her agreement. "When there's nothing between you and starvation but the Lord, you learn real quick how to pray for good crops and healthy herds."

"I think most of my acquaintances in England have never thought of it that way." Evan drizzled honey on the biscuit, considering the last time he had attended church services. It had been for Twelfth Night, and he'd walked with his brother's family down the aisle to their reserved pew at the front of the largest church in London.

A clatter behind him made Evan look over his shoulder in time to see Clark shoot into the kitchen, laughing as he fell into a chair across from Evan. "I beat Travis." With that explanation offered, he snatched up a biscuit.

Travis appeared a moment later. "Only because you didn't shine your boots."

Clark shrugged. "I don't need to shine my boots. I'm not sweet on anybody."

The tips of Travis's ears turned red. "I'm not sweet on anyone."

"Yeah? What about Jessica Harper? Pretty sure she's sweet on *you*." Clark grinned broadly. "Ain't she, Lee?" Then he took an enormous bite of his food.

Lee raised both hands. "I don't know nothing."

"I'd stay out of this one, too," Ruthie said, her eyes bright. "Make sure you give Mrs. Harper a howdy from me."

Travis walked out the back door, muttering something about getting his horse ready.

Clark swallowed loudly. "Where's Dannie?"

DANNIE HELD A DEEP BLUE SHIRT TO HER CHEST, ALONG WITH A string-tie her father had offered with the shirt when she'd told him what she needed. He hadn't done more than lift one eyebrow at her when she explained that Duke needed a clean shirt to wear to visit the neighbors.

She counted herself lucky, as she was fairly certain her brothers would have plenty to say at some point.

Not that something so simple as getting a shirt for their hired hand ought to stir up conversation. She certainly meant nothing by it. It was a kind thing to do, really. The man wouldn't want to make a poor impression on their community, wearing a shirt he'd already worked in, smelling like sweat, leather, and horses.

Although she hadn't minded the look or smell of him when they'd stood outside together only minutes before. With his sunburn faded to a tan, his features growing sharper with work, she had found the sight of him somewhat appealing.

Dannie hesitated outside the kitchen door when she heard Clark ask where she'd gone, wondering what the explanation would be and who it would come from.

Evan answered. "I'm borrowing a clean shirt from your father, so I don't embarrass the lot of you with my ragged appearance."

Clark snorted. "As soon as you open your mouth, no one will care what you're wearing. We've never had someone from England in these parts. They'll be so busy asking you questions, you won't even get the chance to answer half of them."

Dannie relaxed and allowed herself to smile. She walked into the kitchen, folded shirt in hand. "Here you are, Duke. You can freshen up and meet us at the barn. You'll drive the wagon so Travis and Clark can ride."

"Thank you, Miss Bolton." He stood and accepted the shirt with one large hand, a biscuit in the other. "I'll join you shortly." A quick stretch of his legs had him out the door, with just enough of a swing in his gait to make her blink. He'd walked so stiffly, held himself so properly, the first time he had entered the house. Now he walked like a cowboy, but with some added grace.

Clark tipped backward in his chair, a wide grin on his face. "Travis is gonna be mighty sore at Duke."

Ruthie narrowed her eyes at the boy in a way that made him immediately bring all four legs of his chair to the ground. Only then did she nod her agreement. "I reckon he'll feel like he has to crow a bit more for attention."

"What are you two on about?" Dannie put her hands on her hips. "You're not making a lick of sense."

"It's a good thing you're not like most of the girls around here, Dannie." Clark stood and swept his hat from a peg by the door. Then he left the door to swing shut behind him.

Dannie raised her eyebrows and turned to Ruthie and Lee. The boy had resumed reading the Bible in front of him while Ruthie wore a somewhat skeptical expression.

"What is it?" Dannie dropped her fists from her hips.

"Young lady, if you can't see that man's as handsome as a prince in a fairy tale, you oughta have your eyes checked."

Lee snickered, then turned the sound into a cough.

Dannie's cheeks warmed. "Even if that's true, what's that to do with Travis?" She tried to sound like she didn't care, but the way Ruthie smiled at her said Dannie wasn't that great of an actress.

"All the females in the territory, aged anywhere between the cradle and the grave, are going to take notice of him. Even Travis's little Jessica Harper will take notice."

A small twist in Dannie's gut made her wince. Ruthie had a point. She scooped up a basket from the countertop. Ruthie had filled it with jars of preserves to take to neighbors as presents. "I'll be back in a few hours. The boys will likely be out until the sun goes down."

Ruthie nodded, her attention already back on her grandson. "Have a good time."

Dannie walked out with her head high and the basket tucked close.

Ruthie didn't visit the neighbors often. Mrs. Perkins had always come with them in the past. Before her father got sick, he'd come, too, riding in the wagon with Dannie and the house-keeper. He'd not gone visiting since Mrs. Perkins left, even after recovering from his illness.

The wagon waited in the dusty yard, with Duke working to hitch the mules. Travis helped, his own horse already saddled and at the ready. Clark had to be in the barn, seeing to his mount.

Duke's hat bobbed up and down on the other side of where Dannie stood. She gulped and averted her eyes, going to the back of the wagon instead. She slid her basket into the wagon bed. The boys had added a crate of Abram's carvings to give out, with everything from a little wooden dog to a set of square blocks stacked inside.

Abram gave away toys every few months, which usually led to their neighbors paying him to create more for their family or friends as gifts. His skills with carpentry tools had always come in handy, but since the droughts, he hadn't worked on larger projects much.

She'd asked him about it only a month ago. His answer had put another crack in her heart. "People don't have the money or interest in new tables and chairs when they're just trying to make ends meet."

Shaking herself free of the memory, Dannie went around to climb into the buckboard. She put a hand to the seat and put one foot on the wagon's hub, ready to haul herself up, when a pair of hands took hold around her waist.

The Englishman's voice, low and nothing more than polite, accompanied his touch. "Allow me, Miss Bolton."

He assisted Dannie easily into the wagon, with her doing little besides making certain she landed in the right place. She moved all the way over to allow him room to swing up beside her.

Then she looked down, catching sight of him all cleaned up, in the blue shirt brought made the green in his eyes stand out.

He had his black coat over one arm, and he shrugged into it before coming to sit beside her. He looked like he was taking her to church, or on a formal visit, rather than just coming along for the ride.

He slanted a glance at her from below the brim of his hat, and one corner of his mouth turned upward. "You all right, Dannie?"

For that brief moment, Evan Rounsevell sounded a little less British and a little more American than usual.

When her mouth went dry, she blamed the arid desert air. "Perfectly well, thank you." She turned to face forward. "Let's be on our way."

The boys rode through the adobe corridor, and the buckboard wagon followed behind. Dannie folded her hands tightly in her lap and kept her spine straight as a lightning rod. Whatever had come over her that morning? Deciding to take her father's advice, trying to act with a little kindness, shouldn't have turned her into a fool.

Certainly, she had thought Evan Rounsevell handsome the first time she had laid eyes on him, but she hadn't had time for a fine-feathered peacock. She still didn't. Even if he'd proven there was more to him than his fancy way of talking and his stories about the queen. He was just a man, like any other. And men were at best a distraction, and at worst, no-good thieves.

Someday, there might be a man for Dannie. But he'd be a man with as much love in his heart for ranching and the wide-open ranges and skies as she held in her own.

Not a man who intended to go on his way after a cattle drive.

Duke's steady voice spoke over the sound of horse hooves clopping against the dirt. "You've grown quiet, Dannie."

"Sorry. Just thinking." She let out a sigh. He wasn't flirting. Wasn't trying to be a distraction. The poor man had no idea what went through her mind, and he'd be shocked if he knew about the tangent her thoughts had taken her on. "Are you glad to get off the ranch for a while?"

The abrupt introduction of the new topic didn't seem to worry him at all. He gave an easy shrug. "As I haven't been on your ranch long, I cannot say I've grown weary of it already. I will say that I am interested in meeting more of your neighbors. This isn't an easy way of life. I should like to know how people find themselves drawn to it."

"Maybe it's just nice to have a choice. In England, don't most people just take up their father's trades, if they aren't born into titles or wealth?" Dannie watched her brothers ahead as they passed beneath the sign marking their father's property. "My father's father—I never met him—owned a blacksmith shop in Texas. He had three sons. The oldest went back east as an accountant, the second son went north to open a restaurant in Chicago, and my dad joined the army for the War Between the States."

"Did that upset your grandfather?" He guided the mules to follow after the boys down the hard-packed dirt that made up their road. They went toward Sonoita, a loose collection of build-ings that didn't even merit a place on the map. They weren't headed to the tiny town but would stop instead at three houses along the way.

"Dad said the only thing Grandad was upset about was Dad

joining the army. The older two brothers left for good jobs, for careers. And to escape the war. The family lived in Texas, which joined the Confederacy, even though not everyone believed in it. Dad says his family didn't own any slaves, and he didn't actually know anyone who did, since they lived in a little farm town. So when the recruiters came through, they didn't talk about the right to keep a slave. They talked about state rights verses federal rights." Dannie never much liked talking about that part of her family's history. "Dad joined the Confederate Army. That's what upset his father."

The quiet stretched between them, growing uncomfortable for Dannie.

Without meaning too, she became defensive. A whole nation had been at war. People had made foolish choices, done things without knowing what it would mean for the history of their country.

"Dad says he was young and foolish. He fell into enemy hands shortly after signing up; as a prisoner of war, they apprenticed him to a farrier. Dad already had a lot of the skills, growing up as a blacksmith's son. After a while, they let him join the Union Army, but it was toward the end. He joined the cavalry to come west. That's how he met Abram and found out about Arizona."

"I think that is something I admire about your nation," Duke said, a hint of wistfulness in his voice. "I admire their ability to forgive a man and let him change. The war here was, by all accounts, a thing of horror. Yet here your family is, not embittered, but moving forward."

"It's not like that everywhere." Dannie felt the urge to hunch her shoulders, well remembering her time in Boston. She had done all she could to hide the accent she'd partly inherited from her father. For a time, she'd been ashamed to sound like a girl from the southern half of the country. People made assumptions about her intelligence based on her accent, about her prejudices, too.

The gentleman at her side bent a little, drawing her gaze to him as he peered beneath the brim of her straw hat. "I think that's what makes your family all the more admirable, Dannie."

A hawk dove low across the road, making one of the mules flick its ears backward nervously. Sensing a way to break the heavy tension in the air, Dannie pointed at the bird as it swirled upward in a circle. "Look at that. Can you imagine what it would be like to fly?"

Duke sat back again and tipped his head back to watch the rising hawk. "I imagine it would be as exhilarating as riding a horse at a full gallop through a meadow or diving into a cold spring in the middle of summer." He chuckled. "That sounded rather fanciful."

"I liked it," Dannie admitted, nudging him with her shoulder to lend a little friendly weight to her words. "We might not have wings, but there are ways in life to produce that kind of feeling. Things that make us feel alive."

Duke nudged her back, but then his shoulder remained there, brushing hers. "What sort of things do that for you? Make you feel alive?"

Without warning, her whole face burst into flame. Due to his nearness or her immediate, somewhat ridiculous, interpretation of his question, she didn't know.

"Riding, for certain," she said, perhaps a little breathlessly. But her thoughts had produced a different answer, one she had to keep to herself. *Dancing with a man I fancy. Kissing him beneath the moon.*

Not that she had ever kissed anyone beneath the moon. Not even David. He'd stolen a few kisses here and there, but never beneath the stars. Why then could she imagine what it would be like to stand on her toes and kiss the man beside her, the full moon hanging above them like a lantern?

Travis looped back and drew even with them. "Is it all right if we visit the Masons first?"

Dannie bobbed her head up and down in answer, not trusting

herself to speak another word until she had control over her mind and its foolish, romantic imaginings.

What was wrong with her?

The ranch came first. She couldn't afford the distraction, in her head or otherwise, of a handsome Englishman who would be gone come winter, if not sooner. Off on another adventure, a place more interesting, or home again to England. He'd said it himself. He wasn't staying. He wasn't cut out for ranching long-term. Even if he did wind up having a love for it, he had plenty to call him back to England.

Maybe that was her problem. Knowing he was leaving meant knowing when his place in her life would come to an end. That made him safer than a man who'd show up and disappear unexpectedly.

She fully expected Evan to disappear, just like everyone else without roots in the Arizona dust.

CHAPTER TEN

Riding beside the lovely daughter of his employer, Evan thought that something in the air had shifted. During their conversation, for one long moment, a charge of electricity had built between them. But the strange tingling along his arm abated as he turned the mules down the lane to visit the Mason family.

Dannie started explaining who they were meeting first.

"Mr. and Mrs. Mason have only lived here three years. They bought the land cheap after the first drought and started farming black-eyed peas, sweet potatoes, and half a dozen other things that put up with the weather. They've got some cattle, but not enough to consider them ranchers. Mr. Mason keeps increasing his flock of sheep."

"I can't imagine sheep would survive this heat much better than cattle."

The young woman at his side shrugged. "He sells them local, mostly."

A house came into view as their wagon reached the top of a rise in the land. "What is the family like?"

"Nice enough. They have five children together, and Mr. Mason has two older sons from his first marriage." Though she spoke almost carelessly, Evan caught the slightest wrinkle upon her brow. Something about the family, or perhaps the eldest sons, bothered her. "They lived in Tombstone for a while, working for one of the silver mines. Then Mrs. Mason told Mr. Mason she didn't want *her* boys to grow up to be miners. So here they are."

Evan wouldn't want anyone he knew to spend their days below ground, digging up treasure for another person to grow rich. "Farming is a noble profession."

Dannie's gaze flitted away from him, to the house and outbuildings growing steadily closer. "Feeding a family is noble, no matter how you do it."

Though Dannie didn't make her statement a challenge, Evan turned it over in his mind as though she had. The tenant farmers on his family's land worked hard, year after year. His father employed household servants, too. Many of whom lived in the village near the country estate with their kin. Even scullery maids and shepherd boys brought pennies to their tables.

"I never thought of it that way before." Evan didn't realize he'd spoken aloud until Dannie shifted to peer at him from beneath the brim of her hat.

"What way?" Her honey-brown eyes collided sternly with his gaze. He'd seen the woman smile, and heard her laugh, yet she wore sobriety most often. Had she always been a serious woman, ready to weigh each word she heard, each action she witnessed, against the moral compass in her mind?

Things to ponder later. For the moment, Evan needed to give her an answer. They had nearly reached the house. "I never thought of the maids and grooms and under-gardeners as noble for doing what they must to feed themselves. My father always made our family sound noble for providing employment to dozens of people. As though we ought to be honored for creating positions and paying people what they had rightly earned." That viewpoint no longer sat well with him.

"The employer serves in that function. Providing jobs for people isn't a negative, so long as there's fair treatment and fair pay for the work done." Dannie sounded certain of every word she spoke.

"But who determines what is fair?"

At that question, he saw a hint of her elusive smile again. "As our friend Hamlet would say, 'there's the rub.' Employer and employee, lord and servant, rancher and drover, all have to come to an agreement as to what's fair."

He considered her quoting of the English bard, trying to form an enquiry to pursue that topic without sounding as though he questioned her education. The woman would likely prickle up again if she thought herself slighted by his conversation, but he'd never heard *Hamlet* referenced in anything other than a crisp British accent.

A shout from the direction of the house stole Dannie's attention away. "Dannie! I'm so glad you came to visit."

Dannie waved chipperly at the salutation; her smile brightened at the sight of a woman standing on the porch of the Mason house. "Felicity, good morning."

The house they approached was smaller than the Bolton ranch house, only one story with a porch wrapping around its side. It was the only structure made of wood; an adobe barn and other outbuildings stood behind it.

The woman's shout drew others out of the house, and a couple of young children came around the corner of the porch. When Evan stopped the buckboard before the porch steps, a small crowd had gathered to greet the visitors.

Dannie turned to lower herself from the wagon. Without thinking, Evan held his hand out to her. She looked up at him, brown eyes flashing with an emotion he couldn't name, but she accepted his hand and the strength of his arm as she stepped backward to the ground.

He climbed down on the same side, then went to check the mules. Travis and Clark had dismounted and handed off the reins of their horses to two boys.

As Travis passed by Evan, he pointed to the adobe barn.

"Duke, tie up the mules by the trough. Then come inside."

It was the first time the young man had treated Evan as a hired hand rather than an equal, giving orders as he did. When Evan raised his eyebrows, Travis slowed his step and winced. "If that's all right...?"

Though inwardly he chafed at the younger man's ability to command him, Evan forced a smile and quick nod.

"As you say, sir." How many times had Evan had such a phrase spoken to him, even as a boy, when he commanded his father's servants?

The boy's cheeks flamed red, but he nodded tightly and went on into the house, following the family inside.

Evan's stomach soured, the boy's humiliation increasing his own.

Travis hadn't done anything wrong. Not really. Evan was a hired hand under the employment of the boy's father. In the natural order of things, Travis had every right to order him around. And it hadn't been an order in the strictest sense of the word.

Perhaps the weeks of constantly receiving orders had stretched his patience. Frosty, Ed, and Buck all had a greater right to it, given their experience and age, but a mere boy of seventeen telling Evan what to do?

The boys with the horses tied them up outside the barn, near a trough, leaving a second for the mules. After securing the animals, Evan turned to see the two children staring up at him. They both had white-blond hair, blue eyes, and more freckles than he'd ever seen.

"Who're you?" the taller of the two asked.

Evan almost gave them his proper name but remembered himself in time to substitute the cowboy pseudonym. "They call me Duke. What do they call you fine young fellows?"

The boys exchanged a look, then the shorter one wrinkled his nose up at Evan. "You sound different."

He had to chuckle at that, the last of the tension slipping away from him. "Likely because I am from England." A whole ocean and world away from where he stood. Things were different in America, in Arizona. He wasn't the son of a high-ranking nobleman here. He was just another cowboy. The freedom that thought brought eased the irritation he'd felt earlier.

"You still haven't given me your names."

The taller boy jerked a thumb toward his chest. "I'm Tom. This here is Pete." He clapped his hand on the younger boy's shoulder. "Want to come inside and meet everyone else, Mr. Duke?"

"We have cookies," Pete added, eyes going wide. "With nuts and raisins."

Realizing this must be an uncommon treat, Evan bowed as he would to a peer, purposefully seeking their amusement. "I should like nothing better. Please, lead the way, gentlemen."

Exchanging grins, the boys scampered toward the house. Evan had to lengthen his stride to keep up with them. They were good enough to wait at the door, the taller boy holding it open for Evan.

He entered a small corridor with doors on either side, the corridor stretching to the back of the house with another door in sight. The boys opened one of the doors on the right and Evan followed them into what must count as a parlor in that particular house.

The room full of people quieted when he appeared. Chairs, wooden stools, and a sofa were all occupied, as well as the stones of the hearth. A table in the center of everything held a pitcher of lemonade, glasses and mugs, and plates of cookies. An open doorway at the back of the room led to the kitchen, given what he could see above the heads of Dannie and the young woman who had greeted her from the porch.

For a moment, he stood, the awkwardness of silence stealing his wits, but then he made eye contact with Dannie, and she jolted forward to stand beside him.

"Mr. Mason, Mrs. Mason, may I present our new hand, Mr.

Evan Rounsevell. He is lately arrived from England." The formal introduction loosened the tight knot growing in his midsection, and he gave Dannie a brief, grateful smile before he swept his hat off and bowed to the room.

"It is my great pleasure to be in your home today, Mrs. Mason." The words flowed naturally from his tongue, and they seemed to break the spell. The Mason family began speaking, most at the same moment.

"Oh, what fine manners," Mrs. Mason said, approaching him with a glass of the lemonade.

"I can see why your brothers call him 'Duke.'" Mr. Mason chuckled and stepped forward with an outstretched hand.

Evan accepted the lemonade with his left hand at the same moment Mason gripped his right in a firm handshake.

Dannie's friend appeared at his side, her eyes round as a wagon wheel. "What a lovely accent." She batted her eyelashes at him prettily. "And you came all the way from England. How adventurous of you."

Before Evan knew it, Mrs. Mason and her eldest daughter had him sitting between them on the only couch in the room. Travis and Clark were in conversation with a boy of about fifteen years in age, Mr. Mason sitting in an overstuffed chair speaking with them.

The two younger boys who had led Evan inside went to sit at a small table by the window, a plate of cookies and a checker-board between them. A little girl with blonde plaits sat on the rug, practically at Evan's feet, copying her elder sister with her rapidly batting lashes.

He had everyone in sight except for Dannie. He turned to look over the back of the couch, toward the kitchen door, in time to see her disappear through it. Though he hadn't thought himself lacking in social abilities, realizing she had left him on his own made his collar feel a touch too tight around his throat.

"Dear me, Mr. Rounsevell. How did a gentleman such as yourself decide to come this far west?" Mrs. Mason folded her hands politely in her lap. "I can't imagine Arizona is anything like your home country."

Miss Mason, who had yet to be introduced to him properly, eased a bit closer to him on the couch. "What is England like, Mr. Rounsevell?"

"Your mother is quite right, Miss Mason, that it is not at all like Arizona." He sat stiffly, posture correct, and put on the charming smile that had worked well in ballrooms and salons for most of his life. "Which is why I felt the need to travel. I have heard many stories about the great American West, and I wished to see it for myself. England is beautiful but old. There isn't a corner of my country unexplored. But here, everything still feels open and new."

"Ah, he's got the call for exploration in him," Mr. Mason said from across the room. "That's what brung us out here. My family is from Virginia, originally. But it's too crowded there, these days."

"Though it's a far easier place to farm," his eldest son added with an impudent grin. The whole family laughed with an ease that told him this was an old joke amongst them. "What's farming like in England?"

"Fraught with trouble, as I imagine it is everywhere." Evan turned his lemonade glass about in his hand. "While here the seasons are all dry, there, everything is forever wet. Flooding and rot are common difficulties for crops, so irrigation is an important facet of farming in England. Though I am no expert, as our family leases the farmland to tenants."

"Oh, you'd be a landowner over there?" Mrs. Mason leaned back slightly. "My family came over to the states fifty years ago when my grandfather was evicted from his lands. The lord who leased to them decided to convert to sheep farming."

"And then your grandfather went to Virginia and did the same thing." Her husband chuckled and then gave Evan an easy smile. "I'm not sure when my family came over. We've forgotten whatever story it was that brought us here. But my ancestors fought in the Revolution."

"Ah, yes. The rebellion of the colonies." Evan softened the words with a smile. "I cannot say I blame them. The English way of life is stifling compared to the freedom of your country. Though I suppose every government is fraught with its own difficulties."

Mr. Mason nodded sagely. "That's the nature of politics."

"Frank." Mrs. Mason shook her finger at her husband. "No talk of politics on Sunday."

He raised both his hands. "Yes, ma'am."

"Now, Mr. Rounsevell." Miss Mason touched his forearm to gain his attention. "Won't you tell me about London? I've read so much about it, but I'd like to hear everything. Does it really have fog so thick you cannot see more than a few feet in front of you? Does the queen hold court for anyone to visit her?"

Evan took one sip of his lemonade, then shared the stories he thought they would most appreciate. "I have spoken to the queen a dozen times in my life, but she has grown to an age that prohibits her from being as available to the public as she once was. The last time I saw her hold a grand occasion was during her Golden Jubilee, several years ago now. The entire nation celebrated with parades, parties, and fireworks."

"Sounds like Independence Day," one of the younger boys said, the checker game forgotten. "We went to Tombstone last July."

Miss Mason briefly narrowed her eyes at her brother. "I imagine these celebrations were bigger than what you saw in Tombstone, Tom." She leaned toward Evan. "Tell us more about the queen."

Falling into the comfort of a familiar topic, Evan relaxed as he shared his favorite anecdotes about Queen Victoria's court. For all that the Americans proudly touted their independence, they had a great fascination with the English monarchy.

DANNIE LEANED AGAINST THE KITCHEN WALL, LISTENING THROUGH the open doorway as Evan spoke of his noble background without actually coming out and declaring himself an English lord. Though she might admit to herself some curiosity regarding his history, the sophisticated tilt to his words and the rich timbre of his voice was what drew her to listen when she'd rather pretend disinterest.

Felicity's cooing over nearly every word spoken didn't much surprise her, though her irritation with her friend came unexpectedly. Felicity was barely eighteen, two years younger than Dannie, and far less experienced with the world outside of her family farm. That entitled Felicity to curiosity, but the girl ought to rein in her flirtatious giggles.

Striding to the Mason's long kitchen table, Dannie went back to unloading the basket of things they had brought to share. She took out jars of preserves, a few of the wooden animals sent by Abram, one of Ruthie's delicious loaves of bread—

A roar of laughter from the other room made her freeze, her hand wrapped tightly around one last jar of rhubarb preserves. A light, tinkling laughter that carried on longest belonged to Felicity.

Dannie slammed the jar down onto the table with more force than necessary, then winced.

"What is wrong with me?" she whispered into the quiet of the room.

If Felicity wanted to act like a fool over a man, Dannie could abide it. Her friend was young. She didn't understand men. She had no idea that someone wrapped up as pretty as a present, with an English accent acting like a red ribbon on the top, could leave tomorrow without so much as a blink.

Another round of laughter from the other room came through the kitchen doorway.

Evan Rounsevell might dabble all he liked in the art of flirting. Let him paint blushes across the cheeks of every girl in the territory. Dannie didn't care. She'd already lost her heart over a fancy-talker once, and she didn't mean to make that mistake again.

She already knew *this one* would move on. And it wasn't as if he'd shown any interest in flirting with her, anyhow.

Gritting her teeth, Dannie whirled on her best boot heel and went striding right back into the parlor. She wore her smile with confidence and took the last remaining stool near the front window. No one paid her any mind. Or so she thought, until she'd fluffed out her skirt and raised her gaze to collide with Evan's.

His mouth hung partway open, and his brows drew down as he stared at her.

"Then what happened, Duke?" Felicity asked, moving to the edge of her seat and putting her hand on his arm near his elbow. "What did the princess say next?"

Princesses? In an Arizona parlor, *that* was what they were talking about?

Dannie couldn't help arching her eyebrow at him.

The Englishman glanced down at Felicity's hand on his arm, then back up at Dannie.

Go on, Evan. Tell us all about the princesses and knights in shining armor. Dannie crossed her arms over her chest and waited, along with everyone else, for the conclusion of whatever story he'd been telling. Thanks to his natural charm and beautiful accent, everyone ate up his words like chocolate cake at a Sunday picnic.

Evan's tone remained light as he finished his story, his attention pointedly turning to Mrs. Mason rather than her daughter at his side. "The princess declared herself unfit for company and left the banquet hall, and as she walked from the room, the split pea soup left a trail behind her."

The people surrounding him laughed again, and Mrs. Mason wiped away a tear when she had finished. "The poor woman. I daresay, we've all had something like that happen at least once in our lives. Princess or not."

His smile tightened, and Dannie caught his quick glance in

her direction. Perhaps he remembered her objections to his nobility-laced anecdotes?

He abruptly stood, Felicity's hand falling back into her lap, and he walked to the mantel to examine the rifle hanging above it. "We are far from England, Mrs. Mason, and I am a stranger here. Won't you tell me what it is your friends and neighbors do for entertainment?"

Everyone turned with him toward the family matriarch. She appeared surprised at the change in topic, and attention. Mrs. Mason looked helplessly at her daughter.

"Tell him about the dance, Mama." Felicity tossed her head, letting her blonde ringlets fall back over her shoulder. "Do you dance, Mr. Rounsevell?"

"On rare occasions, Miss Mason."

Mrs. Mason clapped her hands happily. "Wonderful! We have an opportunity for that coming this very week. Everyone is invited—Frank even sent word to his two oldest boys to come and join us. They don't meet nearly enough nice young people in Bisbee, you understand. The whole town mines from dawn until dusk."

Perhaps sensing her mother was about to lose the most important part of the conversation in family details, Felicity leaped into it. "We're going to have a big dance in town, outside the church if the weather is fine. We'll have hanging lanterns, lots of food, and wonderful music. Will you come?"

This was the first Dannie had heard of the coming dance, but one look at her brothers told her they'd be present. She went to most of their community socials, but more to see other women-folk than anything else. They came together once a month when the weather was right.

Evan looked in her direction. "I must check with my employer, Miss Mason."

"Oh." Her shoulders dropped.

"Dad and Frosty will let him come," Travis said from where he sat, his elbows on his knees and an easy grin on his boyish face. "Frosty will stay at the ranch, like always, but Dad will want to show Duke off to everyone."

Travis was right. Dannie couldn't imagine her father declining to let the Englishman attend. He liked Evan's sense of adventure far too much and would introduce him to the whole territory, if possible.

"Then you simply must save a dance for me, Mr. Rounsevell." Felicity put a hand to her chest and tilted her head endearingly to one side.

Dannie briefly contemplated staying home.

"It would be my honor, Miss Mason." Evan *bowed*. No one in Arizona *bowed*. She'd seen it back east plenty of times, and his deep nods to her were near enough. But Felicity's cheeks went pink, and her hand fluttered up to touch her hair.

Evan abruptly turned to Mrs. Mason. "What sort of dances are typical on these occasions? I'm concerned what I've learned in ballrooms at home will not meet your standards."

The remainder of the visit passed with the young people explaining reels and dances to Evan; he nodded knowingly and said he would be capable enough. Good thing, too, since Felicity appeared on the verge of offering to give him dancing lessons. By the time the visit was over, Dannie wasn't certain she could manage another house full of people cooing over Evan.

She made it out to the wagon ahead of him easily, getting up without his assistance. When they started for the main road, Dannie still hadn't glanced at him. But she kept a pleasant expression on her face. She wasn't about to discuss Felicity's obvious interest in him, or the dance, or anything else.

Her insides were too knotted up. Though why she cared so much when she was determined to not care at all Dannie couldn't say.

Evan was the one to break the silence. "What have I done to vex you this time?"

"Nothing." She shrugged and brushed a loose strand of hair

out of her eyes. "I'm thinking of the dance, is all. If the older two Mason sons are going to attend, I might just stay home."

Although his expression carried a hint of skepticism, he followed that line of conversation. "You'd forgo an evening of enjoyment based solely upon who is in attendance? If we did that where I'm from, no one would ever go anywhere."

She smiled despite herself. "Have you so many people you dislike?"

"Not just dislike. There are plenty of people in Society whom I loathe." He flashed a brief grin that made her forget herself enough to laugh at his flippant statement. "I'm afraid that's one cost of my upbringing. There are plenty of old grudges and gossip reaching back generations. There are fortune hunters, social climbers, and people who want to use my position to get to someone else in my family or social circle. There is little trust, and less friendship, among the nobility of England."

"That sounds miserable." She let her gaze find her brothers on the road before them. Then she sighed. "Mr. Mason's oldest sons are managers at the Copper Queen mine in Bisbee. They're doing well for themselves, as they are certain to tell any who will listen. Sometimes, they think a lady's favor should come with their prosperity. Whether the lady thinks so or not is irrelevant."

Evan snorted, an unrefined sound she hadn't heard leave him before. "Boorish cads, then. That sort seems to exist at every level of every society."

"You might be right." Dannie leaned back and looked upward, where the sun climbed toward the noon hour. "Are *you* looking forward to an evening of dancing?"

He considered her question long enough that she turned to look at him, uncertain if he had heard her. He watched her from the corner of his eye, the slightest smile turning his lips upward. "It depends on the young ladies attending the event, I think. If the cads keep away the lady I most wish to partner in a dance, I cannot imagine enjoying myself."

Dannie felt heat creep into her cheeks. She jerked herself to face straight again, hardening her spine and lifting her chin. "I hope you are not flirting with me, Mr. Rounsevell."

He chuckled, apparently not at all intimidated by her. "I would not dream of such a thing, Miss Bolton."

She couldn't let him have the last word, especially given his smug tone. "I am not like Felicity Mason. A handsome face and foreign accent isn't enough to turn my head."

He had the audacity to tip his hat back and turn the full force of his summer-green eyes and curving mouth toward her. "You think I'm handsome, Dannie?"

Dannie bit her tongue and glared at him.

Her brother turned into the lane of their next neighbor. Dannie snapped out her orders to the Englishman quickly. "We're visiting the Coopers next. Mind your manners if you expect to come on visits with us again."

"How do your drovers say it? With that long drawl of theirs?" He settled his hat back in place, then attempted to mimic her accent as he drew out the polite words. "Yes, ma'am."

She crossed her arms over her chest and glowered at the tops of the mules' heads. Assuming that stern expression was the only thing that kept her from admiring his somewhat self-assured—and entirely too handsome—face.

AFTER THE COOPERS, EVAN SQUIRED DANNIE AND HER BROTHERS to a family with the surname Harper. He'd kept himself appropriately quiet through both visits, in the spirit of an experiment. The ladies of both households still spent their time gawking at him, even a young woman introduced as Miss Jessica. Travis kept most of that girl's attention with his conversation, betraying the fact to anyone with eyes that he had a *tendre* for the girl.

Evan stood in the corner of the smallish house, shoulder against one wall and back against the other, listening to the conversation turn to the upcoming dance. Dannie came out of the kitchen, easily seen through a large double-sized doorway. This house was simpler than the others he had visited, smaller, and the outer walls bricked adobe.

Dannie held her hat in one hand and the handle of a basket in the other. Her gaze slid across the middle of the room, where her brothers and the elder Harper children sat in a circle of chairs, until she met Evan's eyes.

With a tip of her head, she indicated she wanted him to step out of the front door with her. Evan straightened from his relaxed position.

"Clark, Travis, I'm for home."

"We'll be back by sundown," Travis promised, rising to his feet with the other men in the room.

Dannie turned to take her leave of their hostess while Evan slipped outside to bring the mules and wagon to the front.

The sun bore down on the desert, the hours creeping into the hottest time of the day. Evan put his hat back on his head, then found the mules dozing with their heads near the water trough. They flicked their ears and tails to keep flies off, and when he came near, only one raised its head to look at him.

"No time for napping, gentlemen." Evan gave the red-colored mule near him a pat on the rump. "Let's get you both home to your barn. Then you can rest where it's cool and dark."

A crunch of gravel and dirt behind him had Evan glancing over his shoulder. Dannie swung the basket in her hand, and she walked around to the opposite side of the wagon.

Apparently, she hadn't liked him assisting her to her seat.

The woman had a contrary streak the likes of which he'd never encountered in an English lady. At home, the female members of his set flirted, acted either coy or disinterested, and rarely disagreed with the men among them.

Evan checked the harnesses and reins before climbing up to his seat next to Dannie. She put the basket in the wagon bed, then twisted around to face forward again. The smile she wore, slight though it was, extended to a twinkle in her eyes.

What had pleased her this time?

"Travis is smitten with Jessica," she confided in a low tone, though there was no one about to hear her besides him and the mules. "He's not going to want to come home for hours."

"And that's appropriate courtship out west?" Evan flicked the reins to get the mules moving down the lane.

"So long as they're surrounded by family, no one minds if they spend all day together." Dannie brushed a wisp of hair away from her forehead before wincing up at the sun. "It's not like England, or even the eastern states, out here in the middle of nowhere. We're lucky to see our neighbors once every week or two. When I was younger, it wasn't even as often as that. We're working too hard and live too far apart. I imagine you could pay a call to a lady multiple times a week with little trouble where you're from."

"It is expected, sometimes. If I were to attend a ball, for example, I would call upon or send flowers to every lady I danced with nearly the very next day." Evan wrinkled his nose as the heavy scents of hothouse flowers drifted into his memory. "Not only would I be exhausted from dancing near to dawn, but I would then have to remember who I owed what sort of visit or risk the wrath of Society matriarchs."

She made that unique sound, a sort of light snort which signaled her disapproval, before passing her usual judgement. "That sounds like an awful waste of time. But I suppose people of your class don't have much else to keep them busy."

"People of my—you know, Dannie, you sound quite prejudiced against my *class*." He leaned away from her to better take in the disdainful wrinkle of her nose. "What have we ever done to deserve your censure?"

Her lips parted as her eyes widened, but it took a moment for her to speak. She obviously hadn't expected the challenge in his words.

"I've been unkind again." The realization seemed to trouble

her, but her expression became contemplative rather than apologetic.

Stubborn woman.

"I must confess myself often befuddled by your remarks, Miss Bolton."

Her honey-brown eyes flicked in his direction. "Befuddled?"

"Quite." Evan focused on the thin road ahead, the dust and rock of the desert clear and narrow where wagons made their way from one side of the large valley to the other. "You have your moments of being—as you say—unkind. Yet I sense much more to your character."

"Really." She drew out the single word with a large dose of skepticism. "You barely know me. Perhaps I'm just as mean-spirited as a rattlesnake with a toothache."

Evan didn't bother to fight back his smile. "That is precisely the sort of thing I have alluded to. You have all the charm of any lady I have ever met, but the moment you feel threatened you put up a shield; whether it is constructed of charming colloquialisms or your disapproving frowns, you hold it between yourself and the world just the same."

For several moments she made not a sound, and when Evan dared to glance at the woman, he saw a storm cloud growing in her eyes. She crossed her arms over her chest. "Charming colloquialisms?"

"As I said." Evan swung his attention back to the road, though the mules seemed well aware they were making for their stable full of oats and hay, given the liveliness of their steps. "You express yourself colorfully when you are distressed. Or feeling hostile."

The spring beneath the buckboard bench creaked as she shifted, scooting away from him while turning in his direction. With one arm still tight across her chest, she released the other in order to shake her finger at him.

"You listen to me, Mr.-High-And-Mighty-English-Lord—I'm not afraid of you, so I've got no reason to put up any shields—

constructed of words or otherwise. If I have a thing to say, I say it. That's a fault of its own, I'll admit, and I'm trying to be better about minding my tongue. But if you think for one minute that I treat you any differently than any other greenhorn sticking his nose in my business, you're wrong."

Evan raised his eyebrows, not giving her the satisfaction of an immediate response.

She bristled up even more. "I'm not the one who crossed half the world to show up where I wasn't wanted—or needed. Though why you'd choose to kick up your heels in the desert, I don't know."

"You could ask." Evan's voice was soft, contrasting her brittle-ness, and extending an olive branch he felt certain she would slap away with more barbed words.

Instead, she took his words as a challenge. "Fine then. I'm asking. Why are you in Arizona territory? And don't give me that story about Buffalo Bill or the penny dreadfuls you read in England." She faced forward again, shoulders drawn up and arms folded tight.

Evan measured his words carefully before speaking, sifting out the truthful parts he'd rather not share with anyone from the sincere desires that had brought him across an ocean and into the desert.

Dannie didn't deserve to know his reasons. Yet if she did, he'd welcome her pretty smiles in place of her suspicious frowns. Given what her brother had said of her past, of Dannie being hurt by a man full of charming words and little else, Evan had some sympathy for her suspicions.

"Those were part of the reason. I can't take them out of the equation all together." Evan let his wrists rest against his thighs, the reins loose in his gloved hands. "And though you've not asked your question with sincerity, I'll do my best to answer with such."

She opened her mouth to protest, but when he raised his eyebrows at her, she clamped her lips shut again, allowing him to continue. "For as long as I can remember, my life hasn't been my own. My family's expectations took me through my years of school and dictated my actions and my relationships with others. Yet, as a second son with a healthy older brother and nephew now between me and my father's title, I'm superfluous. There is nothing for me in England. Nothing that is really mine, save a small inheritance. There is no land, no house waiting, and it is unacceptable for me to dabble in business ventures given my lineage. As much as you might scoff at that, it is the way things are in England. The way they always have been. I am as trapped by my father's title as a sailor pressed into service."

His throat went dry from the road's dust, making his next words come out more gruffly than he meant them to. "It's different here. I'm far from my father's influence and from the rules of my birth. For the first time in my life, I can work with my own two hands. I can discover if I am a man of any worth or value outside of the shadow my father's title has cast upon me. If I prove this to myself, I can go back, knowing I'm capable of standing on my own two feet."

Nothing passed between them, and though a breeze came rustling through the dry grasses and across Evan's skin, he sat stiff and still in the heat. Dannie stared ahead, those dark eyebrows of hers drawn together, but no other sign gave away what thoughts ran through her head.

The quiet stretched on, and Evan let it.

Finally, Dannie released a sigh full and heavy with whatever conclusion she had drawn about him.

"You haven't complained about the work once, have you?"

"Not out loud," he admitted, cocking his head to one side.

Her smile slid sideways. "That's better than most manage." Then she pointed to the northwest. "Did you know if you go that way you get to Tucson? My father has taken us there a few times. It's a nice place, for Arizona. The Santa Cruz River is full of fish, and it comes from the Santa Rita Mountains all the way to the Gila River, and then to Mexico. I've heard tell that the river is over two hundred miles long."

The woman perplexed him. "Is that so?"

"Yep." She didn't look directly at him as she spoke her next surprising words. "Like the River Thames. They're about the same length, from start to finish."

Evan pushed his hat back and stared at her profile, at a loss for words.

Dannie slid her gaze to his and gave him an innocent quirk of the lips. "My dad has an encyclopedia. I've been doing a bit of reading since you arrived."

A laugh startled him as it escaped his lungs. "Ought I to be flattered or terrified of you?"

She shrugged. "I thought you should know. I'm not prejudiced against you, Evan Rounsevell, or Duke, or whatever you want to be called. I'm just careful. Because there was a time when I wasn't—when I took every word a man said as truth." She shifted in her seat again, stretching her legs out a little more before her and leaning against the single-board back of the bench. Her eyes took on a faraway look. "I hope you'll be patient with me. I don't trust easily, or all at once."

Evan didn't say another word, nor did she, the rest of the way back to the ranch.

CHAPTER ELEVEN

It was four days after the somewhat uncomfortable Sunday ride that Dannie couldn't find Fable on or under the porch. With evening coming on, turning the sky from blue to purple and then to black, Dannie went to the barn.

It didn't matter how cozy a spot she made for the beautiful shepherd dog, Fable liked to do things her own way. Maybe that was why the two of them got on so well, despite the fact that Fable was a working dog and not a pet.

The sun had barely gone down, with a purple smudge hanging heavy in the west to show its passing. Dannie carried a lantern in one hand and clean towels tucked under the other arm, but no sooner did she slip the barn door open than she saw her light was unnecessary. A lantern already hung in the far corner above the space where they kept blankets and tack.

A deep, rumbling voice came through the quiet. "There's a good girl, Fable. You're doing well. Not much longer."

Evan. They hadn't spoken to one another since Sunday.

The whine of a dog followed his words. Dannie picked up her pace, skirts dancing around her ankles. Gus sat under a wagon, his eyes watchful, and his presence steady and patient. It was almost as if he knew his mate brought his posterity into the world. But dogs couldn't know or care about such things, could they?

She rounded the last stall, and the sight that met her eyes squeezed at her heart. Fable had made a bed out of straw and horse blankets, and she already had two little balls of fur tucked against her side while she licked a third puppy clean. And stretched out near her, propped up on his elbows and facing the dog, was the Englishman.

From where she stood, she saw his profile clearly. His dark hair in disarray, and his beard a little thicker than before, he still looked utterly charming. His eyes were soft, though his eyebrows knit tightly together as he concentrated on the dog's strained movements.

There must be another pup still to come, given the way the muscles in Fable's legs and rump still strained.

Fable finished cleaning the gray puppy and pushed him with her nose to where his siblings nursed and whined. This wasn't her first litter. She knew not to panic.

Dannie barely raised her voice above a whisper when she spoke. "I didn't know they taught English lords dog midwifery."

The green of his eyes flashed toward her, and one corner of his mouth slid upward. He matched her tone, speaking slowly. "My education was quite thorough. I learned Latin, Greek, and dog nursing." Then he winked at her. "I think we have at least one left."

Fable strained again, lifting her head before nosing at her hindquarters. Evan touched the dog's head gently while his other hand helped guide the puppy out into the light. This one was black everywhere except its little snout. He gave the puppy to Fable for her examination and attention, then moved backward until he pushed himself up to his knees.

Dannie came forward and knelt beside him, handing him one of the clean towels. He smiled his thanks as he started to wipe down his hands. "She's an old hand at this, isn't she?"

"This is her fourth litter. Dad wants to retire her." Dannie hugged the remaining towels to herself, admiring Fable's efforts to clean up her youngest pup. "Her first litter, the poor thing seemed to think the world was ending. We had to trap her in a stall and whisk the puppies out of the way until she'd had all six. Then she settled down and fed them and licked them all over like she couldn't ever get enough of kissing her babies."

They sat in silence for a long moment, staring down at the mother and her offspring. Fable finished cleaning her little black pup and tucked it up close to her. Then she met their gazes and her mouth gaped open in a yawn before she offered them what could only be a satisfied grin, her tongue lolling out on one side of her mouth.

Evan chuckled and Dannie laughed, then leaned her head against Evan's shoulder. The sheer peacefulness, the wonder of new life in even this small and familiar form, overwhelmed her with gratitude and hope.

He went still beside her, and as stiff as a fence post.

Shifting quickly away, Dannie went to Fable with her towel.

Resting against him had felt natural in that moment. She hadn't thought about her movement, only acted on instinct—sharing that blessed feeling of rightness with the only other human present.

That's what she tried to tell herself, anyway. *I would have leaned on Dad, Abram, on Travis or Clark, the same way.*

Another part of her mind pointed out the fallacy of her thoughts. *But not Frosty, or Ed, and certainly not Buck.*

Shoving those thoughts to the back of her mind where they belonged, Dannie gave her full attention to the task at hand.

Carefully, she checked each puppy to be sure they were all breathing. That they were well formed. She wiped them down with her towel, though Fable had done an excellent job tidying them up. She threw a question over her shoulder, trying to sound as though nothing awkward had happened. As though she hadn't let her guard down at his side. "Could you get our mother some water, Duke?"

A pan of water appeared in his hands, almost by magic. "I filled it when I first saw her in the barn." He put it near Fable's head, necessitating that he lean in close beside Dannie, their shoulders brushing.

When she sat back on her heels again, he was still there. But Dannie felt his stare on her rather than the lovely sight of new life.

"Thank you for helping Fable." Though she tried to sound business like, her words came out breathy and soft. She winced.

"I wanted to come and find you." He leaned a little closer, his elbow brushing her shoulder. "Since I know absolutely nothing about dog midwifery. But I didn't want to leave her alone too long."

Dannie nodded smartly. She could talk about the dog all night long without embarrassment. "You did the right thing. Even though she managed well, it's important someone knows where she is and what she's doing. I'd hate for something to go wrong, or for her to be afraid and on her own."

Soft footfalls made them both turn to see Gus appear in the circle of light, his head lowered and nose testing the air. He didn't get too close, but he advanced farther than Dannie and Evan before lowering himself to the ground. His watchful eyes took in Fable and their pups and he huffed as though pleased.

Evan scratched the male dog behind his ears, and the stubby tail of the cattle dog wagged. "I suppose the family ought to enjoy the moment without interlopers."

"Gus can keep an eye on things from here." Before Dannie could push herself to her feet, Evan rose and held his hand out to help her. She hesitated, staring at his large hand with its new calluses. Then she slid her slender hand into his, and noticed, without wanting to, the strength in his arm, the warmth of his fingers wrapped carefully around hers.

When she came to her feet, standing no more than a hand's breadth away from him, Dannie couldn't bring herself to look up into his eyes.

Something changed between them. Had one frank conversation damaged her ability to behave as a rational creature? No. If she were honest with herself, things had shifted before the ride home on Sunday. Before she had even seen Evan in the deep blue shirt that made him look like he belonged on the open range. She didn't know when the change had started, or even if it had finished yet.

When Dannie was a little girl, she went walking along the edge of a canyon with her father. She thought she stood far enough back from the edge to be safe, but then she had taken a step onto what she believed was solid ground, only to feel it give beneath her. Back then, Dannie had jumped away at nearly the same moment the ground crumbled and fell, sliding down the canyon walls to hit the stream below.

"Dannie." Evan's voice was low and magnetic. It nearly pulled her gaze up to his.

She had that sensation from the canyon again now, in the quiet of the barn, with Evan standing so close she could feel the warmth of his breath stirring her hair. The ground was shifting beneath her, beneath *them*, and if she didn't jump away now, she'd wind up falling. And falling hard. Then she'd be swept away by forces she couldn't control. Getting hurt in the process.

Dannie stepped back as far as she could in one quick movement. Then she smiled up at Evan, forcing cheerfulness into her words.

"I'm glad you were here, Duke. I hope you rest well tonight. Good evening." She had the absurd thought that she ought to curtsy before taking her leave, but instead she just ducked her head and hurried around him, forgetting her lantern and the unused towels.

Forgetting everything in her need to get away from him.

Evan watched Dannie practically run from the barn, and the warmth that had built in his chest as they stood together vanished completely. In its place was a cold, hard slab of rock that made him ache. He rubbed at the spot just below his collarbone. Somehow, the rancher's daughter had wounded him. Left him feeling tired and homesick.

Homesick?

Evan shook his head at the notion and went out to the paddock to find his horse. The big black fellow hadn't seen nearly enough time outside of the homestead. Evan needed to change that. He needed to get away from the house, from the barns and outbuildings, and do something. Something other than drive a mule-pulled buckboard.

He'd thought he and Dannie had come to an understanding of some sort. That they'd agreed to be friends, or that he had at least risen somewhat in her esteem. But she'd avoided him since their Sunday wagon ride.

Frustration welled up in him as he leaned over the fence, watching his horse snuffle and sleep. The creature, full of fire and energy, was nothing more than a dark shadow in the night. Wasting his time instead of fulfilling the promise of adventure that Evan had felt when he'd purchased the gelding.

"What am I even doing here?" Evan whispered into the night.

The temperature fell as the earth beneath him released all the heat it had soaked up during the sunlit hours. Before long, it would be almost cold.

That was the nature of a desert, Evan knew. Some days it felt as though the ranch existed inside an oven, but then night came on as frigid as the icehouse on his father's estate.

Dannie reminded him of the desert. She went from warm and soft, her head upon his shoulder in the barn, to cold and aloof, as though they were nothing to each other.

"Which is true." Evan rubbed at his eyes. "We're not even friends. Not really. When I leave, I doubt she'll ever think of me again."

The truth of that thought increased the ache in his chest.

Which was ridiculousness itself. The acquaintance of one woman ought not have such an effect upon him.

He didn't want to be anything special to Dannie Bolton. In the adventures of his life, she was nothing more than a footnote. A paragraph, perhaps.

When he told the story of his venture into the great American West, he would only speak of her as the rancher's daughter who hadn't wanted him, hadn't trusted him, to work as a hired hand. In his tale, the triumphant moment would come when he proved himself to Mr. Bolton, collected his pay, and went on to another of the famous places he wanted to see before returning home to England.

He would see more before he locked himself into his familial duties.

Like the Grand Canyon, or the Great Salt Lake of Utah. The Rocky Mountains in Colorado. The Gold Fields of California. Perhaps he would travel all the way to the Pacific Coast, then down to Mexico itself.

Once he had the money from his work, and the cattle drive behind him.

He didn't need Dannie's friendship, esteem, or regard.

Even if there had been that moment when her head touched his shoulder and all he'd wanted to do was wrap her in his arms and hold her close. Those were the reactions of a man too long away from the refined ladies of England. He missed feminine companionship. Perhaps the coming dance and social would cure him of that.

A little flirting, a little dancing, and he'd be content once more.

Somewhat convinced, Evan went toward the bunkhouse. The long day had done its job, exhausting him to the point that he could fall into bed and immediately enter a dreamless sleep. The best kind of sleep.

After taking only a few steps into the zaguán's corridor, a cool and steady breeze filling the darkness, he realized someone leaned against the wall opposite the bunk room.

"Duke." The somewhat arrogant tone in the greeting belonged to Buck. No one else Evan had met spoke quite that way to him. "You're out a bit late."

Evan paused in his steps. "I had chores to see to."

"Right. In the barn. With Dannie."

How long had the cowboy stood there in order to see first Dannie and then Evan leave? The man had something of an obsession with Dannie. Evan saw it plainly and saw how the woman worked to avoid being near Buck.

"The dog had her litter. I was keeping an eye on her when Miss Bolton walked in." Evan tried to relax his arms at his sides, though instinct made him ball up his fists as he stared at the dark outline of the other man. "What have you been up to? Besides spying on people, that is."

"Spying?" Buck snorted. "Nah. Just noticing things. You two seem to wind up in the same places pretty often."

"We could say the same of you and me. Meeting here. Like this." Evan shrugged. "It's not as though we have infinite room to avoid one another. People bump into each other."

"Right." Buck's skepticism dripped from the single word rather like poison from a bottle. "You oughta be more careful about that. You never know when you might bump into the wrong person at the wrong moment." The cowboy shoved away from the wall and stalked off, further into the darkness and out the other end of the zaguán.

Evan watched him go and then went to the bunk room, his thoughts heavy. Though Dannie meant nothing to him, Buck had made Evan into an enemy. In England, the worst thing an enemy did was gossip behind his back. In Arizona territory, an enemy might prove far more dangerous.

Frosty sat with his legs propped up on a barrel near the stove, boots off and stockinged ankles crossed. The foreman looked up from his book, then uncrossed his ankles and lowered his feet to the ground with a thump. "You look a mite troubled, Duke."

Ed rolled over in his bunk, the shifting of blankets drawing Evan's gaze. "He'll be troubled plenty if he doesn't turn in. You're riding with me at dawn," he informed Evan. "It's our turn to check the fence line and count our cattle."

Evan perked up somewhat at that. Any chance to work, to really prove himself, could not be wasted. "I'll be at the ready."

Ed nodded and turned back to face the wall, pulling his blankets up over his head. "Good. Go to bed."

Frosty still stared at him, concern in his gaze.

Evan made a show of getting ready to turn in, and eventually the heavy stare of the cowboy fell away. Ignoring the ache in his chest, and the way Buck had disturbed his thoughts, Evan climbed into his cot and gave in to his exhaustion.

CHAPTER TWELVE

Ed didn't say much as they rode out with the rising sun. He only required Evan to carry his pistol and one of the ranch rifles with him. Evan had sheathed the rifle in its place by his right leg, and he wore his revolver on his hip, though he doubted he'd have any use for it.

The novels he read made it seem as though men in the west went about drawing their guns every day, but he'd had no cause to use his nor had he seen any of the other men brandish their weapons.

Despite the lack of trees, the morning was full of birdsong. Small yellow-feathered creatures flitted from one scrubby bush to another, and the grass danced with the sound of insects. Though Arizona lacked the rain to which Evan was accustomed, the desert welled with life and creatures aplenty. Vibrant sunsets, cool starry nights, and the open plains stretching into the distant mountains gave him reason enough to admire the new world he'd found himself a part of, too.

The cowboy finally spoke to Evan when they crested a small hill, a meadow of sparse desert grass between them and a group of cattle beneath a mesquite tree. "Our job today is to check on heads of cattle, count any new calves we see, and note any unusual sign that might mean unwanted company."

"Unwanted company?" Evan's eyes swept the grasses before them. "Of the human or beast variety?"

"Both." Ed nudged his horse forward and Evan followed, keeping watch for holes or snakes that would cause harm to his horse.

Though Ed was a man of few words, he pointed out things about the cattle he noticed, giving Evan a practical education even if not a thorough one. He showed Evan their brand, the maverick cattle that had mingled with their own, and pointed out the ancestry of the herd as mostly Spanish and Texan longhorns.

"They're hearty. Strong. Mean, too, if the wrong predator comes at them sideways. But they don't hold their bulk." Ed shook his head, leaning over the horn of his saddle as he wiped at the sweat on his forehead. "They're rangy, and their meat tastes like it."

The cattle barely paid them any heed as they rode by, except to raise their heads lazily from grazing a moment or two, still chewing. Evan studied their builds with interest. "What other cattle breeds have the ranchers tried in this territory?"

Ed tilted his hat back and took a large bandana from his pocket to wipe at the dust and sweat on his forehead. "Short-horns. And Hereford. Both breeds originally from your part of the world, Duke." Ed chuckled and shook his head. "Must not be that odd a thing, Englishmen and their cattle coming to Arizona territory. Actually, there's this cattle baron over on the border. Cameron. I've heard he's trying new things with his breed."

Evan turned over an idea in his head. His father's holdings did little with cattle, other than the few dairy cows on tenant farms. "The KB Ranch breeds the cattle and sells them direct to the markets in California, correct?"

"Right. We feed them up, then drive them to the railroad twice a year, pay the fee, and the cattle go to California. Mostly." Ed stuffed his bandana back in a vest pocket, then nudged his horse into motion again. Evan followed. "The railroad fee is steep, and the cattle aren't nearly as big as they should be by the time they get to market. Some die in transportation. The railroad doesn't feed them any, of course. So they aren't worth as much when they get there as they were before they left."

Evan nodded his understanding while his eyes swept the dry, dusty landscape before them. Long yellow-green grasses crackled in the breeze, the buzz and call of insects the only other constant sound.

They rode further out, toward the northern end of the property. Evan hadn't enjoyed a ride on his newly purchased gelding since coming to the ranch. He'd been in a wagon behind mules every time someone had need of his set of hands. It felt good to be on a saddle again, despite the unfamiliar curve and shape of his seat. English riding saddles were nothing like the monstrously sized saddle that kept a cowboy comfortable riding across the plains and mountains.

A windmill came into sight ahead of them, near a rise in the land covered with dense bushes and large boulders. Ed jerked his chin ahead at the contraption. "That windmill powers a pump for a cistern up ahead. Keeps it full enough for the cattle. We'll check to make sure it's still in good shape."

The cistern was tall enough to keep cattle from climbing into the water and fouling it, and the windmill powered the water pump to keep the cistern full enough for them to reach the water. It was an impressive piece of ingenuity.

When Ed dismounted, Evan followed suit, and they allowed their horses to drink while Ed checked the equipment. A handful of cattle made their way through the grass toward the watering place, several calves among them making bawling sounds as though they disliked having to follow their mothers.

The normally quiet cowboy started talking as he walked around the windmill's base, shaking at the struts on which it stood. "King hired a geologist some time back, asked him to find where the water came from. Turns out we've got a bit of an underground pond. An aquifer. At the eastern end of King's property, there's a bit of a swampy patch of land where the water is closer to the surface. It's what kept the ranch from folding during the drought."

"That sounds most fortunate for Mr. Bolton." Evan looked up at the spinning metal blades of the windmill and noted a hawk in the sky, circling lazily above them. Likely hoping to find a rabbit or quail for a meal.

Evan's horse snorted nervously, pulling Evan's attention back to the animal. The gelding backed away from the water, the whites of his eyes showing. His nostrils flaring. Ed's horse jerked its head up, too, and swung it to one side, then the other, nose in the air.

The cattle stopped where they were, heads swinging from side to side, though after a moment they kept moving to the water. Whatever had bothered the horses hadn't had the same effect on the cattle.

Ed knelt, muttering to himself as he tugged at a rope that dropped into the covered part of the ground. "This is how we measure the water, to make sure the well hasn't dried out."

The horses' sudden change in demeanor gave Evan pause. He approached his animal, putting a hand to the beast's neck and looking out over the water tank to the long, dry grass between the water and the oncoming cows and calves.

"Has something frightened you?" He kept his voice low, attempting to soothe the animal's agitation. His horse flicked its ears forward and back, as though uncertain. The muscles on its flank bunched up tight beneath his hand. "Ed?"

Evan drew his rifle slowly, though his pulse increased to several times its usual speed. Anything could have alarmed the animals. But given the number of times he'd been warned about everything from cougars to rustlers, he felt better with the weapon in his hands.

Ed was studying a mark on the rope, likely making mental

note of the measurement, when Evan stood beside him with his eyes on the brush.

"We need the rains to come. They're late this year." Ed frowned up at the blue sky. "If the drought pattern keeps repeating, I'm not sure any amount of underground water can keep KB Ranch going."

A twitch in the grass, the sharp call of a bird somewhere on the ground, made the hair on the back of Evan's neck stand up. He tucked the butt of the rifle into his shoulder and waited.

"Something wrong?" Ed asked, slowly rising from his heels and undoing the leather hammer loop of his holster, readying the gun for a quick draw.

"Our animals seem to believe so." Evan waited and watched.

The cattle were only yards away.

Ed took a long look at the same grass where Evan stared. "The wind's coming from that direction. They could've scented a skunk, or an old rabbit carcass. The cows don't seem bothered, and they'd know if there was trouble."

"Perhaps." Evan relaxed his hold on the rifle, though the tension along his spine remained the same. "Is the windmill in acceptable condition?"

"Yep. We can move on." Ed turned and walked back around the tank to their mounts. Evan followed, when a flash of tawny fur leaped snarling from the brush as the cattle passed.

Evan reacted on instinct, tucking his rifle into his shoulder, sighting along the barrel, and squeezing the trigger. The rifle roared, the crack of his shot echoing across grass to the ridge, and the cougar fell. The cattle bawled terribly, twisting around and stampeding away, making more noise than Evan had ever heard a domestic animal make. The horses whinnied behind him, and Ed started swearing.

Evan sighted down the rifle again, watching the now-exposed cougar on the ground. It didn't move, but he waited another beat before beginning his approach.

"I've never been that close to an attacking puma," Ed muttered, his gun in hand as he came around the opposite side of the tank. He spared Evan a quick look. "Or seen a man take one down like that."

When they stood over the dead animal, Evan lowered his weapon and released his breath. His knees momentarily weakened, and he took a single, staggering step backward. The beast was enormous. Beautiful in its fierce size and shape. He'd shot it through the back of its head, and the ribs of the animal stood out enough for him to realize the predator had been desperate for its kill.

"Young male." Ed didn't touch the predator but lowered himself to one knee to study it. "Inexperienced with hunting, maybe. That's why he's all the way down here after our cattle instead of in the hills where there's wild game." He shook his head. "But if he'd gotten that calf, and figured out the easy pickings, we could've lost dozens of animals."

Ed rose and walked back to the horses. "We need to bring this in with us. No use leaving it out here to spook the cattle or pull in other scavengers. The hide isn't in great shape, but it might still fetch you a decent price."

"Fetch a price?" Evan bent to touch the animal's golden flank. "For me?"

"You shot it, didn't you? I don't know too many men who could make such a clean shot. The animal didn't suffer or limp away. Stopped it mid-jump, didn't you?"

Years of practice on his father's property, of fox hunts and setting up targets to hit with rifle and handgun alike, hadn't exactly prepared Evan for the moment. At least, he never dreamed of using his untried skills on an animal of that size. He'd acted on instinct, and the rush of fear and dread still remained a cramp in his gut, though the moment had passed.

Evan shook himself and stepped away as Ed came back with rope to tie the animal's legs together. "We'll finish checking the line. My horse can carry this without balking. Your gelding is a bit too green to carry a kill."

"As you say." Evan helped lift the cougar up, listening as Ed speculated the beast was around a hundred pounds in weight. They secured it to Ed's horse while Evan's gelding danced further away at the sight of the dead animal.

Then Ed resumed the ride as though carrying a cougar home bothered him not one whit. Evan followed, more alert than before, and relieved that the sharpshooters from his youth had inspired his continual target practice.

THE END OF MAY HAD EVERYONE AS ILL-TEMPERED AS HORNETS, like normal. The air was too dry, the plants too brittle and brown, and all of Arizona territory baked in the early summer sun. When Dannie woke that morning to check on Fable and her puppies, with dawn's light turning from a lemonade yellow to a brighter gold, she felt the itch on the back of her neck that meant she'd gone too long without rain, too.

But the rain would come.

After completing her morning chores, Dannie spent time in her father's study, going over the accounts. He wouldn't hear of delaying Travis's enrollment at Baylor University in the fall, which left few enough places to pinch pennies.

Dannie sat at the desk with the sheet of paper she had worked several figures over. "How much did you say we have left in savings?"

Her father was in his favorite reading chair near the window, his eyes following a single tumbleweed as it rolled across their property. His thoughts had seemed far away of late, though when he spoke to her it was with his usual focus. "Enough for a year of school for the boys. Enough to buy a little more stock." He opened a small box on the table beside his chair and took out pipe and tobacco. "Enough to live like this another year. You know that, Dannie-girl."

She rubbed the bridge of her nose before slumping back in

her chair. "Something has to change, Daddy." She rarely called him that anymore. Daddy was something little girls called their fathers, not the term of endearment or respect full grown women used to discuss business. Though she rarely called him that, she seemed to be doing so more frequently as funds ran low and the rains remained unseen.

Her next comment she made with caution. "Mrs. Perkins being gone has helped a bit, paying half her salary to Ruthie for helping. But maybe we oughta find a new housekeeper? Ruthie's getting on and shouldn't have to do more than tend her own family."

His shoulders stiffened. "Mrs. Perkins hasn't given us notice, one way or the other, what she intends to do."

Dannie folded her hands in front of her on the desk. "I know that, and I know that Mrs. Perkins is practically family. She's been with us for years. But if she was coming back, wouldn't she have done so by now?" She waited, watching her father's expression carefully. His eyes had gone dark, his gaze lowering to the pipe in his hands. He turned it about a few times before finally releasing a deep sigh.

He lit his pipe, puffed on it, and opened his mouth to respond at last—

A gunshot cracked through the air like thunder.

Dannie leapt up. "That was close to the house."

Her father rose, only a second slower than she. "Near the barn?"

Another shot had them both running out the front door and around the fenced in corral to the barn. Neither had grabbed a hat, though both had taken rifles from the case in the study.

Dannie barely remembered the last time there'd been an Indian attack. Rustlers were a more common foe now and rarely did that class of criminal come near a homestead as large as theirs.

She slipped along the side of the corral and came around to the barn, where Dannie saw the cowhands standing in a row, facing northward. Abram, Lee, and her brothers were there as well. All of them stood casually except for broad-shouldered Buck. His stance was that of a man taking aim and squeezing off a few rounds.

"Those boys." Her dad sounded both relieved and disapproving as he marched past her, his rifle still clutched in one hand. Dannie sighed and followed, her heart slowly falling from where it had risen into her throat. Bullets might be cheap, but the sound of them going off was as exciting as fireworks. So long as one knew the fireworks weren't going to explode directly overhead.

Abram leaned against the barn wall with one shoulder, Lee standing close to his grandfather. As Dannie and her father approached, she could hear her father's business partner chuckling.

"I thought you said you never missed, Buck?"

Buck swore more viciously than the situation merited.

"Buck," Frosty snapped. "King doesn't tolerate that language on his land."

They were close enough now that when Buck swung around to snap at Frosty, Dannie easily saw how red-faced he was. He caught sight of her and her father, though, and the red vanished. He straightened his posture.

"Mr. Bolton. Dannie."

The other men turned, Ed, Frosty, Travis, Clark, Abram, and Evan.

Duke.

She had to think of him the same way she did the other cowboys. They called him Duke. That was his name, so far as she or anyone else in the Territory was concerned.

Dannie's gaze lingered on his carefully composed expression, but she pulled them away to meet Frosty's gaze as he explained the situation.

"Duke here got off a good shot today. Buck thought he'd prove Duke owed the shot to luck."

Her eyebrows raised, and she looked past the men to a long table—an old one, scarred by tools and time—someone had drug out about fifty yards away. The men had put glass bottles and metal cans on the table. Someone had even included a rusty tin pail.

Her dad sounded more amused than gruff when he spoke. "Next time we're having a shooting match, make sure the house is warned." Then he chuckled. "We thought there'd been a good old-fashioned raiding party."

Abram looked down at Lee. "I thought I told you to warn the folks."

Lee's grin turned sheepish. "I told Granny. I guess I thought she'd tell the others. Sorry, Mr. Bolton."

"No harm done." Her father joined the line of men with a good-humored grin on his face. "Ruthie is the only one who'd rain trouble on us if we were shooting without her knowing why." The rest of the men chuckled while her father came to stand next to Evan. Duke. The Englishman.

Drat.

Dannie wrinkled her nose, disgusted with herself. She hefted her rifle over her shoulder and joined the line between Travis and Clark.

"Tell me about your 'lucky shot,' Duke, if you will." Her dad was always happy to take part in a friendly competition.

Duke shifted his weight but looked to Ed to answer. To Dannie's surprise, the mostly quiet cowboy took up the explanation with a wide grin. "It happened earlier today, out on the range. Duke brought down a cougar. Maybe twenty yards from where we stood."

Her stomach dropped at the same moment her father whistled in appreciation. He spoke with genuine admiration. "That's a shot, all right. Was the mountain lion after you or the stock? Rabid?"

"Hungry," Evan—Duke—answered quietly. "He was going after a calf. We just happened to be in the right place to stop it."

"I didn't have time to draw on him," Ed said, already shaking his head. "Duke reacted faster than most anyone could."

"That sounds like practice. Not luck." Her father turned to look at Buck. "So? What've you been doing? Proving our Duke is lucky or that you need to spend more time shooting at jackrabbits?"

Buck went red again, but he didn't answer. Her dad didn't wait for him to, either. Instead, he pointed to the row of targets. "Hit one of those cans for me, Duke."

"Yes, sir." Duke didn't sound pleased about it. Maybe it had been a lucky shot that took down the cougar. He put the butt of his rifle in the cradle of his shoulder. "Third from the right." He squeezed the trigger not a second after speaking, and the can went flying off the table.

Dannie's eyebrows raised at the same moment Travis and Clark whistled, slightly higher-pitched variations on her father's favorite note of surprise. She was tempted to whistle, too. If ladies did such a thing. Which they didn't.

"Who else can make that shot?" King tilted his head to one side and regarded his sons. "Boys?"

Travis and Clark stepped forward, took aim, and after the echo died away from their dual shots, a bottle and another can had disappeared from the table.

"Lee?" Her dad winked at him. "Better go get your gun. I'd loan you mine, but it's likely to blow you backward."

Lee cracked a grin. "Sure. I'll grab more cans, too." He took off running for his family's house.

"Abram?" Her father handed Abram his weapon. "Let's see the range of talent we've got on my ranch."

Dannie barely refrained from snorting. Men and their arrogant, prideful ways. "I'll go get more rounds," she said.

By the time she returned to the impromptu competition, the table had been moved back a few more yards and everyone was waiting. She passed out ammunition, then stood back with her arms crossed as one after another of the men took shots. They were given two opportunities at each distance to hit a target, then the table of targets was moved back again.

Given the way her dad kept smiling in her direction, Dannie remained silent and bided her time. Of those present, Ed, Buck, and Evan had never seen her shoot before.

One by one, the men dropped out. Lee, though no longer in the competition himself, was grinning with pride that his grandfather put a hole through every target he aimed at. Evan and Travis stayed in. Dannie's Dad and Frosty. Then it was only Abram, Evan, and Travis.

Abram missed his first shot, the targets far enough out that he put on his glasses before attempting the second. He made that one.

Then with a clang of metal, Evan knocked a can off, too.

Travis aimed. Lowered his rifle. Aimed again. Sighed. "Reckon I've got a bit of dust in my eye. Dannie, could you hold this for me a second?"

She bit the insides of her cheeks to keep from laughing, accepting the rifle while Travis made a show of wiping at his eyes with a handkerchief. He hemmed and hawed dramatically a moment, then shook his head. "It's no use. You'd better take the shot for me, Dannie."

"Sure thing, Travis."

She registered a laugh—Buck's—behind her as she took aim.

She'd not warmed up like the rest of them. The shot would be partly skill, partly luck. One gentle exhale, her mind clear and eyes focused, and then a squeeze of the trigger—

BANG. The bullet knocked through the can with a satisfying clang. Her shoulder absorbed the recoil of the gun the way it was supposed to, keeping her from falling backward like a fool. Travis favored a Sharps rifle, which suited her fine, it seemed. She lowered her weapon, pretended to consider the targets, then handed the weapon safely back to her brother. "Hope that suits you, Travis."

"Yep." He grinned at her, obviously pleased with his part in their little drama.

The other men clapped, including Evan.

Duke, she reminded herself. *Or Mr. Rounsevell.* But when she met his gaze, the warmth in his eyes went straight to her heart, curling around her like a cat. It was genuine admiration. Not shock. Not even surprise. His was a gentle, kind regard.

"Duke's turn," her father said.

The Englishman stepped forward as she stepped back, and he spoke in a low voice as they passed. "Fine shooting, Miss Bolton."

Why the simple compliment made her cheeks heat up like a firecracker, she didn't know. But it did. And she didn't bother hiding her smile as she took her place between her brothers again.

"Fancy shooting for a lady," Buck said behind her.

Clark snorted. "For anybody."

Dannie exchanged a grin with her brother. Women in the Territory needed to shoot just as well as the men. Her mother had taught Dannie the importance of that when she'd shot a coyote invading their henhouse when Dannie was a little girl. She'd heard stories all her life of women hunting when the menfolk were away or defending their homes from invaders who thought a cattle drive the perfect distraction to make homesteads easy pickings.

Most of her friends could shoot well enough. But King Bolton hadn't been happy until his children shot with the same accuracy he did. Abram had been a fine teacher, even if none of them had ever quite matched his skill.

Evan made the last shot of the day, but no one moved the table back to decide between the three with the best aim. It was getting late. And they had a dance to go to.

CHAPTER THIRTEEN

T he water in the hip bath cooled quickly, before Dannie had even finished scrubbing the day's dust off the back of her neck. There wasn't much call to primp on the ranch, and she worked as hard as any of the cowhands, but that didn't mean she rushed the process of getting ready. Not in the privacy of her room.

She didn't have any rosewater or expensive perfume, but she had soap that smelled of orange blossoms and ginger.

She dressed in a clean chemise and petticoats and took her favorite dress from her closet. The sky-blue gown would have appeared rather plain back East, without all the frills and expensive fabrics one could find in a large city. Dannie and Mrs. Perkins had worked for weeks on the gown during the cold winter months, before the housekeeper left to visit her sister. The project brought them both a measure of hope for the year ahead of them, or so Dannie had thought.

Donning the dress without Mrs. Perkins present made her miss the woman who'd cared for the house and the family for a decade of Dannie's life.

A row of little mother-of-pearl buttons on the bodice brought shine to the tailored gown, the sleeves had enough shape to appear elegant, and the lace and ribbon Mrs. Perkins had added to the elbow-length sleeves made Dannie's heart flutter with feminine pride every time she wore it. Which hadn't been often enough.

The dress felt light and soft, perfect for an evening of dancing. Before the mirror above her little dressing table, she twirled once and then smoothed the fabric at her hips.

She sat down at her small vanity and took down her hair. She brushed through it, again and again, until satisfied with its smoothness. The girls at her school in Boston had spent hours brushing their hair, only to apply crimping and curling tongs after, singeing the strands until they looked like dried up straw.

Dannie had other plans.

Gathering her hair just above her ears to the crown into a tail, she braided it long and straight down her back. The braid she twisted up into a bun, turning her head one way and then the other to be certain it looked right, jabbing pins as cleverly as she could to hide them. The hair still loose, falling halfway down her back, she divided into two thin braids. One at a time she wrapped them around the larger bun, loosening the strands along the outside after she secured the braids themselves. The effect would be elegant but practical in keeping her hair away from her face while she danced.

Not that she planned to dance.

Much.

Dannie glared at her reflection. "Don't be silly about this," she admonished herself. "You've been to dozens of these dances. There's nothing special about them."

She leaned away from the mirror, carefully tugging a strand of hair loose so it would drape down her cheek and curl toward her ear. Then she huffed. "Nothing special."

What did it matter that Evan would be there? Buck would, too. And the Mason boys. Truthfully, there were more reasons to keep away from the community gathering than there were to attend. The moment she arrived, she would find her friends.

They would stand in a row beneath the paper lanterns and talk when the musicians weren't playing. The rest of the time, the other girls would dance. And she would watch, remembering when she used to enjoy dancing with a handsome gentleman from the East. Before he'd left her for better pickings.

A knock on the door brought her out of her dismal thoughts.

"Dannie? I need your help with the pies." Ruthie rapped on the door one more time.

"Yes, ma'am. I'm coming." Dannie pushed away from her table, gathering her slippers in her hands. They weren't like dancing slippers from the east. Really, they were more akin to boots, but they were the sort of shoes a woman wore in the west.

The first time she had danced with David, her shoes were satin, with clever little heels and a bow above the toes. Her pink satin gown and hair loose down her back had marked her as young, innocent, and entirely too trusting. Too willing to let him follow her home and pretend to care about her family, her ranch, when he had only wanted her father's money.

Thank goodness her father had thought her too young to marry, and insisted David learn the family business. Nearly two years had gone by before they could even announce an official betrothal with her father's blessing.

Then, David left. With no more than a letter to explain he had a girl in Oklahoma, and he didn't think himself cut out for the ranching life.

Coming down the steps, Dannie heard Ruthie chatting with someone in the kitchen. Hesitating on the stair, she thought at first Ruthie spoke to her grandson, but after a moment Dannie realized someone else was on the other end of her lecture.

"I expect you to behave yourself, young man. Be polite to every girl you dance with, and don't go giving any of them false hope of roping you in. Oh, a little flirting is healthy, but Territory girls always have marrying on their minds. If you haven't fixed yourself to stay put, you shouldn't let anyone fix their hearts on yours."

Evan's rich voice answered the former slave woman, speaking as respectfully to her as if he spoke to a lady of rank. "Of course, madam. I would never wish to give the wrong impression to a young lady. I thank you for the advice."

Dannie looked down at her stocking feet, then sat on the steps to put her shoes on. The idea of walking around barefoot near Evan—Duke—felt entirely too informal.

"What are the women like where you're from?" Ruthie asked, her light step crossing the kitchen floor.

"Elegant. Sophisticated." The Englishman sighed, and the table bench creaked. What was he doing, sitting in the kitchen while Ruthie worked? While the other men doubtlessly prepared themselves, the horses, and wagon for the trip into Sonoita? "Stiff. Formal. Lacking a sense of humor, and often a sense of purpose outside of ensnaring a husband for their very own."

Dannie tied up her shoes as he spoke, listening to the carelessness of his tone.

Ruthie chuckled. "Not all of them are like that, I hope. If they are, you oughta find yourself a wife before you go back."

Taking care to make a racket on the stairs, Dannie came the rest of the way down and entered the kitchen. She kept her eyes on Ruthie when she walked inside. "It smells wonderful in here, Ruthie. I hope you made enough to keep a pie back. There won't be anything left over from the dance."

"You're sweet, Dannie." Ruthie's warm smile appeared as she looked Dannie up and down. "And a pretty sight, too. Look at you. That a new style for your hair?"

"Yes. Do you like it?" Dannie finally turned, allowing Ruthie to inspect her hair, and her gaze collided with Evan's stare.

His deep green eyes darkened still more, reminding her of shadows in a forest. He rose from the table, leaving behind jars of lemonade he'd been securing with lids. He'd shaved for the first time since they'd first met, revealing again the high cheekbones, the cleft in his chin, and the angles of his strong jawline that had made her think him handsome in the first place.

"Miss Bolton." He bowed to her. "You look—" He hesitated, and for one awful moment Dannie wondered if there was nothing about her appearance he could find to compliment. "—Excessively pretty."

Ruthie clicked her tongue against the roof of her mouth, and Evan's cheeks went red beneath the tan he'd earned working in the sun.

"Pretty is as pretty does, Duke." Ruthie pointed to a tall wooden box on the table. "Put the pies in the crate, Dannie."

"Yes, ma'am." Dannie went to the table, standing on the opposite side from Evan. She kept her gaze down, sliding the pies into the clever box Abram had made his wife. He'd used a crate with multiple slats as his inspiration for a box full of shelves, each just wide and tall enough for a single pie to rest safely within. Then another pie above that one, and another. Once all five pies were in, she slid the box closed with a smooth piece of wood.

Evan's quiet voice brought her gaze up at last. "Dannie?"

"Duke." She raised her eyebrows at him.

He winced. "Can't you call me Evan?"

Though she had certainly been calling him that in her mind, she stuck her chin out stubbornly. "Why?"

The left corner of his mouth turned upward. "Because you and I are friends." The twinkle in his eyes bespoke admiration more than friendship. Or was that just her wishful thinking? "Are we not?"

"Perhaps." Dannie pointed to another box with multiple compartments for the glass bottles of lemonade. "Do you need help with that?" She came around the table and started filling the crate, and he did the same.

"Have you changed your mind about the dance?" he asked, voice low.

Dannie hesitated, hand on the last jar. "Changed my mind?"

"You didn't seem enthusiastic about dancing this evening. I thought, if you changed your mind, I might secure your hand for at least one turn about the dance floor."

Her stomach leapt like a jackrabbit, and heat warmed her cheeks. "I suppose I could stand to partner with you at least once."

His fingers brushed hers as he took the lemonade jar gently from her grasp. "Your generosity does me great honor, Dannie." She couldn't rightly tell if he was teasing or not.

Then he put the last jar in the crate before lifting the whole of it; hefting the weight caused his shoulders and arms to tense beneath his clean white shirt. "I'll take this out to the wagon now, Ruthie."

He strode out the door, pushing it open with his shoulder.

Dannie met Ruthie's suspicious gaze. "Why are you looking at me like that?"

Ruthie shrugged. "Just thinking."

"About what?"

"Mostly I'm wondering how much longer you'll hold on to the memory of that rat when you've got a man handsome as a fox making eyes at you." Ruthie laughed when Dannie gasped and protested, then she waved Dannie away. "I won't argue with you. I've got eyes, and I've known you since you were a little girl. Let's get the wagon loaded. The day isn't getting any longer."

Cheeks burning, Dannie gathered up a basket full of food and hurried out the door.

David had been a rat.

Evan as a fox, handsome and mannerly as he was, was still not someone she should trust. Though she found herself very much wanting to do so.

EXCESSIVELY PRETTY. IF HE COULD FIGURE OUT A WAY TO STRANGLE himself with the tie around his throat, he would. The lukewarm compliment he paid to Dannie didn't at all capture his thoughts upon seeing her enter the kitchen. Evan wore the fine clothing he had first purchased upon his arrival in Texas before taking the train to Arizona. He had only traded out the cravat-like tie for a thinner, ribbon-kind of tie Frosty had loaned him.

On his gelding, riding behind the wagon with the other men, he kept his eyes on Dannie's figure. She had a loose cotton bonnet over her hair, likely to protect it from the dust, and she maintained her near perfect posture despite the sway of the wagon.

The woman's appearance always distracted him. Split skirts and a braid, Sunday calico, and now the enchanting blue gown proved she could wear a gunny sack and still look like an angel. A strong-willed angel, with divine fire in her eyes and a biting tongue.

What else could he have said, though? She wouldn't take compliments from him kindly. If he said an admiring word, she'd find a reason to suspect him of idle flattery.

Asking to dance with her had nearly resulted in a set-down for him. Something he'd never experienced in his life. But there had been enough playfulness in her answer that he suspected her defenses were breaking at last. Not that he had been working to such an end. Not really.

It would be futile to form a connection with a woman as captivating as Dannie Bolton, knowing that he would leave her behind, eventually. Likely at the end of that cattle drive that had seemed so important a mere four weeks before.

More people and wagons appeared on the road ahead and behind them. They all kept a distance apart, so the dust wouldn't fly up in their neighbors' faces. Everyone called out to one another cheerfully, heading south to Sonoita as the sun sank lower in the west.

"You know every girl attending expects you to dance all night, don't you, Duke?" Travis asked, bringing Evan out of his thoughts. The boy's grin stretched across his youthful face.

Evan feigned nonchalance, keeping his gaze steady on the horizon. "Even your Miss Harper?"

On the other side of Evan, Clark snickered. That brought on a verbal battle between brothers that allowed Evan to slip back into his thoughts until they arrived at the church - the only white-washed building in Sonoita, and one of the few made of wooden planks rather than adobe bricks.

The doors to the church were closed, but the expanse of hard-packed earth next to the building blazed with light from strings of paper lanterns. The sky had turned purple and orange; the sun slowly sank behind the mountains. Trestle tables lined one side of the clearing, covered in tablecloths of various fabrics and patterns, and weighed down by pots, pans, bowls, and pitchers of drinks.

After leaving their horses at a corral across the thin dirt road, the men from the KB Ranch unloaded Ruthie's contributions to the evening. Evan lost sight of Dannie nearly the moment she slipped off the wagon, disappearing into a crowd of her neighbors.

The music had yet to begin, though Evan heard the quiet slide of a bow across strings as a musician tuned an instrument.

King Bolton put a hand on Duke's shoulder. "You've met some of our neighbors. Let me introduce you to the rest. This way." He gestured to a knot of men standing near the wall of the church, several of them with instruments in hand.

Casting one last glance in the direction Dannie had gone, Evan nodded. "Of course, sir. I look forward to meeting your friends."

The old rancher chuckled, and a gleam appeared in his eye. "And their wives and daughters. I predict you'll be a busy fellow this evening."

Evan didn't allow the sigh building up in his lungs to escape him. Everyone accepted that his accent and bachelor status would make him a sought after partner. The forgone conclusion didn't chafe as it would have in England, when he appeared at Society events. He'd wanted to be around female company again, hadn't he?

How else would he distract himself from the increasing

attraction he felt toward Dannie Bolton? A bothersome thing, considering she'd barely agreed to treating him friendly, instead of like an invading pest. He had to adjust his smile from amused to polite as he shook hands with the men Mr. Bolton introduced.

Shaking hands had become one of his favorite American traditions. In England, he bowed more often than he clasped hands with another man. He didn't make deals that required the seal of a handshake. Here, a handshake indicated the character of the man behind it. Hard worker or lazy, calloused hand or smooth, firm or lackluster.

Mr. Mason, one of the few men standing who Evan already knew, came forward with his hand extended and a large grin on his face. "Ah, Duke. Men, you'd best keep an eye on your pretty daughters this evening. My Felicity's been talking about nothing but Duke's accent and charm all week long."

Some laughter followed the statement. Evan drew upon years of social training with ease, keeping his smile polite. "On my honor, gentlemen, you have nothing to fear from me. The women of this territory are impressive in many ways, and I would stand between them and a whisper of harm."

Another man took a pipe out of his mouth, gesturing to Evan with the stem. "Handsome words from a handsome fella. You mind yourself they're the truth and you'll have no trouble from us."

"The other young bucks might not agree," someone else in the circle said.

Mr. Bolton stood at his ease, hands in his pockets. "A little friendly competition never hurt anyone. Besides, Duke here isn't a permanent threat to their dancing days. He's only staying on through the fall roundup. Then he's off to see more of our great country. Isn't that right, Duke?"

Evan had never kept his intentions a secret, not even from his employer. With all the men looking at him, waiting, he nodded his agreement to the statement. "Indeed. I have more I wish to experience before I return to England and my family responsibilities."

"Family? You got a girl back in England?" Mr. Mason asked, crossing his arms and grinning widely.

"What else would draw a man back?" someone else said, elbowing his neighbors. "Having a bit of fun before settling down?"

Shifting a little uncomfortably at the lightness in the statement, Evan shrugged with his answer. "Something like that. Though there isn't a lady at home."

"Oh? Ailing parents, then? Taking on the family business, maybe?" the man with the pipe asked.

Evan shook his head. "My father is a titled lord. I have an elder brother who will inherit the title and all the responsibilities that go along with it."

A few blank stares met that statement. An older gentleman, the only one with white hair and a scraggly beard to match, started shaking his head. When he spoke, his accent, though soft from years away from home, was working-class English. "Son, you listen to me. Family is all well and good, but a man has to eventually strike out on his own. Stand on his own two feet."

Evan hadn't heard a familiar accent in long enough that he immediately trained all his attention on the man, though he stood back a bit from the group and was diminutive in size. "Sir, I do not believe I caught your name. You sound as though you come from the same shores as I do."

"Folk around here call me Sparks." He grinned, showing a few gaps between his teeth. "I came for the mining and stayed for the fresh air."

"He was a blast specialist for the Tough Nut mine in Tombstone," Mr. Bolton explained, stepping back to allow the slight-sized man to come in closer to the group.

The man shook Evan's hand, his eyes narrowed. "You're quality folk, aren't you? One of the nobs."

"My father is a marquess," Evan said with a shallow nod.

"And you're a second son." The man nodded, understanding maybe better than most where that placed Evan in society back home. "I can't say that I wouldn't go back, if I was you. It's a good life for your kind, even if you're not at the top of the pecking order. But I can say, knowing what I do about the Territory, that it's a good thing to build a life with your own two hands, instead of having an old life handed down. The coat might be cut of fine cloth, but if it's ill-fitting, it's still uncomfortable."

Evan stared at the man for a long moment, the strange advice turning over in his mind. "And you'd trade it for something homespun?"

"And made to fit." The old codger grinned again, then snapped his suspenders with one hand. "If you men'll excuse me, I see my missus looking thirsty. I'd best fetch her a lemonade."

They parted for him, conversations starting up again, while Evan watched the old man make his way to the refreshments.

"Sparks doesn't talk about England much. He came over as a boy." Mr. Bolton shifted, watching the old man along with Evan. "He said most of what he remembers is the mines. He worked them with his father, until his father died. Then Sparks hid himself on a ship bound for our fair shores."

"He was young when he made his way in the world," Evan murmured.

"Young, brave, probably foolhardy. But then, that's how a man has to be to carve out a piece of land or a business of his very own." Mr. Bolton turned to the group of men and raised his voice. "Are we going to jaw away the evening, or are you fiddlers fixing to play us some music?"

The musicians laughed and moved away from the group, carrying fiddles and guitars, someone put a harmonica to his lips and blew a scale, and people all around the lit churchyard started clapping and whistling.

Mr. Bolton clapped him on the shoulder. "Now, Duke, you'd best get started on learning how Americans dance."

Evan forced a smile, and the next instant Miss Felicity Mason was at his side, hooking her arm through his. "Duke, you ready?"

He turned his smile her direction. "As ready as I can be, Miss Mason." She practically dragged him to where men and women were lining up, and Evan sent a quick prayer to heaven that he'd not make a fool of his partner, or himself.

CHAPTER FOURTEEN

When Dannie's closest friend saw the musicians finally coming to order, she had squealed in delight and disappeared without a word from the small circle of unattached women. There were only a dozen of them at the dance, unmarried but eligible, between the ages of seventeen and twenty-three. Several of their friendships had been born of necessity rather than true amicable feelings.

When the group began to partner off, Julie Dashwood, the eldest of the group, sidled closer to Dannie. They were the only two who weren't spoken for with the first dance, and the eldest two. Julie had lost her fiancé to an accident two years before. A stampede. She hadn't allowed another man close to her until recently.

"Felicity's dancing with your new English hand?" She put her hands on her waist as she watched. "He's a fine looker."

Dannie's lips twitched upward. The women hadn't wanted to talk about anything else. Thankfully, Felicity and Jessica Harper had been willing to share everything they knew about him from their brief time with him on Sunday. Dannie hadn't needed to say a word.

"He's handsome," Dannie agreed, turning to watch as Evan

went down the line of couples with a smile as stiff as a starched shirt on his face. "And fairly charming."

"Why haven't you staked a claim, then?" Julie didn't sound anything other than curious. "Is he all hat and no cattle?"

Dannie snorted. "He's clever enough. And he doesn't swagger like the Mason boys." She wrinkled her nose as her eyes landed on those two men. One danced with his step-mother, which was almost admirable. The other danced with one of their set. "But he's not staying."

"Oh." Julie understood better than anyone that a brief flirtation wasn't reason enough to get involved with a man. She turned back to the table, adjusting a pie server, then spreading out the forks a bit more. "Why does it always seem like the best ones are either temporary or uninterested?"

"I don't know." Dannie walked around the table, pulling the checkered cloth on top a little straighter. "But I'm not worried about it at present."

"You're young." Julie shrugged. "You've got time."

"You're not exactly ancient." Dannie squared a pan of cornbread with another by its side.

"Oh, I know." Julie's eyes came up, a faint sparkle in them. "I haven't put myself on the shelf yet. And I know you've been in love, which is a sight more than most of those girls could say." She pointed over her shoulder with a toss of her head. "I think I'm finally ready to take a chance at it again."

Dannie's hands fell to her side. "Really? But—you loved Pete." Everyone had liked her fiancé. The whole community had mourned him. He'd been a hand at another ranch, with enough money put aside to start his own spread. Especially with so many selling out cheap.

"I did, and it's hard to imagine loving someone else like that again. But he'd want me to be happy." Julie looked up, meeting Dannie's gaze with a sincere expression on her face. "Of the two of us, I feel like I'm the lucky one. Pete didn't leave me." The words were like a slap in the face, but before Dannie could fully register the hurt, Julie continued. "What happened to you was horrible, Dannie. Everyone knows it."

Dannie swallowed. "Is that what people say about it?"

"Not mean-like." Julie made a placating gesture with her hands. "And none of us think the less of you. You were tricked, plain and simple."

Which made Dannie sound like a fool. She swallowed back an angry word and moved down the table, pretending to check on the lemonade. Julie followed, determined, it seemed, to say her piece.

"Dannie, hold on a minute. I wasn't trying to poke at you. Just listen to what I have to say." Julie came around the table and put her hand on Dannie's shoulder.

"Seems like you've said what everyone else is saying and thinking." Dannie had to remind herself that Julie was one of her few friends to keep from shrugging her off.

Julie turned Dannie to face her. The girls stood almost eye-to-eye, thanks to both having towering fathers. "Listen. You're one of the best of us. We all know it. Your father owns more land than anyone, and he's always been there for the rest of us. You have, too. You were the first friend who put her arms around me after Pete died." Julie swallowed and looked away, her eyes going to the dancers a moment. "You'd been hurt around the same time, and still you came and held me together. All I want to say is that I think you're special, and you could probably have your pick of the good men in the territory. If you'd let yourself try again."

"I don't know why you have to say that now, or here." Dannie folded her arms over her chest, trying to ignore the tightening in her throat.

"Because we're at a dance." Julie squeezed her shoulder gently. "And everyone knows that you don't dance. All the men here know. So I'm thinking maybe you should. Enjoy yourself, and show them that you might be ready to entertain a few callers." She smiled coaxingly. "Come on, Dannie."

"Times are a bit hard right now." Dannie hated that she

sounded uncertain, though Julie wouldn't know it was about the idea of courtship rather than the same uncertainty everyone else in the Territory faced.

Julie wasn't about to be deterred. "All the better to find someone to share the burden with, don't you think? When I look at my parents, and I see how much help they are to each other, it makes me want that, too."

At that remark, Dannie's eyes found her father. He stood alone, at the edge of the dance floor. Most of his cronies were either playing instruments or dancing with their wives. Her father didn't appear to be watching his sons dancing with girls their age, nor did he seem to hear the music spilling into the night around him. Was he missing her mother? Wishing he had someone to share his burdens with him?

Evan danced with Felicity, and Dannie found herself watching them with a start. She hadn't even been looking for Evan. The music had come to an end, and he smiled down at Felicity politely, nodding when she gestured to another of their friends. He'd found his next dance partner, it seemed.

"Maybe I should dance tonight," Dannie murmured.

Julie put her arm around Dannie, squeezing her in the casual embrace. "That's the spirit. It's time for both of us to reach for a little happiness. Come on. Let's find ourselves partners."

That made Dannie laugh, albeit nervously. "That's why you had to talk to me. You don't want everyone to notice you dancing again."

Her friend's smile went a touch wicked. "The gossips will have to divide their attention between the two of us, that's for certain." They made right for Dannie's father and Ed, who'd come to stand beside his boss for the moment.

"Good evening, Mr. Bolton." Julie smiled widely at Dannie's dad, then turned her smile on to the hand. "Ed. I see you're not dancing yet."

Ed exchanged a nervous look with Dannie, so brief Julie may

have missed it, then smiled at her friend. "Not yet, Miss Julie. I'm making my way around, talking to our neighbors."

Ed didn't dance much. Dannie knew well enough that not everyone would be thrilled to have someone of his complexion dancing with their daughters. Julie obviously didn't mind.

"I like to do my talking while I dance," she stated boldly. "And I intend to do a lot of talking tonight."

Oh. Dannie realized what her friend was up to with a wince. She wanted word to get around that she'd be willing to dance with anyone who asked. It seemed she took no real interest in Ed. He seemed to realize that at the same moment Dannie did, as his shoulders relaxed.

"Is that so? I can think of a few fellows who'd like a chance to have a conversation or two with you."

Julie's smile beamed all the brighter. "Wonderful. You'll let them know, won't you?" Then she gave Dannie a pat on the shoulder. "And maybe mention Dannie, too."

Someone called Julie's name—her mother. Julie excused herself, moving away with a lightness in her step Dannie hadn't seen in years.

"You want me to put the word out you'd like to dance, Dannie?" Ed asked.

Dannie looked from Ed to her father, who'd stood quietly the whole time, eyebrows raised. She swallowed, then shrugged. "I guess."

The music was starting up again. "Hold on, Ed. I think I'll take my daughter on the dance floor first." Her father held his hand out to her. "It's an easy one, for us older folk."

"You're not old, Dad." She took his hand and he led her out to the others. It was a slower song, an easy two-step. "Thank you," she said more quietly.

"Miss Dashwood seemed insistent about this." Her dad raised his eyebrows. "I haven't seen you dance in years. Are you really up to it tonight?" He sounded hopeful.

Dannie shrugged once. "I suppose we'll find out."

The music started and her father led her through the steps easy-like, his expression thoughtful. "You should dance more, Dannie."

"That's what Julie said."

"Not because of what Julie said." Her father huffed. "Because you want to dance. I've seen you, at all these events, watching others have their fun. You oughta have fun, too."

"When's the last time you danced, Dad?"

"Before I got sick. Last December." He smiled a touch. "We danced inside the Hackett's new barn, at Christmas."

"I remember." Dannie let her father lead her, keeping her eyes on him. Decidedly not looking to see who noticed her dancing, and *not* noticing how near Evan and his current partner were to her and her father. "You danced with just about every one of your friend's wives. And Mrs. Perkins."

Her father's hand stiffened a moment, squeezing hers. "That's right. And you sat in a chair all night next to Mrs. Renner."

"Who had her baby the next day and should've been resting." Dannie laughed. "But she was so determined not to miss the evening."

"You were kind to keep her company." Her father spun Dannie so her back was to him, as the dance called for. "I wish you would've danced more. Maybe I should've said something before. You can't let one man steal all the light from your life."

It was Dannie's turn to stiffen. "That's not what I've done, Dad. I'm just putting the most important things, the most important people, first."

"You could do that your whole life." Her father turned her around to face him again, easing his way through the couples surrounding them. "Then wind up all alone. Sometimes, you have to put yourself first." He said it firmly, but his eyes didn't meet hers. It was almost like he was talking to himself or reminding himself of something he'd forgotten. "You can't go around tending to others when your heart isn't whole or spreading joy when you've lost your own happiness."

Dannie peered up at him, confused by the serious turn in conversation. "Dad?"

He looked down at her again, and his eyes brightened. "You have to take hold of your own happiness, Dannie. Promise me that you'll try, and I'll do the same."

As confused as she was by his statement, she'd always done what her father asked of her. This was no different. "I promise, Daddy."

"Good girl." He turned her about one last time as the song ended, and Dannie found herself face-to-face with Evan, who'd just released the hand of his last partner.

Her father stepped forward, his usual cheerful expression in place once more. "Duke, it appears you've got the knack of our way of dancing."

Evan's gaze flicked from Dannie's up to her father's. "I hope so, sir. I should hate to disappoint my partners with less than satisfactory grace."

Her dad laughed and gave Evan an approving nod. "Good. How many of your waltzes are spoken for? Or your reels?"

Again, Evan's eyes met hers, and this time there was a question in them. "I haven't made any promises to the other young ladies yet."

Dannie's heart skipped. For a moment, she wondered if he meant something more than dancing. But that was ridiculous. She knew he was leaving. Not to mention that they had a tentative truce between them, at best. She'd agreed to be kinder and more friendly, but that didn't mean anything more.

"Really?" Her dad looked down at Dannie with mischief in his smile. "Did you hear that, Dannie? Our guest might need another dance partner."

Her mouth went dry. Subtlety hadn't ever been her father's strong suit. "Dad—" She didn't disguise the warning in her voice.

"Oh, there's George Whittaker. Excuse me. I need to see him about something." Her father walked away without any more warning or excuses, and Dannie watched him go with her lips pressed tightly together.

She looked again at Evan, whose smile was as wide as the Rio Grande. "I thought you didn't dance." He edged closer, those green eyes of his laughing at her.

"I usually don't." She tilted her chin higher, daring him to tease her and see what happened. "A friend of mine persuaded me to make an exception this evening."

"Really?" Evan lifted one hand toward her, his lips parting as he smiled. "Then maybe—"

"Oh, Mr. Duke?" Annie Greene put her hand in the one Evan had almost extended to Dannie. "You must let me show you how we square dance. Didn't you say you'd never square-danced before? Dannie, tell him how fun it is!" Annie batted her big blue eyes at Evan, not even glancing in Dannie's direction.

Evan's smile turned tight-lipped, and his handsome eyes were suddenly wide with alarm. He looked up at Dannie, but she grinned back at him. "You really must let Annie show you how it's done, *Duke*." She waved them away, determined to enjoy his discomfort. Decidedly not thinking about the sudden stab of disappointment in her gut. "Enjoy."

She stepped back, clearing the way for Annie to drag her reluctant Englishman back into the swirl of couples. Dannie pulled in a deep breath and released it, along with the hurt she wouldn't acknowledge for a single minute more.

Instead, she would let it go and get on through the evening.

Dannie went in search of Ruthie, or anyone else, who might let her join their conversation away from the dancing and the temptation to watch Evan learn the sometimes-complicated calls of the square dance.

Perhaps Miss Greene had saved Evan when she inserted herself between him and Dannie Bolton. He'd been about to ask his employer's daughter to dance with him, without knowing which steps the next song would require. Such a thing surely would end in disaster for him, with Dannie laughing at him for his missteps. Miss Greene didn't laugh, though she did frown now and again when he misinterpreted what the "caller" meant by certain instructions.

Dancing with Dannie, even had he known where to put his feet, seemed like a bad idea the more he thought about it. She'd finally warmed up to him, and obviously considered him a friend. But one of the reasons he had looked forward to this evening of simple entertainment was to get her out of his thoughts.

But despite the flirtatious smiles of the women around him, or the kindness of his dance partners, his eyes kept seeking Dannie Bolton out among the crowd.

Perhaps his lack in female companionship and conversation wasn't to blame for his increasing interest in the quick-tongued woman at the KB ranch. But the implications following that thought—he couldn't possibly entertain them. She was too fine a woman for a casual dalliance, even if he behaved as a complete gentleman toward her.

"Mr. Duke?" Miss Greene spoke as though she'd been trying to get his attention for some time. He smiled apologetically at her.

"I beg your pardon, Miss Greene."

She blushed prettily. "Can I introduce you to my sister?"

He didn't let himself think about finding Dannie, about trying to ask her to dance again. "Of course. Please, lead the way."

He spent the next half hour keeping his gaze away from the knot of women near the corner of the church, refusing to watch Dannie as she laughed and spoke with them. Young ladies came and went from that little crowd, several of them to dance with him. But he never met Dannie's eyes. He didn't seek her out.

When he'd managed to finish dancing with one partner without her setting him up with another, Evan withdrew to the table of lemonade and coffee. He took up a glass of yellow-tinted liquid and gulped it as quickly as he could while still retaining his manners, uncertain when he'd have another chance to quench his thirst.

Ed sidled up next to him, picking up his own glass. "Seems we were right, and you're the belle of the ball tonight."

Evan choked on his drink. "I am *what?*"

The cowboy laughed. "No hard feelings, Duke. But you've got to admit, no one else has had nearly as much attention as you this evening."

With a scowl, Evan sipped at his drink, now more than half gone. "I haven't seen you dancing," he accused, between drinks.

Ed winced. "Not too many here who'd say yes if I asked. But that's fine by me. I've got two left feet anyhow." Ed knocked back the rest of his drink. "You oughta ask Dannie. Pretty sure people will notice if you don't."

"She hasn't danced with anyone except her father." The moment the words left his mouth, Evan clamped his jaw shut and widened his eyes in terror.

"Noticed, have you?" Ed chuckled. "Don't worry. Your secret is safe with me. But the word is getting around that she wants to dance. Her friend, Miss Dashwood, is making sure of that."

Evan put his empty cup in a large crate full of other used glasses. A group of youth were washing cups and bringing them back to the party, apparently taking turns attending to the need for clean dishware.

"Good. She'll have plenty of partners without me making a fool of us both. I don't know half the steps." Evan backed away from the table, but Ed followed with his loping steps.

"You really want to take the chance that ignoring her won't be seen as an insult? Here you are, the most sought-after partner of the evening, and you haven't asked Miss Daniella Bolton, daughter of the most successful man here, to dance. That sounds like the way to make a woman into an enemy—and weren't you two finally getting along?" Ed grinned wickedly.

Evan stared at him, shocked the easy-going cowboy had paid

enough attention to notice the tension between Evan and Dannie. "You have given this far too much thought."

Ed shrugged. "I have five sisters at home," he said, as though his words were enough of an explanation. Then he swaggered away, lemonade still in hand, whistling along with the music as he went.

Evan's gaze went immediately to where Dannie stood. He'd been aware of her all evening. Making excuses why he shouldn't seek her out. The night Fable had her pups came to mind, when they'd been together in the quiet, and she'd let her guard down. And laid her head on his shoulder.

A twist in his chest made him take a step in her direction. Then another.

She bent to speak to a child, a little girl half Dannie's size. Dannie listened to the child, nodded, and took the girl's hand. The two of them went toward the back of the church.

Though he told himself seeking Dannie out was a bad idea, Evan followed.

Around the back of the church, lit with a lantern hanging on a hook outside its door, stood an outhouse. Dannie opened the door for the little girl, took the lantern down and put it inside, then allowed the child to go in. Dannie closed the door behind her, then crossed her arms, obviously waiting for the child.

Smiling to himself, Evan leaned against the back of the church wall and waited, too. Dannie saw him and lifted her hand in a wave. When the girl popped out a minute later, lantern in hand, she wore a big grin.

Evan could hear her from where he stood. "Thank you, Miss Dannie. It wasn't as scary with you standing here."

"Run back and tell your mama." Dannie hung the lantern back in its place and watched the girl skip away, then she meandered over to Evan with her hands tucked behind her back. The low light from the lanterns several feet away didn't disguise her amused expression as she raised her eyebrows at him.

"Do you make it a habit to follow ladies to the necessary, sir?"

She batted her eyes at him, affecting a curious expression. "Or are you merely hiding at the back of the church from your many admirers?"

The light made strands of honey-colored curls stand out in her otherwise dark hair, and the way one corner of her mouth pulled to the side as she teased him made his stomach flip. Evan tried to sound confident, tried to tease her right back. "A man needs to take a breath now and then, I suppose. Especially dancing in boots." He pointed down to his leather footwear. "This isn't anything like what I'd wear to a dance in England."

"Did you forget your dancing slippers when you came over on the boat?" Dannie sidled up next to him, leaning her back against the white-washed church wall, too. Their shoulders were only inches apart.

"Among other things," he responded. "I left behind my valet. I think I miss him most of all. Only think how much more the cattle would respect me if I was turned out in style every day, with a shine to my boots and freshly shaven."

She laughed, then covered the sound with a finger on her lips. "I beg your pardon. I forgot we were hiding."

With an easy grin, he turned so his left shoulder was against the wall and he could better look down at her. "So now you're hiding, too?"

Dannie tucked a loose strand of hair behind her ear. "Might as well keep you company as stand around out there." For a moment her gaze drifted away from him, back to the lanterns hanging along the outskirts of the party. "You know, I've never actually asked you much about your home. I've heard enough about the queen." She cut him a narrow-eyed look, and it relieved him her gaze lacked the distrust from their original meeting. "Do you miss it?"

The question took him a moment to answer, as he had to truly consider when the last time he'd thought of his home with any longing had been. "Only when I'm mucking out the stables."

That tilted her lips upward again. "That can't be true. I've heard that England is greener than green, that it rains all the time. Arizona is so different. Here it's dry and brown."

"That's true." Evan considered how to explain himself, his thoughts turning back to England's green shores. "England is beautiful, and I am certain many in my situation would pine away wishing for the damp. But I find I like the clear air here, and how open and beautiful the plains are. In England, even the countryside feels crowded. Tenant houses, farms, row upon row of tiny villages, ruins of castles and abbeys... And the cities are cramped and overcrowded. Out here, there's more room to breathe, and more opportunity to think."

For a long moment, she said nothing, though he waited for her usual quick-tongued response. It didn't come.

"I can understand that feeling, too." Her tone softened, her gaze returned to him. "I went to school in Boston for several years. It was something of an adventure." She lifted one shoulder and dropped it again. "But I have never felt so hemmed in before or since."

"Boston." Evan chuckled. "You went to finishing school, didn't you? That explains a few things." Like the way her tone changed from time to time, to something more elegant and business-like, and how she knew certain things, and called attention to his behavior in an intelligent way. It also explained why she'd never been much impressed by him.

"Finishing school." She snorted, more the rancher's daughter than a socialite. "I can't say that I felt all that finished when I left. There weren't a lot of things I learned that I actually use these days, except maybe for addressing letters to my father's business associates."

He narrowed his eyes at her. "It probably taught you more than you think, but I understand what you mean."

"The other girls at the school weren't all that impressed with what I tried to tell them about ranching." Dannie waved at the darkness around them. "And yet they expected me to be wide-eyed with wonder when they talked about shopping for hats and gloves with their mothers and meeting their fathers' business partners."

"I find people rarely want to look beyond their own experience in the world, for fear they'll find the place they occupy is much smaller than they had thought." Evan put his hands in his pockets, his fingers brushing against the silver dollar. "My family always laughed at the idea of anyone running off to America to seek their fortune. Given my father's place in Society, he and my brother couldn't imagine why anyone would want to step outside that world for another." His heart sank an inch or two with the thought, and he wondered for a moment what they had thought when they found he'd gone with only a letter left behind, saying he was going to America.

He'd thought about sending a letter, or a telegram, to tell them he'd arrived and where he was. But, knowing his father, they'd find a way to send the U.S. Army after him to drag him back to New York and a boat bound for Great Britain.

"I didn't feel that way," Dannie said quietly, her gaze distant. Perhaps her thoughts had turned as far away as his had. "If anything, I saw the value in another way of living. As different as Boston was, as much as I missed home, I'm grateful I experienced what I did. I learned that there's a world beyond my father's ranch, and that it's there if I ever want to step into it. There are other choices that I'd never been aware of before."

"Precisely what I've always thought." Evan studied her profile, the way her nose turned up at the tip, the scattering of freckles barely present in the semi-darkness, and the way she pursed her lips while she thought.

"It makes my choice to stay here feel..." She narrowed her eyes, searching for the right word. "Feel like it means more. I know there are other paths, and I'm sticking with this one. Not out of ignorance. Because it's where my heart belongs."

Then she turned the full force of her deep brown eyes upon him, her expression gentle, her brows drawn down. "Does that make sense, Evan?"

Nothing made more sense in that moment than the two of them standing close, the rest of the world far away and quiet. "I understand it," he responded, barely aware of what he said, lost as he was in her gaze. "I think—"

"Here's Miss Bolton!" The raucous shout made Evan start, but he stepped in front of Dannie rather than away.

One of the men he'd been introduced to earlier, the eldest Mason son up from the Bisbee copper mines, had appeared at the corner of the building with his brother.

Dannie's hand went to Evan's shoulder as she peered around him. "Rodger. Herman." She sighed. "How have you two been?"

They were a matched set. Not as tall as Evan, but wide through the shoulders, with white-blond hair and wide grins. They held themselves with the easy confidence of men reliant upon physical strength.

"Just fine," the elder said, putting his thumbs behind his suspenders. "Herman and me were talking and realized neither of us have had the pleasure of dancing with you tonight, and we hear you're happy to dance."

"Is that right?" Dannie stepped around Evan, and something in his chest tightened. The men weren't a threat, yet he wanted nothing more than to step between Dannie and the brothers. "I'm not sure where you heard that. I danced with my father earlier, but I haven't had another partner tonight."

Herman spoke up, eyeing Evan. "That's a real shame. You'd think there'd be a line clear to Mexico of men wanting to stand up with you, Dannie." He jerked his chin up at Evan. "Like this fellow. Is he bothering you back here?"

"Not at all. We were enjoying a discussion on the topic of our shared travel experiences."

Was it Evan's imagination, or had Dannie lost her usual accent in favor of something more refined?

"You've been to England?" Rodger asked, his eyes widening. "I didn't know that. Thought you just went back east for a bit."

"Indeed. But traveling outside of one's homeland is an experience best shared with others who have done the same." Dannie smiled at Evan, then back at the other men.

Rodger shared a glance with his brother, then pointedly ignored Evan's presence when he snapped his suspenders. "You're gonna dance with us, Dannie."

She put a hand to her chest. "At the same time? Dear me. What would people say."

Herman's forehead wrinkled and he rubbed at the back of his neck. "Well, of course not. We figured we'd take turns."

"Did you?" Dannie sounded completely at ease, and the quick look she darted in Evan's direction made it clear she didn't need his help with the brothers.

"We've danced with nearly all the girls already," Rodger said importantly, puffing out his chest some more. "Even though this here isn't as big a party as we have in Bisbee. There are a lot more girls there, of course."

Evan had to bite his tongue against entering the conversation, if only to find a way to get Dannie out of it. The arrogance with which both men spoke reminded him far too much of English ballrooms.

"Are there?" Dannie tucked her hands behind her demurely. "I wonder then why you came to our little get together."

"Pa asked us to," Herman said. "We have to be back to work on Monday, though. The foreman depends on us." He grinned, showing all his teeth. "You oughta come to one of our dances. We'd show you around."

"Very kind of you to offer, but I doubt I'll find my way to Bisbee anytime soon."

Rodger appeared to finally lose his patience, as he huffed. "Nevermind Bisbee. We're here right now. Come dance with me, Dannie."

"And then me," Herman added as his brother reached for Dannie's arm.

She side-stepped him neatly. "Not tonight, boys. Perhaps you ought to give that honor to another girl."

Evan's shoulders stiffened when both men only stared at her, jaws agape.

"You saying no to us?" Herman asked, astonished.

Rodger glowered at her. "Typical Dannie Bolton, always acting like she's better than everybody."

Evan's hands came out of his pockets, and he folded his arms across his chest. "I don't think that's necessary, gentlemen."

"Nevermind, Duke." Dannie waved his help away, then turned fully to the brothers again. "Considering neither of you asked me politely, but just assumed I'd fall all over myself for the honor, I'd say it's you who think yourself above your company. But as I said, I've only danced with my father tonight, because he's the only *gentleman* who has *asked* me." She shot a pointed look in Evan's direction, though he couldn't be sure what she meant to communicate by it.

Perhaps she was upset he hadn't asked her to dance.

Or she was communicating she didn't intend to dance with him either.

Whatever she meant by the hard stare, he didn't act quickly enough. Dannie turned her polite smile back on the brothers. "If y'all will excuse me, I had better go help with the pies." She swept up her skirts and stepped directly between the brothers, not so much as brushing either one of them with the hem of her gown, and then she was gone.

Herman huffed. "You said she'd say yes."

Rodger cast Evan a dark look. "She never dances at these things. C'mon. Let's go ask the Harper girl again."

Evan had to bite back making a remark on whether they intended to *ask* anyone, or keep demanding partners, but the Mason brothers were none of his concern. Dannie had dealt with the situation more deftly than a debutante at a London ball. Of course, she'd as good as stated she wouldn't be dancing with anyone else that evening.

Which was a shame. Because he'd dearly love to ask her, and he'd wondered what it would feel like to hold her hand in his as he waltzed her around beneath the stars and lantern light. But he'd missed the opportunity, and possibly a thorough set-down, by holding back.

He brushed the silver dollar in his pocket again, the coin reminding him why he'd come to Arizona in the first place. He was looking to prove himself equal to the cowboys, to their style of living. Not to flirt with a woman, no matter how witty or beautiful he thought her.

As he came around the corner of the church, approaching the crowd, he caught sight of the old man. Sparky. He stood next to a woman as white-haired as himself, her arm looped through his. They were smiling at one another as they spoke, their eyes on each other rather than their neighbors. The woman's shawl dipped down from her shoulder, and Sparky was quick to put it back in place, smoothing the material and smiling with his eyes as much as his expression. His wife put her hand to his cheek, the gesture small, but full of years of devotion and affection.

The old man had said he'd prefer homespun made to fit instead of the finest suit of clothes made for another.

Evan's eyes went to Dannie, somehow knowing where she was without needing to search for her. She stood next to Ruthie and another woman, a smile bright upon her face as she laughed with them.

Maybe there was something to this way of life, and to working with his hands and his heart rather than merely accepting what his father handed to him. His dust-covered boots and wide-brimmed hat fit more comfortably than any fine suit of clothes by London's finest tailors. Maybe this way, Dannie's way, deserved a little more thought.

A Miss Lamberth appeared at Evan's side, eyes bright and hopeful. He put his thoughts aside and asked the eager young woman to dance. His musing would keep for another time.

CHAPTER FIFTEEN

Dannie went through the motions of visiting her neighbors on Sunday, this time with her father and brothers. Travis and Clark were full of conversation, which covered Dannie's own silence quite nicely. But she noticed her father said as little as she did. Whatever thoughts he had, they seemed heavy, and she had no wish to burden him with her own.

When Monday morning came, Dannie still hadn't sorted out her feelings the way she wanted. Nothing in her head was as neat and tidy as she liked. She couldn't stop thinking about Evan and the night of the dance.

Why hadn't he asked her, even once, to accompany him on the floor? Hadn't she given him a strong enough hint that she'd welcome the invitation? She lay in her bed, watching the shadows in the early morning light dance across her ceiling. Playing with the end of her braid, she thought over the evening yet again.

What more could she have said or done short of asking him for a dance? That sort of thing was too forward, even for her. And why did it bother her so much that he hadn't attempted to draw her into even a simple reel?

She huffed and rolled over, bunching her pillow up underneath her chin.

He'd been on duty Sunday since he'd had the previous day of rest without work. Evan and Ed had ridden the fences, counted calves, and come back with news that no more of their herd had disappeared. They reported to Frosty, of course, who let her father know. She'd been in the room when Frosty appeared, hat in hand.

Since the dance, today was the first opportunity she'd have to speak to Evan. Travis and Buck were going to cut some cattle out of the herd to take to Benson that week, and Evan was supposed to be taught how to do the same.

There were plenty of beef suppliers to Benson, of course, so they wouldn't get a high price on the animals. But it would be enough to settle the pay for the men for a time, which was what mattered. Frosty and her father had discussed it briefly the previous evening.

Maybe Dannie ought to go watch Evan's lesson. Just to make sure Buck taught him properly, instead of posturing or crowing about his own skills as he was apt to do.

She rose from her bed with that thought, flipping her braid over her shoulder. She could be dressed and out the door in no time. She made her bed up before throwing open her wardrobe and finding clothes that were suitable for the day's work. When she realized how few fresh shirts she had hanging up, she winced.

With Mrs. Perkins gone, Dannie had taken up the responsibility of laundry for her family. It wouldn't be fair to ask Ruthie to do the backbreaking work. And it looked like Dannie needed to apply herself to that chore sooner rather than later.

"Can't wait any longer," she said aloud with a firm nod. She'd wash the clothes later that day.

Once she'd dressed, brushed her hair out and braided it neatly again, she took up her favorite working hat and went out the door. She skipped down the stairs and prepared to swing into the kitchen, but her father's voice stopped her before she cleared the doorway.

"Dannie, you're awake. Perfect." He motioned for her to join him in the parlor. "I need to ask your opinion on a matter."

Though she fairly itched to get out into the sunshine, and to oversee a certain Englishman's lessons, she put on a smile. "Good morning to you too, Dad." She followed him into the parlor. "You're up early."

"I don't sleep much these days." His tired smile made her think his sleeping habits had more to do with worry than anything else. He motioned for her to sit on the couch, and he took his place beside her instead of in his chair. "I need to speak to you about something that's weighed heavily on my mind, and on my heart, for some time."

Restlessness fled beneath her father's soft gaze, her whole mind tuning to his words. Dread circled her stomach with a rope and tightened, the ranch's trouble looming in her thoughts. "What is it, Dad?"

For several seconds, the ticking mantel clock made the only sound in the room, counting each moment her father hesitated to speak.

The knot around her stomach grew even tighter.

At last, he cracked a smile at her. "This isn't a conversation I know how to start, even with all the time I've spent thinking on it. It has to do with Mrs. Perkins."

Dannie released a confused, breathless laugh. "Mrs. Perkins? What about her?"

She knew no letter had come since the last. Mail received at the ranch was never a secret, brought in as it was from the Sonoita store that acted as an unofficial postal drop. Mr. Holloway in Sonoita had contracted as a postal agent through Wells Fargo; given that he traveled to and from Benson with regularity, he was the closest thing they had to a mailman. They hadn't seen Holloway in days.

"Well. I have a decision to make about Loretta." He rubbed at the back of his neck, and Dannie's curiosity grew. Had he finally decided to hire a new housekeeper?

Dannie turned her hat around in her hands, fingers gentle against the brim. "How can I help?"

"She left because I told her I had feelings for her." Her father met Dannie's stare with a rueful smile. "And she said she had feelings for me."

Her jaw dropped like a newborn calf. She knew her eyes had gone wider than the full moon, too, but Dannie couldn't change either of those things in her shock. A sound escaped her throat, but it wasn't one that made any sense to her, let alone her father, who started talking a whole lot quicker.

"You needn't look so flabbergasted, Dannie. I know I'm getting on in years, turning fifty next year. And I've not looked at a woman since your mama passed. You children and the ranch kept me busy. Loretta—Mrs. Perkins was a godsend when we hired her on as a housekeeper. I was only ever thankful she agreed to come work out here in the middle of nowhere. Until the last drought."

Dannie found her voice, enough to squeak out, "That was two years ago."

King Bolton, her father and her hero, turned more than a little red in the face. "I didn't mean for it to happen, Dannie. You were hurting after Robertson slithered off, and the entire family grieving over our losses with the drought, and Loretta was steady as a rock. She kept us all going, with her faith and warmth. I fell more in love with her every day, but I didn't say a word. I wouldn't make her uncomfortable with unwanted attentions."

The idea of her father silently pining after a woman as prim and orderly as their housekeeper made it difficult for Dannie to think through what he said. Her dad. In love with the well-starched, white-aproned, housekeeper? The woman who had washed their laundry, dusted his study, helped Dannie learn to sew, and baked the boys cookies....

The more she thought on it, the more it made sense. Mrs. Perkins had cared for the family for years. They had paid her to do it, of course, but a man might well look at all she'd done and feel affection for her.

Dannie loved Mrs. Perkins, though she rarely thought of her affection for the older woman in those terms. Mrs. Perkins had held Dannie on more than one occasion while she'd cried over David Robertson's faithlessness. She'd also been the one to insist to Dannie's father that Dannie was too young to marry the sidewinder. Maybe she'd even seen David for what he was—someone looking to cash in on a family's success.

Dannie pushed aside the uncomfortable thoughts of her own lovelorn past. "When did you finally speak up?"

"When she started to notice things." Dad shrugged, that tired look coming back into his eyes. "She guessed at what I felt. After I got sick, on one of the worst days, she told me she felt the same. When I got better, I told her I couldn't ask her to hitch her wagon or hopes to me. Not with the ranch in such a state. I wouldn't propose without the ability to provide for her and make certain her future is secure."

Things started to fall into place in Dannie's mind, and the world almost made sense again. "Mrs. Perkins loves you back, but she couldn't stay here without marrying you. Because she's not just a housekeeper anymore." Dannie watched as her father nodded about her assumption. She folded her arms and leaned back against the couch. "So she went to see her sister and clear her head."

"That's about the lay of it." Her father rested his elbows on his knees and slumped forward. "And I've been downright miserable ever since she went away, even though I told her it was probably for the best."

The easy thing to say, to do, would be to tell her father he'd made the right choice. No one ought to risk their future on the ranch outside the family. Except Mrs. Perkins had become family.

In the time she'd been with them, the housekeeper had worked as hard as they all had to make the ranch successful.

And her dad, honorable and good as they came, had put aside his happiness for years to make everyone else comfortable.

"Daddy," Dannie spoke softly, putting her hand on her father's shoulder. "When you and mama got married, you didn't have the ranch. You didn't have much of anything."

Her father lifted his gaze to hers, one of his eyebrows raised. She smirked and mimicked the expression. "That's true," he said. "But we were younger."

"So now you're a lot older and a lot smarter than you were back then. Did Mrs. Perkins say she couldn't marry you unless the ranch was secure?"

After a brief hesitation, her father shook his head. "She said she didn't care what the ranch's future was, as long as she was part of it."

Dannie's reservations fell away. "Then maybe you should stop being miserable and ask her to marry you already." It cost her something to say the words, regardless of how she felt about Mrs. Perkins or her father's happiness. The memory of her mother clung to Dannie in a thousand ways. "Mama would want you to be happy."

"I can't offer any kind of stability," her father reminded her. "Not yet."

"Sure you can." Dannie picked up her hat again, running her hand along the crease on the top. "Daddy, love is stability, isn't it? You'd offer yourself to her. That's the best thing any woman could ask for." Her eyes pricked with tears, the ghost of her own hurts making the words hard to say.

Her father stared at her a beat. "When did you grow so wise, Dannie-girl?"

Her laugh came out weak and damp. "Mrs. Perkins actually taught me that."

"When?"

"After David." Dannie's entire life was divided into three pieces. Before she lost her mother. After she lost her mother. And after David left her broken. "I was up late crying. You may remember I did a lot of that."

"I remember. I didn't know what to do. If I could've tracked down that man after he hurt you—" Her father shook his head and came closer, wrapping his arm around her shoulders. "I was grateful Loretta was here for you."

The sunlight had started streaming through the curtains. If Dannie didn't finish her thought quickly, she'd cry, give herself a headache, and cast aside her plans for the day. "I told Mrs. Perkins that I wasn't enough for David, so I wouldn't be enough for anyone. Without the ranch, I wasn't someone a man would want to love. And she told me that I was more than enough. That offering myself, my heart, to the right man would be more than enough. Even if I didn't have a penny to my name."

Unbidden, the memory of Evan in the barn came to her. How nice it had felt to lean against him. And the night of the dance, standing close and talking. Being near him had made her feel less alone.

Noises started up in the kitchen, Ruthie's humming announcing her presence. She had likely fed her husband and grandson and had come around to make certain the Boltons were eating properly. Since none of them had even entered the kitchen yet, she'd likely fuss at them for not even putting the coffee on to boil.

Her father wiped at his eyes, and Dannie dug into her vest pocket to find her handkerchief. She offered it to him, keeping back her own tears.

"Write to her, Dad. Ask her to come back and marry you. She's been part of the family a long time. You should make it official."

He chuckled. "I hadn't thought you'd prove so wise. I only meant to ask if you thought I should let her go."

Dannie stood, determined to stay cheerful despite the bruised feeling in her heart. "Don't let her go, Daddy." She bent and kissed him on the cheek. "You both deserve to be happy, and it sounds like you will be if you're together."

She left him behind to his thoughts, almost eager to escape into the kitchen for a scolding from Ruthie.

CHAPTER SIXTEEN

Evan sat back in his saddle next to Travis, watching Buck round up twenty head of cattle. Buck had spent the morning belly-aching about having to teach Evan how to cut heifers from the herd. Travis leaned forward, one elbow on the horn of his saddle. He'd loaned Evan one of his best cutting horses, since the gelding Evan had bought hadn't ever performed that particular duty.

They were in a paddock in the middle of the ranch, near a natural watering hole. Travis and Buck had driven the cattle into the fenced area, a place they used often to sort cattle and tend to other needs the animals had while on the range.

"Sorting cattle is an essential skill. You gotta part cows from calves, sick from well, mavericks from branded." Travis said, chewing on the end of a long piece of dry grass. "The more time you spend practicing with a horse, the better for both of you."

"Sounds like everything else in life." Evan cast the boy a grin, but it faded quickly. He tried to focus on Buck again, but the man's arrogance made it difficult to learn from him. Travis's narration of Buck's movements helped.

Travis shrugged one shoulder. "Most of the work you do should be with your legs. A good horse will go the direction you press him with your legs, and the reins are a way to keep him in line if he wants to go a different direction or gets distracted. But Colorado"—he nodded at the horse—"he's an old hand at this. He likes the work as much as we do. And then you've got Gus."

The dog was sitting between their horses, watching with his ears perked up and waiting for the command to join the fun.

"It's a game," Travis added. "But a game that can get you killed if you don't play by the rules. Cowboys like to compete against each other all the time, to prove who has the best cutting horse. Training up a horse that can do it practically on their own is a mark of honor."

Buck went after a dark red heifer with a white face, and once his horse realized which cow they were after, the mare moved in sync with the quarry. The cow jolted forward; the horse kept pace alongside, coming near enough to the cow to force it away from the rest of the small herd. When the cow jerked to a stop, the horse stopped too.

The cow, a good twenty feet away from the herd, tried to come back. The horse had to mirror the cow's darting left and right to stop the cow. Then Buck took out his lasso, swinging it through the air until he let it fly. The rope whizzed through the air and caught the cow around the neck.

Evan shifted in the saddle. The horse snorted and shook its head, sensing his tension. "Cutting isn't something I've ever tried before." He touched the rope Travis had given him that morning, the stiffness reassuring to his gloved fingers. He'd practiced roping nearly as often as he had marksmanship. He'd thrown Travis's lariat at a fence post a few times to remind his wrist how to twist and his fingers to release at the right moment.

"The horse does the work," Travis reminded him. "Think of him as your partner."

The sound of galloping hooves in front of them covered the sound of approaching hooves from behind, but when Gus looked backward Evan and Travis twisted around in their saddles.

Dannie rode up on a piebald mare, the horse's black and

white splotches making it stand out prettily against the brown of dust and dry grass. Dannie wore a bright green shirt and a black split skirt, with a faded straw hat covering her head.

"I hear you men are out here having fun," she shouted as she drew nearer. "Cutting heifers."

"Teaching Duke here the fine art of cattle work," Travis said with an air of correction and a sly grin. "He says he can rope, but we're watching Buck to make sure he knows what we expect."

When Dannie stopped her horse alongside the gate, Evan noticed that her broad smile was a mask. Her eyes weren't bright and smiling but dim and perhaps sad. They hadn't spoken since the dance two nights before. What had made her pensive and reserved?

"Well, look who's joined us," Buck called out, riding over to them with his rope in hand again. He'd released his cow while Dannie's arrival had distracted Evan. "Dannie. You come to watch the greenhorn run in circles?" His impudent grin flashed in Evan's direction.

Rather than rise to the bait of a verbal battle, Evan shifted and used the reins the way Travis had told him to make the horse back up.

"Take Gus," Travis added.

Though he'd rather prove himself with no outside aid, Evan knew his limitations. Evan whistled for Gus to join him, and the dog took off.

They'd already told Evan which two yearlings they wanted to take to town, and Gus followed his lead when Evan worked to cut the first from the group. The horse knew its business, responding quickly to Evan's subtle nudges. Then Gus got between the chosen heifer and the rest of the herd, lying low on his belly and watching, ready to spring into action if the cow tried to rejoin the group.

The cow paced the fence, and Colorado stayed with it while Evan took hold of his rope. His fingers remembered where to grip and house loosely, then his wrist twisted, and for one brief moment, Evan was back in England, chasing after ornery sheep. A cow wasn't really all that different. Just higher up from the ground.

He released the lasso and—before the rope slid through his fingers—he knew he had aimed true. The lasso sang through the air and settled around the heifer. Colorado stopped and pulled with Evan, tightening the rope and moving backward to hold the calf still. Gus came up from his feet, slinking toward the cow, getting the animal's attention on a familiar-looking predator rather than Evan.

The heifer tossed its head, backed into the fence, and from there Travis was ready with a second rope. The boy's grin stretched ear to ear. "Get the other one."

Evan's heart, he realized, was pounding fiercely despite his success. Or perhaps because of it.

Gus followed Evan to cut the next yearling out, and Colorado cornered it quickly. Evan kept his attention on the heifer, trusting Gus to keep the other cattle back if needed. But the herd wasn't interested in picking a fight with a man on a horse. With the cow in the corner, Evan snapped the lasso to the animal's head, catching it with the same speed as before.

The morning sun blazed hotter, causing a line of sweat to break out along Evan's back. With rope in his hands, a horse beneath him, and surrounded by bellowing cattle, Evan's heart settled. He looked up from his work, across the paddock and milling animals, and met Dannie's gaze.

The world stilled, and time stretched out behind and before him. Evan had never felt more at home than he did in that moment, and that sensation had everything to do with Dannie Bolton's warm brown eyes and encouraging smile.

Gus barked, and Evan forced himself to get back to work.

Buck opened the gate, Travis called to Gus and started chasing out the other cattle while the two yearlings remained tied to the fence.

No one spoke much until all four of them on horseback were

headed back to the homestead, the two yearlings spurred on by Gus ahead of them.

"Where'd you learn to rope, Duke?" Travis asked, riding between Evan and Dannie. Buck was on Dannie's other side, apparently sulking.

The truth sounded like a tall tale, or something Dannie might call bragging. But it was still the truth. "Buffalo Bill gave me my first lesson." He darted a glance at Dannie and caught the corner of her mouth listing upward in a smile. "After that, I practiced until I drove my family mad. And then practiced more."

Travis shook his head. "You've got a clean throw. I'd like to see you do it at a run."

Buck snorted. "Big difference in a cornered yearling and a bull on the prairie."

"I have no doubt of that," Evan agreed easily. "Still, I look forward to trying my hand at it."

Dannie faced forward, that contemplative expression returning to her face. "You're turning into quite the cowboy, Duke."

"I hope that's a compliment."

She arched one dark eyebrow at him. "We'll see." The words were teasing, not disapproving as they would've been weeks before.

Hours later, Evan carried an armful of clothes out to the washing shed. The building only had three walls at present. Ed told him that they put a fourth in place in winter. Evan used a water pump and bucket to fill the washtub— a smallish wooden barrel that stood on four tall legs.

He got there to find a fire already stoked beneath a pot full of clothes, and he frowned at it for a moment. Someone had beat him to the massive pot. Ruthie's laundry day was every Tuesday, which meant only one other person would think to use the pot that afternoon.

Dannie came around the corner, toting a bucket of water from the nearby pump. She'd changed clothes. She wore a faded blue cotton dress and a striped apron over it. The sleeves of the dress were short, and the skirt of the gown fit close against her legs. She smiled when she saw him standing there with his hands full of dirty laundry.

"I'm not washing that for you." She sounded amused rather than irritated.

Evan dropped the clothing on the table against the washroom wall. "I wouldn't expect you to. It's not an easy or diverting task."

"We certainly agree there." She dumped the bucket of water into the washstand, then put the washboard against the inside. She took a paddle to her boiling laundry. "Lucky for you, though, I'm done with the hot water." She took things out with the paddle, dropping them into a large woven basket on the ground. Evan hurried to help, using a large pair of iron tongs hanging on the wall.

"Thank you." Dannie dragged the basket closer to the washstand, but Evan hurried to lift it for her, then lowered it with a grunt on the table beside the stand. At that point, his eyes caught on the drying lines stretching from the back of the washing shed to a crossbeam. She'd already washed several sets of sheets and hung them up.

Dannie followed his stare. "I've been at it since we came back from your roping lesson. I think we all expected you to take a bit longer to get the hang of things." When she met his gaze, he caught the sparkle in her eyes. "You're full of surprises, Lord Evan."

He hadn't heard his title used in months and hearing it from her mouth brought him up short. "Evan is good enough for me." He wasn't a lord here. He had none of the rules of his father's title guiding his behavior or actions. The freedom of his circumstances came to him anew.

Dannie checked over a shirt in her hands, then put it through the clothing wringer. She turned the crank, then shook out the cloth. That done, she walked it to the line and hung it up. She returned and examined the next shirt, then put it in the vat of cool water, scrubbing it up and down the washboard.

Evan dumped his load of clothing into the boiling water, then used the discarded paddle to stir them into the water. He watched Dannie from the corner of his eye, the two of them working alongside each other without speaking for several minutes.

One long, limp strand of hair fell forward from behind her ear while she worked at scrubbing a pair of denim pants. With her hands occupied, she tried to blow the hair out of her face. "You did well today, with the cattle."

"Thank you." He took off his hat to wipe at his brow, then hung the hat on a peg in the wall behind him. "I confess, I wasn't sure what to expect. I'm grateful it went smoothly."

"You must have practiced a great deal." She looked up at him, a tilt to her head. "On moving targets, I think."

"On sheep."

Dannie's light laugh brought an answering smile to his lips. "I remember now. That's one of the first things you told us when you came. I suppose your practice paid off beautifully." She pulled up the clothing, looked it over, then put it through the wringer. "Every day I grow more aware of how unfair I was to you." She tried to blow that strand of hair away again. "But I didn't think you'd make it here. Because you weren't born to this way of life."

The apology in her smile, the softening in her expression, put him at ease. Tension he hadn't realized he carried fell from his shoulders. "I imagine there would be those who would object to anyone stepping off one path and onto another."

"I'm glad you had the chance to prove me wrong." She took the trousers gripped in her hands to the laundry line, pinning them up with wood pegs. He watched as she pushed that loose strand of hair behind her ear again, using the back of her hand.

Evan put the paddle aside; letting the clothes soak for a bit wouldn't do any harm. He intercepted Dannie at her bucket of water and soap and pulled out another shirt from her sopping pile. "Hm. This one needs attention. Looks like Clark spilled jam down his sleeve."

He raised his eyebrows at her, watching as her smile went from soft to amused. His pulse jumped as it had with the cattle, though this was an entirely different pursuit. One for which he hadn't had nearly as much practice, nor a proper plan.

DANNIE STUDIED THE SHIRTSLEEVE, RELIEVED THAT THE RED SMEAR had mostly come out in the boiling water. It just needed a little extra attention to come clean. "I think that's exactly what happened." She reached for the shirt, but he held it away from her. "Mr. Rounsevell, that's *my* laundry."

"Evan," he reminded her. He stayed between her and the scrub board, dropping the shirt into the water. Then he held out his wrist and unbuttoned the cuff of his shirt. First on one side, then the other.

"What are you up to, Evan?" She blinked, watching as he rolled one sleeve up to his elbow, revealing well-shaped wrists and sun-browned forearms. Then he rolled the other sleeve up to match the first. Then he flexed his hands, large and liberally calloused after all the work he'd done on the ranch. Her mouth went dry for no reason she could think of, and she stood staring at him like she'd turned into a statue.

"It might be your laundry, but I'm going to help you with it." He pulled the shirt out of the water and ran it down the scrubbing board and into the water a few times, giving attention to the sleeve.

Her mouth opened wide, and she stepped back, hands going to her hips. "Why would you do that?"

"Society raised me to be a gentleman. That means coming to the assistance of a lady in distress. Can you think of anything more distressing than laundry?" He cocked his head to the side, and Dannie was torn between laughing at his superior expression and protesting his kindness.

"I can't let you do that."

"Oh, but you can." He checked the cloth, gave it another swirl in the water, then put it through the wringer, driving the crank with better speed than she had before he snapped the shirt once and handed it to her. "I will allow you to hang the articles to dry."

Dannie stopped protesting. She took the shirt to the line and then came back to perch on a stool someone had left in the shed. "Who taught you to do laundry? Calamity Jane?" She kept levity in her tone.

"Frosty." Evan snapped another shirt and put it to the side of the table, beginning a pile for her to take to the line all at once rather than bit by bit. "On my third day here."

"I'll bet that wasn't your favorite lesson."

"Given that the end result meant I no longer smelled of manure, I did not mind it too much." He grinned at her, then scrubbed a handkerchief along the board. "Who taught you?"

"My mother." Dannie tugged at the long strand of hair she'd somehow missed when she braided her hair earlier. With a huff, she pulled the end of her plait over her shoulder and momentarily considered redoing the whole thing. But with Evan near, watching her every move, the thought of taking down her hair became far too intimate. No one had seen her hair loose in a long time. Not since her girlhood. "Mama, Ruthie, and I used to do laundry together. Until my mama died. Then we hired Mrs. Perkins, and she took over all the laundry. She said she had more than enough time, and I had to learn other important things."

"The mysterious Mrs. Perkins," Evan murmured, giving his attention to one of her divided skirts. Should it embarrass her for him to handle her clothing? Somehow, she didn't mind. She'd already taken care of her underthings. They were drying on the line hidden behind the billowing sheets. With those unmentionable items out of the way, nothing else gave her worry.

Dannie folded her arms over her chest as she watched him,

musing to herself that the muscles of a man's back and shoulders looked just as attractive washing clothes as they did when a man swung an axe or hauled buckets of water. And Evan, who hadn't looked poorly to begin with, had uniquely refined muscles after his work on the ranch.

"I hope she won't be a mystery to you much longer. She might be back before the end of June." Dannie hoped for that outcome. She hoped Mrs. Perkins would be a June bride, marry her dad, and be the new Mrs. Bolton. Her father deserved that happiness. They both did.

A breeze swept through the yard, twisting around the two of them and the heat surrounding the boiling vat of cowboy linens. Dannie looked up and to the east, then she came to her feet. "Evan, look! Clouds. An entire line of them."

He stopped his scrubbing, turning to the east, too. "Nimbo-stratus clouds."

Somewhere in the back of Dannie's memory, she knew she agreed with him. When had she learned the names for clouds? At some point in her life, she'd forgotten, and learned only to iden-tify if the coming clouds meant rain or not.

These clouds, dark, gray, and featureless, and rolling out like a blanket, were rain clouds.

He looked at the laundry on the line, then at her. "Do we need to get the wash inside?"

Dannie shook her head, grinning at him. "Nope. These are monsoon clouds. They'll come and get things wet, then they'll go away, and it'll be as sunny as it was this morning. The clothes are already wet. A little rain won't hurt, and they'll dry just as well after." She grinned up at the clouds again. "We'd better hurry so we can get undercover."

She snatched up the pile of clothes and went to the line, digging wooden clothespins out of her apron pocket to get every-thing up quickly.

"What about wind?" Evan asked, hurrying alongside her. "It won't ruin your laundry line?"

"Shouldn't." Dannie gave him a handful of wooden pegs. Between the two of them, they were done quickly. "See the storm, how it's moving nice and slow? It's not bringing much wind with it. Just water." Beautiful, precious water.

It wouldn't be another drought year.

"Every day for a few weeks, we'll see this happen. Usually around the same time, too."

"An unusual phenomenon." Evan made the work go twice as fast, and they still had time to get his clothes out of the boiling water and scrubbed before the first raindrops fell. She helped him get them on the line when droplets started hitting the dirt.

The nearby cattle lowed, and the horses were tossing their heads. Everyone went a little crazy before the first rain of the season fell, but now—now they'd all have clearer thoughts and easier moods.

Dannie stepped back from the line and looked straight up into the sky, Evan beside her doing the same.

"Do you need to go inside?" he asked over the sound of rain hitting the tin roof of the laundry shed and other outbuildings.

"Only if there's lightning." She held her hands out to either side, feeling the droplets along her skin like kisses from the sky. Evan held one hand out in front of him, probably thinking she'd lost her mind over a little change in the weather. Dannie looked up at him, somewhat sheepishly, ready to defend herself.

Except she didn't need to.

His eyes were closed, his head tipped back. The man wore a smile as soft and sincere as she'd ever seen on his handsome face. When he spoke, barely loud enough to be heard over the sound of water hitting every surface around them, his tone was reverent. "I've never thought about rain as much in my life as I have in these past weeks. It's beautiful, isn't it?"

"And life-saving." She watched the drops collect along the ridge of his nose and across his dark eyelashes. A shadow along his jaw showed he'd need a shave again soon. His sleeves were still turned up and almost transparent with the rain soaking through the fabric. All along his shoulders and the top of his chest the same thing happened, gluing his damp shirt to his skin.

Why didn't rain do things like that to women? All she could feel was the way her hair had started to stick to her cheek and the back of her neck.

His eyes opened, and he turned a wide grin to her. Then one of his hands came up, unexpected, and he stroked back that bothersome lock of hair behind her ear for her. Then that same hand touched the inside of her arm, and his fingers slid down the inside of her wrist until their palms touched.

Her breath froze inside her lungs and her pulse sped up as Evan's fingers twined with hers.

Far away, she heard someone calling her name. Travis, maybe.

Evan grinned and gave her hand a tug, and she let him lead her away. Away from the wash shed, around the outbuildings and past the paddock. The rain fell faster, almost cold, but the sky stayed bright enough behind the layer of clouds that she knew the rain wouldn't last long.

She laughed along with Evan, memories of playing in the rain as a child making it far too easy to skip through the rain at his side. They came to the meadow, the long dry grass crunching beneath their feet. The earth soaked up as much rain as it could. Elsewhere, there would be sudden streams where there had only been dry creek beds. The rain, when it came on fast, could cause all sorts of mischief.

But the first rain was special. It was relief from the heat, from the dry air and dust.

When Evan released her hand, Dannie spun around in a circle. "Tomorrow, this field will be green," she predicted. "And full of flowers."

Evan untied the bandana from around his neck and shoved it into his pocket, then twisted around in a tight circle. "I can't even imagine this place green."

"It's beautiful," she assured him. "Just like the rain."

He met her gaze squarely, his expression serious. "It turns out there's a lot in this desert I find beautiful."

He might not have meant her. Pretty words did not a truth make, either. Yet Dannie felt those words and the intensity in his stare strongly enough to make her blush.

They walked back to the house, the rain already slowing. The first rain rarely reached torrential strengths, though it had soaked both of them through.

"Do you think it necessary to wash this shirt after the soaking it received?" Evan asked as they approached the front porch of the main house.

Dannie studied the shirt critically. She blushed more than she liked and admired his physique far more than appropriate. Then she looked away, cheeks still burning. "I'd say it still needs a little soap."

Evan chuckled, then he shuddered. "The desert isn't as stifling when you're walking around soaked through."

Dannie stepped up on the porch, then turned to look down at him as she leaned against the supporting beam. "Do you have anything dry to wear?"

"I'll manage, never you fear." He looked out over the horizon, watching the rain clouds begin their retreat from the sky. He took his bandana out of his pocket and gave it a flick before tying it back around his neck, then he shoved his hands in his pockets and leaned against the rail.

A question that had tugged at her for some time rose again, and for the first time, she felt like she could ask it. "Evan?"

He turned his full attention to her, hands still in his pockets, his expression open. Expectant. "Yes?"

Her arm wrapped around the porch, anchoring herself to her home and land. "Why did you finally come to America and the Territory? You've made it sound as though you waited your entire life to be here. What finally brought you?"

Over the weeks since meeting him, she'd imagined every possible scenario. Had he been spurned by the woman he loved and ran away to let his heart heal? Perhaps he'd had a falling out with family. Or maybe he'd broken a law and needed to lie low.

"This brought me." Evan pulled his hand out of his pocket, his fingers holding something that flashed silver at her. He put one foot on the lowest step and held his hand out to Dannie.

Frowning, Dannie opened her palm. He dropped a coin into her grasp. She stared at it, then brought it closer to examine it. "Evan. This is just a silver dollar."

"Given to me by Buffalo Bill, newly minted, in 1879. Directly after he performed for Queen Victoria." He raised his eyebrows at her, a challenge in his eyes. "Do you believe me?"

She folded her fingers over the coin, its ridges smooth and warm from his pocket. "I believe you."

And she did. She'd stopped doubting his stories some time before. She'd even wondered, curious, about what tales he could tell of England and the people he'd known.

She opened her hand and studied the coin again, holding it with two hands to turn it over and over in her grasp. "If you've had the coin for so long, why come now? The year is 1895, not 1879."

"Because a man is more prepared than a boy to take up his courage and leave home." He answered without apology or shame, his voice warm. He stood with a relaxed posture, his head tilting to the side as he considered her. "Where I am from, it is no inconsequential thing to walk away from family, even for a short time. They have expectations of me and for my future. My father brought me up to fulfill certain responsibilities. No one ever stopped to ask what I wanted. So I stopped waiting for them to ask, and I took it."

Dannie's stomach sank as she took in all he said. Those expectations would inevitably pull him back to his family, to his responsibilities, and to England. She smiled, quick and with her lips pressed together. Extending her hand, she returned the coin to him, noting the way his expression shifted from sincere to surprised.

"Your silver dollar obviously means a lot to you. Like a good luck charm." She winced at the careless tone she'd used, then quickly smoothed her expression to one of disinterest. She had allowed herself to get too close to him. She felt it already—the tug inside—pulling her toward him. It wasn't fair. She'd been tricked into giving her heart to a rat, and now she was in danger of handing it to a lord.

But his words reminded her that she couldn't expect life to treat her fairly.

Dannie babbled on, her hands shoved deep in her apron pockets. "I better go inside and change. You should dry off, too. Dad wants you to go to Tombstone with him on Friday, and you can't afford to catch a cold before that trip." She took one step back, then another. "Thank you for your help with the laundry."

She turned on her heel and hurried into the safety of the house. The screen door slapped loudly, and she shut the thick wooden door too quickly, making it slam.

"Dannie!" Clark snapped, hand over his chest. He'd been standing in the hall, book in hand. "What're you always telling us about slamming doors?"

"Sorry, Clark." She started untying her apron and rushed by him to get to the stairs.

"Why are you all wet? Were you out in the rain?"

"Doing the laundry," she answered over her shoulder, then ran up the last few steps to get to her room. Once inside, she shut the door slowly. Locked it. Then leaned heavily against the wall.

Evan had a lot of things waiting for him back home. He might play in the rain with her, but a heavy weight of foreboding had settled in her chest. He'd leave. He'd go back to England, just as he'd originally said. All he was really waiting for was the cattle drive in the fall.

She swallowed, but the burning sensation creeping up her throat only increased. She shook her head and hurried to undo the buttons of her dress, then stepped out of the wet fabric. All the while, she kept her head down and her thoughts away from the Englishman and his gentle eyes, his soft words, and even his far too charming accent.

"I'm a fool," she whispered, pulling on dry underthings. She slid into her bed rather than bother with another layer of dry clothes.

The sun had come out again, judging by the light coming through her window. Yet Dannie couldn't stop shivering. She pulled the blankets overhead. "A silly girl. He never said he wanted anything but friendship, and here I am, losing myself to him piece by piece." She burrowed deeper beneath the blankets. "I just can't. He's leaving." She hiccupped, then realized she had tears burning in her eyes.

Evan had conducted himself honorably. He'd only been friendly. He knew he had to leave.

"He doesn't want me," she whispered. "He just wants a friend."

There was a world of difference in those two things.

She just needed to make her foolish heart understand, preferably before she had to emerge from her bedroom for dinner. But she wouldn't avoid Evan. She'd enjoy what time she had. Heaven knew they had little variety in the company they kept.

Dannie curled up in as tight a ball as she could, trying to stuff all her feelings back where they'd come from. But that only made her heart hurt all the more.

CHAPTER SEVENTEEN

His distracting thoughts regarding Dannie's sudden shift in behavior plagued Evan for a couple of days, rather as though a bevy of troublesome flies had swarmed him. He went through all the motions of his usual chores, tidying the barn, checking tack, and tending to the animals in the paddock. The work he did by rote, which left his mind free to overthink every move Dannie Bolton had ever made, and every word she had ever said.

Something had changed, for him at least. And he had thought there was—had *felt* there was—an answering change in her, too. Yet she had darted away from him, rather like the antelope he'd seen on his last ride with Ed. The beautiful creatures watched them approach, then fled before the men came too close.

Evan went into the barn as night fell. Fable had made a cozy nest, which she'd tucked into a corner with fresh hay surrounding her and her litter. The four pups with their patch-work coats of black, white, and tan, had barely opened their eyes. They crawled about, pink noses nudging each other, and tiny paws kicking at the air as they slept.

"How is the family, my lady?" Evan kept his voice soft, not about to startle the mother or her offspring.

Fable watched him come near, and she opened her mouth in her usual grin. He settled on the ground next to her, reaching in to give her ears a gentle rub. Then he picked up one of the little ones, rubbing his finger down the puppy's nose. It grumbled before curling into a ball against his chest.

Gus trotted in a moment later and flopped onto the ground, several feet from Fable, and huffed. Apparently, the mother had kept him at bay. Perhaps not trusting him to treat her little ones with care.

Evan didn't move for several minutes. The quiet company of animals had always been soothing, but was even more so as he tried to understand the new world he inhabited. It had rained, as Dannie had predicted, the last two afternoons. The mud churning up, while unpleasant, didn't even upset him since it came with the pleasure of cool air and gentle storms. The more he considered what he'd seen of Arizona Territory, of its landscape and weather, the more he liked it.

Would it be so terrible—would his family be bereft—if he didn't return to England right away? He'd thought to stay at the KB Ranch until after the cattle drive, then make his way somewhere else, to see more of the country. But what if he stayed? What if he spent the autumn learning to track game in the mountains surrounding the ranch? Then he could hole up for the winter months, when travel wouldn't be ideal, and learn more about Fort Huachuca? He'd heard there were still men around who had been present when Chief Cochise surrendered to the United States Army. He could find them, maybe, and learn about what happened to the native people of Arizona.

And he could make the ranch his center, returning between adventures to a place of security. Then take part in the spring cattle drive. Then he'd have an entire year's worth of experiences on a true cattle ranch in the wild west.

The idea spun out before him, like a tapestry unfurled, presenting him with images of what could be. Campfires glowing in the night, riding a strong horse across the range, climbing to the top of a mountain peak, and sitting in front of storytellers with gray beards and wide-brimmed hats. Each imagined scene came from the books he had read, but they would be real, and it would be him in the place of every protagonist he'd envied during all those years of reading.

But he didn't see himself alone at those campfires. And he imagined a woman with a long braid and a wide grin racing him across the desert on a piebald horse, black and white, galloping a horse-length ahead of him. Had Dannie climbed the mountain range visible from the porch of her home?

"I bet she has," he muttered aloud, stroking the furry creature against his chest. "I bet she's done all the things I want to do, and she'd be better than me at all of it." That made him grin, especially as he remembered when she'd made that shot with the rifle the week before. People in Arizona called a woman like her a *spitfire*. The descriptive term fit. Dannie was full of fire, ready to stand toe-to-toe with anyone she thought a threat.

She was as passionate about the things she loved as she was in defending them, too. And Evan...he wondered how passionate she might be if she were *in love*.

The barn door opened, but Evan didn't move. If someone was looking for him, they'd call out. Otherwise, he was happy to stay put.

A light step came closer to where he sat, and a gentle voice crooned. "There's my Gus. What are you doing in here, boy?"

He stilled and watched as Dannie appeared, bending down to give the male dog a pat on the head. In the moment before she saw him, Evan took in her expression. The tired look in her eyes, the gentle tilt to her lips that signaled a smile about to appear. She wore a calico dress, her hair pinned up in a braided circle, and her usual boots peeking out from beneath her skirt.

Pretty as a picture, he thought, smiling at the sight. If he drew it, or painted it, he'd call it, "The Lady of the Ranch."

She looked up, her eyes going to Fable's place, but she stilled when she saw Evan sitting there instead. Her mouth opened, but before she spoke someone called her name from just outside the barn.

"Dannie? You in the barn?" It was Buck.

Her eyes went wide, and she dove closer to Evan. "Do *not* tell him where I am," she hissed, then she tucked herself behind Fable's nest and the barn wall. The hay had been stacked up enough that she was well hidden from view, even though Evan could've easily stretched out his hand and touched her nose.

He could smell her, too. Despite the scent of fresh hay, dirt, rain, and leather, he caught a whiff of apples and roses. Whatever she'd been up to that day, he liked the results of it.

The barn door opened again, and louder footfalls came quick across the floor. Dannie stilled and squeezed her eyes shut, as though that might somehow help her maintain her hiding spot. Evan had to bite his lip to keep from laughing, but he had schooled his features into a look of indifference by the time Buck came around the corner.

The cowboy stopped upon seeing Evan. "You. What are you doing in here, greenhorn?"

Evan shrugged, not taking offense to the term they'd all labeled him with at one point or another. "Sitting down a spell. Enjoying Fable's pups. It's relaxing. You ought to try it."

The man folded his arms. "The more I know about you, Englishman, the more I wonder if your whole nation is full of men like you. You look like you're made of butter."

Evan raised his eyebrows. "Is that supposed to be an insult of some kind?"

Buck scowled and planted his feet wider apart. "You're so green you don't even savvy cow when it's in your stew. Of course it's an insult. You're soft, you're weak, and you don't belong out here."

"All interesting conjectures," Evan said quietly. He placed the pup back with its mother, then came slowly to his feet. "I'm fairly certain I've spent the last month of my time proving that I'm as capable as the next man."

"They just feel sorry for you, so they won't send your sorry hide on its way." Buck glanced around. "Dannie didn't come through here?" He looked at the small door at the back of the barn.

"She did not pass through the barn." Evan leaned against the wall, most decidedly not looking at Dannie laying in the straw below him. "I wonder why you are so often in pursuit of Miss Bolton. The lady seems either weary of your company or averse to it."

Buck snorted. "What do you know about anything? A rooster's got more sense than you do."

"Perhaps. But I cannot say I have seen a more likely coxcomb than yourself, sir." Evan grinned happily when Buck only stared, his expression a blank.

"What's that supposed to mean?" he said at last, apparently unaware of the insult given.

"Nothing for you to worry over." Evan held his hands out. "As you do not see Miss Bolton in the barn, perhaps you had better take yourself elsewhere. I highly doubt the two of us are capable of a pleasant conversation, or any sort of meeting of the minds."

"Sure." Buck narrowed his eyes at Evan, glanced around once last time, then turned and went out the way he had come, muttering something about Evan's parentage that Evan chose not to hear.

Only after the barn door slammed shut, and remained so for several moments, did he look down at Dannie. Her eyes were open, and she stared up at him with a sympathetic smile. "I'm sorry about that."

"I'm not." Evan crouched down, putting his weight in the back of his heels as he studied her. "The man is a base miscreant with only a handful of uses. If he were not excellent at the part of his job that matters most, I have full faith that Frosty would send him on his way."

"You're probably right. I'm not sure anyone particularly likes him." She sat up at last, then ran her hands over her hair checking for straw. Her fingers found a few stray pieces and she tugged them out.

Evan stretched out his hand to take another piece off the very top of her head, where her searching hadn't reached. She sat back, the hay rustling beneath her. "Thank you for not giving me away."

With a hand to his heart, he nodded deeply. "I am always happy to act as your champion, Dannie."

Her light laugh, almost a giggle, made his heart lighter. He contemplated how best to make her laugh again as she responded.

"I've never had a champion before. What does that mean, exactly? That you'll fight duels for me? Slay dragons?"

"Among other things," he answered with a lofty tilt to his head. "A champion stands between his lady and anything or anyone that would distress her. You have but to point me in the pertinent direction, and I will act as your sword or shield, as need be."

"That sounds lovely." She pulled her legs up close, wrapping her arms around them. "But what qualifications do you have to hold such a position? Have you served as a champion many times before?" The slant to her eyebrow added a teasing aspect to the question. A question which had a serious answer if he dared to give it.

Evan looked back at Gus, who hadn't moved much, still staring mournfully at his mate and their progeny. The dog wanted to get closer to his lady, but Gus knew he'd be unwelcome. Evan knew exactly how the animal felt.

Evan cocked his head to one side and spoke slowly, watching Dannie carefully. "I have not, in fact, offered that service to any woman of my acquaintance before now."

She offered him a weak smile in return, a pink flush coloring her cheeks. "I am surprised at that, *Lord* Evan. There must be many ladies in England eager to have you return to their parlors and ballrooms."

He grimaced and looked down at the straw on the barn floor. "Not many. While a second son is a prize for a few, most set their sights on larger game." Then he met her gaze again. "What about you? You say you've never had a champion, but I've heard—"

"About David," she interrupted. "Yes, I know. You've heard enough, even if all you've heard is his name." Dannie picked up one of Fable's puppies and tucked it just beneath her chin.

"Are we friends, Dannie?"

Biting her lip, she nodded without looking at him.

"Then tell me, as your friend, anything you'd like about David." It was a risky invitation. She might well fold up on herself again, or lash out at him, or run away.

But Evan needed to try. He needed to understand more because Dannie drew him in. She made him consider things about himself he never had before. And he wondered if leaving the ranch, and her, might be a mistake of enormous proportions.

"DAVID ROBERTSON." DANNIE'S EYES FELL TO THE PUPPY IN HER hands. The black and white splotched little creature, with a pink nose and soft paws, was a much safer place to look than into Evan's searching gaze. "I met him in Boston when I was seventeen. The other girls at my finishing school had finally accepted me. One of them invited me to a cotillion ball. I understand they're similar to your balls when debutantes make their grand entrance into society."

"A grand occasion, then." Evan's accent made her smile, especially when he added, "A place to see, be seen, gossip, and win *beaux*."

"Precisely." Dannie shifted, trying to get more comfortable despite the uncomfortable conversation. "This friend, Samantha, she wanted everyone to know that I was worthy to be there. She had told people, without my say-so, that I was the daughter of a wealthy Arizona cattle baron."

"Ah, thus granting you an exotic air."

Dannie felt her cheeks warm as she remembered that evening, and the way so many people had pretended an interest in *cows* just to talk to her. To find out if Samantha had told the truth. "Precisely."

"And you met Mr. Robertson at the event, I surmise." Evan didn't sound judgmental or bored. He sounded...concerned.

"I did. And danced with him. He was the only one who *didn't* want to talk about cattle or rattlesnakes that night." She shivered and placed the puppy back with its mother, then wrapped her arms around herself. "He was absolutely charming. He only wanted to talk about *me*. What I thought of Boston, of the ball, and what I liked to do when I wasn't at the boarding school. I felt like he was the only person who saw me." She laughed, releasing a bitter note impossible to keep back. "Of course, I realize now that he was trying to get in close, and fast, to secure my interest in *him*."

Evan shifted, then moved so he sat beside her. "Not an unusual tactic for a fortune hunter."

"So I've learned." She tilted her head back against the barn wall, staring up into the rafters. One of the barn cats looked down from a beam, twitching its tail above her. "At the time, I was flattered. He visited me every week when the boarding school matron allowed callers. I wrote home about him. He met me at every social event he could, when we could both get invitations."

"A clever invasion." Evan sat with his knees pulled up just enough that he could rest his wrists against them, leaving his hands free. She watched as his fingers curled and uncurled into fists as she spoke.

"When my father sent news of the circumstances on the ranch, with everything pointing toward another hard year and a drought, I knew I needed to return home. I planned to tell David and ask him to write, but he didn't like that I was leaving. In fact, he insisted he escort me home. I had a paid companion, for my reputation, but he bought his own ticket and joined us."

"Impertinent," Evan muttered, his hands closing again. Then he looked at her, his eyes soft in the low light of his lantern. "What did your father think of the man?"

"That he was impertinent," she answered, a smile tugging at her lips. "Uninvited. A pest. Underfoot. But Daddy—he tried to be reasonable, too. To understand what I saw in a Yankee city-slicker." Dannie could almost laugh about that phrase now, and how mournful her father had looked in his study when he'd called David all those things.

Evan bumped her shoulder with his. "Sounds familiar. I'm surprised your father didn't take one look at me and send me on my way."

"My dad strongly believes that people should get the chance to prove themselves before passing judgement. But maybe you can understand why I wanted you gone," she said, then bit her bottom lip.

Evan nodded with a slow, deliberate bow of his head. "I do. This Robertson fellow—he must have convinced you well of his affections."

"He asked my father for permission to marry me." Dannie shivered, and Evan leaned a little more into her shoulder, offering warmth and support without saying a word. "Lucky for me, Mrs. Perkins convinced my father to make him wait. If I had doubted her love for me, I would've been so angry. Instead, I knew I just had to convince her of everything—that it would all work out."

The hay rustled as Evan reached into his pocket and revealed a large white handkerchief, unadorned by initials or embroidery. A man's handkerchief. Clean, plain, and kindly meant to dry her eyes when she'd barely realized she was crying.

What was wrong with her? Monsoon season started and that meant she had to be as damp as the clouds?

Dannie laughed, the sound too watery for her liking. "I hate crying over that man. I've wasted far too many tears on him."

"You should not think of it that way." Evan didn't sound uncomfortable with her tears or her tale of woe. Instead, his voice was gentle as ever, his words kind. "You aren't crying or mourning for him, but for the beautiful thing he stole away."

"What did he steal?" Dannie asked quietly, staring at the now damp handkerchief in her hand.

Evan's hand appeared, and he wrapped it around hers. "He stole your trust. And maybe a little bit of your hope."

Dannie tried to grin, but it felt wobbly on her face as she lifted her gaze to Evan's. He stared back at her, his eyes warm and glowing with intensity. "I thought you were going to say he stole my heart."

"I don't think anyone can steal that, Dannie. Hearts are for sharing, or giving. But they can't be stolen." He lifted her hand to his lips, pressing a kiss to her knuckles with his eyes closed. "At least, I hope not. If someone like him made off with your heart, it leaves someone like me with little hope of winning it for myself."

A rush of warmth flooded her, from the tips of her ears down to her fingertips and toes. *He didn't mean it. He didn't mean it at all.* Dannie gulped, but the barn was too warm. He was too warm. "Evan, don't—"

"When did he leave?" Evan asked, not allowing her to reprimand him. "What finally drove him away?"

She stared at him, uncertain how to escape from him when he held her hand. And she didn't really want to escape, either. She just knew she couldn't sit next to him much longer. "My dad sat down with him in June, when the rain didn't come. He told David that the cattle would die soon, and that David needed to prove himself able to provide for me when the ranch no longer could. He left that night. One of my friends from school wrote later that he went to Oklahoma and married a girl on a ranch there."

Evan snorted, and his hand pressed hers more firmly. "Likely using every trick he'd learned here to make himself look good. Poor girl."

"I've often felt sorry for her. Whoever she is." Dannie stared at their hands, then gave an experimental tug to get hers back. She couldn't hold his hand. She couldn't sit with him like this, not knowing when he would leave, believing he would never come back when he did.

He released her hand, then stood. "Thank you for telling me." His tone was even, not hurt or mad, not flirtatious either. Just friendly.

Dannie rose without his help, though she leaned heavily against the wall. "Have you rescinded your offer of championing me?" she asked, trying to sound light and teasing, but failing miserably. Unburdening herself to him had made her tired. Terribly, emotionally exhausted.

And yet...it hadn't hurt her to talk about David. It had felt—not necessarily good, but—right.

"On the contrary, my lady." Evan swept off his hat and bowed to her, as courtly a bow as he might give the Queen of England herself. Or so Dannie imagined. "I am only more determined to be of service to you in these trying times." Then he winked at her.

She'd never seen him wink.

Dannie allowed herself to relax, and then she shook out her skirt to rid herself of any lingering straw. "Do I look all right?" she asked, smoothing her hair again. "No more hay anywhere?"

"You look exceptionally fine to me, Dannie." Evan stepped back. "You ought to go out one side of the barn, and then I'll go out the other. Buck watches you too closely, and I don't want him to get the wrong idea."

"Thank you for that." Dannie bent to pick up the handkerchief she had dropped during their conversation, then held it out to him. "Would you like this back, or—?"

Evan took a step back, that earnest look in his eyes again. "You keep it. Just until the next laundry day."

That brought the blush back into her cheeks. He let her leave first, out the rear door of the barn, after he made certain no one would see her go. As Dannie went back to the house, skirting buildings and avoiding notice from anyone, she clutched the handkerchief tightly in her hand.

What did he mean, offering to be her champion? Evan couldn't possibly be considering staying on the ranch. Could he?

He'd mentioned winning her heart as though that was something he actually wanted. But then he hadn't let her say a word on the matter and perhaps thought she had forgotten about it by the end of their conversation.

The carefully constructed arguments she had made against love dissolved like sugar in the rain. Evan had dismantled one of the last walls between her heart and his, getting her to talk about David and admit how much that horrid man's treatment of her had colored her opinion of Evan.

Everything was out in the open between them. She had nothing more to hide from him. She didn't *want* to hide anything from him.

In fact, Dannie very much wanted to tell him *everything*. Her hopes, her dreams, and the silly things she kept to herself in case someone else thought her odd. Maybe Evan wouldn't mind sharing the same with her.

Maybe.

CHAPTER EIGHTEEN

Tapping the pencil in her hand against the sheet of paper on the kitchen table, Dannie looked from Abram back to her father. The two of them always got to talking when they were supposed to be making the shopping list for the approaching trip. Usually their conversation ended up stretching backward in time as they remembered the first time they'd set foot in Tombstone or reminisced about adventures they'd had on the trail to one of Arizona's largest towns.

She sent a frustrated glance to Frosty, who was representing the needs of the cowboys and animals, but he only smiled at her in that calm way of his. He wasn't in any hurry. He leaned back a little more in his chair, until Ruthie caught his eye and shook her head. Then he adjusted his posture and sighed.

"Do you remember," Abram said with a suspicious glint in his eye, "that time we caught the sheep rustler because he didn't have any idea to get them to move?"

"We rounded up the animals easy as you please with Gus's grand-daddy." Her dad laughed. "And he just kept cussing at us for getting the job done right in front of him."

"What was that dog's name?" Abram asked, eyes narrowing as he tried to recall. "Shep?"

"We didn't ever have a Shep. We had a Whip, though. I think that was him."

"Dad?" Dannie interrupted their musings with exasperation. "We don't need to talk about Whip, we need to get this list finished. You're leaving before dawn for Tombstone, and I'd rather not have to remind you of any last-minute purchases when we're all still half asleep."

Her father had the grace to appear apologetic. "Of course, Dannie-girl. S'cuse us. Ruthie, did you get everything you needed on the list?"

Ruthie wore a half-lidded, none-too-amused expression as she eyed the menfolk. "Dannie and I finished the household lists before you men even sat down."

Abram folded his arms on the table and leaned toward his wife. "You trying to say you women are more efficient than us?"

"Not trying." She sniffed. "I'm just saying it plain."

He laughed and took her hand across the table, and Dannie hid her smile behind the paper she picked up. "We've got all the necessaries written out for us. The boys put in their two cents worth, too. What about you, Frosty? Any bunkhouse and barn needs?"

"The usual things." Frosty sat up straight again and started ticking off items that Dannie jotted down, nothing at all out of the ordinary. Until he named the final item. "Oh, and a new washboard. Duke's request."

Dannie's pencil hovered over the paper, and she raised her gaze slowly as heat crept up the back of her neck.

Ruthie, Abram, and her dad all stared at Frosty, and he shrugged at their confused gazes. "He asked."

"Why? Something wrong with the other board?" Ruthie glanced to the back door as though she wanted to dart up to check on the small but essential piece of equipment herself.

"Not that I'm aware." Frosty lowered his gaze to the tabletop, his words a slow drawl. "All he said was that the washing would be easier to get done with two."

The pencil slid out of Dannie's hands, clattering to the table. She picked it up without meeting anyone's eyes and wrote *washboard* on the paper. Evan hadn't meant for her to know what he said, had he? Or for her to be aware of his request? But maybe he did want her to know that he was thinking of their silliness over the wash. Maybe it was his way of saying he'd keep on helping her.

And maybe she saw too much of what wasn't there in an innocent request.

After a few more minutes discussing the Tombstone trip, Dannie rose to get everyone a cup of chamomile tea. The men didn't protest the beverage choice, since this was something of a tradition. They needed to get a good's night rest. Ruthie would send them off with hot coffee in the morning to fortify them for their long trip to Tombstone.

As she walked by the back door, with only the screened-in door closed, she looked through to the yard and saw Evan. He had two buckets full of water, walking from the pump near the barn to the bunkhouse. He wore the blue shirt, sleeves rolled up, suspenders taut over his shoulders. His hat was on, pulled down low.

She caught a sigh in her throat before it could slip out, then hurried to serve the others at the table.

Frosty drank his tea quick enough Dannie thought he'd scald himself. Then he rose and put his hat on his head. "Thank you, ladies. I'll make sure Duke's ready to head out early, King."

Her father nodded his thanks, and Frosty went out the door.

"Checkers, Abram?" her father asked, rising from the table at the same time as his old friend.

"I think I'd like a game or two. Ruthie? All right with you?"

Ruthie waved him on, and the two left the kitchen for the parlor. Then Ruthie poured herself and Dannie more of the relaxing herbal tea. "Now they can get their jawing done without the rest of us as a captive audience." She flashed one of her indulgent smiles as she spoke.

SALLY BRITTON

"I love listening to their stories, most of the time." Dannie sipped at her tea. "The early days at the ranch were something else."

"That they were." Ruthie chuckled. "But we're still seeing unusual things. Good times and bad. The older I get, Dannie, the more I realize life isn't ever easy. But if we put in a good day's work, live by God's word, and love each other, things are a lot more bearable."

Dannie lowered her teacup, her finger tracing the delicate handle. Her mother had brought the china from her home in Texas, the only gift her family had given her when she left home. "I'm glad you're here to remind me of that, Ruthie."

"Me, too." Ruthie stretched out her hand to lay it against Dannie's wrist, making Dannie look up to meet the warmth in the older woman's eyes. "Abram told me about your daddy and Loretta Perkins. That's not bothering you none, is it?"

"Oh." Dannie shook her head quickly. "No—not at all. It'll be an adjustment if she says yes and comes back to marry him. I know that. But—but it'll be good for both of them. I think she and Dad will be happy together."

Ruthie studied Dannie for a long moment, measuring and weighing the sincerity of Dannie's words, before she nodded. "I think so, too. I'm glad you're grown up enough to see the good in the match. But Dannie"—Ruthie narrowed her eyes—"Something is bothering you."

"No." Dannie released a laugh, though it sounded shaky even to her. "I'm fine. I promise." She shrugged one shoulder upward. "I've just been helping Dad with the accounts. My mind is full of numbers and ideas that I can't quite make work just yet. But I'm fine."

"Hm." Ruthie sipped at her tea, not appearing entirely convinced. "You know you can talk to me whenever you want, Dannie-girl."

Dannie's heart constricted at the old term of endearment. It normally only came from her father, but anyone she loved using the term made her heart happier. "I know. I'm fine, Ruthie. I promise." Fine as she *could* be, anyway, with the future stretching out before her as dark as night. No clear path to take, and uncertain of who'd be by her side on the journey.

EVAN HAD THE BATHTUB SET UP IN THE STOREROOM ADJACENT TO the bunk room. The other cowboys washed up in creeks and cattle cisterns when they wanted to do an "all over," as Ed called them. But Evan had found a tub large enough to sit in. Even if it wasn't luxury, it was better to be near a fire and indoors than out where he had to be wary of snakes, skunks, coyotes, and who knew what else.

He poured in the last few buckets of cold water from the pump, missing his valet again, but at the same time, just glad to get clean. There were only a few inches of water in the tub, but that was all he needed. He stripped out of his work clothes and lowered himself into the copper-bottomed bath. Using soap, a cloth, and a tin cup to rinse, he did a better job of washing than he had since the dance the week before.

Shivering his way into clean clothes, Evan looked out the window to the paddock. His gelding grazed alongside the two heifers they were taking to Tombstone the next day. And though he hadn't been on the range long, he could see now what the others had when he'd arrived on that horse.

"Pretty is as pretty does," he muttered to himself; it was a phrase he'd heard Ruthie use. Then he shook his head. The horse, a finely bred creature, didn't belong on a working ranch. "Fit for Sundays and not much else." He chuckled when he recalled those words describing his horse, and likely meant for him, too.

Maybe he could trade the horse for something else in Tombstone. Get two range horses out of the deal, if he was smart.

Frosty might help him with that kind of trade. The man knew his way around horses better than most.

He tipped the tub to scoop water out with one pail, then poured as much as he could back into the other. Then he lifted both and made his way out of the bunkhouse. Ruthie had caught him throwing water out of a wash basin his first week at the ranch, and she'd told him in no uncertain terms of a dire fate that she'd bring down upon him if he wasted water again.

"Pour it on the gardens where it'll do some good," she snapped at him, snatching away his empty basin as though it was a mistreated infant.

Tonight, he hauled the pails all the way around the front of the house. To the tree that stood in front, where he'd seen Dannie linger from time to time. That tree meant something special to the girl. He didn't understand how he knew it, only that he did. So it was there he went, willing to aid that tree in any way he could.

The pails were heavy but dumping them out along the tree's roots satisfied him. He took up the buckets and turned around to go get the rest of the water, then stopped when he saw movement on the dark porch.

Dannie stepped out of the darkest shadows, her hand on the railing. She stared at him, waiting.

Evan slowly lowered the buckets to the ground, then approached her with his heart in his throat. How did she always manage to look like she'd just stepped from one of his dreams? Whether she wore dresses or split skirts, aprons or boots, she always looked ready to take on the world. And him, too, if he stepped in her way.

Tonight she wore a split skirt and cream-colored blouse with shiny white buttons going from her waist up to her throat. Her hair was loose, too, with the waves created by her usual braid. It hung down her back, dark with silver streaks in the moonlight.

"Dannie." He stood beneath her on the porch. "How did the list-making go?" Frosty had made it sound like a chore when he took suggestions from the men on what to bring back from town. Or maybe the chore had been listening to Buck bellyache about not being chosen to go to Tombstone.

"Fine." She stepped down, lingering on one step and then the next. "Frosty said you needed a new washboard."

He tipped his hat back on his head. "I did make that request, yes." He'd wondered if she'd think it strange, if she would ask questions about it, or if Frosty would simply add it to the list without a word.

Dannie took another step down, now only one step above the ground where he stood. "He said you thought laundry would be easier to do with two." She was eye level with him, and she didn't shy away from meeting his gaze.

"I thought it was easier with two. Most things are." He wasn't talking about the laundry.

The gleam in her eye said that she knew it, too. "It made the list."

"Good."

"Yes." She kept staring at him. "I went and saw Felicity Mason this morning. Did you know? She asked after a recipe from the dance."

"That was kind of you to take it to her." Evan wanted to lean forward, wanted to take her hand. She stood so close. But what would he do with her once he had her? That indecision kept him still.

She lifted one shoulder in a shrug. "That's what neighbors do. She wanted to talk about the dance, too. Especially about enjoying when you led her around the floor."

"Did she?" Evan shifted back on his heels. "As I recall, your friend was a fine partner. Most of the ladies did well."

One dark eyebrow lifted. "They did well?"

Evan rubbed at the back of his neck, pretending to consider her tone and the insult it implied. "American steps are not the same as what I'm used to, and American women dance *differently* than Englishwomen."

That made her eyes blaze, and she huffed indignantly. "Oh, do we?"

"That is my assessment, yes." He grinned at her. "Of course, I didn't dance with *every* American lady present. Perhaps I should ask Ruthie if she'd like to prove me wrong."

Her eyes narrowed. "*Ruthie?* Evan Rounsevell, you know full well you didn't once ask me to dance. And you've not said a word about it, even now, a week later! And don't think my friends will let me forget it, either. Felicity said they were all confused as to why you didn't even ask me."

Evan held up a hand to stop the quick, sharp flow of her words. "I apologize, Dannie. I didn't mean to offer up an insult. I didn't think you wanted to dance with anyone. You made that plain to the Mason brothers."

She sniffed and folded her arms. "I made it plain I didn't want to dance with *them*. They're presumptuous, and often don't behave themselves."

"So if I would have asked...?" He let the question hang between them; his breath stilled in his lungs waiting for her answer.

Dannie's glare abated, and a tired look replaced it. "I would've said yes. We *are* friends."

"That we are." Evan held his hand between them, palm up. "Will you dance with me now, my lady?" He met her eyes, unflinching, unsmiling. She needed to understand just how serious he was. And he needed her to say yes.

Her warm, slight hand slid into his. "It would be a pleasure, my lord."

With nothing more to guide them than the sounds of the desert night, Evan tugged her off the last step and into his arms.

CHAPTER NINETEEN

Waltzing beneath the starry skies of a desert felt like dancing amid the Milky Way itself, Evan's partner a woman well suited to the soft starlight. His right hand cupped her shoulder, his left held hers in a gentle grasp. She held herself with the skill of one used to the proper dancing forms. From the waist up, she held firm like a goddess, but stepped as lightly as a nymph across the ground, following his lead as though it was all she had ever known.

Evan kept time by instinct alone. His whole attention was taken up by the way Dannie had enchanted him. What else could he call the spell cast over him whenever she came near but magic?

Dannie had beauty in abundance, and her clever tongue had amused him from the first time they met.

"Have I proven myself to you yet, my lord?" she asked, her voice soft in the night's velvet shadows. "Or are you still of the opinion that English women dance better than the uncultured Americans?"

"You turn my words against me, my lady."

She snorted at the term of respect, her nose wrinkling.

"You do," Evan insisted, deftly bringing her into a gentle turn.

"I never said English women are in any way superior to Americans, not even that they dance better. Only differently."

Her chin lowered, as did her gaze. "Differently. I am certain the ladies last week were astounded by your technique. I will not say anything against the men of the Territory, except that they sometimes forget there is a difference between dancing with a girl and wrestling a heifer to the ground."

Evan laughed, guiding her back with him, away from the tree and to the flat expanse of grass before the house. "I did note the rough handling from time to time, but it appeared as though the women in the Territory were equal to the task."

They said nothing for several steps, their only music the crickets and birds.

While the sounds of London had often drowned out Evan's thoughts, the stillness of the wilderness around them allowed him to hear himself think as never before. The scent of dirt, hay, sun-dried cotton, and leather clung to him instead of the heady soaps and perfumes of Society, all of it covering the stink of cobbled streets teaming with horses and masses of people all scraping and striving for even a small measure of happiness in the life they'd been born to live.

Things were so different here. He could breathe. For the first time in his life, he could take in a lungful of air and release it in laughter, in satisfaction of a good day's work completed.

His muscles frequently ached, his hands were brown and calloused, and he was stronger than he'd ever been in his life.

One month had changed him. One month of sunshine and dust had taught him what a lifetime of perfume and silk never could.

And Dannie....

His steps slowed, and he placed Dannie's hand on his chest, holding it there. "Why were you outside all alone?" he asked her.

Dannie did not protest the end of their dance, nor did she pull away from him. Her other hand remained on his shoulder, enough room between them for the wind to whistle around and between their still forms.

"I needed to think." She averted her gaze to the tree. "My mother planted that tree and kept it alive, even though a Spanish oak like that one has no call to be out here in the middle of nowhere." The humor in her voice, bitter-sweet though it was, made him smile.

"You feel closer to her when you stand beneath the branches." Evan studied the sweep of her lashes, the curve of her cheek, the tilt of her lips.

"Yes." Dannie looked up at him, the silvery light of the moon bathing her face in its glow. "I feel like she's still keeping watch over me, and the ranch, my brothers. My father."

Evan's heart softened still more at the peek into her soul, the vulnerability in her voice. "She must be very proud of you."

Her hand fell from his shoulder to his chest, resting against it like the one he held over his heart. "What makes you think that?"

A breeze swept around them, stirring her hair, settling a few loose strands gently against her face. Evan stroked her cheek, sweeping the hair back behind her ear as he considered how to explain to her what he saw. What he knew about her.

"You possess an abundance of strength, Dannie. Yet for all of that confidence, that strong will, you have a gentle heart. I've watched you in your role as a cowgirl, a true picture of the American West in your hat and spurs, in your split skirts. But then I see the way you study your family, watching them, ready to steady them with your hands and your compassion, should they need you. I am...overwhelmed by you."

She blinked up at him, and her smile turned tremulous. "That's not exactly what a girl wants to hear, even if everything that came before was pretty as a picture."

He chuckled, cupping her cheek in his hand, amazed that she hadn't pulled away. Instead, she leaned in closer.

"Dannie, please trust me when I tell you that I could not be more admiring, more in awe of you. Every word is a compliment.

I have never met a woman like you in my life." He put both hands upon her waist, drawing her nearer with deliberateness.

Her breathing hitched, her gaze dropped momentarily to his lips, and the thought of kissing her consumed him. The desire had flickered once or twice in his mind, but he'd dismissed the idea as an impossibility. As something that could never happen. Something she would never allow.

She certainly meant to allow it now.

Dannie rose up on her toes, and he held her to him. He fit himself to her, from his arms around her waist to the tilt of his head, the slant of his lips against hers. She sighed and wound her hands up to comb her fingers through his hair.

Evan pressed his fingers into the soft fabric of her dress, her skirts brushing the tops of his boots. His awareness of her sharpened intensely. He felt her take in a breath between one press of lips and the next, and he knew she had to feel his pounding heart.

Her lips against his, her arms holding him close, and the sweet softness of her body molding to his was more perfect than he could've dreamed.

Evan had been created for this moment. He knew it, deep in his soul. Never before had he felt the touch of heaven as he did when he held Dannie.

When they broke apart, both needing more than a quick breath to regain their senses, he exulted further in the moment as her cheek laid against his chest. They recovered together, when he'd half expected her to reprimand him or else make one of her cutting, witty remarks. Perhaps she would find a way to compare him to a rattlesnake or a cactus.

He chuckled.

"What's so funny?" she demanded, snuggling closer to him by wrapping her arms around his waist.

"Me," he said aloud, inhaling the smell of the wild Arizona sky and wind, closing his eyes to seal the memory safely away. "I cannot begin to explain to you how my time in this desert has compared to what I expected. In so many ways it has been worse, but at this moment—everything is better than I could have dreamed."

He kissed the top of her forehead, then leaned back the better to study her expression.

Evan's heart shuddered, and the peaceful moment shattered.

Despite the darkness, he saw clearly the glint of tears in her eyes and the shine of their tracks upon her cheeks.

"Dannie?" he whispered, confounded. "You're crying, love. Did I do something wrong? Say something unkind?"

A KISS IN THE STARLIGHT SUCH AS THE ONE SHE AND EVAN SHARED was the stuff of dreams and fairy tales. Unfortunately for Dannie, she knew she must wake from her dream. There was no happily ever after for the handsome Englishman and the rancher's daughter.

The endearment he used when he spoke, sounding terrified of the tears upon her cheeks, didn't make what she had to do next any easier.

Dannie stepped back, her hands trailing down his shoulders to his chest. She put her palms flat against him, hesitated, then pushed him away. Slowly. Gently.

He staggered back a step anyway, as though she'd shoved him a lot harder.

"Thank you for the charming moment, Duke."

"Evan," he corrected, then snapped his jaw shut with an audible click.

She smiled at the correction, though she lacked the energy to make the expression at all convincing. "Evan. You didn't do anything wrong. But we both know—you aren't staying here. Not on this ranch. Not in Arizona. Not even anywhere on this continent. You're going back to England."

His head jerked up as though she had slapped him. He didn't

argue, though. Didn't say a word against what she'd stated. They both knew the truth. He could never stay.

"Whatever it is you came out west to find, this isn't your home. It isn't your world." She crossed her arms over her chest, holding herself together. "You have family and a place somewhere else. Your fun will come to an end."

The man drew himself up as though insulted. "My fun? Is that what you think this has been? An immature attempt at entertaining myself?"

She forced herself to laugh. "Now who's twisting words around? I think fun is a fine thing. Everyone should have an adventure or two if they can stand them. The way you talked about being here, about coming West looking for cowboys and gun fights, I know that's what you were after. And I'm not sorry for my part in it."

"And what, exactly, do you think your part entails?" He sounded almost bitter when he spoke, or disapproving. She couldn't tell which and refused to examine his tone closer than she must.

She rubbed the tops of her arms. The air had grown cooler in the sun's absence, sending a chill across her skin.

"I'm the rancher's daughter," she said, sounding timid where she had meant to come off as confident. "The personification of the desert. Wild and unpredictable. Prickly as a cactus. Just waiting for the right man to come along and kiss her senseless." She averted her eyes, looking up at the moon and then toward her mother's tree. Anywhere but at him. "You see, I read dime novels, too. I know the type of character I'm meant to play."

"You aren't a character in a cheap story," Evan said abruptly, coming closer and taking her by the shoulders. The intensity of his gaze sent a jolt of warmth through her. "You are the most real person, the most astounding woman, I have ever met. Dannie—"

She pulled away. "Stop. Please." She stepped around him, walking for the house.

He tried to walk with her, but she shook her head. "You need to go back to the bunkhouse where you belong."

He stopped when they came to the porch, but his words reached after her. "I care about you, Dannie."

She hesitated, her hand on the door. Dannie didn't turn around. There was no point in seeing the earnest expression that accompanied his words. She'd already seen it, every time he set out to prove himself. "You're a good man, Evan. I'm lucky to count you a friend. But that's all we can be." She opened the door. "Goodnight."

Dannie slipped inside the dark house and immediately removed her shoes, then ran up the steps to get to her room. No one stirred; no sound or movement revealed anyone else awake.

There would be no one to witness her heartbreak as she climbed into her bed, curled around her pillow, and cried for the loss of something too precious for her to ever possess.

Evan's heart, as good and honorable as he was, could never be hers. She had already broken once, into a thousand pieces when she was left behind. Not that Evan was anything like David had been. Evan was better. Honest. Kind. Mindful of her in a way David had never been. An honorable man.

He wouldn't ask her to return to England with him because he knew her. He knew she couldn't be part of that world. Boston had given her a taste of high society, of the "proper" way of doing things. She'd never measure up to the expectations of the English peerage.

She belonged on her father's ranch, far from lace tablecloths and silver teaspoons. A girl in spurs had no business waltzing with the son of a marquess.

No matter how much she wanted to keep him.

WATCHING DANNIE DISAPPEAR INTO THE DARK HOUSE OPENED A wound Evan hadn't known he possessed. Before they had kissed, he had imagined what it would be like. During the kiss, his soul had called out to hers. But when she stepped away, when she'd said nothing could ever happen, all the hope and rightness building in his chest had collapsed like a house of cards.

Great. He was even starting to *think* like her.

The troubling knowledge that she spoke the truth arrested him, made it impossible for him to call her back. He'd left England determined to prove he could make it in the American world of mountain ranges and cowboys. His dreams weren't the eccentric ramblings of a spoiled peer, as his father had always said. Evan was capable of more than running a small estate for the marquess until he died.

Evan backed away from the house, finally questioning the wisdom of seeking out Dannie. Beautiful, prickly, stubborn Dannie Bolton.

There was so much more in the world he could do and be, if only he'd been born in another place. Another time. If he'd been the son of a gentleman or a farmer or born on the range itself.

A fist tightened around his heart and squeezed, making him stop with a sharp inhale. He rubbed the spot on his chest, the same place she'd put her hand to push him away. And he'd let her. Because that was what an honorable man did.

And she was right.

As much as it galled him to admit the truth, she had only told him what he had tried to ignore.

He walked along in the darkness, though he'd rather do something more physical to release the tension building in his shoulders and the frustration curling within him.

Even if he wanted to stay in Arizona, even if the call of responsibility to his family didn't pull him, he had to go back to England. He didn't have the funds to stay in America forever, and while he could work and scrimp and save, starting from nothing to build something of himself, he couldn't ask Dannie to wait around while he did that. She deserved better.

His realization stopped him in his tracks. If he could stay, if his duty to his family didn't exist, he *would* stay.

For one glorious moment, he imagined a world in which he lived on the ranch, worked alongside Dannie, took the evening meal with her. At night, they'd sit by the fire in the parlor and read, laughing about their cheap novels, holding hands on the sofa. Then they'd go upstairs far earlier than he ever retired in England, knowing the new day would bring new work and challenges to overcome. Together.

Evan's throat tightened up as the vision swam before him.

As Lord Evan Rounsevell, son of the Marquess of Whittenbury, he had to return to England.

Evan's feelings for Dannie, new and bright, weren't what they needed to be to ask her to come back to England with him. She wouldn't do it. She'd never leave her family or the land she loved. With good reason. The gatekeepers of English society wouldn't allow her to step foot in their drawing rooms. Even if she was every inch a lady in her conduct and virtue, they wouldn't look past her birth.

He kicked an especially large stone out of his path. It slammed its way through the dirt and struck a fence pole.

A sharp bark came from inside the fence, and a pair of eyes gleamed through the darkness at Evan. Gus recognized Evan and gave another quick bark, perhaps a reprimand, before bounding to the gap in the fence and sliding beneath it.

The dog opened his mouth in a yawn, adding a whine to the movement, before bumping Evan's thigh with his shaggy head. Evan crouched down to bring his face level with the dog's as he rubbed the animal's ears. "You are a fine fellow, Gus."

The dog's tongue lolled out, and he tipped his head to the side, as though trying to understand Evan's words.

"It's perfectly all right, boy. I don't understand myself, either." He looked up at the night sky and realized the ache in his chest wasn't only due to the thought of leaving Dannie. But the knowledge that when he left Arizona behind, he'd lose something of himself in the process. Something valuable and bright. Something he had spent his life yearning to find, and here he had found it at last. But he had to give the piece of him up to return to England.

Didn't he?

CHAPTER TWENTY

They left at dawn. The cattle made the going slower than if the men had taken themselves and a wagon. Since there were only two heifers, they tethered the animals to the back of the buckboard wagon rather than herd them with the horses. Mr. Bolton drove, and the pace wasn't terrible. But the long road left Evan far too much time to think.

Frosty rode close to Evan, quiet for the most part. The cowboy said little most of the time. But after a while, he must have tired of being left to his own thoughts.

The ranch foreman addressed Evan. "You know, Benson is near the same distance as Tombstone."

The small talk surprised Evan enough that he stared at Frosty in silence. Though the two of them had to be close in age, Frosty's tendency to stay close-mouthed and taciturn made Evan forget the man wasn't a decade his senior.

"King prefers Tombstone, though. The train doesn't go through there. I think he might have something against it." Frosty shrugged one shoulder, as though he didn't think it was odd for someone to resent the idea of trains.

Even an odd conversation was better than being trapped in his thoughts of Dannie and how hurt she'd looked when she left him the evening before. "I came through Benson, then took a stagecoach to Tombstone."

"And that's where you met Dannie and the boys." Frosty nodded, thoughtfully. "I've wondered about things like that. S'pose you hadn't been in Tombstone that day. Or they hadn't. Where do you think you would be?"

"Working odd jobs somewhere else, I imagine." Evan directed his gaze across the wide expanse of desert before them, noting the green that had sprouted up with the arrival of the rains. The whole desert had bloomed, just as Dannie said it would. There were tall flowers, strange sprouts shooting up from oddly shaped cacti.

Unlike some of the more rural roads in England, the path to Tombstone hadn't turned to mud. He could see cracks and crannies where the ground had swallowed up the rain, but he saw no sign of standing water anywhere along their path.

A lazy bumblebee flew alongside Evan a moment before it broke off toward a patch of pink flowers, where several other insects already hummed.

"If I wasn't in the Territory," Frosty said, "I'd be in Missouri. That's where my family's from. St. Louis, Missouri."

Evan's mind took hold of the city name and shook out a few memories until Evan realized why that place sounded familiar. "Wasn't that the starting point for people who went west on the Oregon Trail?"

"Sure was." Frosty waved a hand at a passing horsefly, and his horse danced a step to the side. "My grandaddy thought about going west, but then stayed put in town and opened a dry goods store. He made a small fortune selling to the pioneers and trail bosses. Missionaries. Migrants. My pa did the same until they built the railroad. Then he turned the family store into a restaurant to serve people who stopped along the rail."

The uncharacteristic chattiness of the experienced cowboy hinted at some motive behind the sharing of his story. Or perhaps

Evan had turned too suspicious. He'd worked alongside Frosty for over a month. Maybe he'd finally earned the man's story.

"Does your family still own the restaurant?" Evan asked, curious as to what had taken Frosty from a comfortable life in Missouri out west.

"My sister and her husband took over a few years ago." Frosty stated the fact easily, without reservation or anything to indicate he minded that fact. "My pa passed away ten years ago. My ma went east. My sister was the oldest, and she wanted to run things. She writes, from time to time."

Evan kept his eyes on the trail, noting the familiar hills ahead. They were near enough to Tombstone that he could see wisps of smoke in the air from the mines and homes of the city. "Do you ever miss it? The city, or your family?"

"Not often." Frosty's eyes swept the surrounding land. "I knew that wasn't the life I wanted. Serving other folks three meals a day, and running myself ragged to do it? Dying behind a desk in some back office. That wasn't for me. My ma and sister understood. I left home with their blessing."

"A fortunate thing. Family support would mean fewer regrets." Evan forced a smile, his mind circling back to his own worries. He couldn't imagine his father condoning Evan doing anything other than returning to England to live out his life doing the family's bidding. Dying behind a desk in a study that didn't truly belong to him.

Frosty rubbed at his chin, casting Evan a look heavy with meaning. "It made it easier, but I would've left anyway. I think we get too tied up trying to be the person folk want us to be. In reality, that just makes for a long, hard, miserable existence. And I'm not saying I'm the man to advise you on things. Just to hear you talk, anyone would know you've got a better education than most men. But I've watched you since you arrived, Duke. You've taken to our way of life, our work, like you were born to it."

The compliment, unexpected as it was, made Evan sit straighter in the saddle. "Thank you, Frosty."

The cowboy waved Evan's thanks away with an impatient gesture. "It's not flattery, but an observation. If you like it here, stay. There. I've spoken my piece." Obviously uncomfortable with saying so much, and possibly regretting it, Frosty nudged his horse's sides and went ahead of Evan and the wagon.

Evan heard him speak to Mr. Bolton, then Frosty jabbed at his horse again and rode ahead of them both at an increased speed. He'd make it to Tombstone ahead of them.

Mr. Bolton threw a glance over his shoulder and waved Evan forward. After applying a quick kick to his gelding's sides, Evan and his horse came alongside the driver's seat of the wagon.

"Did you need something, King?" Evan asked, referring to his employer the way everyone else did, despite the oddity of the name feeling a little too much like thumbing his nose at his upbringing in the peerage.

The older gentleman pushed his hat back, then gave Evan a square look. "Frosty's gone ahead to sort out a buyer for the cows."

"Yes, sir." Evan had no idea what that had to do with him.

Mr. Bolton raised one dark eyebrow at him, which resembled Dannie's habit of doing the same whenever she felt the least bit skeptical toward Evan. The woman had obviously learned it from her father.

"Frosty's of the opinion you might decide not to come back to the ranch with us."

Evan's head jerked to meet his employer's stare again. "What? Sir, I assure you, I have every intention of continuing at your ranch until after the cattle drive. I would not leave without giving proper notice, either."

"That's what I said." Mr. Bolton's smile didn't quite reach his eyes as he turned forward again. "But Frosty knows we need the extra hands right now. And honestly, son. I've been preoccupied, but not blind."

Those words made Evan's entire body go cold, from his head

to the toes in his boots. "I never thought you were, sir." But he knew exactly what Mr. Bolton wanted him to know.

The cattleman said his next words with a slow, certain kind of cadence. "Dannie likes you, Duke. I'm not about to threaten you or forbid her from feeling what she does. But you've only promised us your time until August. That's coming on quick. You'll both have to live with yourselves, whatever happens between now and then."

Evan gripped the reins in his hands tighter, and his horse flicked an ear back at the movement. "I understand you, sir." And Evan did.

"I trust my daughter to sort out her life on her own. I won't interfere." King Bolton took off his hat, then wiped at his brow with a bandana. When he spoke again, it was with a brighter tone and a new subject. "Once we get to town, we'll drop these heifers at the stockyards. I've got a telegram to send. You can take care of your own needs after you help Frosty gather our supplies. If you go drinking, keep it light. We'll meet up around four o'clock to start back the way we came, or else make plans to stay the night."

That gave Evan several hours to himself, if he wanted them. "Thank you, sir." He let his horse fall back again, trailing behind the wagon.

Though he hadn't actively tried to hide anything from Mr. Bolton, or anyone else at the ranch, it galled him to know his interest in Dannie hadn't stayed a secret. They had an audience watching their romance unfold. While that knowledge made him wary, Evan had to admit to himself it also relieved him. Dannie had a supportive father and family at the ranch. Whatever happened, there would be people to look after her.

The business part of the trip didn't take long. By the time King and Duke had arrived at the stockyard, Frosty had already negotiated a price with the manager of the place. Money changed hands, the cattle joined a larger group in a pen, and King dismissed the men after giving them their pay.

"Fifteen dollars a week, and bonuses at Christmas and after

drives," Frosty said, reminding Evan what he'd agreed to weeks before.

A month's pay came in at sixty dollars. It was a small fortune for most men. Small enough that many a man likely drank or gambled it away almost as soon as it hit his hand. But Evan stowed the money away in a pouch tucked inside his shirt and tied around his neck.

Sixty dollars was enough for a train ticket all the way back to the eastern states. Possibly to New York. He could leave that very moment. No wonder Frosty had been concerned.

Evan followed the cowboy on the errands, while Mr. Bolton left them for the telegraph office and his own business. It didn't take long to put what they needed in the wagon, and then Frosty turned to Evan with narrowed eyes.

"What else you need to do today, Duke?"

Evan didn't hesitate before responding. "I'd like to sell my horse and see if I can get something better-suited to ranch work. Maybe two horses. I was wondering if you could take the time to help me with that purchase."

The worry that had darkened Frosty's gaze lifted, and his expression became almost friendly. "Horses? That's easy enough. Your pretty gelding will fetch a good price with the city folk who want to impress their neighbors."

Frosty knew what he was about, too. An hour later, Evan had a work-worn saddle, a cutting horse, and a mare who'd been on the range for four years. They were both horses of dubious parentage but were sturdy and used to the work.

"They'll still take some handling, so they know you and you know them. But there's good lines on them. I think they'll serve you well." Frosty looked over the horses, nodded to himself, and then pointed down the road. "Want a bite to eat? I'm paying."

"Then I will accept your generous offer."

They made their way over to a restaurant, the name on the front nearly worn off from wind and dust. *Smith's* was all it said. A waitress in a dark dress and clean apron had them settled at a table by the window, with coffee and soup, in the blink of an eye.

Frosty had gone back to his quiet ways, which left Evan with little to do other than people watch out the window. Tombstone, despite its gloomy name and sordid past, was a thriving town. The people were rising from the mining industry to make something of themselves, and Evan had to admit he liked the energy in the atmosphere.

He watched couples strolling down the boardwalk, arm-in-arm, and children skipping behind their mothers, laden with purchases. How so many people had come to make a life for themselves in the desert, he didn't know. But he liked feeling like he belonged right in the thick of things with them.

And he couldn't help but glance at a barbershop at the edge of the street, nearly out of his vision, and smile at himself. He'd met Dannie a month ago, in that town, down the street. She'd looked him up and down, found him wanting, and took him home under protest.

Given how their relationship had changed, blossoming like the desert after the rain, Evan wondered what she'd say about their first meeting now.

The waitress came back with plates filled with mashed potatoes, thick slices of bread, and steaks that covered half the dish. The waitress flashed both of them a flirtatious smile before mentioning she had apple pie, too. If they wanted something sweet.

Frosty said they'd think about it, and when she sashayed away he fixed Evan with one of his hard looks. "These town girls always seem to know when a man has money in his pockets, and they try to get you to spend it on 'em as fast as they can. I promise, if we say yes to that pie, she'll start trying to wheedle an invitation to the theater out of us. Or a visit to the drugstore for cream soda, at the very least."

Evan laughed, unable to help himself given Frosty's disapproving frown. "My dear sir, I must ask how you came to act like a man of sixty when we cannot be more than a few years apart in age."

Frosty snorted. He took up his steak knife and sawed at the meat. "I s'pose living a hard life ages a man." A glimmer in his eyes was the only thing that betrayed his amusement with Evan's question.

People came and went while they ate, and traffic on the road outside the window never ceased. Which was why Evan paid little notice to the two men in black suits who entered the restaurant, sweeping the room with hard stares.

"Uh-oh." Frosty saw them first. "Those two look like lawmen on the hunt."

At the same moment Evan looked up, one of them looked his way. He elbowed the other man, and the two of them came to where Frosty and Evan sat.

"You in any trouble I should know about?" Frosty asked quickly, voice low and his eyes on the men coming their way.

Evan shook his head, the movement small. "No."

But the men in black suits stopped at their table. They stood there, wearing bowler hats and gruff frowns. They were a matched pair—both in their mid-forties, with mustaches well-groomed, and suits that belonged in finer establishments than where they stood. They both wore guns on their hips, too.

"Evan A. Rounsevell?" one of them asked gruffly.

Exchanging a look with Frosty, Evan slowly came to his feet. "Yes, I am he."

The men relaxed, and one reached into his coat. "We have been charged to find you, by your brother, Lord Rothley." He held out a piece of paper to Evan, which he took and glanced over briefly. It was signed by his brother's hand, on paper bearing the name of a hotel in New York.

Evan couldn't keep the shock from his voice. "William is here? In the United States?" Never had William said anything complimentary about the country or expressed even the faintest curiosity about traveling over the Atlantic. He enjoyed visits to

Berlin, Paris, and occasionally Rome, but Evan thought such enjoyment had more to do with what Society expected than his brother's actual preferences.

The other man took up the explanation with a wide grin. "The earl is on his way to Arizona at this moment. His train will arrive in Benson next week. We sent word to him when your trail went cold here in Tombstone."

"Not cold," the other man said with a scowl at his partner. "We figured out you'd gone to work with a family west of here, but no one could remember the name of the ranch."

The other man didn't seem as perturbed as his companion. "We were going to ride out after your brother arrived to check the smaller settlements." Then he extended his hand. "Forgive us. I'm Steinman, and this is Shelby. We're investigators with the Pinkerton agency."

"Pinkertons." Evan gestured to the two empty chairs at the table. "Please, join us. I have always wanted to meet men from your well-established detective agency. The stories that make it to England about what you fellows have accomplished are incredible."

Frosty snorted. "Betcha they're all hat and no cattle." He eyed the agents with unconcealed suspicion. Evan loosely interpreted the phrase to mean the Pinkertons had a reputation they didn't deserve.

Shelby, the sterner of the two, glared at Frosty before taking a chair at the table. "We aren't here to regale you with stories, Lord Evan."

The title made Evan's gut twist most unpleasantly. "No. Forgive me. My brother sent you to find me. Is something wrong? His wife delivered their second child safely, did she not? Our father, he isn't—?"

Steinman spoke with a calm smile. "We are not aware of any of your family's circumstances in England, Lord Evan. Lord Rothley sent us to find you, so he can fetch you home."

"Home?" Evan repeated the word, and his imagination

conjured a pair of honey-brown eyes before he reminded himself of the rolling green hills dotted with sheep that were supposed to be his home. "He wants me back in England? Why?"

Shelby made a snuffling sound behind his mustache. "We do not question our employer's motivations where it is unnecessary to the case."

"My impression of the circumstances," Steinman said, giving his partner a somewhat exasperated look, "is that your family is concerned that you do not mean to return at all, given the abrupt nature of your departure."

Evan opened his mouth, momentarily ready to deny that possibility, but he hesitated to speak. Hadn't he imagined, quite vividly, what it would mean to stay in Arizona? His mind had conjured up images of staying, living as a cowhand, traveling from place to place doing odd jobs. And that had been before his kiss with Dannie. Before he'd awakened to his growing affection for her.

All three of the men at the table with him were staring at him with varied expressions; Shelby looked suspicious, Steinman appeared intrigued, and Frosty had a crooked grin in place of his previous scowl. Evan leaned against the back of his chair, considering the Pinkertons. "What were your orders, should you find me?"

They exchanged a glance before Steinman answered. "Our orders were to find you and tell you that your brother is looking for you. He implied that would be enough."

Shelby growled. "He said knowing he was here would mean your cooperation."

That sounded like William. Assuming compliance based solely upon his whims, much like their father. Not that William was a bad sort. Only irritating, from time to time. And a bit high in the instep.

"While I recognize my brother's expectations in this matter, I am afraid his lack of knowledge regarding my current situation means his inevitable misunderstanding." The multiple-syllabled words felt strange on his tongue. He'd spoken more casually of late, counting on his actions rather than his vocabulary to stress his points and impress upon others his capabilities. No wonder Dannie had thought him pretentious when they first met. "I have an agreement in place with another gentleman. I will not return to England earlier than September. And I may choose to stay considerably longer than that."

Frosty covered a cough that sounded like a laugh, and his cool blue eyes sparkled across the table at Evan with a fair amount of good humor. He'd earned the foreman's approval before that moment, but Evan had the feeling their relationship had veered into friendship with his statement.

The Pinkertons stared at him, Shelby looking thunderous and Steinman appearing confused. Shelby spoke first. "Our employer isn't going to like that, Lord Evan."

"I apologize for putting you both in a difficult position." Evan could well imagine William's shock when the agents delivered the message that his younger brother had refused to toe the line. "But my honor requires that I fulfill my promise to my employer. If Lord Rothley wishes to communicate with me in the future, he may direct all correspondence to the KB Ranch, care of Mr. King Bolton, in Sonoita."

As they stood, the Pinkerton agents did as well. Steinman wore an uncertain smile, while Shelby's countenance had darkened considerably. The friendlier of the two spoke first. "We understand honor, Lord Evan. But you must understand that our agency always delivers on our promises."

Frosty shifted, his posture changing to something most observers might see as casual. Yet Evan felt the tension in the way the cowboy leaned a little away, taking a stance that would allow him to spring into action without knocking Evan over in the process.

Taking his cue from Frosty, Evan let his arms hang more loosely at his side. "You promised my brother you would locate me, and you have done that. No one could speak against that."

Shelby's lip curled. "You pretentious types, always trying to use fancy words to get around the truth of a matter. Your brother paid us to insure you return to him. We mean to meet those expectations."

"My brother falsely assumed I had nothing better to do than adhere to his whims." Evan directed his words to Steinman, obviously the more reasonable of the two men. "I have my own business to see to, and I doubt either of you want to make my life or yours more difficult than necessary."

The restaurant around them had quieted, though at what point in their discussion anyone else started listening in, Evan couldn't say. They certainly had the attention of the room at present. A chill went through Evan as he realized how closely the situation resembled scenes he had read in his novels. Scenes of gunfights in Deadwood and Tombstone.

Except they were in a restaurant occupied by upstanding citizens instead of a saloon filled with ruffians. And if guns were drawn, Evan had no intention of fighting. His pride wasn't worth anyone's life.

Steinman brushed his fingers along the edge of his coat, as though thinking about the gun he likely kept on the belt beneath it. His gaze flicked from Evan's to Frosty, then back. "Let's not make a scene, gentlemen. Perhaps we could step outside—"

Shelby didn't wait for his partner to finish the suggestion before he grabbed for Evan's arm. Evan stepped away, hands coming up defensively.

Frosty stepped between the Pinkerton's and Evan, glaring. "You'd better listen to your friend here, Mr. Shelby. We don't want any trouble."

"You get outta the way and there won't be any," the Pinkerton snarled.

Steinman attempted to intervene, his gaze sweeping the room full of people. "Shelby, perhaps—"

But his partner's short fuse had burned up. Shelby put a hand on Frosty's shoulder to shove him out of the way, but Frosty ducked the shove—and the left-handed punch Shelby threw grazed Frosty's cheek.

Quicker than Evan could react, Frosty had rocked to the side and shot his own fist upward, catching Shelby beneath his chin. The Pinkerton stumbled backward, knocking over a chair and catching hold of the tablecloth, pulling it and everything on it to the floor with him.

Evan's reaction was to snatch both his and Frosty's hats up before they could join the agent on the floor. He pushed Frosty's hat into his chest. Steinman stood over his partner, eyes on Evan and Frosty, and his hand reaching into his coat.

Evan put his hat on his head and raised both hands, palms facing out. "Mr. Steinman, my brother didn't give you leave to take me by force. We've already caused that scene you wanted to avoid. I'm leaving with my friend." He tilted his head in Frosty's direction. "And that's an end to it."

Shelby sat up, hand on his jaw and eyes swirling with anger. Steinman looked down at him, concern on his features. "Perhaps it would be best if we confer with Lord Rothley before proceeding further, Mr. Shelby."

The downed agent swore and lurched to his feet. "No one lays a hand on me, you two-bit cowboy." Then he propelled his right fist directly at Frosty's face, but the cowboy had dropped his hat and easily deflected the punch with his left arm and swung up with a right hook that would've made any bruiser proud. He landed the hit in Shelby's face and the Pinkerton went down a second time, groaning and covering his nose with both hands.

"Maybe you better stay down there, Shelby," Frosty said, shaking out his hand with a smirk.

Evan saw the waitress in the doorway to the kitchen, as well as a middle-aged man coming in their direction with distress written clearly upon his features. Likely the owner of the establishment. Evan took several bills out of his pocket and dropped them on the empty table. His next words he directed to Frosty. "I think it time we meet with Mr. Bolton, if you are finished with your meal?"

Frosty grinned crookedly. "Sure am. Let's go. So long, fellows." He nodded at the Pinkertons as he retrieved his hat from the ground. Frosty dropped his own coins on the table, ignoring the way Shelby cursed from the ground. "Have a drink on me, boys. One for the road."

They left the restaurant without another word, and the moment they stood in the sunshine Frosty started to chuckle. "Duke, for a minute there, I thought you'd be crazy not to leave with them."

That caught Evan's attention. "Would you have gone with them?"

"Nope. But I'm not an English nobleman." Frosty shrugged and pointed down the street. "King's going to be pleased when he hears this."

Evan wished he could keep the Pinkertons' visit to himself, but that wouldn't be possible. Mr. Bolton needed to know that Evan's brother was in the Territory, in case strange letters or demanding telegrams started arriving at the ranch. But if Dannie found out, she'd be even more determined to keep away from Evan. His brother's insistence on Evan's return would reinforce Dannie's decision to maintain her distance.

She was the more intelligent of the two of them. He wanted to pursue the feelings he had for her. Nothing had ever compared to what he felt when he'd held her in his arms, kissed her, or even stood by her side in the rain, and at the laundry. A hole in his heart filled when Dannie sent her smiles or sass in his direction.

He hadn't even known his heart bore such a wound until he met her.

If only he could stay. Perhaps then, Evan might work to make Dannie's heart whole again, too.

CHAPTER TWENTY-ONE

June 1, 1895

When morning came, Dannie watched the sun rise with it. The beauty of the gray dawn promised an early start to the rain that day. Her father, Frosty, and Evan might be caught up in it. Arizona rainstorms weren't something to sniff at, given that a dry wash could turn into a flooding river within a few minutes.

The oncoming clouds meant she wouldn't get much of a chance to leave the house, either. Animals and people alike hunkered down on cloudy days. Usually, she didn't mind it. Rain came so seldom, and even rarely lasted all day long, that most people sat back and enjoyed the rest from their usual toil.

A full day of rain meant catching up on indoor chores, like mending hems or sewing a few stitches on something new. But Dannie needed more of a distraction than that. She'd spent the entire day before working outside, with the animals. She'd taken Gus out, Clark accompanying her, to give the younger cattle a lesson in minding the dog. The physical exertion necessary for that activity had kept her mind occupied and away from trouble-some thoughts of the Englishman.

By the time night fell, she'd rejoiced in her exhaustion. She would sleep, she had thought, deeply and without dreaming.

In reality, Dannie had laid awake for hours, watching the shadows on her wall. Thinking about Evan. Reliving his kiss.

When she finally slept, it was a shallow, restless kind of sleep. Filled with memories that became dreams, and dreams that followed her into waking. She left her bed almost as tired as when she'd entered it.

"Maybe some reading," she said aloud while she brushed her hair. Dannie sat before her mirror, dividing her hair into two sections to make a pair of long braids. "I could give Mr. Holmes another go."

They didn't have any new books. They hadn't purchased any in months to save money for the books the boys had to have for their schooling. The opportunity to spend time with a new novel was something that Dannie had missed before the days got longer, meaning more outdoor work and less time curled up by the fire to read.

She ran the brush through her hair, smoothing out the ripples from the night's sleep. "Or maybe I'll read some Jane Austen. Or Alcott." Women's stories were her favorites, of course. She'd liked Jane Austen, too, even though the writing was a touch old-fashioned. One of her few friends at boarding school had handed over a copy of the book *Emma*. The characters were witty, despite being flawed, and had to navigate a world in which the men made all the decisions.

Thinking about Jane Austen led to thoughts of England, which of course led to thoughts of Evan. What must he be like at home? It was difficult to picture him in an elegant drawing room, like those she had entered in New England. Not because of any lack on his part, of course, but because she had grown used to the sight of him in denim pants and leather gloves, with his shirt-sleeves rolled up while he worked. She'd seen him wear exactly that clothing when he hauled water, pushed a wheelbarrow, shot a gun, and slung a pitchfork.

Not to mention when he'd been elbow-deep in soapy water, a crooked smile on his face while he flirted and teased.

Dannie started when she recognized the look of longing in her reflection, then scowled and shook her brush at herself. "Stop that, Dannie. You can't imagine him in England? Ha. Try picturing yourself there."

She couldn't. Because she couldn't imagine her life away from the painted night sky or the sun-bronzed days of work. A horse beneath her, purple mountains in the distance, and the landscape wide and open as far as she could see. She'd been in Boston, with houses and people crowded in on one another. And there were merits to living that way.

"But not for me," she whispered, putting her brush down on the table. "And if I can't imagine running off to England to be with Evan—not that he's even *asked*—I sure don't expect him to stay here, eating Arizona dust and grit the rest of his life."

Giving herself one last stern look, Dannie twisted her hair into a bun atop the crown of her head. If she wasn't wearing a hat to go out, she might as well enjoy a different hairstyle. She put on her most comfortable dress, left her feet scandalously bare, and went down to the kitchen to find food.

Travis and Clark were already in the kitchen, with uncombed hair and in their stocking feet, books spread out on the table along with a plate of toast and bowls of oatmeal. Both looked up and said good morning when Dannie entered.

"Can you make the coffee, Dannie?" Travis asked. "Yours tastes better than mine."

"Sure thing." Dannie went to the kettle on the stove. "You boys studying all morning?"

"Until Ruthie kicks us out so she can cook," Clark answered.

Ruthie always cooked on the big supply days. She said it was a good way to reward those who left home and bring them back quicker. Mrs. Perkins had always agreed, then slyly added it was the best way to finish off any of the old supplies that might not keep.

As she worked on preparing the coffee for herself and her brothers, Dannie focused on that aspect of her father's trip. The fact that they'd stayed in Tombstone overnight meant the response to her father's telegram hadn't been immediate—if it had come at all. For her father's sake, Dannie hoped Mrs. Perkins still cared for him.

A broken heart didn't heal easily.

She sat down to enjoy her coffee with the boys, though their quiet work left her too much room for her thoughts. She wanted to confide in them. Tell them something of her worries. But her father hadn't shared with his sons about Mrs. Perkins yet, and it wasn't her place to tell them that news. Considering that they'd spent most of their growing-up with the affectionate older woman, Dannie couldn't think they'd mind her place as a stepmother.

Clark groaned, closing one of his books. "I hate algebra. The numbers and letters all mix together until I'm not sure whether I'm figuring out a square root or how to buy tickets to Chicago."

Dannie gave him a commiserating smile. "Dad says it's valuable knowledge. Calculating wages, cattle prices, percentages to give to partners—all of it is important."

"Maybe to you and Travis," Clark said darkly.

Travis wrote something out in a notebook on the table, then closed his textbook, too. "Even if you don't stick with ranching, you'll be grateful for the complex math."

Clark snorted. "Not likely." He rose from the chair and fetched the milk pitcher, pouring quite a bit of it into his coffee. "I'm not going east, either. I'm going north. Where it's cold and I only have grizzly bears for company."

"I suppose grizzly bears aren't known to bother themselves with algebra," Dannie drawled over the rim of her cup.

"What about you, Dannie?" Travis asked, crossing his arms over his chest and leaning back in his chair. Ruthie wasn't there to glare at him, though. "You staying at the ranch, or going off to England?"

Dannie nearly choked on her swallow of coffee, the hot drink going down her throat at odds with a different heat filling her cheeks. "What on earth—Trav, what are you talking about?" She put her cup down and covered her mouth, coughing more to try to get rid of the uncomfortable sensation in her throat.

Clark gave her a flat look, then looked at Travis. "They think 'cause we're young we don't notice things."

"You didn't notice anything. Jessica had to spell it out for you," Travis said with a smirk.

"Jessica? What does Jessica have to do with this?" Dannie looked between her brothers, confused and trying her best to avoid answering their questions or knowing stares.

Clark answered before Travis could. "Jessica said that Duke spent the entire dance mooning after you."

"Even when he was dancing with other girls, he kept trying to see where you were in the crowd," Travis added. "I saw it, too. Thought for sure he'd ask you to dance."

Acting too defensive would only let them know they were onto something. Instead, Dannie gave a single-shoulder shrug and tried to sip her drink again. More carefully this time. "He didn't ask me to dance, though, did he?"

"Not until two nights ago," Clark blurted.

Dannie's whole body went cold, then hot as an Arizona August. She spoke slowly, deliberately, horror in her tone. "What do you mean?"

Travis leaned across the table to punch Clark in the shoulder. "Now look what you did. Dannie, it wasn't that bad. We only saw the two of you under the tree, then I made Clark shut the drapes."

She rubbed at her temples. "You were both *watching* me?"

"Not on purpose," Clark said hastily. "I went to open the window, 'cause it was too hot in our room. Then I saw you and Duke talking."

"We couldn't hear anything," Travis added. "And I didn't let him open the window, or watch."

"Even though it was probably our duty to make sure you were safe." Clark grinned, the horrid imp. "Trav said you'd want privacy."

Dannie groaned and covered her face with both hands. She stayed that way as she spoke. "You saw us talking, then you saw us dancing. Is that really all?"

"Yep. Why? Did something else happen?" Travis asked, sounding deceptively unconcerned. "Anything we should know about, as your brothers?"

"Nope." Dannie dropped her hands and glared at him. "Nothing you need to worry about at all. And nothing else is going to happen, either. I told Evan—" She gritted her teeth. "Duke. I told him that he's going back to England, so nothing can happen at all."

"You could go with him," Clark said with a grin. "Then I could come visit the two of you."

"There is no 'two of us.'" Dannie averted her gaze to the table-top. "There isn't going to be, either. I belong here. He doesn't. That's all there is to it."

"If you like each other...." Travis let the words hang in the air. He was still a boy, for all that he thought he knew what love was, thanks to sweet little Jessica Harper. He probably thought the world was full of happily-ever-afters and sweet endings. But everything, *everything*, was more complex than that.

With those thoughts in mind and wanting to spare her brother's view of the world a little longer, Dannie gave him a tired smile. "I don't want to go anywhere but here."

"Duke will stay, then," Clark declared, opening another text-book. At fifteen, he wasn't as invested in conversations regarding the future or love as his brother was.

Travis didn't agree with Clark, but he met Dannie's eyes with a little more solemnity. "I like Duke a lot. I think he's smart, too. Maybe he won't go back to England."

"Who would choose Arizona over England without being born to the way we live?" she asked. Dannie took her coffee cup and stood. "I'm going to do some reading. You boys let me know if you need anything between now and dinner." With that, she closed the subject and took her leave of the room.

Their innocent observations, their surety that Evan might actually give up his life for hers, made her feel even worse. The tightness around her heart, the icy feeling in her stomach, remained there to keep her thinking more realistically.

Even if Evan stayed, it wasn't as though he'd made any declarations or promises to her. Suppose he didn't go back to England right away. Did that mean his future plans would include her after *one kiss*?

She settled on the couch that faced the window, looking out over her mother's garden and tree.

There was more to it than the kiss. She knew that. But it was easier not to think of all the little glances, the teasing conversations, and the way her heart sped up every time she caught Evan smiling at her. David Robertson had slowly lulled Dannie into thinking she loved him. But Evan had come into her heart like the storms, with a relentlessness that was as alarming as it was exhilarating.

Thunder cracked overhead, making her jump, and the rain finally broke over the house. Raindrops fell, the speed at which they ran off the porch increasing in seconds. Dannie sent a prayer to Heaven for the safety of the men coming from Tombstone. If they'd left at dawn, they'd be about halfway home by this time.

She watched the rain, then realized she'd sat down without selecting a book. Her mind had been too preoccupied. Too wrapped up in Evan.

Dannie watched the tree sway in the wind and rain, and she imagined what it would be like to have Evan beside her at that moment. And why not? She couldn't rid her thoughts of him anyway. Perhaps indulging herself, just a tiny bit, would help. She'd watched her parents sit where she sat and seen the way her father put his arm around her mother, their heads tilting toward each other. As a little girl, she'd been comforted by their obvious love. And she had taken it for granted that one day she'd have a husband who put his arm around her, who adored her, the same way.

It was so easy to picture Evan as that man.

With her eyes closed, Dannie listened to the rain and wondered at her sanity for falling in love with an Englishman.

THE STORM KEPT THE MEN TUCKED UP AGAINST THE SIDE OF A boulder for two hours, a tarp stretched over their heads and the wagon. The rain didn't trouble the animals, and Evan's new horses kept looking back at him with boredom. The wagon mules seemed exceptionally pleased to take the opportunity to nap, still in their harnesses.

Frosty and Mr. Bolton took their cue from the mules. They sat with their backs to the rock, hats over their eyes, resting. As if they hadn't had enough sleep staying in Tombstone the evening before.

Mr. Bolton had come back from the telegraph office when they closed at five o'clock, a spring in his step and a smile stretched wide across his face. He'd paid for their hotel rooms at a modest establishment, then took himself off without saying a word as to his important business. While Evan wasn't one to pry, it would've been nice to know what kept them overnight in Tombstone.

The Pinkertons had come to see him again at the hotel. They informed him they sent a telegraph to Benson for his brother, and Steinman politely asked Evan to accompany them. Shelby glowered when Evan again denied them.

He was going back to KB Ranch. Back to Dannie. And he'd not leave again until he'd fulfilled his agreement with Mr. Bolton. It already hurt to think about leaving, and he wasn't going to let anyone rob him of the time he had left in Arizona. Not because he wanted to keep playing cowboy, like a child refusing to leave toys behind in a nursery. But because he knew the moment he left this new life he'd discovered, all the weight of his previous life would fall upon his shoulders and heart, never to fall away again.

Generations of his family's affairs would smother him, his responsibilities toward his family would imprison him, and he'd have to live up to the expectations and strictures of English society for the rest of his life. Walking the path carved in stone before him, as everyone in the peerage must. Standing behind his father first, and later his brother, a silent and supportive shadow to the more powerful man.

Keeping watch over a little estate full of sheep that weren't even his.

The damp and his thoughts combined to make him cross. Life itself chafed at him, and the only thing that would make it better would be to see Dannie.

He'd fallen in love with her.

The knowledge had come to him full force the previous evening when he bid farewell a second time to the Pinkertons. He'd lain in bed for hours, thinking through every reason he had to return to England when the seasons changed.

Dannie had entered his mind again and again, disrupting his thoughts with her smile, the spark in her eyes, and the way she'd felt in his arms. He didn't want to leave her. And he knew—with a sureness he couldn't explain—that walking away from her would be the worst mistake of his life.

When the rain finally let up enough for them to travel, Evan moved at double the speed of the other two men to put their animals and gear back in order. He didn't bother to conceal his rush, either.

"Someone put a burr in his blanket?" Frosty sounded amused when he spoke to their employer. Evan ignored him.

"It's probably the idea of his brother nipping at his heels," Mr.

Bolton answered in his lazy drawl, climbing up into the wagon seat to drive the team. "Take it easy, Duke. No one is coming to drag you off to England."

Evan again kept his mouth shut. He wasn't about to correct Mr. Bolton, or to inform him that Evan's mind dwelled on his pursuit of Mr. Bolton's daughter rather than the Pinkertons' pursuit of *him*. Once they were well underway, soaked by the light rainfall and hot beneath the oiled rain slickers Mr. Bolton had provided, Evan relaxed.

He needed to speak with Dannie.

They had to go slow over several low patches of ground where the rainfall had created mires of Biblical proportions. Finally, they came to the now-familiar road from Sonoita to the KB Ranch.

The cutting horse Evan had purchased sensed his hurry and responded with irritation, flicking its ears and trying to move faster than Evan thought polite. He stayed with the slow-plodding wagon, grateful the mules had picked up a little more speed when they realized they were close to their barn and their feed.

When they passed beneath the iron KB Ranch sign, something deep within Evan shifted. And when they crested that last rise, the ranch house ahead of them, antelope to the north leaping through the tall grass and the mountains stretching out in either direction to the east, Evan's soul shifted. Everything fell into place.

The rain had abated, though the clouds remained hanging over their heads. The gray sky didn't bother Evan in the slightest. Not when he caught sight of a woman coming out to the front porch to wave at them. Then she disappeared inside again, likely to wait for them out back, or to tell others of their arrival.

Getting a moment alone with her, Evan realized, would take careful planning. Especially if she still felt skittish about their kiss. For her, nothing had changed since they last saw each other. For him, the world continued to shift, and he couldn't be certain when it would stabilize once more.

Ed and Buck met them in the dry cover of the zaguán. Travis, Clark, and Lee waited, too, to take the purchases inside while the men saw to the animals. When Evan came through to the back, leading his horses to the dry barn, he saw Abram and Ruthie on the back porch. But no sign of Dannie.

"When everything's squared away, you men come in for something warm to eat," Ruthie called from the porch.

Evan's stomach growled, reminding him he'd barely eaten his breakfast in his agitation to be on the road that morning. Mr. Bolton left the men to see to the animals. Buck took the mules in hand while Frosty and Evan took care of their own mounts.

At last they left the barn for the house and crossed the gravel-and-mud strewn yard to the porch. Evan, despite his hurry, wasn't the first inside.

The table bore a few of the goods they had brought back. Ruthie went through it all, handing things off to the boys with instructions on where everything went.

Dannie and Mr. Bolton were nowhere to be seen.

"Let's get this table cleared up. Ed, Buck, Frosty, and Duke—you just have a sit-down. The boys will finish up. I'll get you men some coffee and then put a meal on the table in a bit. We weren't sure when you'd be back."

The men obeyed, and Ed immediately started asking about Evan's new horses. Frosty wasn't about to answer for him, so that left Evan talking about exchanging his thoroughbred gelding for two new creatures. His eyes stayed on the door leading from the kitchen to the rest of the house.

The minute he saw Dannie enter, he was on his feet.

The other men stared at him like he'd lost his mind, but Dannie's gaze meeting his put everything else out of focus. Her expression wasn't easy to read, but he saw the glow of welcome before she turned away to help Ruthie.

Mr. Bolton entered a moment later and cleared his throat, bringing all other talk and movement to a halt. He surveyed the room with a gleam in his eye. "I have some news for all of you.

First of all, I want to thank everyone for taking on more than their share these past months. Despite being short-handed in the bunkhouse, you men have done well keeping things going on the ranch." He nodded to Frosty, then turned his attention to where Ruthie and Dannie stood near the large oven.

"And Ruthie, we'd be lost without your help in our home. Thank you for everything you've done to help Dannie and the boys, too. I'll be forever grateful for you and Abram's friendship."

Ruthie's usual knowing smile turned gentle. "That's what we do, Mr. Bolton. We take care of each other."

He nodded his understanding, then swept the room with a serious expression which slowly changed to a smile as he spoke. "Now for the news. You all know we remained later than usual in Tombstone while I awaited a reply to a telegram. Well. The reply came minutes before the office closed for the evening. You see, I sent a message to Mrs. Perkins, asking her if she'd come back. Not as our housekeeper, but as my wife." The gleam in his eye spoke clearly of his feelings as he regarded his children. "She said she'd be on the next train home." Emotion choked the end of the man's statement, and his joy was apparent in his voice.

Everyone clamored to congratulate him at once, including his sons. The men rose from the table to shake his hand. The boys and Dannie embraced their father. Ruthie gave him a congratulatory kiss on the cheek. Evan shook his hand like the others, but something about the way Mr. Bolton looked at him was different. Then the old rancher subtly nodded toward Dannie, who wiped at her eyes near the door.

"Told her about the Pinkertons," Mr. Bolton said, too quiet for the others to hear in their excited chatter. "Be kind to her, Duke."

"Yes, sir." Evan went back to his place at the table, giving Dannie plenty of room for the moment. He tried not to stare at her during the impromptu congratulatory feast, too. But his eyes kept finding hers, and every time he looked up he discovered she was watching him, too. She'd blush and turn her gaze away, never addressing him during the meal. But she was paying attention.

And she probably had some questions for him. While Evan didn't have all the answers yet, he at least knew the most important one.

He loved Dannie Bolton. He'd fight to keep her in his life as long as possible.

CHAPTER TWENTY-TWO

A voiding a man in order to keep her heart intact would've been much easier in a town. But on a ranch? Dannie couldn't possibly keep clear of Evan for more than a day. She managed, all day Saturday after lunch, to keep to the house while he went back out to do his usual chores. She finally found a book and curled up in her room, successfully avoiding everyone for hours.

With the arrival of dawn on Sunday, Dannie woke with a determination to guard her heart while showing Evan she wouldn't belabor their kiss. They were friends. And with the news the Pinkertons brought of his brother's presence in the territory, their days were numbered anyway.

Evan seemed to think his brother would leave him alone, knowing he intended to fulfill his family obligations at some point, but Dannie doubted it would be that easy.

She put on her Sunday best. The first Sunday of June meant a visit from the pastor in Patagonia. Their small community had tried, and thus far failed, to find someone permanent. But they didn't have enough funds to support a man with a family, and few men wanted to come out to the middle of nowhere to preach to a handful of cowboys and their wives.

Dannie entered the kitchen to find her father already at the table, a plate of eggs and toast in front of him, and a newspaper spread out between him and his food. He always picked up back issues of the newspaper when he visited a town, then read everything in the appropriate chronological order. He called it "playing catch up" with the world at large.

Dannie poured herself coffee and slid into the chair at his right hand. "You going to speak to the pastor about getting married soon?"

"Sure am." He folded up the paper and put it aside, smiling at her with an easiness she hadn't seen in some time. He'd been holding his feelings close for so long, and she hadn't even realized it. "I think first week in July should work. Loretta has you in the house as a chaperone, like always, and Ruthie on the property. I doubt we'll scandalize too many people."

"I've been thinking about you getting married. I was wondering if you and Mrs. Perkins are going on a honeymoon." Dannie kept her gaze on the dark liquid in her mug, blushing despite herself. "Or if you'd rather me and the boys go visiting so you have the house to yourselves for a while."

"That's mighty generous of you." Her dad sounded amused, but he thankfully didn't tease her about the subject. "I'll ask Loretta what she prefers when she returns. She's been gone so long, I'm not sure she'll want to leave again right away. But we'll see."

Dannie relaxed and smiled away her discomfort. No one really *wanted* to think about their parents going on a honeymoon, despite the facts of life involved. Putting aside the discussion gave her more time to get comfortable with the idea of her father marrying again, and all that such a thing implied for their family arrangements.

The housekeeper's room had been across from Dannie's, and down the hall, the brothers shared a bedroom across from the guest room.

"We'll have two guest rooms now," Dannie said, then laughed. "Not that we've ever had many guests to use them."

"Ain't that a fact." Her father pushed his cold eggs around his plate, a sharp v forming between his eyebrows. "I've been thinking, too. About your future, and the boys. Your mama and I always said when y'all grew up to courting age we'd start building houses. I thought about it when you were away at school. But with the droughts, it never happened."

"Houses are expensive," Dannie said with an easy shrug. "And it's not as though I'll be tying the knot anytime soon." She didn't mean for her voice to fall, to sound so disappointed, in that fact. The memory of Evan hanging laundry at her side came to mind, along with the fresh smell of clean cotton, and the feel of his hand wrapped around hers while they stood in the rain.

Her father's words intruded on the memory. "There's that new lumber mill just east of us, by Fort Huachuca. I bet I could work out a deal with the owner, get a discount in exchange for some calves or some such thing."

Dannie raised her gaze to his, noting the gentleness in his eyes, the hopeful way he smiled at her. "Maybe someday." Her throat threatened to close up, but she forced herself to respond without sounding too wistful.

A house of her own, on the ranch. Wouldn't that be something.

Her father nodded, allowing her to let the subject rest. "Everyone's to church today," he said abruptly. "Except Buck. I asked him to stay back and keep an eye on things." As Buck usually volunteered for that duty, and got it half the time, this wasn't a surprise.

The ranch required that their cowboys attend services once a quarter, at the least. Their choice of where they went. Ed often rode out to a Catholic church, established in the sixteenhundreds by Spanish missionaries. Sometimes he stayed to listen to the pastor, too. He'd once told Dannie it depended on what kind of direction he needed at the moment. He'd been raised

Catholic by his mother, Methodist by his father—who thought the Methodist way allowed him the most leeway to apply his ancestors' beliefs to the faith he'd accepted into his life.

Frosty didn't seem inclined to care about religion, at least not enough to discuss it.

Dannie sipped at her coffee, reflecting that she needed a little more peace in her life at present. Evan had thrown her out of her comfort zone like a greenhorn thrown from a bronco. And she'd reacted poorly to him from the beginning, lacking the compassion her mother had always shown to others.

When the time came to go to town, Dannie, Ruthie, and all three boys climbed in the wagon. Abram drove, his wife next to him, and the rest of them sat in the back. King Bolton, Frosty, Ed, and Evan rode horses. Everyone wore their Sunday best.

"We really need a permanent pastor," Abram remarked in the quiet of the drive.

"Good luck finding one." Ruthie adjusted the wide-brimmed straw hat she wore, a beautiful creation topped with cherries that looked entirely real. "It takes a special kind of person to make this place home."

Dannie watched Evan from the corner of her eye, where his horse kept pace next to the wagon. It did take something special to bring people to the desert, and something more to make them stay.

The sermon that morning, delivered with the pastor's usual deliberateness, didn't ease Dannie's heart much. Though she agreed with everything said, applying the principles of ministering to the sick didn't quite stick to her current situation. And, though she felt a stab of guilt at realizing it, her mind wandered many times during the hour-long discourse.

Since Mr. Barnaby only made it out to them once a month, if that, he tended to run long in his sermonizing.

The rain clouds had gathered by the time they walked out of the building, but no one had planned on staying for a picnic in the middle of monsoon season. Only a few families had small children, and they lingered to let their little ones play together.

Dannie went to the wagon ahead of her family, while they stopped to mingle with the Masons.

Only when she prepared to climb in the wagon did Dannie realize Evan had followed her. She put both hands on the open back of the wagon, to push herself up and in as she had since girlhood, when warm hands went around her waist and lifted her upward.

The noise that escaped her lips—*not* a squeak, she told herself—was followed by his chuckle. "Sorry, Dannie. I couldn't help it."

She turned, sitting on the back of the wagon her feet dangling. She straightened her skirts, relieved they had stayed in place. "Evan, you've got to warn a girl before you go around manhandling her."

"Yes, ma'am." The cowboy-like drawl with which he spoke made her head come up fast, and their gazes met. He wore a smile without any sign of repentance. "Even though I find it immensely entertaining to surprise you, I will refrain from doing so in future."

Her lips twitched. "I don't mind some surprises. Just not the ones that startle me, like a rattler underfoot."

His eyebrows raised. "Are you comparing me to a snake?"

Dannie relaxed, welcoming his light tone. "Nope. I don't think you're mean enough to compare to a rattler."

"That sounds like a rather dubious distinction. Which desert animal, pray tell, would you equate with my character?" He crossed his arms and leaned against the side of the wagon, a handsome sight in his clean white shirt and dark vest. He'd taken off his coat during the sermon, which wasn't uncommon in the Arizona heat. "A *javelina*? Coyote? Perhaps some type of buzzard?"

Folding her hands in her lap, Dannie considered the question carefully. "I can't be sure. Those are all irritating interlopers on a ranch."

"Ah, so you don't see me as an interloper anymore?" His eyes sparkled at her, and his smile went crooked. "That's a relief."

"If I had to choose," she said, ignoring his charming grin as best she could. She couldn't afford to swoon over his charm. Not right in front of him. And she needed to keep a straight face. "I would say you're something like Gus."

His eyebrows drew together. "Gus. The dog?"

"The *ranch* dog." Dannie affected a tone she'd heard often enough from her instructors at the school in Boston, lecturing him. "He wasn't born to the desert, but he's adapted, and even proven himself useful. I would say that comparing you to Gus is a compliment. He's a fine animal. Handsome, too, for a dog." He snorted when she said that, but she kept on speaking. "He's loyal and hardworking, never complains. And just look at how fine a father he's proving, looking after Fable and the pups even though she's a grouch."

The only warning Dannie had that his next words were more than teasing was the flicker of mischief in his green eyes. "You think I would make a fine mate and father? A very fine compliment, indeed. Even if a tad inappropriate."

Heat rushed into her cheeks, and Dannie sputtered for a moment before getting a word out. "Evan Rounsevell, that isn't what I said—"

"But what you implied with your compliment. Thank you." His eyes still twinkled, and he slid closer, bringing their gazes almost even. "For what it's worth, I would consider it an honor to look after *you*. Even when you're a grouch."

The wagon rocked suddenly, with Travis climbing in from the side. Evan stepped back, giving Dannie room to breathe at last. The other members of their homestead had appeared, all talking at once, mounting horses and climbing into position on the wagon. Evan and Dannie's moment had passed.

Disappointment settled heavily in her chest as he mounted his horse.

On the ride back to the ranch, Ruthie went over the sermon with the boys. Dannie listened with half an ear, grateful for Ruthie's help with her brothers, but unable to bring herself to join in the conversation. She stayed quiet, and she noticed Evan didn't take part in any talk, either, though he rode between Ed and her father.

When Abram pulled the wagon to a stop in the yard, Dannie's brothers and Lee spilled out over the sides of the wagon like puppies crawling out of a nesting box. Abram walked all the way around the front of the wagon, speaking light praises to the mules before assisting his wife to the ground.

Dannie slid as gracefully as she could so her legs went over the back of the wagon, and she almost looked to see where Evan was. Maybe he'd help her down the way he'd helped her up—

Buck appeared in front of her, hand outstretched. "Welcome home, Dannie."

She had to swallow her disappointment and force a smile onto her face. "Thank you, Buck." Her hand went into his as she slid off, her feet hitting the gravel with a crunch.

"What did I miss today?" Buck asked, expression eager and a big grin on his face.

"Admonishment to care for the sick and needy," Ruthie answered abruptly, walking behind them toward her house. "And reminders to do good works."

Buck raised his eyebrows. "Fine words to live by."

"Right." Dannie shook the dust from her skirt and wished she could get rid of Buck that easily. She turned toward the house. "Hopefully you can come next time, so you won't miss anything."

"Yep." He walked a few steps with her. "Dannie, I was wondering if you'd come for a walk with me later. Maybe after supper."

It took a great deal of self-control to keep her expression calm. "A walk?"

"Sure." He grinned and swept his hat off, as though just realizing it would be more polite to address her with his head uncovered. "Before the sun goes down. I'd like to talk to you about something."

Dannie had once stuck her foot in her boot with a frog waiting for her inside. This conversation was nearly as unpleasant and just as uncomfortable as that situation had been. But it presented her with an opportunity to have her say, and possibly let Buck down gently. "After dinner, I'll meet you on the front porch."

He looked entirely too pleased with himself. "Good. See you then." He plopped his hat back on his head and ambled away.

When Dannie turned back toward the house, she caught Evan watching her from the back porch, where he spoke with her father. He made eye contact with her, his expression momentarily solemn, then gave his full attention back to his employer. Had he heard anything Buck said? Or guessed at it?

Not that it was any of his business. But it would be nice to talk to him about it. Maybe get his opinion on what she ought to say to Buck, to let him know she wasn't interested in any romantic entanglements with him. Or anyone in her father's employment.

Except Evan. Who, for all she knew, still planned to leave.

At war with her thoughts and her heart once more, Dannie brushed by Evan and her father and went directly inside and upstairs to her room, to change her clothes so she could prepare the Sunday meal for her father and brothers.

Maybe cooking would take her mind off things.

Then she burned the cornbread.

"It's all right, Dannie. If we just scrape off the bottom, it's not so bad," Clark said, attempting to be helpful.

Travis wasn't nearly so diplomatic. "Mrs. Perkins will be back soon. Then you won't have to worry about cooking."

"Boys." Her father's smile had twitched beneath his mustache. "Your sister is a fine cook. Burning one batch of cornbread out of twenty isn't something worth kicking up a fuss. Take it easy on her." Then he'd eyed her, a bit of concern in his gaze, before excusing himself from the table.

The boys helped her clean up, and Travis offered to make the evening meal. Perhaps feeling penitent. Though that meant beef stew and leftover biscuits from the day before, Dannie accepted and went on her way.

Of course, that left her with time on her hands. Again.

Time she spent thinking about Evan rather than fixing on what to say to Buck.

After dinner, she checked her hair once in the mirror, then wrapped her favorite shawl around her shoulders. She went to her father's study and knocked. "Dad? I'm going on that walk with Buck now."

The door opened, and she looked up to see her father's deep frown in place. "You'll be all right?"

"Sure, Dad. We'll be right by the house."

He nodded once. "Give a shout if he gets moody on you. My window's open."

Dannie sighed. "I don't think he's going to take the conversation well, but I doubt it'll cause any problems. I'll be nice. I promise."

"I'm not worried about your behavior, Dannie-girl." Her father put his arms around her in a quick embrace, then kissed her forehead. "I taught you how to handle yourself, didn't I?"

At her affirmative nod, he released her, and Dannie went to the front door with the feeling that she had walked into a blind alley.

EVAN'S SKIN CRAWLED WITH IRRITATION OVER BUCK'S SMUG behavior. The moment he'd had the chance, the swaggering cowboy had told Evan he had invited Dannie on an evening stroll, and she'd accepted. The fact that he wanted to get a rise out of Evan actually kept Evan calm.

Dannie had enough intelligence and good sense to know what Buck was after, and given that she'd hidden from the cowboy the other day, she'd likely been avoiding a conversation of the very kind Buck likely wanted to have. It didn't take someone of Evan's education to realize she meant to clear the air with Buck rather than encourage his pursuit of her.

Which meant things might get uncomfortable for Dannie during their little walk.

In the hours that passed between their return from Sunday services and sundown, Evan debated with himself what course of action he should take, or if he had any business involving himself at all.

When the evening crept in upon them, and Buck went off through the zaguán with a whistle to circle to the front of the house, Evan waited a few minutes before standing to follow. He'd been reading in the bunkhouse, a book he'd picked up in Tombstone.

Frosty watched him stand, his head tilted back and expression somewhat disapproving. "You going to stay out of trouble there, Duke?"

"I hope so." Evan picked up his hat from his bunk. "At least, I don't intend to make any of my own."

After considering this, Frosty nodded and turned back to his newspaper. "Keep in mind, you both have to work together come morning."

Evan slipped out of the bunk room and through the cool corridor of the adobe structure, then circled around to the front of the house. He didn't slink into the shadows, or crouch secretly behind a bush. He just stood at the corner of the house and listened, arms folded, and stance relaxed, in case Dannie had need of him.

Not long after he arrived, he heard Dannie and Buck's voices. They weren't speaking loud enough for him to hear, and he made it a point to focus his attention on the hills in the distance. With the house facing east, from where Evan stood, he could already make out a few stars on the horizon.

They were close enough to the house that Buck wouldn't dare raise his voice.

But no sooner had that thought crossed Evan's mind, lending him some relief, than he saw the two of them walking eastward, away from the house. Their backs to him.

Alert now, Evan debated another moment if he should follow. How far would they go with darkness coming on? He knew as well as anyone how dangerous it was to walk in the tall grasses without the benefit of clear sight. Snakes were one of many dangers someone might stumble upon in the dark.

As they became silhouettes in the distance, easily a few hundred feet in front of him, Evan followed.

A woman in England would never step out with a man, with dark approaching, unchaperoned. Such an action would ruin her reputation. While rules were more lax in America, Evan wouldn't leave Dannie alone in a compromising situation with a man who'd shown a lack of honor.

They stopped ahead of him, with Evan standing silently, and started talking again.

Buck reached for Dannie's hand, but she tucked it behind her back. Evan heard her speaking, though he couldn't make out what she said.

Buck's response was considerably louder. "What do you mean, you don't care about me?"

Dannie's voice was only a little louder. "I said *in that way*, Buck. I'm not of a mind to court you."

The cowboy answered tersely and more quietly, and Dannie took a step away from him.

"I don't see how that's any of your business," she said, sounding as high and mighty as the first time Evan had met her. Putting on that Boston polish with her stubborn cowgirl tongue. "I understand you are upset, and I am sorry that I cannot return your feelings. But I believe you're a good man."

"Isn't that cold comfort," he said, voice raised again. "You'll make eyes at the greenhorn but won't give an honest American a chance? What's wrong, Dannie? Ain't I smart enough for you? Is it the accent? Or maybe you just like wanting what you can't have."

"That is enough, Buck." Dannie didn't sound distressed. But she sounded plenty angry.

Evan shifted from one foot to the other, frowning at the situation as a whole. He didn't like being brought into the argument, especially given Buck's point. Evan wasn't going to stay. Everyone knew that. Dannie knew it.

"Maybe you just don't know what it's like for a real man to care about you. First you had that Yankee people won't stop jawing about, and now an English rat. Let me show you how it's done in the territory." Buck grabbed her arm before she could step out of reach, and Evan started forward at a run—

Dannie's movements were efficient, and quick enough that it took Evan a moment to realize what had happened, but Buck suddenly doubled up, groaning, and fell to his knees. Then he started cursing, and by the time Evan came to stand next to Dannie, Buck had fallen sideways on the ground.

Dannie didn't even look up right away, though her hands were on her hips and her posture spoke of a battle-hardened queen rather than a frightened maiden. "Think you can get him back to his bunk?" Dannie asked without so much as glancing at Evan.

His lips twitched. How long had she known he was there?

"Indeed, madam. It would be my pleasure."

"Thanks." She whirled on her heel and stomped away, and Evan watched her go with a grin. He'd been prepared to lay Buck out flat, but Dannie had the situation handled. Maybe he should have known that would be yet another difference between her and the sort of ladies he had known in England. A different kind of life meant a different way to prepare for those sorts of unpleasant encounters, he supposed.

"Come along, Buck." Evan bent and took Buck by the arm, hauling him to his feet. "Let's get you back—"

A fist flew into Evan's jaw. Buck had thrown a vicious right hook, and Evan had let his guard down too soon.

He stumbled back, nearly landing on his rear, but caught his balance. He glared at the man in front of him. "I don't wish to fight you, Buck. Frosty said it's not allowed."

Buck swore colorfully, if not entirely intelligently. "You're to blame. She'd been friendly enough until you showed up."

"I doubt that." Evan put one foot back, stabilizing himself against another swing if it came. "You need to calm yourself. Think before you make a mistake."

"Mistake? Knocking you down a peg would do everyone a favor." With that, Buck charged Evan, fist swinging upward.

Evan bobbed away, his guard up, and experienced a wave of gratitude that William had insisted they box together at the club. "I have no quarrel with you, or anyone else."

"Yeah? Because you're a chicken-hearted limey." Buck charged and swung again. This time, Evan caught Buck's wrist with his right hand and delivered an uppercut to Buck's jaw with the left.

Buck went flying backward, and Evan realized Dannie had returned. He saw the flash of her skirts from the corner of his eye and held his hand out, silently commanding her to stay back. He didn't take his attention off his opponent.

Staggering to his feet again, Buck let out an undignified roar and charged, coming for Evan's midsection like a bull bent on goring him. Evan dropped his shoulder right as Buck hit, sending the cowboy flying over Evan's back, and onto the hard-packed earth.

"Stay down, Buck."

When Buck only answered with another string of profanity, then rolled onto his knees, Evan prepared for another charge.

A deep voice came from behind, the Texan drawl unmistakable. "Buck. That's enough. Take your horse and camp at the northern point."

Even in the semi-darkness, Evan could see the color leech from Buck's face. Mr. Bolton had arrived, and clearly saw enough to know it was Buck causing the problem and had issued his command with the same authority a king exercised over his court.

King Bolton stepped up alongside Evan. "Don't come back until Tuesday. That will give me a chance to decide what to do with you."

Buck stood, picked up his hat from where it had fallen to the ground, and slunk away. Evan watched him go, alert for another unexpected attack, and Mr. Bolton stayed beside him. Dannie was still at the edge of Evan's vision, too.

Only after Buck disappeared around the corner did she approach them. "Daddy, I'm sorry. I didn't think he'd take it so hard."

"You're a pretty girl, Dannie. Some men think that means you oughta be grateful for that kind of attention." King Bolton shook his head. "You all right?"

"Yes, Daddy."

Then he looked at Evan. "And you, son?"

Evan worked his jaw a moment, testing the damage done. "Bruised, but otherwise fine."

"Good man." Mr. Bolton looked from Evan to his daughter. "Maybe you should sit on the porch a bit. Get some fresh air and clear your head." He looked at Evan, appraising him openly. "You too, Duke." Then he strode away, his walk that of a man with great confidence regarding his place in the world.

"He's bossy sometimes," Dannie said, sidling up next to Evan. She adjusted her shawl and avoided his eyes when he looked down at her. "You don't have to come sit on the porch with me."

A lamp burned on the porch, likely left there by Mr. Bolton when he'd come out to join their dramatic scene.

"But I want to." The words had slipped from his lips before he even thought about saying them. When she looked up at him, he tried to grin. "Besides keeping a lovely lady company, it will mean avoiding Buck until he leaves. I'd rather not confront him twice in one evening."

Dannie laughed, the sound light and easing him into a more relaxed stance. "Your true motivation comes out, sir."

He shrugged, then offered her his arm. "May I escort you, Miss Bolton?"

She slipped her hand through the crook of his arm, taking hold of him. "You may, kind sir." With her free hand, she held the front of her shawl together. The house wasn't far, and when they climbed the porch steps together, Evan could almost imagine the former unpleasant confrontation hadn't even occurred. It certainly didn't seem to have held any lasting effects for Dannie.

"Do you know who I'm named after, Evan?" she asked, settling herself on the long bench against the house.

He leaned back against the porch rail. "Daniel Boone."

She nodded. "An American hero. I asked my mother once why she let my father pick our names. I'm Daniella Abigail—the Abigail after Abigail Adams. Travis is named after William Barret Travis, who died at the Alamo. Clark is after Merriweather Clark, of the famous westward exploration."

"What did your mother have to say about it?" Evan asked, tilting his head to the side.

"That she liked his choices." Dannie leaned back against the wall, her eyes sparkling up at him in the lantern light. "She said children ought to be named with a purpose. My parents meant our names to remind us of the noble people who came before us. Heroes who fought for the right thing and followed their hearts to explore the world around them."

Evan considered that reasoning a moment. "And do you live up to that expectation, Dannie?" Evan put his hands behind him on the rail, watching her still, admiring the way the flickering light from the lamp made her eyes stand out in golden shades.

"I try." Her smile faltered a moment. "Though lately, it's been a bit harder. Especially when it comes to following my heart."

"I can't imagine your heart would ever take you away from

this ranch." Evan knew the truth of his words, and he didn't mind them. He couldn't picture her happy anywhere else. Her laughter in the rain, the way she rode her horse across the swaying grasses of the meadow, and her easy way with the day-to-day work on the ranch all showed how happy and at home she felt in the desert.

Dannie shifted, her gaze falling away from his. "I didn't think it ever would, either. But lately, I wonder. If the right circumstances came about, or if the right person asked..." Her voice trailed away to nothing.

And Evan knew.

She loved him, too. Enough to offer, however shyly, to come with him. Back to England. If he asked.

He tried one last time to picture her on a settee in his mother's parlor, sipping tea and speaking politely of the weather. She'd be beautiful in an English rose garden. She'd match any old English tabby word for word with witty remarks. She'd stand her ground when people questioned whether she belonged, and forge friendships through her strength of character alone.

But would she be happy, hemmed in by English towns and hedgerows?

He never had been.

Evan crossed the porch, lowering himself to sit beside her. Then he took both her hands in his. "I wish I could ask you to come with me, Dannie. But I can't do that to you. To both of us."

She adjusted her hands, twining her fingers through his. "I could try, Evan."

"My dearest lady." He lifted their joined hands to kiss her fingertips, then he met her eyes squarely. He tried to smile. "You understand duty and obligation to family, I think."

She nodded, no answering smile on her face.

"Those things call me back, and reluctantly I must go, when the time comes. But I would rather stay here with you."

Her lips trembled. "Then stay." She laughed the moment she said the words, without any true joy or humor. "I shouldn't make this harder for you. Or for myself. But I've known—I've known for a long time that you would leave. That you have to go because you're an honorable man. I think that was one of the reasons I tried so hard to not like you. I'm so tired of being left behind."

"I'm sorry, Dannie." He bent to kiss her forehead, his lips lingering at her hairline as he breathed in the soft, lovely scent of her. Soap, wind-dried cotton, and the desert wildness he loved. "What do we do now?" he asked in a whisper.

"Enjoy what time we have." She leaned her head against his shoulder, keeping one hand locked in his. "And hope it won't hurt too much when we say goodbye."

He tilted his head against hers and let the silence stretch out, long and comfortable between them, while more stars appeared above, and the night grew deeper.

CHAPTER TWENTY-THREE

Nothing in his life had prepared Evan for the bittersweet joy of loving Dannie. For the next several days, they found every possible excuse to spend time in each other's company. She met him at the barn, or he walked around to the front of the house to sit on the porch as the sun set. Each moment they were together, he could forget for a time that his days at her side were numbered.

They hadn't kissed again. Though he wanted nothing more than to hold her, there were lines they couldn't cross. He treated her as she deserved; Dannie was a lady, through and through.

When Buck didn't come back, Ed and Frosty had ridden out to find him. The man was long gone. Perhaps too humiliated to return and ask for forgiveness, or face being turned out by Mr. Bolton.

Nearly a week after his return from Tombstone, Evan woke in the bunkhouse. He thought of Dannie before he even opened his eyes. As he had for weeks. Now the emotions following his initial moment of curiosity—*I wonder what Dannie is up to today?*—were a mixture of excitement to see her and a stab of pain reminding him the autumn cattle drive came ever nearer.

And he hadn't heard from his brother yet, either.

Evan left the bunkhouse early, the sky gray and yellow as the sun rose, and went to the barn to begin his chores. He hummed to himself a song that had been popular for several years, with the more daring young people he knew singing along to it as they waltzed at private balls. An American song, he'd learned to his great delight.

The melancholy lyrics struck him more poignant now.

After the ball is over,
After the break of morn,
After the dancers' leaving
After the stars are gone;
Many a heart is aching
If you could read them all
Many the hopes that have vanished
After the ball.

Love stories rarely ended well in song. Perhaps in life, too. Evan tried to shake the lonely feeling that had settled and went out into the early morning light with Gus waiting for him. The big dog peered around Evan into the interior of the barn. Perhaps the animal wondered if Fable would welcome him. Or he was only curious about the new inhabitants of his domain.

Evan scratched behind the dog's ears. "She just needs a bit of time, then the two of you can teach those pups how to round up the cattle."

The screen door at the back of the main house clanged shut, and Evan looked up to see Dannie approaching him. She wore a bright smile that lit her entire countenance. That he was the reason behind that smile was humbling.

She was dressed to ride, he realized, in a split skirt and dark blue blouse, with a dark vest on and a long rifle in her hand. She tipped her felt hat back with her free hand when she stopped before him. "Good morning."

He hoped his answering grin sent her heart dancing the way his was. "Good morning, Dannie. Are you going for a ride?"

"Yes. Would you like to come?"

He tilted his head to the side, studying her rifle. "Do you expect any trouble?"

"None, actually. But you know the rules."

He touched a hand to the gun belt on his hip. "Never leave the homestead without a weapon. And walk around with one, when you can." He'd seen Ed shoot a rattler not twenty feet away from the bunkhouse the week previous.

"Just so." She nodded to the barn. "Are you coming with me?"

"I must inform Frosty first." And the foreman would likely give him the same stare he had the day before, when he'd asked Evan what he was thinking, courting a girl he knew he had to leave behind.

No one had stopped Dannie and Evan from spending time together. Apart from that one remark from Frosty, no one had mentioned it, either. Not to Evan.

Once he had Frosty's approval to ride a fence line, Evan returned to the barn and started saddling his horse. Dannie finished ahead of him and went out the door, which spurred him into moving quicker. Every second counted.

They rode out through the zaguán, then went toward the property line near the road. Dannie's horse cantered ahead, and Evan enjoyed watching her. She rode with great ease, as a woman born to the saddle, and with more abandon than any Englishwoman he had ever met. Daniella Bolton on horseback embodied his idea of freedom, because watching her made him long for it all the more.

As they came to the long stretch of barbed wire fence, Dannie and Evan slowed and rode side by side at an easier pace.

Dannie nodded to a knot of cattle in the distance. "Did you know that the first time you put a cow in a pen—no matter how big or small the pen is—that cow will walk the whole fence just to see if they can find a break in it? Every new cow I've ever seen will do that. Then they'll never check it again."

Evan stared out at the animals, again surprised by just how enormous the ranch was even compared to his father's holdings. "I suppose it is in the nature of most living things to test their boundaries."

"We all want to know where the line is," she said with a quick nod.

They enjoyed the silence for a time, the sun getting higher and warmer with each passing minute. In a few hours, it would rain again, giving them respite from the heat.

"What will happen to the ranch, Dannie?" Evan asked, his tone heavier than he meant. When she turned to look at him, he tried to offer a reassuring smile. "I know you have cause for concern, for the ranch's future. Has your father set upon a way to secure things yet? Have you?"

The way her expression fell and her chin lowered told him the answer before she spoke. "We haven't come up with much. Maybe we'll get lucky and the demand for beef will rise again. Maybe the train prices will go down. I don't know."

And he wouldn't be there to help her through it, to find a way to set things right. The guilt made his chest grow tight and his shoulders heavy. "What about bringing in that new breed of cattle? Ed was telling me about the Herefords."

"We've talked about that. But until the fall drive, we won't have enough capital to add to our herd." She lifted her shoulders in a shrug, and her gaze drifted away. After several moments of staring into the distance, she added, "And we'd still have the same trouble with shipping the animals, even if Herefords stayed fatter longer."

"Of course." Evan tilted his hat down his head a little more, settling into his thoughts. If he could only stay. He might find a way. Might help them.

They were already down to too few cowhands. Bringing on more animals, trying new things, might overcomplicate matters too much as they were. Evan didn't have a quick solution. He doubted anyone would, but serving as only a pair of extra hands didn't sit right with him, either.

"Evan?" She turned to him, reining her horse to a halt. "Can we just pretend there isn't anything to worry about? Just for a little while. Please." Those gold-brown eyes went soft, as did her smile. "I've time enough to fret about it all later. And you don't need to concern yourself about it at all."

That stung, given that he doubted he'd ever stop thinking about Dannie and her family. He'd likely think about her, them, and the ranch for the rest of his days. Unable to do a thing about it except watch the sheep on the estate grow fat and wish they were cattle, instead.

"You're a good man, you know." Dannie nudged him with her leg, side-stepping her horse to make the movement possible. "You have to go back, Evan. It's the right thing to do."

"The honorable thing, perhaps." He took her hand and bent so he could kiss the back of her wrist, just above her leather glove. "But not right, Dannie."

Her forced laugh reminded him they weren't supposed to talk about the future that way. "C'mon. I'll race you back."

He wheeled his horse around with hers and together they went flying across the range, back to the ranch house. Outracing their worries, if only for a few moments.

Halfway between the KB Ranch gateway and the house, Dannie saw a pair of unfamiliar riders. She drew her horse up, the mare dancing beneath her and reluctant to come to a stop. Dannie twisted in her saddle to look at Evan, then pointed at their visitors. "Company."

Even from their current distance, she knew the men were strangers to her. She'd grown up with everyone in those parts coming and going on familiar horses, wearing familiar hats, and carrying themselves in a unique way. But these riders had never been on her father's land before.

Stopped beside her, Evan peered from beneath the shadow of his hat-brim, studying the men riding toward the ranch. Evan released his next word as more of a growl. "Pinkertons."

That didn't mean anything good. Though she'd suspected his brother wouldn't leave without a word with Evan, she'd thought there would be a letter, telegram, or maybe the man would show up at the ranch himself. But instead, he'd sent hired men. The Pinkertons, trained to hunt better than any lawmen she'd ever heard of.

Dannie looked up at the man beside her, noting the tightness in his shoulders, the way he'd clenched his jaw. He didn't want to see those men any more than she did. Their presence meant saying goodbye.

The goodbye had come far too soon.

They kept riding, but at a slow pace.

"Maybe they just brought word," Evan said quietly.

"We both know that's not likely." Dannie tried to keep her voice light, but emotion had already started to clog up her throat. Her eyes stung, too. But she didn't even try to blame the dust.

The Pinkertons rode around to the front of the house to come through the front door like civilized people, most likely.

"I could ride away. They haven't seen me yet." Evan turned to look down at her, his smile wavering. "Wouldn't that put a knot in their rope."

She laughed, the sound startled from her by his use of one of her *colloquial* phrases. "It would've been so much easier to just keep on disliking you," she said.

He squared his shoulders somewhat dramatically. "Ah, but my charms are irresistible, Miss Bolton. As you well know."

Despite the fact that he had to be hurting as much as she was, Evan tried to make her laugh and smile. Tried to make their last moments alone together more than woebegone.

She loved him all the more for it.

When they stopped at the front of the house, Evan held his hands out to Dannie to help her down. She slid from the horse into his arms, then laid her head against his chest. She closed her eyes and took in a deep breath, committing the moment to memory. The way the sun felt on her back, the strength of his hands at her waist, and the leather and sage scent of him.

"I love you," she whispered.

He held her tighter.

Then the front door flew open and boots clomped along the porch.

"Lord Evan, we have come to take you to your brother."

Dannie looked up into the deep-set, blackened eyes of a man who scowled as though he'd never known a happy day in his life. The swelling in his nose evidenced he solved problems with force rather than words. Behind him, dressed in a similar dark suit of clothes, was someone with a more cheerful look to him.

"Our job description changed, you see," the cheerful man said. "We are to bring you to Benson, by force if necessary."

For one wild moment, Dannie's gaze went to the rifle holstered at her saddle. She could hold them off. She could make them leave.

"My obligation is to Mr. Bolton until the cattle drive," Evan said slowly, releasing her and stepping away. "Did you make that clear to my brother?"

The man with the scowl stepped forward, looking as though he'd jump right off the top step to throttle Evan if he thought it necessary. "Your brother made it clear that you are to come with us, no matter your excuses." He moved his coat aside, clearly showing a revolver.

"Of course he did." Evan relaxed, then gave Dannie a smile over his shoulder. "William is almost as stubborn as you, love."

"Mr. Bolton has assured us he understands the situation." The cheerful man gestured to the doorway where Dannie's father stood, watching her with a sympathetic expression.

Evan took her hand and walked her up the porch to her

father, ignoring the Pinkertons for the moment. "Mr. Bolton, I apologize for leaving. Perhaps I can make my brother see reason, and I'll return after I have spoken to him. But if not, I hope you will know that my whole heart is here." He looked down at Dannie, giving her hand another gentle squeeze. "And I wish things were different."

Her father nodded, then held out his hand. Dannie stepped close to him, grateful when her father's arm went around her shoulder. She'd started to feel lightheaded right along with brokenhearted.

Her father extended his right hand to Evan, then shook the Englishman's hand with his usual firm manner. "It's been an honor to know you, Duke. Make sure you don't forget about us. And know that you're always welcome at my fire."

"Shelby. Steinman." Evan looked at the two men, his expression cold. "I'll get my things from the bunkhouse, and then we can be on our way."

The gruff one actually looked rather disappointed that Evan wasn't going to fight their orders. The cheerful one clapped Evan on the back and followed him through the house and out the kitchen door.

Dannie stood beside her father, leaning into him for strength, and waited.

Travis and Clark arrived, eyes wide and demanding to know what was going on. Everything around Dannie filled with fog, though. Her thoughts, too. Until she wasn't really hearing her father's deep voice quietly explaining the situation to her brothers. Then explaining it again to someone else—Ruthie, maybe.

She didn't know how long she stood there, or who else came onto the porch.

"Thank you, all of you." Evan's voice broke through the haze and she jerked away from her father, hurling herself into the arms of the man she loved one more time.

A clatter around her indicated Evan had dropped several things in favor of wrapping his arms around her, burying his face in the crook of her neck. Dannie shuddered with the first sob, her face in his shoulder.

It wasn't fair. Or right. And she wanted to rail against the world. Losing Evan was so much worse than she thought it would be. Partly because she thought the weeks and months before he left would make it easier. That they could find a way to smother their love into friendship alone. A false hope, but one she'd clung to.

But there just wasn't any more time.

"I love you, Evan," she said softly.

He kissed her forehead. "I love you, too. Always will." Then he stepped back, his eyes on her, ignoring everything and everyone around them as she did. "Keep this for me." He took up her hand and slid a warm silver dollar into her palm. "Please."

She looked down at the silver dollar he'd claimed had brought him all the way to Arizona, and to her. "But Buffalo Bill—"

"I don't care about Buffalo Bill, or Wyatt Earp, or Calamity Jane, or any of them. It's only you, Dannie. And I want you to keep the silver. To remember me." He closed her hand around the coin and stepped around her with deliberate speed. He stooped to gather up his things, then went out the door. Dannie kept her back to him, and she was vaguely aware of Ruthie slipping an arm around her waist.

"Oh, sweet child. I'm so sorry."

Dannie shuddered, and she listened. Listened until she heard the last murmured farewells, and then the sound of hooves in the dirt, drawing away from the house.

Finally she let herself give in, she let the loss and the heartache win. Dannie crumpled to the ground in a heap of skirts and tears, clutching the silver dollar to her chest. Ruthie came down with Dannie, arms around her, murmuring words of comfort.

"It hurts, Dannie. I know it does. But it's all right. It's all right."

Ruthie rocked Dannie back and forth, right there on the ground. "You men scat," she said hoarsely. "Let us alone for a while."

Footsteps went away, though Dannie felt her father's hand atop her head a moment before he withdrew.

Her heart just kept breaking into smaller and smaller pieces.

All the while, Ruthie held her until Dannie's sobs went silent.

"To grieve is to pay the price of loving someone," Ruthie said quietly.

She had said the same thing when Dannie had lost her mother. This was almost as terrible as that.

Then Ruthie moved back and wiped at Dannie's eyes with her own handkerchief. "'Weeping may tarry for the night, but joy comes with the morning.' We know this is true, don't we?"

Dannie nodded tightly. She'd heard the Psalm many times, applied to everything from the drought to a broken toy. It was how Ruthie lived her life. She believed strongly that every grief would fall away, one day, and joy would replace the loss. She'd always been right before.

"Thank you, Ruthie."

"Dear little girl." Ruthie stood, and Dannie hobbled to her feet, too. "You've gotta have some hope. Things will work out as they should." Ruthie patted Dannie's cheek. "Go on upstairs. We'll get you a bath, and then you better go to bed. Some rest will help your weary heart."

Dannie climbed the stairs to her room, a shadow on her heart and Evan's coin in her hand.

CHAPTER TWENTY-FOUR

Evan entered the hotel in Benson, covered in dust, saddle-sore and heart broken. The Pinkertons were behind him, promising that his brother waited inside. And he did. The hotel wasn't as grand as some of those in Europe that Evan had seen, but it boasted a sizable room with red carpet and tables scattered about for meals or leisure.

William D. Rounsevell sat at a table near the center of the room. Heir to a marquess. A peer. And the most irritating brother on two continents.

Evan stormed over to the table, heedless of the dust on his clothing, and sat abruptly in the chair across from his brother.

William startled, nearly spilling his tea. He blinked once at the man in front of him, and Evan wondered how strange he had to appear to his brother. He was bronzed from time in the sun, rough around the edges from work and a lesser diet, harder than iron from hauling his weight in hay, water, and leather. And he hadn't shaved in days.

"William." Evan narrowed his eyes at his brother, seeing in the baron all the things Dannie had likely seen in Evan. No wonder she hadn't trusted him to step foot on the ranch.

He already missed her fiercely.

"Evan? Is that you?" William put down his cup, then grinned and reached out to punch Evan's shoulder. "It is you! You look as wild as that American did—what was his name? The one you liked so much. Never mind. I appreciate you have less buckskin attached to your person than he did. Amazing."

Evan didn't even smile, he just slumped forward with his elbows on the table. He put his face in his hands. "William, what do you want? Why are you even here?"

"Why am I—? How ungrateful." William chuckled, as though the whole thing was a lark to him, of no more importance than fetching his brother home from school. "When you left, with nothing but that note telling us you meant to go see the west, Father and I thought you had lost your mind. Not to mention poor Roberta—"

"Your wife?" Evan lifted his head. "How is she? And did you really leave when she was about to have a baby?"

"She had the baby two days after you disappeared." William's chest puffed up like a rooster's. "Another boy. Healthy and nearly twice the size his brother was at birth. We've named him after you."

A second son, named after a second son. And now, Evan was fourth in line for his father's title. God willing, it would never come to him now. "Congratulations."

William waved that word aside, though he still grinned. "Roberta said I had better come and find you. She says a father is only in the way the first months of a baby's life, anyway." William snorted. "So here I am, ready to take you home, back to your responsibilities."

"I have responsibilities *here*," Evan stressed, gesturing out the door. "I agreed to work for a gentleman through the fall. He took me on in good faith, had his men teach me everything they could about ranching, and now I've left him a hand short during an important season."

"He'll find a more qualified cowboy soon enough." William leaned forward, studying Evan's clothing. "I really cannot believe you even dress like they do. Well, what was it like? Your dream? It wasn't as wonderful as you thought it would be, was it?"

Evan sat back, glaring at his brother across the table. He didn't answer. He couldn't. William wouldn't understand. And Evan didn't need him to. Not anymore.

"I have an obligation to Mr. Bolton, William. I can't leave this way. It's wrong."

"An obligation?" William appeared confused. "Have you a contract or something to prevent you from going back on your word?"

"I promised him I would see things through, work my best, and take part in the autumn cattle drive. He is already short on drovers." Evan took off his hat, which he should've done the moment he sat down, and placed it on the table. "It is a matter of honor, William."

William sat back, his expression hardening. "Evan. Father isn't well. He sent me with explicit orders to return with you. You must come home."

Evan's insides twisted unpleasantly. "Father is ill?" He wasn't close to his father. The marquess had always been somewhat aloof, aside from imparting the occasional lordly command or advice to Evan. "How bad is it?"

His brother averted his eyes, looking down at the table. "Ill enough. The doctor says he has a weakness of the lungs, brought on by too many cigars, or not enough medicinal tobacco, or some such. They don't actually know."

Had the marquess ever struggled with his lungs before? He'd always had a rasp in his voice, a cough when the weather changed. But never anything serious. "What is being done?"

"Come home, Evan. Father demands it. And if he worsens, this would be your last chance to see him. You must take hold of your duties, too. There is an estate to manage."

Evan closed his eyes, his mind whirling, and at the center of it all was Dannie. He'd held out hope he'd return to her. That he could somehow reason with his brother. But—he had an obligation to his own flesh and blood, did he not?

"I must send word to Mr. Bolton." His voice sounded weak, even to him. He cleared his throat. "I have to fulfill my promise to him."

His elder brother sobered somewhat as he stared at Evan, his eyebrows drawing together. "What do you think your promise is worth to him in silver?"

The silver dollar flashed through Evan's memory, shining as he'd placed it in Dannie's palm. "What do you mean?"

"I have the full weight of our family fortune behind me." William held his hands out in an expansive gesture. "Name your price. We'll make your loss up to him, so he can hire whatever help he needs."

Evan stared at his brother while his mind churned that thought about, twisting and pulling at it, and then he tapped the table with one finger. "A moment, please." He looked away, out the door through which he'd entered the hotel. The Pinkertons were outside, flanking the door, as though Evan might try to make a sudden bid for freedom. But beyond them was the town, and somewhere, there would be a stockyard.

Evan's mind buzzed as the possibilities presented themselves, one by one.

"How much of my money do you have access to?" he asked quietly.

"Your entire portion, if you wanted it." William laughed, somewhat uneasily. "But you aren't worth that much as a cowboy."

"Maybe not. And I don't need all of it." Evan met William's gaze squarely. "I will make you a deal, brother. I will come home to England, take up all my responsibilities and be there for Father, without any trouble. If you give me a fortnight more here, and three-thousand pounds against my inheritance."

William stared, aghast. "What are you going to do with all that money?"

"You'll see." Evan rose to his feet. "Do we have a deal?" He held his hand out.

William looked at Evan's hand as though he'd never seen anything so strange in his life. Finally, he realized he was meant to shake it. He stood, putting his cup of tea on the clean white linen tablecloth. "Why not?" He shook Evan's hand. "But only a fortnight, Evan. We have to return to England directly after. And the money comes out of your portion."

For the first time since the Pinkertons showed up in Tombstone, Evan had hope on his side. If he couldn't stay with Dannie, he could at least relieve her of some of her worries.

"Wonderful. Let's get going." He swiped his hat off the table and started for the door, then realized William hadn't followed. Evan turned around and went back to take his brother by the arm. "There isn't any time to waste, William."

"There isn't?" William drug his feet, his fine shoes snagging the edge of the carpet.

"No. And after we get my money, we need to get you a pair of proper boots."

William appeared horrified as he looked down at Evan's dust-covered footwear. "Like yours?"

Evan laughed, his heart light enough to manage it. "Exactly like mine."

He couldn't fix everything, but he could make things better for Dannie and her family.

That would have to be enough.

CHAPTER TWENTY-FIVE

Dannie sat beneath her mother's tree, waving off the occasional fly, with her back against the tree trunk. Clark sat next to her, a book in his hand, studying for the entrance exams again. Travis and her father were in the house, going over the account books together for the first time.

And Dannie's mind was far from home.

Two weeks had passed since Evan had left. In that time, no letter had come. No wire brought to them by a contract Western Union employee. No word at all. It almost made her feel she had imagined Evan and their connection.

But the silver dollar she kept tucked close reassured her. Evan loved her. He'd left with reluctance. He would write when he could.

In two weeks, could they already have traveled to New York or Boston? Maybe they would board a ship in the southern states. But he would write before he left the country completely. She knew that.

"Look at this." Clark held up his book in front of her, blocking her view of the road. "It's a map of England. Where does Evan's family live?"

She took the book in both hands and held it in her lap,

studying the rivers and borders of Evan's homeland. "Here," she said at last, pointing to the county where Evan would keep sheep the rest of his days. "But they spend most of their time in London, Evan said." She tapped one of the largest dots, the word *London* in bold red above it.

"Like Sherlock Holmes or Charles Dickens?"

Dannie smiled, though the expression didn't fit quite like it used to, and leaned back against the tree. "Like the Queen of England." She closed her eyes, releasing a sigh.

"Why don't you just go to England, Dannie?" Clark asked, sounding innocent and far too young. "If he can't stay here, you could go. We want you to be happy, even if it's not with us."

"It's more complicated than that." Dannie didn't open her eyes as she spoke. "In Evan's world, I'd be shunned. I don't have the right pedigree, or enough money, or anything like they would expect in a lord's wife."

Clark took his book back from her lap. "Sounds less than ideal, I guess."

"You could say that."

"Travis said he thinks Duke will come back."

Dannie shook her head, the rough bark behind her snagging her braid. "I don't think he can. He's a loyal, honorable man. If he has a duty to his family, he'll see it through."

Clark snorted and shifted away from her.

It was nearly time for supper. Though Dannie had done most of the cooking since Mrs. Perkins left, Ruthie had taken to cooking for all of them again. She claimed it was as easy to make extra as to feed just the three members of her family. But Dannie knew the truth. Ruthie didn't think Dannie was taking care of herself. That she was falling apart. And maybe she was, just a bit.

Dannie didn't have much of an appetite. It would come back in time, she was sure. But with her heart gone, her stomach didn't seem to care whether it was empty or full most days.

Love did strange things to a person.

The front door opened and shut, and Dannie looked toward the porch to see her father coming out. He walked with a new spring in his step and obvious joy in his heart. Though he was careful how he spoke around Dannie, she could see the hope he held for his future with Loretta Perkins.

A letter had come from her only the day before, stating that she'd return as soon as her sister's house was put in order again, but not giving an arrival date. Dannie's father had fretted some, but Dannie had a feeling their former housekeeper meant to surprise them. Though she was a steady woman, she had a touch of mischief to her. She claimed she'd inherited it from an Irish grandfather.

Dannie called out to her father, "Do we need to come help with supper?"

He looked up, started to speak, then frowned and looked over Dannie's head into the distance.

She turned to see what he stared at and saw a cloud of dust hanging above the road. A big cloud.

Dannie stood and stepped out from the tree, shading her eyes. Not much could stir up that kind of cloud during monsoon season. And it was a cloud, not a wall of sand or spinning dust devil. That meant a lot of animals coming down the road.

None of their neighbors had mentioned driving animals into or out of their community. Had someone decided to fold up and sell what was left of their herd? Or had rustlers gotten enough animals together to make a run for it out of the mountains?

"Horses and guns," her father said. "Clark, get your brother."

Dannie turned to her father. "Want me with you or on the porch?"

"Stay with Ruthie and Lee. Abram will join you in the house." Her father turned and loped back into the house at a steady run, and Dannie only looked back one more time before she followed. She found herself a rifle, ammunition, and a hat. Then she took it all out to the front porch to wait.

Abram arrived at her side, and Ruthie opened a window to look out.

"It's not moving fast enough to be a stampede," Ruthie said, eyes narrowed. "But my eyes aren't what they once were. What do you think, Dannie?"

"I think you're right." Dannie glanced at Abram. "Whatever it is might pass us by entirely."

"Nope." Abram nodded. "Whatever it is, it's coming straight to us."

Dannie faced the dust again and noted that it grew rather than passed by along by the road. He was right. She swallowed and moved the bench, tipping it on its side so she could kneel behind it and peer through the porch rails. Abram did the same on his side.

It had been years since Dannie had been through a raid, and they'd never lasted long. But in the past, her father had been younger, and they'd had a lot more men to guard the homestead.

Ruthie and Lee shuffled around inside, likely getting more weapons ready to load and hand out the windows.

The men rode away from the house, led by her father. Frosty and Ed fanned out on either side of him, while Travis and Clark followed behind. Gus appeared on the porch, coming up the steps and then sitting down next to Dannie.

"For heaven's sake, it's 1895," Dannie muttered as she looked at the dog, his hackles raised. "It can't be an Indian raid, or rustlers. That just doesn't happen anymore."

Ruthie snorted from inside, and Abram interpreted his wife's thoughts. "So long as there are bad men in the world, Dannie, trouble will keep on coming. Doesn't matter how modern or advanced our ways of thinking are. But the good news is that so long as there's good men, we'll get along all right."

Pressing her lips together, Dannie watched her father disappear over a rise. Then her brothers. And she waited.

The minutes stretched longer and longer, and the cloud of dust grew above the horizon.

Finally, noises started drifting close enough to make out more than a general sound. There were shouts, yips and whistles, and the rumble of hooves. Indignant cows lowed, too.

A wagon appeared at the top of the hill, with a man driving it and a woman sitting alongside him, hand to her bonnet. The woman saw the people on the porch and started to wave.

"It's Mrs. Perkins," Dannie whispered, trying to make sense of the scene before her.

As they watched the oncoming wagon, cattle appeared behind it. All black cattle, a few with white faces, sounding irritated about being driven along. With the cattle came men on either side of them, yipping and shouting, keeping the cattle bunched together and driving them forward.

Then some of the men broke away from the herd. Dannie saw her father, recognizing his broad shoulders and easy way in the saddle. He rode up to the wagon and jumped into the back of it, and the wagon stopped. Mrs. Perkins stood and climbed in back, throwing her arms around him in an embrace.

"Loretta Perkins did *not* bring a herd of cattle home," Ruthie said, sounding confused.

"Sure looks like she did," Lee said, his head out the window. "Can we put the guns away now?"

"Yep." Abram stood his long rifle against the porch. "This here's a homecoming, not a raid."

"Thank the Lord," Ruthie said, and Dannie silently echoed her words.

A cowboy broke away from the herd to ride alongside the wagon, which was moving toward the house again.

Dannie recognized the rider at once, and she took a step down the porch while her mouth went dry and her heart sped up.

"Evan," she whispered.

But why? And how? And if it was Evan, why was he coming toward her so slowly with the wagon?

If he wasn't going to hurry, she would.

Dannie ran to him, ducking beneath the tree and leaping through the tall green grasses like an antelope. She wanted to shout his name, get his attention, but she didn't spare the breath for it. Getting to him was more important than shouting at him.

But he did see her coming. She likely looked a fright, running wildly toward him.

He hesitated. She saw it, clear as day, when he debated with himself for that single moment before he made up his mind. The hesitation hurt, but immediately healed when he spurred his horse and shouted, "yah!" to get the animal moving.

He hardly slowed down enough to jump off when he reached her, and Dannie had the briefest moment to realize he wore a shirt as green as his handsome eyes, and then he was crushing her to him and kissing her.

Dannie knocked off his hat in her hurry to twine one hand around his neck and the other around his waist, holding them together.

The hows and the whys could wait.

She'd never thought to see Evan, let alone kiss him, again.

He tasted like summer and thunderstorms, and he smelled like clean cotton, and the dust of the trail mingled with leather. His lips against hers felt like home and sunshine, warm and bright. Then he broke away to kiss her on both cheeks, her forehead, and finally, back to her lips.

Dannie cried, all her emotions mingling together and overwhelming her. She murmured to him between kisses, not disguising her shock. "Evan. You're back."

The kisses slowed, and then he pulled back and tucked her into his side. "Oh, Dannie. I wish it was for good."

She hiccupped and turned her face into his shoulder. All her hopes crashed to the ground like a bird with a broken wing. He'd come back, only to leave again. And she'd start the grieving all over from the beginning, and—and she didn't care. He was real, and by her side, and if he left and it hurt again, what did that prove, but that she had a heart capable of loving someone?

The others in the wagon had joined them. There was a man she didn't recognize, but he looked like an old hand with animals. He tipped his hat to her. "Ma'am. Boss, these two asked me to drop 'em here before goin' on back to the paddock."

Dannie's father climbed down from the wagon, then held his hands out to take hold of Mrs. Perkins's waist and helped her down. The housekeeper looked exactly as Dannie remembered her—blonde-haired with streaks of silver, fair blue eyes, round cheeks, and a kindly smile.

Dad kept her arm tucked through his. "Thank you, Mac."

The wagon driver nodded, then flicked the reins to get his mules moving again.

"What's going on?" Dannie asked, looking from her father up to Evan, then to Mrs. Perkins. "I'm dreadfully confused. Evan, what are you doing here with all these cattle?"

Another man on a horse came forward, and when Evan's full attention swung to him, hers did, too.

The man mopped at his face with a white linen handkerchief. He wore brown canvas trousers, a long-sleeved red shirt, and a straw hat pushed back to the crown of his head. He had dark brown hair, and startling green eyes. Not to mention a horrible sunburn.

Her mouth popped open. This man could only be Evan's brother.

"We've got a lot of explaining to do," Mrs. Perkins said, sounding entirely too chipper. "But these men are thirsty. Let's go inside and get them something to drink, Dannie." She released Dannie's father only to loop her arm through Dannie's, tugging her away from Evan with far too much efficiency.

Dannie looked back over her shoulder, her gaze locked onto Evan's. "But Evan—"

"He'll come inside in a minute. I think he needs to explain a few things to your father." Loretta smiled gently as she spoke, that motherly expression reaching her eyes. "You picked a wonderful man, Daniella."

"I don't get to keep him," Dannie replied, facing fully forward at last. "Mrs. Perkins, how did you wind up coming home with Evan?"

"I ran into him in Benson. I was trying to secure a ride to Sonoita, and he overheard. He really is a darling man, so thoughtful and kind. When he offered to escort me home, but said I needed to wait a few days, I agreed. He's been quite busy, it seems, arranging all of this."

"I still don't know what all of this is," Dannie reminded her. "Oh—Mrs. Perkins, I'm so sorry." She freed her arm in order to wrap it around the other woman's shoulders. "I should've congratulated you first. Things are just so confusing right now—"

"I know, darling." Mrs. Perkins smiled, not the least put out. "And thank you. I know it's unexpected. But I hope you truly don't mind. I love your father, very much. I love you three children, too. Even before I realized how in love I was, you were my family."

By this time they had arrived at the front porch, and Ruthie interrupted them to throw her arms around Loretta Perkins to welcome her home and offer her own congratulations. When they bid Dannie come inside, she followed, only looking over her shoulder once to see that Evan still stood with her father and his brother, who had finally dismounted, the three of them looking at one another with earnest frowns.

"What are they talking about?" Dannie murmured. But if anyone heard her, they didn't bother trying to answer.

KISSING DANNIE SENSELESS THE MOMENT HE SAW HER HADN'T BEEN Evan's plan. Not in the least. But then, he hadn't expected her to come charging at him across the desert. The moment he'd laid eyes on her, all his plans for a thoughtful, careful approach had fled. Holding her in his arms had become as much of a need as breathing.

Letting her go had left him drowning again, too.

Until his brother smacked him on the back. "You didn't tell me about a lady." He grinned impudently. "Though that explains a lot more about your behavior of late."

"That lady," Evan said slowly, "is Daniella Bolton. Mr. Bolton's daughter." He nodded to King Bolton, who stood with arms crossed staring at them both. "Mr. Bolton. It's good to see you again."

"And you, son." Mr. Bolton looked back at the cattle now being driven to the paddock through the adobe house's corridor. "You, your brother, and six cowboys. Not to mention a hundred head of cattle."

"I know it's not a lot," Evan said quickly, "but there's more coming. They'll be delivered later. This is just what I could bring with me. And the men have pay for this drive, and we've left the rest under your name at the bank in Benson. There's enough to pay them for the next five months."

Mr. Bolton let out a low whistle. "You'd better come inside and explain exactly what you mean by that. Because I'm not about to accept a load of cattle and money and call it a Christmas present." The tall Texan gestured to the house. "Come along, gentlemen."

One of the cowboys came riding up to them. "Duke, Lord Bill, it looks like they'll all fit for now, but they'll be loud if we don't get 'em out in the fields by nightfall."

"Lord Bill?" Mr. Bolton said, looking askance at William.

William shrugged. "I'm afraid the name is rather stuck."

Evan waved the cowboy away. "We'll have things settled soon. Go water the horses."

Mr. Bolton chuckled. "Let's go get something to drink and you can tell me all about it."

They entered the house, and Evan's posture stiffened. Dannie was already waiting in the parlor, a tray of lemonade in her hands. Her eyes met his and the longing within them matched his own. Seeing her one last time, on his own terms, had been an immensely satisfying thought. But maybe he'd only made things worse. Maybe he should've sent the cattle and not come himself.

Mr. Bolton handed lemonade glasses to Evan and William, then took his own and settled in a chair. William sat down, too, releasing a satisfied sigh. He probably felt like the stuffed chair was pure luxury, given his complaint over spending the last several days in the saddle. They had rounded up cattle from several locals, getting a few here and a few there. Evan had made his brother do all the work with him.

Evan stared at Dannie, keeping to his feet even after she slowly lowered herself into a chair. Abram entered the room, took a glass, and a seat near Mr. Bolton. Evan nodded his welcome, pleased that someone had told Abram this discussion would need him present.

"Mr. Bolton," Evan began, "Mr. Steele. I've come to you both with a business proposition. As you are aware, I have always had great respect for the men of the west. During my time here, I have come to realize a great deal about your work and livelihood that never occurred to me before. I've also developed a great deal of respect and faith in your methods. That is why I would like to become a partner in the ranch."

"A partner?" Dannie said aloud as that elegant eyebrow of hers raised. She looked at her father, confusion written on her face.

"Yes. And since I can't be present in this partnership, and since I have far less knowledge of how to run things, I would be a mostly silent partner. I know the ranch is split four ways at present. Abram's share, then three shares for Mr. Bolton to split amongst his children. I propose that I take only an eighth of a share. I'll buy my way in with the cattle I brought today, and the salary for the men in my company. If the men prove helpful, you can decide to keep them on after their contracted period with me ends."

Evan tried not to shift his stance, but to keep his posture stiff and tall, his shoulders back. He had to look confident.

"We weren't planning on taking any more partners." Mr. Bolton looked first to Abram, who nodded slightly, and then to Dannie. "And this is a huge buy-in. You said there are more on the way?"

"Three hundred more cattle, mostly cows." Evan put his cup down without taking a drink, then put his hat on the table next to it. "So four-hundred head and five months of pay for six drovers and a bunkhouse cook."

Abram chuckled. "Frosty would like that. That man can't boil water without burning it."

Evan glanced at his brother, who seemed content to drink his lemonade and stay out of the conversation. Though William kept glancing in Dannie's direction, a glint of speculation in his eye.

"My brother and I have spent the last two weeks making all the arrangements in Benson." Evan tried not to smile at this point in the explanation. People around Benson had taken to calling them the English Outfit, thanks to their distinct accents and mannerisms. Evan had introduced himself to the cowboys they hired as Duke, and though he'd used his brother's correct title, they soon were calling him Lord Bill.

The most surprising part of that was that William hadn't seemed to mind.

Though his brother had frequently reminded Evan of their father's illness. Of their need to return to England. Despite Evan's heart pulling him back to Dannie every waking moment.

Evan cleared his throat and continued to outline his plan. "We've even secured a buyer for your yearlings. Rather than sell direct to market in California, I suggest you raise yearlings and ship them north to Wyoming. The fare is less expensive, as are the taxes. The Wyoming ranchers have more grass and ground, and a gentler climate for the animals. They'll fatten them up the rest of the way and sell them to the highest bidder."

Mr. Bolton looked at Abram, his eyes wide. Abram pursed his lips thoughtfully before speaking. "And for all of that, if the venture does well, you'd be content with an eighth of the part-nership?"

"I don't expect to make my investment back all at once." Evan let his hands hang loose at his side and he screwed on a smile. "I'll not be a bother to you since I'll be all the way in England. We'll wire from time to time, but a silent partner doesn't get consulted regularly. If ever."

William tugged at the bandana around his throat, loosening it with a sigh. "Gentlemen, I should also let you know that we have contracts drawn up for your perusal. They're in my luggage. We've set up the necessary accounts in Benson if you wish to move forward with my brother's investment. However, we have a second set of contracts available if you are uncomfortable with the arrangement. Tell them, Evan."

His shoulders sank a little. "Of course. The second option, if the first is truly unappealing, is that the cattle and payment for the hands is seen as a loan. As soon as it is paid back, with minimal interest, you would never have to worry about my involvement again."

Mr. Bolton leaned forward in his chair. "You seem reluctant to talk about that deal, Duke. Why is that?"

He didn't have to answer. But he wanted to be honest. "This ranch means a great deal to me, as do the people who live and work here." He met Dannie's gaze and managed a smile, which she returned somewhat sadly. "If I am reluctant to let go of my last connection to it, even if it's only an eighth of a share, I hope you cannot blame me. This land has taken a piece of my heart." He pulled his gaze from Dannie, meeting Mr. Bolton's eyes again. "All I truly want to do is help, sir. I know that a man must have his pride, standing on his own two feet. That is why there are two offers, and neither one is an attempt to give you something for nothing. I had a good idea you would not stand for such a thing."

"You were right about that," Mr. Bolton muttered, then he looked at Abram again. "May we discuss this for a moment in the study?"

Evan nodded his agreement. Abram and Mr. Bolton came to their feet, Abram with a grunt and muttering about creaky bones, then they went across the hall to the study, closing the door behind them.

William, Dannie, and Evan remained alone in the room. Evan could feel Dannie's gaze upon him, and he saw William staring at her. He sighed at last and made proper introductions.

"William, may I present Miss Daniella Bolton? Dannie, this is my brother, Lord Rothley. William Rounsevell."

They both stood, William to bow, and Dannie to execute a perfectly acceptable curtsy. William sat, as did Dannie, and Evan couldn't help but smile, tired though he was.

Then he lowered himself to the couch next to her, reaching out to take her hands in his. "I'm sorry, Dannie. Maybe I shouldn't have come. But I wanted to speak to your father myself. I wanted to see you again." Even though it hurt, like a poker through the heart.

"Did you?" she asked, that corner of her mouth slanting upward. "Your brother said you never spoke about me. Sounds like you forgot all about me pretty quick."

It had hurt too much. Talking about Dannie wouldn't change things. Only wound Evan further. He glanced at his brother, who appeared to watch them with interest, then he dismissed him from his mind. Let William stare. He didn't care.

"I could never forget, Dannie. Everything I've done, as much as it was for your family and the ranch, it was more for you. I couldn't leave without knowing you'd be cared for, and that you'd have everything you need."

Her eyes sparkled, and her bottom lip trembled before she bit it and lowered her gaze to their joined hands. "Thank you, Evan." She squeezed his hands in her grip. "For everything."

"Wait a moment," William said, sounding cross.

Evan turned to glare at him, though he knew his scowl lacked heat. "What is it, William?"

"You're in love with Miss Bolton." He nodded at Dannie, who

blushed and kept her gaze down. "And she seems to like you well enough, though heaven knows why."

Her head snapped up at that and she detached one of her hands in order to point her finger at William. "You listen to me, you stuffed-shirt Englishman. Your brother is worth a dozen cowboys, and probably a dozen lords, too. He's a kind and honorable man, with a noble heart. Any woman would fall in love with him if given half a chance. The fact that he's here, doing all this for me, just proves that he's wonderful. When he goes back to England with you, you oughta keep that in mind. And maybe, just maybe, give him more than a silly sheep farm to fill his time."

His heart warmed all the more at her defense of him, and Evan could've kissed her right then, too. He had to laugh, instead. They'd already had an audience for their last kiss, and it was probably smarter to avoid pressing his lips to hers again. He'd spend the rest of his days pining for her kisses, most likely.

William put his glass down on the table between them with a loud clink, then he stood up and focused a stern gaze on Evan. "Are you in love with this wild woman?"

Evan was on his feet in an instant. "She is a lady, Will. Remember that when you speak about her."

His brother responded with a befuddled wave of his hands. "Do you love her or not?"

Looking down at Dannie, Evan swallowed past his hurt and nodded. "With my whole heart."

"Then why the blazes didn't you say something?" William demanded. "You fool! You can't come back to England. Not if you have to leave Miss Bolton behind." Then his brother gestured more wildly to the window behind him. "And what about what I've witnessed this past fortnight? You have worked with such single-minded determination to ensure the future of this patch of desert, these cattle, and have shown more pleasure in that work than I've ever seen you show when addressing any of the estate needs in England."

Evan stared at William, shocked by his brother's display. "I have no choice. Our family—my responsibility is to our family. Our father is ill and he would never forgive me if I stayed. Our bloodline—"

William strode forward, taking Evan by the shoulders and shaking him. "Stop being an idiot, Evan. Who cares what Father says? I'm his heir. I have two sons. The estate, the family holdings, have stood for centuries without your assistance. They will stand long after both of us are in our graves. But this place? This place needs work." He glanced at Dannie. "No offense meant, Miss Bolton."

Dannie shook her head, her eyes wide. "None taken, my lord."

"Do you hear yourself?" Evan said quietly. "What about the marquess's illness? Father won't be pleased. My inheritance—"

"Is already gone. Or most of it is, anyway." William grinned impudently. "And Father—he isn't well. That's true. But Evan, whether you are here or in England will not have an effect upon his health. If you come back to England, and he passes away, what will you have? We know how these things go. You will be trapped into running another man's property—looking after my blasted *sheep*. I can't let you do this to yourself. Not even for the marquess." He stepped back, his erratic behavior stabilizing to something Evan recognized. Protectiveness. Affection. The stance of a man looking after one of his own. William switched his gaze over to Dannie. "Do you love my brother, Miss Bolton?"

"Very much," Dannie answered, without hesitation. "But he said he couldn't stay."

William snorted. "Because he has that noble heart you mentioned. The thing about Evan, Miss Bolton, is that he has treasured stories about honorable heroes and self-sacrificing adventurers his whole life. Before cowboys in the west, it was knights fighting for Camelot and King Arthur."

Evan opened his mouth to protest, but William held up a hand to stop him. "I am not saying this is a horrible thing. Because Evan is a man who conducts himself with honor and integrity. But obviously, he's taken the self-sacrificing part of the stories too hard to heart. Evan, you can't come back to England."

Then William's smile turned sad. "Much as it pains me to admit it, I was already thinking I should find a way to make you stay behind. Even before I knew about Miss Bolton. You've come alive here in a way that didn't seem possible. I've never seen you happier than you were when you were talking to ranchers and cowboys and rounding up those beasts out there. This life—I think you were made for it."

Dannie's arm slid around Evan's waist, and he looked down at her, seeing the bright pleading in her eyes.

"If I stay," he said, his words soft and meant only for her, "what does that mean for us?"

"Would you want to stay in the territory if you didn't have me?" she asked, her eyebrows drawn sharply together.

He answered with honesty. "I can't imagine my life anywhere else. Not anymore. This life you have—it's difficult. The labor is hard. But working on the land and making something of myself, it's changed me for the better. I would stay without you, but Dannie, I would much rather marry you."

Her whole countenance brightened, and her grin spread. "Is that a proposal, Lord Evan?"

"Better not be," Mr. Bolton's voice came from behind them. "Because he needs to do a better job of courting you first." The rancher entered the room, Abram at his side. "We've talked it over, and we agree to take you on as a partner. Silent, if you leave. But we'll let you have a say in things if you're sticking around." Mr. Bolton grinned and held out his hand. "What do you say to that?"

Evan accepted the firm handshake. "I say that I accept." Then he shook Abram's hand. "Thank you. Both of you."

"You've proven yourself, Duke." Abram clapped his hands together. "I'd better go see to the meal preparations now that we have extra mouths to feed. Ruthie and Loretta will likely want another pair of hands."

Mr. Bolton's eyes sparkled. "Maybe I'd better join you."

Evan cleared his throat. "Mr. Bolton? Might I have my bunk back?"

"Sure, son. Though that bunk room is going to be awfully crowded." Mr. Bolton glanced at Dannie with a knowing grin. "We've been thinking we need to build on to the property. Make a proper house for the foreman—Frosty shouldn't have to bunk with all the men, given his position. And you're a partner now. Maybe you'll need a house, too."

Dannie leaned her head against Evan's shoulder. "Dad, you promised me the next house we build."

Mr. Bolton sighed. "That's true. I'll let the two of you figure it out. Loretta," he called as he started to the kitchen. "Need any help in there?" Abram followed, chuckling.

Evan's heart fluttered as he looked down at Dannie. "Maybe we could share that house of yours."

William sat down again, pouring himself more lemonade. "This is too much excitement for me. In English parlors, we don't go around proposing business deals, house-building, and marriage all within a quarter of an hour."

"I guess we just do things a little differently here in Arizona." Dannie rose up on her toes, brushing Evan's lips with a kiss.

EPILOGUE

One Month Later...

Dannie walked across the floorboards of her new home, one hand skimming over the wooden frame that would soon be walls. Her silver wedding band glinted in the moonlight.

In the middle of the room she'd decided would be her parlor, Evan had set up a room with canvas on all four sides. Another stretch of it hung limply, allowing them to look up into the night sky at the moon and stars.

"This isn't much of a honeymoon for you," Evan said, slipping into the makeshift room. His hands went to her waist, and she leaned back against him. They'd been married the week before by the pastor from Patagonia, and Evan hadn't wasted any time setting up their temporary home away from her father's house.

"Oh, hush. It's perfect. I have you all to myself." She turned in his arms and stood on her toes, kissing him on the cheek. "It hasn't been difficult, has it?" She pointed to their bed, which had stood in her room at home until their wedding day. "You're comfortable and warm at night, aren't you?"

"Mm." He hummed his agreement and bent to kiss her beneath her jaw. "Very comfortable. Quite warm."

She had to work not to giggle, or shiver with pleasure as he moved his lips to the curve of her neck. "And the view is incredible. Not every bride has a ceiling made of starlight."

"That does sound rather romantic," he whispered the admission in her ear. "In fact, putting up real walls and a roof might actually ruin the whole thing."

"You haven't been through an Arizona winter yet, Evan. I'm fairly certain the first cold snap will change your mind about that." Since he'd stopped kissing her, Dannie carefully slipped away from him to sit at the table and chair, also from her old bedroom. Maybe they'd get new things in a few months, after the fall cattle drive.

He came up behind her and helped Dannie undo the pins and ribbons from her hair. The two of them had pretended the rest of the world didn't exist, though a meal appeared in a basket on their unfinished porch every evening. Loretta and Ruthie had made it a present, to feed the newlyweds so they wouldn't have to return to the main house during the week.

But tomorrow, they'd go back to the usual routine. Working with the cattle. Riding the fences.

She handed Evan her brush, and he carefully set about running it through her long hair. He'd insisted on that duty since their wedding night, claiming her hair down was one of the most beautiful things he'd ever seen.

"Are you sure you want four bedrooms in this house?" Dannie asked quietly. "It really doesn't have to be as large as my father's. He and mother always meant to have more children, which is why they have all the rooms upstairs."

"How many children do you mean for us to have, Dannie?" he asked, leaning close to place a kiss on her temple.

She shivered. "I see your point."

He chuckled, the sound making her want to answer it with a kiss. She stood and held her hands out to him. "Dance with me?"

"It would be an honor, love." He took her in his arms—closer than the proper forms would allow in a ballroom—and spun her through a waltz beneath the starry sky. "You mean everything to me, Dannie. My love."

Much later that night, while Dannie lay curled within his arms, she caught sight of a glint of silver on the small table by the bed. She smiled to herself and cuddled closer to her husband, who kissed the top of her head despite being sound asleep.

Somehow, one little silver dollar had brought him all the way to Arizona. Dannie would always be grateful for Evan's fascination with the American West. Because that fascination had brought them together. She loved him, and she would spend the rest of her life loving him. Her Duke.

Thank you for coming on this adventure with Evan and Dannie. There is more to the story of the KB Ranch. To continue the tale with Frosty and his countess, get your copy of the next book in the series, Copper for the Countess, available Fall 2021.

AUTHOR'S NOTES

I've worked on this book for several years, and I think the first thing you need to know is how much of what is written is real, based on reality, and complete fiction.

The term "Indian" for Native American and First Nations people is inappropriate. However, it was applied here with historical accuracy in mind. The term was used sparingly, and in reference to the characters' understanding of the Native peoples of North America.

Tombstone was a thriving and law-abiding city in 1895 and would be considered sleepy by most standards.

Buffalo Soldiers were stationed at Fort Huachuca for several years, and many retired in Arizona. There is a museum there you should go see if you're ever down that way. I would like to thank Salt & Sage Books for their sensitivity editors, who helped me write Abram, Ruthie, and Lee in a thoughtful manner.

Cattle Rustlers ran on both sides of the national border with Mexico. A border which was invisible at that point in history in almost all respects.

Sonoita is a real town, but all I borrowed from it is its name and general location.

The KB Ranch is loosely based on the Empire Ranch, which

was founded by an Englishman and his Canadian partners in the 1870's and is a working ranch to this day. The letters written by the Englishman home are still available to the public today, and they were immensely helpful in writing this book. I had the opportunity to tour the working ranch and several original buildings, including the adobe structure that served as the bunkhouse in this book.

Many thanks to the Empire Ranch Association for their upkeep of the land and houses. This ranch hosted several Old West style movies and television shows over the years, including those starring film cowboy John Wayne.

The Pinkertons were the forerunners to private security firms. They became feared in the 1890's for infiltrating unions and breaking up strikes. They were also hired to track down famous outlaws such as Jesse James and Butch Cassidy. They obviously had to make an appearance in my novel.

Monsoon season in Arizona has always been a thing. They are absolutely amazing. The rain comes in every day like it has a schedule to keep.

One of the big decisions I made with this novel was to allow my heroine to ride horses astride in the appropriate apparel for the time period: split skirts. There are numerous historical photos, contemporary to the time period, of ranching women in split skirts. It was considered more appropriate attire than a woman wearing trousers, though I'm certain that happened, too!

As this is my first foray into the world of writing Westerns, I've approached it with caution. But I hope readers will feel my deep love for this genre and forgive any missteps. My first introduction to westerns was reading Ride the River by Louis L'Amour. I devoured all his books, then several by Zane Grey.

My grandfathers both loved Western books and movies. I spent a lot of years watching John Wayne stride across a screen, sitting next to my Grandad on more than one occasion, and admiring the sweeping landscapes of the west. This book is dedicated to them, because they passed their love of the American

West to me before I could tell them what it meant to me. Before I started writing. I miss them both. I hope they would have enjoyed my attempts to join the ranks of their favorite authors.

I lived in the area where I based this novel, in a little town called Sierra Vista, for five years. Unlike a lot of Arizona, Sierra Vista rarely hit triple digit temperatures in the summer, and it was a wonderful place to live throughout the year. The Empire Ranch is in an even better position, up in the mountains, with tall grasses and biodiversity you wouldn't expect to find in the middle of the desert state. So if it doesn't exactly fit your mental picture of Arizona, know that I did my best to be accurate to my own experiences in the area.

Now, I must truly thank my dear writing friends for listening to me talk about this book for almost three years. They were patient and kind, encouraging and understanding. Especially my editor, Jenny Proctor, who saved this project when I was ready to give up. Thanks go to my alpha reader and bestie, Shaela Kay, too. And my proofreader and assistant, Carri Flores.

I am most grateful for the encouragement and love from my husband. He's always the hero of our love story. I'm grateful for my children, and their patience with me as I talked about cowboys for a year with them. And my mother, who talked me through several scenes and processes.

Thank you to everyone I didn't mention by name, but helped me through one part or another of writing this thing. Thank you, with all my heart, for helping me tell this story.

-Sally

ALSO BY SALLY BRITTON

CASTLE CLAIRVOIR ROMANCES

Mr. Gardiner and the Governess | *A Companion for the Count*

HEARTS OF ARIZONA SERIES:

Silver Dollar Duke | *Copper for the Countess*

THE INGLEWOOD SERIES:

Rescuing Lord Inglewood | *Discovering Grace*

Saving Miss Everly | *Engaging Sir Isaac*

Reforming Lord Neil

THE BRANCHES OF LOVE SERIES:

Martha's Patience | *The Social Tutor*

The Gentleman Physician | *His Bluestocking Bride*

The Earl and His Lady | *Miss Devon's Choice*

Courting the Vicar's Daughter | *Penny's Yuletide Wish*

STAND ALONE ROMANCES:

The Captain and Miss Winter | *His Unexpected Heiress*

A Haunting at Havenwood

An Evening at Almack's, Regency Collection 12